TODAY WE DIE

THE KILLING SANDS · BOOK 1

DANIEL P. WILDE

Today We Die (The Killing Sands, Book 1)
Daniel P. Wilde
ISBN 978-1-77342-015-8

Produced by IndieBookLauncher.com
www.IndieBookLauncher.com
Cover Design: Saul Bottcher
Interior Design and Typesetting: Saul Bottcher

The body text of this book is set in Adobe Minion.

Also Available
Kindle edition, ISBN 978-1-77342-014-1

CONTENTS

This book is dedicated to my wife Chandi and my six children, Sage, Roston, Aspen, Rader, Porter (deceased) and Loch. They love me unconditionally, and that's more than I deserve.

PROLOGUE

The town of El-Alamein, Egypt is located at the seaward (northern) end of a 40-mile-wide bottleneck that is flanked on the south by the largely-impassable Qattara Depression—part of the Libyan Desert. The Depression lies below sea level and is covered with thick saltpans and extensive sand dunes. This arid region covers about 19,605 square kilometers (7,570 square miles).

The Second Battle of El-Alamein was a historical turning point in World War II. During October and November, 1942, British troops operating under General Bernard Law Montgomery fought German troops led by General Erwin Rommel, one of Germany's most proficient generals. The Second Battle of El-Alamein, one of many battles fought between the Axis and Allied forces in North Africa, was a struggle for control of the Suez Canal, and of gaining access to the Middle Eastern and Persian oil fields via North Africa.

El-Alamein was the only direct land route (avoiding the Qattara Depression) eastward to the Suez Canal. This crucial east-west corridor became a vital defensive line held by the British Army, and marked the farthest point of penetration into Egypt by German forces. This battle is of significant historical interest, and was a major turning point in the war in favor of the Allies.

NOVEMBER, 1942
BERLIN, GERMANY

"Hauptmann Roehm, thank you for coming. I always enjoy our talks. Please, sit down, and share with me this marvelous meal."

"Thank you for inviting me, Reichsführer; the pleasure is mine," replied Günter Roehm, a tall, thin, balding man, 34 years of age.

The room in which they met was relatively spartan save for the white-laced tablecloth draped over the round table where they sat. A single kerosene lamp in the center cast shallow shadows behind the plates and cutlery, doing little to ward off the evening's chill. Pointedly empty bookshelves seemed to decry their state, pleading to be filled once again. But after the burnings . . . well, there was little chance that the shelves would be replenished any time soon. Apparently, Reichsführer Himmler did not approve of personal memorabilia, for no evidence of his family hung on the walls or stood on the desk in the far corner. Could this man even have a family? Who would marry such a man? Günter shuddered at the thought. Only a red German flag bearing a black swastika and a picture of the Führer adorned the walls.

The meal laid out between the men sat in stark contrast to the furnishings of the dark room. Roast beef, steaming boiled potatoes, and several kinds of cheese and breads were piled high—enough to feed Günter's family as well, had they been invited. Germany's ranking officials, it seemed, were getting fat while its population slowly starved.

"While we eat, I would like to discuss with you an assignment of the greatest importance. But please, have some drink."

Günter took a drink, but it did little to calm his nerves. The glass shook slightly in his hand, something he hoped didn't give away his unease at being in the presence of someone he believed to be mostly evil.

"You have been assigned to join Generalleutnant Böttcher in Egypt to aid in our offensive attack at El-Alamein," Reichsführer Heinrich Himmler stated, so matter-of-factly that there remained nothing for Günter, a Captain in the German Schutzstaffel ("SS"), to do but nod his understanding.

Plain to Günter were the consequences of failing to accept Himmler's "request" to join him for supper. However, aware of his lack of combat experience, and knowing the importance of securing El-Alamein from various briefings in Himmler's office, Günter hesitantly asked, "What will be my purpose in such travels, Reichsführer? You certainly must be aware, to my shame, that my combat experience is of little merit."

Reichsführer Himmler *did* know that. It was exactly why Captain Roehm was selected for this assignment. He was not too bright and was known to follow orders. And without real combat experience, he would not get in the way of Böttcher's operation. His real weakness, however, was his dedication to his family. He would do anything to protect his wife and daughters. Himmler needed just such a commitment to ensure the success of this operation. Himmler decided, nonetheless, that a little more insurance was needed. So, in a forceful, but quiet voice Himmler replied, "It is of small importance to you, except that you should obey your orders, and I expect that you will do so."

"Yes," Günter replied, "Of course I will obey orders Reichsführer. I only hope that I am the right man for this assignment."

"Perhaps it will do some good for you to understand your assignment, in order for you to also understand the critical nature of its success, and the consequences of its failure," Himmler thought aloud.

"Perhaps you are right, Reichsführer," Günter replied, so quietly that only one much closer to him than Himmler could have heard it, had there been anyone else in the room. That was usually the scariest part of these kinds of meetings—being alone in a room with a man who had no scruples about killing. The old chair creaked as Günter shifted. The meal had not been touched.

"The purpose for this assignment can be stated simply," Himmler said. "You will carry to Egypt a sample of *bacillus anthracis*, 'borrowed' from the so-called 'Epidemic Prevention and Water Purification Department', which is operated by our Japanese friends in Manchukuo, China. This vial will not leave your person. You will show it to no person and no person will ask you about it so long as you keep it hidden and secure.

"This biological agent has, for the past several months, undergone various adaptations to render it more effective. More lethal. Once in

Egypt, at a location of which you will be informed later, you will release the agent into a nomadic population center."

"Our objective", Himmler continued quickly as if anticipating an interruption by Günter, "is to understand the efficacy of the agent to be able to better use it against our enemies at the appropriate time. Two weeks after you have released the agent, you will return to the site of the release to observe the results of our test, and then report back to me."

Shocked by the contrast between Himmler's demeanor and the cold act of violence suggested by his words, it took a few heartbeats to realize that Himmler was expecting a response. Günter finally stammered, "I understand, Reichsführer," not really understanding at all. "When do I leave?"

"Tomorrow morning. This evening, you should return to your home and tell your family 'good-bye'. We will, of course, see to it that Hanne and the children are cared for in your absence. You will report to Unterleutnant Shafer at 0900 hours. He will have the package and your instructions."

With those final words, ignoring the meal sitting before them, Himmler picked up a paper from a stack on his left and began reading, dismissing Günter summarily. Günter remembered to salute smartly before turning to leave the office. He closed the door quietly behind him, the muffled sound covering the rumbling of his stomach. Himmler never looked up, but a crooked smile played briefly on his lips.

Unlike his failure to understand this bizarre assignment from Himmler, Günter understood *very well* what Himmler meant when he said that he would "see to it that Hanne and the children would be cared for" in his absence. Günter had seen several officers' families removed forcefully from their government housing with just the clothes on their backs, only to be left in the street to fend for themselves when their husbands and fathers failed to complete an assignment given by Reichsführer Heinrich Himmler. Oftentimes, the circumstances were even worse. These words, of course, stirred within Günter an energy and sense of purpose which he would not have been able to describe to another person, if he had tried.

Günter loved his wife dearly, and his two girls were the light of his life. Hanne was just out of school when they met. They had a whirlwind romance and married while Hanne was still 19. To Günter she was beautiful, with blond hair and dark blue eyes that twinkled when she laughed, which she did often. Where Günter was quiet and serious, Hanne was lively and socially adept. Her presence was a delight to her husband, friends and strangers alike.

Günter's daughters, Anja and Klara, six and three years old, looked just like their mother. Günter often marveled that, in a land teeming with hate, bigotry and ugliness, he could be so fortunate to have a home life so wonderful! It was for his family that he joined the SS. Such service to his country ensured his family certain protections not afforded to other "less-patriotic" Germans.

Günter had heard some disturbing reports recently about how the government was treating the Jews—reports that made the apparent solution to the "Jewish Problem" something entirely different than they had been led to believe. But he could see that this was where he and his family needed to be. And even though he questioned some of his leaders' methods, in order to have such protections, he sacrificed certain of his own values. The sacrifice left him internally conflicted, with feelings of guilt despite the happiness that reigned in his home.

He wrestled with his internal conflict daily to ensure the survival of his family. He fully understood that a failure at this assignment could surely end that safety and the protection that he had sacrificed so much for. Even more than this, however, was a new and uncomfortable feeling as he pondered this assignment.

Death.

The unspoken result of the assignment forced upon him by Himmler would be the death of innocent people. Günter heard and felt it between the commander's words.

NOVEMBER, 1942
NEAR EL-ALAMEIN, EGYPT

Three days after his meeting with Himmler, after too many hours on trains and small airplanes, Captain Roehm joined Generalleutnant Karl Böttcher's ranks in Egypt, on their march into El-Alamein. While the temperature of the air hovered around 20° Celsius (68° Fahrenheit), neither the cool air nor the hard winds blowing south from the Mediterranean Sea provided any relief as the heat rose from the sands beneath his feet.

The high humidity in the air was surprising, given his belief about the aridity of desert climates. Günter did not realize before he arrived that El-Alamein's proximity to the Mediterranean coast afforded it a somewhat milder climate than places farther south, notwithstanding the vast expanses of sandy desert in the area. Despite the humidity, swirling dust filled his lungs and dust-caked drops of sweat clung to his brow. The sky lay void of rainclouds that might provide moisture sufficient to dampen the billowing dust that encircled him and his comrades.

General Böttcher, unaware of the purpose for which Roehm was thrust upon him, but understanding, as Günter did, the consequences of any breach of loyalty or obedience to the Nazi party, unreservedly allowed for this change of plan.

"Hauptmann Roehm, while your companionship at this time is certainly of no inconvenience," General Böttcher said, the lie apparent in his voice. "I advise you to stay out of my way!"

Günter barely made out the general's barking through the screams of artillery fire whizzing around their position on the right flank. The look on Böttcher's face spoke more than his words. It was well known that the general did not allow diversions or detractions from the fulfillment of his duty. The man had proved ruthlessly focused in his assignments. Nevertheless, on this occasion, despite his obvious belief that a scrawny SS man from the Motherland could be of no use—and more likely would get him killed—Böttcher apparently thought it wiser to accept the inconvenience than to face Himmler's wrath.

"Indeed, Generalleutnant, I will stay out of your way insomuch as I am able," Günter yelled. He would have crawled into a hole in the sand to hide, so great was his fear for his life. Instead, he crouched low and covered his ears to avoid losing more of his hearing, jumping at every new report from the artillery.

Günter had lost a great deal of the hearing in his right ear as a child following an accident on his bicycle. Since that time, his left ear had provided adequately for his needs, but now, on this great battlefield in Egypt, with the wind howling and artillery and small-arms fire wreaking destruction all around him, he feared that he may lose his hearing entirely. He thought how sad it would be to not be able to hear the giggling and laughter of his young daughters—the laughter that grounded him amid such great internal conflict.

"FALL BACK!" General Böttcher shouted. "FALL BACK TO THE PANZERSCHRECK LINE!"

Being lost amid the commotion of battle, and his own thoughts, Günter had failed to notice the enemy's rapid approach directly in front of them. He responded slowly to the orders given by General Böttcher, who was stooping less than three feet to his right to avoid enemy fire. General Böttcher was not yelling at his men—he was yelling directly at Günter. Seeing Günter respond, Böttcher turned and moved quickly away.

Finally realizing the danger that threatened to engulf him, Günter began running, for his life, following Böttcher back in the direction from which the Germans had advanced. In the chaos, Günter tripped over a downed German soldier, landing heavily on his Mauser M712 and splitting his left hand open from the tip of his thumb to his wrist. Dimly aware of the pain and the blood now pouring from the wound, but not paying either any heed, Günter attempted to leap up. His backpack snagged on his fallen comrade's Maschinengewehr 42, a fairly new, and greatly improved weapon introduced during this battle. Greatly improved or not, the rifle brought him back to his knees, where he struck his left knee on a jagged rock protruding from the sandy desert floor.

"WAIT COMRADES!" Günter shouted, as he whipped a kerchief from his pocket and hastily wrapped it around his left hand to slow the bleeding. He stumbled forward with pain shooting up and down his left leg. He could see that he was falling behind as his fellows retreated from the advancing British forces.

Günter had heard that the Germans were outnumbered at El-Alamein, by at least two to one. From his vantage point, it seemed that the odds were much higher. Between the wind and the retreating feet of his comrades, the dust became so thick that his vision and breathing, along with his hearing, suffered immensely.

Finally, unable to see, choking on dust, and able to hear only the loudest blasts and detonations around him, Günter sank to the ground, desperate for air, and even more desperate for a miracle. Remembering the gas mask in his belt kit, he pulled it out, lifted it one-handed over his head and awkwardly fitted it over his mouth and nose with his right hand to filter the air he was breathing.

Still disoriented from the noise and dust swirling around him, and favoring his injured knee, he crawled in the direction he perceived to be the one that would lead him away from the enemy. Sand filled the voids in his bloody hand, despite its wrapping, as he slowly crawled farther away from the battlefield. Eventually, the cacophony of battle faded—either that or his hearing failed altogether.

After 40 or 45 minutes, that seemed more like hours, Günter barely spied a rock outcropping through the roiling dust. Knowing that it could be hours before the air cleared enough to see, if it ever did, he crawled forward and lay against the rock. During this respite, he checked the damage to his hand and leg. Unwrapping the bloody kerchief from his left hand, he was shocked at how mangled his hand looked. His stomach lurched and he had to swallow quickly so as not to vomit.

With little attention to trying to close the wound or clean the sand out of it, he wrapped it back up and turned his attention to his left leg. The pant leg was torn slightly and there was blood below the knee. He carefully took his knee between his right thumb and forefinger and tested the knee for bone damage. It was painful and the knee felt soft, as if the bone had been crushed. His stomach lurched again and he had to remove his hand.

With a deep sigh, he lifted his right hand to adjust his gas mask, noticing immediately how much sand was in his tangled hair and on his face. He had lost his helmet somewhere in his struggles. *I must look terrible*, he thought. He thought briefly about the mirror he had packed, but the more he thought on it, the more he realized that he didn't want to see what he looked like. He would have laughed aloud at his predicament if he didn't hurt so much. Instead, he closed his eyes and tried to ignore the pain—and to keep his stomach under control.

Günter remembered the pain medicine in his first aid kit and was just reaching for his pack when he became aware of significant ground movement. A quick look to the right revealed the hazy, gray shapes of several Sherman tanks sent from the United States to Egypt to shore up the English forces in the region. Their close proximity did not bode well for his continued safety. The medicine would have to wait until he removed himself from danger.

At that moment, despite his pledge of loyalty to the Führer, and despite the love he felt for his family, Günter's only thought was to save himself. He crawled away, slowly, and with blood from both his crushed knee and his mangled left hand staining the sand and rocks below him.

Through the commotion of battle, and the hasty, unmeritorious retreat of his frightened comrades, and indeed the entire Panzerarmee Afrika led by Field Marshal Erwin Rommel, Günter found himself unquestionably lost and cut off from any person from whom he might expect kindness or sympathy. His wanderings ultimately led him far from the German Army and their English enemies. Almost subconsciously, he felt for the vial still secreted in his pocket, remembering Himmler's warning.

Two days later, on November 6, 1942, while Günter hid in the stifling confines of a small outcropping of rock—the only place he could find that provided shelter of any kind—the British Army finally drove the Germans westward from Egypt back into Libya.

Later, Winston Churchill said of this victory: "Now this is not the end. It is not even the beginning of the end, but it is, perhaps, the end of the beginning." After the conclusion of the Second World War, Churchill wrote: "Before Alamein we never had a victory. After Alamein, we never had a defeat."

1

It was my watch, and it was hard to stay awake. I was so tired. We were all tired. We had been on the run for days, hiding out, trying to rest when we could. We had lain awake, or half awake, night after night, listening for sounds of pursuit. No one was able to sleep tonight either, at least not soundly.

Standing there by the window, desperately trying to keep my eyes open, I sensed another presence almost within reach. Without thinking, I swung my weapon around in that direction.

"It's me," Anta whispered, and I remembered to take a breath. It was two AM, time to change the watch.

"Ok," I mumbled, exhausted, as I stood to face her.

As Anta came closer, to take my place, I realized again how much I care for her, maybe even *love* her. We met just six months ago, but we'd been through so much together, and depended on each other so often, that it seemed like much longer.

Her short, black hair hung straight tonight, but slightly messy. Her dark skin left only the whites of her gray eyes visible in the night. I sensed, rather than saw, a tired smile and realized I was staring at her lips—again. I tentatively moved toward her.

Anta squeezed past me to sit on the chair beside the motel window. I watched her train her eyes on the dark landscape outside, her familiar scent filling my head. She reached for my weapon and our fingers touched. I let go and pulled away, finally turning away from her, drifting to the couch to try to rest.

I didn't know how long I'd been down when the sound of breaking glass crashed into my dulled senses. Anta's startled cry roused me further and I was instantly wide awake. I rushed to her, fear coursing through me. Her clothing and hair had been showered with glass fragments from the broken front window. My attention was divided between concern for her safety and the fear of the possibility that this might be a full-on attack.

"Is it them?"

Angel's excited whisper surprised me, even though I knew she was fascinated by the Skins. She and Street had glided into the room when they heard the crash, silent as ghosts.

"Yes!" Anta whispered, beginning to lose control of her emotions. "And there are hundreds of them!"

I discretely confirmed Anta's report from a position beside the window, careful to stay concealed behind the curtains. Street checked the back through the bathroom window.

"They're out back, too. We may have to fight our way out again."

The situation seemed impossible considering where I was, and what I had been doing only six months earlier. Such a short time really; but man, it seemed like forever ago.

2

"Hello," I said. The man who looked out at me from the Holo was aging, with graying hair and bags under his eyes. He looked like a man who's seen bad things and then worse. His skin was splotchy and the pores on his nose were much bigger than I cared to see this close up.

"Good evening Doctor Bader, I am Abasi Chalthoum, Egyptian Minister of Health and Population. My secretary should have announced me."

"Yes, he did; although he didn't provide me with any context for our conversation. To what do I owe this honor?"

"Your reputation, Doctor. My superiors request your services. They would like you to join a small expedition to investigate some recent reports of peculiar, but isolated deaths in one of the Bedouin tribes in northern Egypt, near El-Alamein."

"I see. *Actually*, I understand, but I don't *see*. Why me?"

"Again, Doctor, your reputation. You have been made known to our government as an expert in archeological anthropology. Your study of contagious diseases, and the impact of epidemics on the course of human history, is what attracted us to you. Of course, your father's work right here in Egypt, at the University of Cairo, has certainly not hurt your reputation among my colleagues."

Minister Chalthoum was wise to bring my father into the discussion so early. I'd always had a difficult time staying away from the things in which my father was involved. My father died when I was only four years old, leaving mom to take care of me and my little sister, Arilee. But before his death, he studied historical biological agents and events during the great wars of the early- to mid-twentieth century. I found his work interesting but elected a different course of study. My sister says it's because I'm a "stubborn arse".

At the University of Colorado, I majored in archeological anthropology. I studied under the wise tutelage of esteemed professors like Doctors Abrahm Goldstein and Maricia Nerond. It wasn't so much the history of the events of humankind that captivated me, but the works of human hands over the millennia. These brilliant anthropologists found a way to make even the old, mundane research of prehistoric cave tools and 14th century American Indian dwellings come alive.

Of course, nobody can fully escape their roots, unless they never really had any to begin with, and I did. Over time, I became more interested in my father's line of work. Perhaps it was because I felt some desire to learn who I really was as well as who my father was. I was determined to carry on his work, despite the arcane and archaic nature of the research. It was a little tedious at times.

As I began my career, I looked for ways to diversify my work and keep it fresh. I finally branched into the anthropological subspecialty of the historical biological and chemical works of man. As a result, I'm an anthropologist by choice and a viral and bacterial historian by fate. I know, pretty boring. My nieces think I'm lame. I'm glad I don't have kids of my own—I'm sure I'd be a real letdown.

"Minister Chalthoum, I may not be the right person for this job. I'm no Indiana Jones—not even close."

Minister Chalthoum didn't laugh. It seemed he didn't know who Indiana Jones was—gasp! Or, worse, he actually did. Dr. Jones probably wasn't a hero in Egyptian lore if the old movies were any guide.

"Doctor Bader, it is not bravery nor heroism that we desire from you; it's your knowledge. You alone seem to have the qualifications that would be of the greatest service in this matter. You have come highly recommended by your father's colleagues and your superiors at the University. And, my government intends to pay you very well for your services."

Oh. Money. That changed everything!

"When do I leave?"

"We've already arranged for your transport. A hovercar will be at your home to collect you and your bags at 8:00 AM on January 2."

Ooooo-kay. They assumed my participation in this little venture. My reputation—my greedy reputation—*did* precede me. "I'll be ready. Thank you."

"Thank *you* Doctor!"

3

The airport at Apion (formerly, Alexandria), Egypt, is a modern structure with all the latest technological advances. Despite its sophistication, we still had to wait on the tarmac for the C5 port to become available due to the high level of air traffic at the airport. I spent most of the three and a half hour flight from Boulder, Colorado to Apion watching the on-board news for any reports of these so-called "peculiar" deaths in Egypt. Nothing.

I didn't know if the silence was because the deaths occurred in one of the few remote places left on Earth, or because the government, as they tend to do, was attempting to control panic. I had a growing suspicion that what I was about to learn was going to be unpleasant. And the generous advance Minister Chalthoum wired to my bank account two days ago led me to believe that my task was going to suck. Maybe I would die. I'm not superstitious. I'm not even very religious, despite my Christian upbringing. In any event, I couldn't sleep on the plane. I hoped that wouldn't bite me in the backside later.

Other than not being able to sleep, the only problem on the flight was the unenergetic, almost robotic flight attendant, with gobs of makeup plastered to her face; and who, unlike her colleagues near the back of the plane, seemed to find little enjoyment in her work. She actually spat on me when asking me what I'd like to drink. *Uh, I'll have a little bag of peanuts to go with that saliva, thank you.* Anyway,

I'd flown all over the world, and in recent years, made many trips to various places in the Middle East, including Egypt. Of all those flights, I couldn't recall a single occasion where more than a dozen seats were empty, or where the passengers and crew were in anything but high spirits. The same was true on this flight, with the exception of *my* flight attendant.

Air transportation is just so inexpensive and so fast now that nearly any person, on any budget, can afford to fly to nearly any place on Earth. Airplanes are so large that even smaller commercial craft hold 800 people or more. Thanks to international security and peace, restrictions on travel through foreign airports have relaxed so much that only one form of identification is necessary to travel to every country but Cuba; whereas, by 2026, twenty-five years after a tragic terrorist attack in New York City, travel to foreign countries was severely restricted, and security measures, with extensive background checks and screenings, were necessary just to travel between the various states within the United States of America. So, of course the plane was full. They always are.

So I didn't sleep on the plane; but we landed anyway, and eventually, we were allowed to get off. I walked out of the C5 Port at the Apion airport and was greeted by a small assembly of aging, yet distinguished-looking ladies and gentlemen wearing dark business suits and sunglasses. They looked like they came straight from an old mafia vid.

"Good afternoon Doctor Bader! I'm Minister Chalthoum," a man said, walking up to me with outstretched hand. He was clearly the oldest of the group and I recognized him by the bags under his eyes. I took his hand and shook.

"These are my colleagues," he said, motioning toward the men and women to his rear. "And this is my daughter, Dr. Anta Chalthoum." He bowed slightly, extending his hand toward a young woman who seemed highly out of place among the group. I wondered how this woman, Dr. Anta Chalthoum, could possibly be the daughter of the Minister. She was exotic and beautiful, and he was . . . well . . . not.

"It's nice to meet you," I replied, smiling widely at Doctor Chalthoum and ignoring the others.

Dr. Chalthoum looked to be about 30 or 31 years old and tall, only two or three inches shorter than me. She was dressed in dark blue jeans and a plain white blouse with the top two buttons left undone. *Whoa!* I thought as my focus drifted away from what her father was saying.

Dr. Chalthoum's eyes were slate gray, but bright and vibrant. She had long, dark eyelashes that could probably swat a mosquito if she blinked at the right moment. She was not made up like so many women around the world, including Egypt. Such raw beauty was uncommon. Her dark hair was pulled back into a single ponytail in the back. She wore a black armband on her upper arm containing the single word, in white lettering, لتاق, meaning "fight" or "combat". I knew that the name "Anta" meant "goddess of war". *What kind of woman is this?* I wondered.

I was mesmerized.

I stared at her, too long. A low "cough" from Minister Chalthoum reminded me that I had looked at his daughter long enough—well past the period of appropriateness for a man hired by her father to participate in State business. She noticed. I saw it in her eyes, and saw a slight upward curve of her sensuous lips; yet, she didn't look away. In fact, she appeared to be using her amazing smile and long-lashed, mosquito-swatting eyes to flirt with me. She was clearly used to being gawked at. I shouldn't have given her so much attention, but who was I kidding?

JANUARY 2, 2093—DR. ANTA CHALTHOUM

Wow! I thought. *This Dr. Bader guy is hot—for a professor!* I'd probably have gotten both of us into serious trouble if he'd been *my* professor at University. Not too tall, maybe six feet or six foot one. Short hair, and some facial hair. So he's probably not too stuffy. He's pretty tan too. Maybe he *is* an "Indiana Jones". Dad said he made that reference during their Holo so I looked him up. Nice!

Dr. Bader looks good for an old man. Alright, he's not old; probably in his mid-thirties. He looks familiar, but I can't place him.

When dad told me that he was hiring an American professor to join me in this expedition, I was worried that I'd be stuck with some old, wrinkly, boring grandpa. This one might be boring—time will tell—but he's certainly not old and wrinkly. Too bad he's my colleague. Can I date a colleague?

JANUARY 2, 2093, LATER—SHIFT

Following these brief and informal introductions, I was led, with Dr. Anta Chalthoum by my side, through the main concourse of the airport's international wing. We traveled through a set of inconspicuous, metal, double doors, then climbed a plain circular, outdoor staircase. After reaching the top of the metal stairs, we walked out onto a quaint little roof-top terrace overlooking the dirty airport tarmac below.

The terrace looked like some kind of private sanctuary for people with special privileges—like pilots, wealthy business executives, government leaders, movie stars, and the mobsters I was with. I was invited to sit with the others, around a large, ornate, glass table, with imbedded digital maps, charts and pictures spinning around on the clear surface.

Dr. Chalthoum looked at me. "Are you feeling okay?" She asked. "You look a little pale." Really? She just met me and could tell I was pale? I was feeling a little dizzy looking at the spinning pictures on the table. I once rode the tea-cups at Disney World. Once.

"Yeah, I'm fine. Just taking it all in."

The air was cool, but not cold. There was a stiff breeze carrying the smell of jasmine, or maybe it was just french fries. I couldn't tell. The sun was warm on my skin, making me wish I was here to relax and not to listen to the Mafiosos. I didn't know what Apion's weather was typically like in January—much different than Colorado for sure—but it felt very nice on that roof.

There were small trees and shrubs along the edges of the terrace and in various planter boxes placed strategically throughout the space.

In summer months, they would have provided some valuable shade. It was nice, and quite unexpected at a place as utilitarian as an airport.

Having settled into our rooftop conference room, Minister Chalthoum made formal introductions. Each member of the mafia was a professor at Cairo University, assigned to the Ministry of Health and Population under Minister Chalthoum. For the next two hours, Minister Chalthoum attempted to moderate this intimidating assemblage, as they bombarded me with what they had learned over the past few days. We looked in detail at maps, charts, data tables, research notes, and some gruesome pictures that, when considered collectively, detailed a "peculiar" set of circumstances indeed.

Two of the professors, Dr. Shehata and Dr. Biljon, took turns interrupting each other in an attempt to educate me on the latest news. I tried to focus, but between their accents and their constant interruptions of each other, it was tough. Plus, I couldn't stop peeking over at Dr. Chalthoum—the way the breeze pushed her blouse against her . . . *anyway* . . .

Ultimately, this was more or less the story I heard: a local tour guide in El-Alamein accidentally stumbled upon (but not literally) two dead human bodies in the dunes southwest of El-Alamein on December 25th while I was at home with my sister and her girls opening presents that Santa left under their tree. The pictures I was shown were apparently taken with an old cell phone camera during a bad sandstorm. Either that or someone took a knife to the camera lens.

The belief was that the tour guide took the pictures, but that hadn't been verified. Minister Chalthoum contacted me within hours of his receipt of the photographs, which was just a few days after the pictures were taken. From the condition of the bodies, the ministry assumed the people contracted a disease of some kind. When asked how they came to that conclusion, all they could agree upon was that they couldn't agree on anything; but that was the one conclusion they couldn't rule out.

The photos were hazy with the blowing sand, but depicted two males, obviously-deceased. They appeared to be desiccated, but nearly-perfectly preserved on the exterior—although partially unclothed and slightly bruised and decayed. They were unlike anything I had ever seen. Through close-up photos of gaping cuts or bites in the torsos, we could see near-empty body cavities. Only bones remained. It looked like the two people had died as a result of being devoured from the inside, like someone stirred up and then scooped out their guts with a big spoon.

One theory among the professors of the Health and Population Ministry was that "some biological agent had infected the men, causing their death through some means wholly unknown to the human race." Amused by their sophisticated language, I almost laughed out loud, covering my mouth and coughing into my hand instead.

I wasn't in a position to disagree with them, and, regaining my composure, I assured them that we could solve this mystery; although I wasn't sure that I was the person to do it. I didn't tell them that though—they're paying me *a lot* of money.

After two hours, I could still barely believe that the pictures I was looking at were not doctored in some way; and yet, I was excited. Sick, I know. I couldn't wait to get started. I couldn't wait to discover whether even a small part of what I'd been told, and had seen, was actually true. I didn't have to wait long. I was excused as soon as the presentation was finished, and led by Dr. Chalthoum and an assistant of some kind, back out the way we had come in, past a McDonald's. Ah, fries, not jasmine.

On our way back down to the concourse, Dr. Chalthoum informed me that she would be my "personal escort and assistant" as I traveled west, past El-Alamein, and into the remote, sand-hilled desert on the northern edge of the African continent. Excellent! I would rather have her as my guide than any one of those stuffy mobster-types I had been with for the past couple of hours. I mean, seriously, if you had seen these people, you'd understand why a trip into a barren desert with even just one of them was the last thing any sane person would want to do.

Dr. Chalthoum informed me that she would stay with me, as the second and final member of the expedition team, until we've completed our investigation into whatever it was that caused the people in those photographs to look the way that they did. Even though it was a bit surprising that Dr. Chalthoum, rather than one of the professors, was to be my teammate, I wasn't going to complain. Plus, Dr. Chalthoum informed me that she is "quite educated in biology and medicine", which may prove useful.

I was taken to the International Apion Hotel by a staff member of Minister Chalthoum's team, Senbeb. I took advantage of the drive through the clean, palm tree-lined streets of Apion to gather information from Senbeb.

Apion, apparently, has been a hotbed for travel and tourism for several decades. The city of Apion, formerly Alexandria, is said to have been founded by Alexander the Great in 331 B.C., one of about 20 cities founded by the same. The name "Apion" was adopted in Egypt by popular vote in 2068 following the discovery of stone slabs containing ancient records under the ruins of the Citadel of Qaitbay.

Maritime archaeology in the Harbor of Apion began over 70 years prior, in 1994. The discoveries revealed details of the city of Alexandria both before the arrival of Alexander the Great, when a city named Rhacotis existed here, and during Alexander's siege of the city in 331 B.C. Previously unknown, the stone slabs told of the existence of one Ptah Apion, a popular peasant leader around 331 B.C.

Ptah Apion held no government position, could not read, and had no wealth. But his vast popularity among the peasant population of northern Egypt provided him with ample numbers of men to rise up against Alexander. The evidence suggested that, under the informal leadership of Apion, the Egyptian peasants nearly overthrew Alexander the Great. But they finally suffered defeat after four months of fighting with Alexander's armies. Ultimately, Apion and his peasant loyalists were defeated, allowing Alexander unfettered access to the city.

After the battles, Alexander changed the name from Rhacotis to Alexandria and established Greek rule over the city. When the citizens of this city learned of the heroics of Ptah Apion, nearly 25 years ago now, they changed the city's name to "Apion", a name reflective of the grandiose achievements of the Egyptian people.

During the decades following Alexander's conquest of Rhacotis, Alexandria became an important center of the Hellenistic civilization. It remained the capital of Hellenistic and Roman-Byzantine Egypt for almost a thousand years until the Muslim conquest of Egypt in AD 641. At that time, a new capital was founded at Fustat (later absorbed into Cairo).

The port city of Alexandria—now Apion—occupied an advantageous location on the Mediterranean Sea. Its advantages originally included numerous trading opportunities and the provision of safe harbor for sea-going vessels seeking refuge and trading opportunities of their own. Subsequently, during World War II, on December 19, 1941, Italian torpedoes destroyed or disabled four war ships (three British and one Norwegian) sitting at dock in the Harbor of Alexandria. That event temporarily turned the tide of the war against the Allies. Senbeb would have shared other historical facts with me as well, but our time was cut short as we arrived at the massive, architecturally-inspiring International Apion Hotel.

Senbeb parked the hovercar and walked into the hotel with me. He insisted upon carrying my luggage—running around to the back of the hover and grabbing my luggage before I even stepped onto the curb. When asked, Senbeb would not divulge whether this was by direction from the Minister, an Egyptian custom, or an expression of his regard for me. In any event, I was definitely not worthy of that kind of attention.

The lobby of the International Apion Hotel was beautiful! The floor was tiled in fine, gray marble that reflected the light fixtures and curved ceiling above. Several crystal chandeliers spread a rainbow of colors across the floors and walls of the luxurious entrance hall. Embroidered, silk seating surrounded a large, welcoming fireplace in the center of the room. The double set of twin doors leading from outside into the lobby was elegant with gray handles to match the tiled floor.

The reception desk, to which I slowly made my way as I gawked at my surroundings, followed by Senbeb and the luggage, was made of dark-colored mahogany and capped with a white-colored marble top. Exquisite paintings of various historical figures (few of which I could name) hung from the dark, red walls. Columns supporting the great weight of the ceiling high above were ornately engraved with various spirals and symbols appearing to belong to ancient Egyptian civilizations.

As we approached the counter, I was surprised by the clerk's kind welcome. Not only did she speak flawless English, but she also knew my name. Senbeb explained that the hotel knew I was coming, and that they'd been given explicit orders, to "take care of" me. So, I got a suite on the top floor of the hotel. *Thank you very much!* After receiving the promise of a meal delivered to my room within the hour, I was escorted by two immaculately-dressed members of the hotel staff. As we walked away, Senbeb called out, "Dr. Chalthoum will be here to pick you up promptly at 9:00 AM! She has your number."

I was then escorted out of the lobby, up a very fast elevator, and to my room.

The top floor of the International Apion Hotel was 88 stories in the air, with mesmerizing views to the north and northwest. From my windows, I had breathtaking views of both the sea and the vast city of over 14 million people. In the northwest, I could see the Citadel of Qaitbay, on the coast of the Mediterranean Sea, with its massive stone walls now falling into the sea. The fabled Lighthouse of Pharos, one of the original "Seven Wonders of the World", once sat in that same location. It was destroyed during an earthquake in the 14th century, but I could see why the location would be perfect.

In the Harbor of Apion, a few small sailing craft were wrestling with fairly large waves which could only be the result of wind rushing across the Sea from the north. The water craft were likely some of the last of a dying breed of independent fishing vessels; or, perhaps, they were half-wits that got some kind of rush sailing in rough waters as night approaches.

As I sat in my room, gazing over the fantastic scene below me, my mind kept wandering back to the feelings of discomfort I had on my flight this morning. I tried to connect those feelings of unease with the information I learned later on the outdoor airport terrace. I couldn't get those gruesome pictures out of my mind, even as I tried to enjoy this beautiful place. Not even the four varieties of huge, juicy, delicious shrimp, pasta and Pepsi brought to me this evening for dinner could overcome my mind's replaying of those images. Ugh.

I knew sleep would probably come slowly this evening, but I went to bed anyway, my trepidation about this whole mess keeping me awake long past midnight.

4

Even though I thought it impossible, Dr. Chalthoum looked even sexier this morning in her travel fatigues than she did yesterday. Sexy or not, though, she didn't have much reason to be pleased with me this morning.

I was awakened at 9:05 AM by a call to my room from the reception desk. The agitated voice informed me that Dr. Chalthoum was waiting for me. I wondered what she said to that poor guy to get him all worked up. But more importantly, why couldn't my MEHD, a multi-dimensional eyeglass holographic display, perform the simple function of beeping at a set time?

Sure, I overslept; but in my defense, I had had a long day. Plus, as expected, images of diseased, molting bodies swam through my dreams in lakes of boiling Mediterranean salt water.

Dr. Chalthoum agreed to meet me in the hotel restaurant at 9:30. After showering—fast—and dressing in my travel clothes, I appeared in the restaurant 22 minutes later to find a very sexy Dr. Chalthoum finishing off a plate of whatever it was she ate for breakfast. I'm sure I would have known what she had eaten had I met her on time.

With more patience than I thought I deserved under the circumstances, she informed me that my meal was on its way. She obviously believed me when I said I'd be here at 9:30, despite my failure to be ready at 9:00. If I had failed for a second time, I would have eaten a cold breakfast.

After quickly eating greasy, undercooked bacon (just the way they like it here, I'm told), and some kind of delicious eggy-sausagey-cheesy casserole-type concoction, I was glad I didn't have to eat it cold. Dr. Chalthoum tipped the server and we were off.

To my surprise, instead of a hovercar, we walked over to an old 4-wheel-drive pickup truck, probably built between 2015 and 2020, and likely powered by gasoline. That stuff is a little hard to get a hold of these days, at least in the United States, but we were close to those old oil wells and refineries of the Middle East. Dr. Chalthoum took my suitcase and tossed it into the bed of the truck. I held tightly to my briefcase. I didn't think my electronic equipment would fare as well as my clothing after a toss like that through the air into the metal bed of a rusty pickup truck.

Dr. Chalthoum (or "Anta" as she soon asked me to call her) started the truck's engine with the simple twist of a key. As she slowly accelerated away from the hotel, my previous feelings of unease returned.

Realizing that this woman was to be my companion for this journey, however long it took, I *felt* like opening up to her, and sharing my feelings. But I was too manly for that. Instead, we discussed Egyptian history, including a history of El-Alamein. I thought, based upon my education and career, that I probably had a superior knowledge of the history of all of Northern Egypt, but I quickly learned that I didn't. Anta was one smart girl! I soon felt pretty stupid and gave up trying to appear otherwise. She smiled.

First things first: I wanted to know why we were traveling in this truck instead of a hovercar, or "hover" as they're popularly known. I was used to traveling in hovercars, floating several inches off the ground. The bumps and rough turns of the pickup truck, on the other hand, rolling along a paved, but cracked road, was foreign and quite nauseating.

I had always been fascinated by human transportation. I had even visited a museum in Las Vegas a few years earlier where I spent a ridiculous amount of money for the opportunity to drive old cars. The place was amazing and had automobiles dating as far back as the "Model A" built by the Ford Motor Company in 1903 to the eventual demise of automobiles as the go-to mode of transportation in the 2050s. Of course I paid the money. When would I ever get a chance like that again? And I had a blast! I drove the Model T, a 1967 Chevrolet Camaro, and a few other classics. While automobiles are not, by any means, ancient relics now, they *are* considered a substandard and slow mode of transportation. They're uncomfortable, to which I could now attest. And, they use far too much of our world's scarce fossil fuels.

The highway between Apion and El-Alamein became progressively worse as we traveled west. It was littered with potholes, cracks, debris, and in some places, weeds and other plants growing through the pavement. Unlike many other countries, Egypt seemed to have decided that the maintenance of automotive travel infrastructure was a waste of money. We arrived in El-Alamein 90 minutes after we left the hotel in Apion. During that time, we saw only a couple automobiles traveling in either direction.

In that same time span, we were passed by hundreds of hovercraft— the predominant mode of travel since the 2050s—likely traveling in excess of 90 miles per hour. The pilots of nearly every craft glared at us as they passed by. It was clear what they thought of this lesser form of travel; and of their attitudes toward those who used it. We were in the way. We didn't get the bird, but I still felt like hunkering down in my seat to hide after the first few passed us by. Anta didn't appear bothered, so I figured I didn't need to worry about being gunned down in the street.

In any event, Anta explained that many people still use cars and trucks in the Sahara Desert because the shifting sands cover the pulsar energy modules imbedded into the pavement of the major roadways. Plus, many of the back roads aren't even modified to hold the modules in the first place. That made sense.

So, there we were, bumping and lurching along a pot-holed and sand-covered road, on our way to El-Alamein. All the while, Anta's broad knowledge of each subject we discussed made me wonder whether I should actually be considered a professor. Obviously, I didn't think I would know everything she knew about this place, since she was a local. I shouldn't have felt stupid, but I was the professor, and every time she said something I didn't know, she smiled. And that smile—wow. When I got up the nerve to ask her, much later, how she knew so much on so many topics, she smiled and told me she didn't really have to know that much, she just had to know more than me. Then she winked.

"I don't know why," I finally said as we neared our destination, "and I can't understand it, but I have a feeling that whatever it is that caused the bodies in those pictures to look that way is a very bad thing. In all my studies, research and travels, I've never seen anything like that—not even in the old days before the vaccines."

"I have had the same bad feeling," Anta replied. "I hadn't seen those photographs until a couple of hours before you did and they grossed me out."

Yeah, she said "gross"—how cute. And there was my chance to regain the upper hand. Call me a chauvinist, I don't care. I explained that humans today were living longer and healthier lives than ever before in recorded history, with an average life span of 109 years for women and 111 years for men. Just 60 years ago, people rarely lived into their 100s. This advancement is partially the result of fewer wars and significant advancements in prosthesis and cloning. But fewer mortal illnesses within the human population are also a significant factor. During the advanced stages of life, now, humans aren't riddled with dementia and the crippling diseases and accompaniments of old age previously known to the race. Thus, the average human, barring some fatal accident or the inability of his body to properly deal with some rare, but not altogether-unknown infectious disease, can expect to live more than 110 or even 120 years in relative good health.

She said she already knew that.

A little more timidly, I continued to explain the interesting part—that biologic and manmade diseases, along with other mortal medical conditions, are significantly rarer today than in previous generations. This is due to tremendous advancements in science and medicine, of course. Numerous diseases and other human conditions that previously plagued the Earth, like the flu, chicken pox and malaria have been largely eradicated. Other conditions, like heart disease, tuberculosis, cancer, and lung disease are now no more serious or life-threatening than the common cold due to advancements in simple, cheap, over-the-counter medications. Biological diseases, like Anthrax and Smallpox, while profoundly feared at various times in the history of the world, haven't been a cause for concern since the early 2050s.

She knew that too. Cripes.

Our discussion ended as we drove into El-Alamein. I concluded my thoughts by remarking that my unease was probably because the bodies in the pictures looked to have succumbed to some crippling infectious disease, which we haven't dealt with as a race for nearly 40 years. Anta agreed aloud. Secretly, however, I doubted it. In any event, she must have appreciated my knowledge in this area because she didn't even attempt to get the last word in. Yes! Nailed it!

I fully expected to learn that the desert bodies' deaths were caused by some war between rival nomadic families. And then maybe some punk kid thought it would be funny or cool to desecrate the bodies and show his friends on the Net. I knew a few kids like that.

Entering the city, Anta headed directly to the office of Mr. Riyad Shafik, the local tour guide who is believed to have taken those gruesome pictures. Anta hoped that he would know where the bodies are and would be able to take us there. Mr. Shafik wasn't at his office. A young, homely woman, with dull, mud-brown hair and vacant eyes— Shafik's bored and underpaid secretary probably—informed us that he wouldn't be back until tomorrow morning.

What could we do?

We did what any traveler would do under the circumstances—we ate. Although it was relatively early in the day, we had dinner at a small, tastefully-decorated, Greek café on the coast—an obvious tourist trap. I ordered stuffed swordfish and a Pepsi. The fish was awesome, and our server gave me only a slightly condescending look as she noted my choice of drink, then spit out the word "Pepsi" when repeating my order. Anta ordered tomato and feta shrimp with a "Louisa" (some kind of lemon herbal tea) to drink. The server showed no animosity toward that beverage choice.

During dinner Anta said, "Dr. Bader . . ."

I cut her off. "Please, call me Shift."

"Okay Shift; but is that really your name?"

"It's what's on my driver's license," I replied.

Anta looked confused.

"Yes, my name really is Shift," I added quickly. "My mom said they made it up so I would feel unique."

"Okay, it's certainly that. I like it."

Following our meal, we walked back to the hotel and said "good night" before separating to adjacent rooms at the Porto Marina Hotel. No kiss, no hand shake, no awkwardness . . . right. I spent the evening wondering what Anta was doing.

"Why am I thinking about Anta when I should be preparing for this expedition?" I eventually chastised myself out loud, shaking my head. But instead of preparing, I looked out the window, again.

The window to my hotel room, some 17 stories off the ground, looked out over the vast desert to the south. It was beautiful in the dimming light as the sun set in the west. Yes, the sun sets in the west everywhere, not just in America. More interesting, however, was a *huge* cloud of sand south of the city! It looked like it was blowing in from the east across the desert.

I'd never seen the infamous sandstorms of the Sahara Desert. As wind power has become more prolific in poorer countries like Egypt, large wind turbines have been built all over the desert to pull water up from deep under the dunes. The increased water flow has led to the development and expansion of farmland throughout the Sahara. Old books of the desert show pictures vastly different from what can be seen in many places now. Tales in the Bible and other historical treatises depicting life in the Sahara seem to indicate that it had been bone dry for centuries. The change is remarkable!

The increase in farming has led to a rapid decline in sandstorms since the Sahara itself has shrunk more than 40 percent since the late 2030s. Here, though, all I could see out my window, once I got past the suburbs of the city below me, was sand. If that storm turned north toward us, I mused, I would get a rare opportunity to see one of the great storms up close! That would be sweet! Probably. Of course, since these storms can last for days, I knew that could put a damper on our expedition.

With my thoughts coming back to the expedition, I remembered that I wanted to follow up on our dinner discussion of the history of El-Alamein. I wanted to get an idea of whether the desert, or the people of the desert, or some characteristic of the desert, had anything to do with the condition of the bodies. Anta shared a great deal of historical information with me at dinner, but I wanted to fill in some of the gaps.

I removed the electronic tablet containing my research log from my suitcase and sat at the desk, touching the control to turn up the desk lamp. Thankfully, I had one of the new "MEHDs" with me, which fit conveniently in my pocket and could communicate with my tablet. I wasn't very technical, but I'd already used the MEHD to communicate with others, via real-time holographic display, which is the MEHD's main purpose. I also had someone show me, before I left Colorado, how to use it to access the Net. I wasn't not too impressed by the alarm clock.

The MEHD functioned like a standard holographic display, or "Holo", but the display was accessed through light-weight glasses, accompanied by tiny ear pieces embedded in the frame of the eyeglasses above the ears. The ear pieces softly affixed to my skin as I placed the glasses on my face, allowing sounds and other sensory information from the display to be sent through my skin into my ear canals.

The glasses, and all of their parts, are meant to project a multi-dimensional image in front of the user, allowing the user to see, hear and actually feel like he or she is in the presence of the person with whom the user is conversing. Because the display is projected via eyeglasses, only the wearer of the glasses can see, hear and feel the holographic display. Of course, there's also a setting that allows the holo to be displayed outside the glasses for others to see, but the user then loses the other sensory information. It's limited to sight and sound in that setting. Either way, it's amazing! I knew it would be very useful for this trip, where my standard holo would be too heavy and bulky to carry.

I started by verifying information that Anta provided. During dinner, Anta told me that the Health and Population Ministry just stopped all tours into the Depression. I asked why. I thought I knew the answer already, but wanted detail to help me in my analysis. She explained that the population of El-Alamein is roughly 29,000. But tourism is the major industry—bringing nearly 250,000 travelers annually—thanks to its "white, sandy beaches and favorable climate". Although moderated by the Mediterranean Sea, the average daytime temperature in El-Alamein is about 88°F (31°C) during the summer months.

Just south of the city, the town meets the Qattara Depression, part of the Libyan Desert. That's the part I'd been staring at for the past half hour. The Qattara Depression lies below sea level and is covered with saltpans, sand dunes, salt marshes, cliffs, and fech fech. I learned that fech fech is very fine, powdered sand. My life was more complete.

The average summer temperature in the Depression is 98°F (37°C); and it's exceptionally remote, with few plants and only isolated water sources. Camelback tours into the Depression are an immensely popular recreational activity. Makes sense—sit on the back of a smelly, bug-infested horse with humps and walk slowly through the heat of the desert to look at dirt. Got it.

Historically, two important World War II battles were fought in the area around El-Alamein. This I knew, but I let Anta explain anyway. I'd given up trying to get the upper hand in our relationship. At the First Battle of El-Alamein (1–27 July, 1942) the advance of Axis troops on

Alexandria (now Apion) was slowed by the Allies. At the Second Battle of El-Alamein (23 October–4 November, 1942) Allied forces broke the Axis line and forced them back, westward, into Tunisia. The Qattara Depression confined the battles of World War II to the coastline. Thus, El-Alamein has significant historical interest to travelers as well.

The Qattara Depression is huge and falls to a depth of 436 feet (133 meters) below mean sea level. That fairly-unique situation led to various proposals, a long time ago, to create a massive hydroelectric project within the Depression. A project was eventually approved in 2019 and was known as the Qattara Depression Project—or "The Project" to the locals. The Project called for the excavation and construction of a large tunnel from the Mediterranean Sea to bring in seawater. The tunnel was created through a series of small nuclear explosions, much to the chagrin of the scientific and political world. *Imagine that.*

Once completed, salt water flowed through a series of hydroelectric penstocks that generated electricity by releasing the water. That water then spread out from the release point across the basin, evaporating by solar influx. Due to the evaporative effect, water could constantly flow into the depression, creating a stable source of energy.

Eventually, The Project resulted in a hyper-saline saltpan as the evaporating water left the salt it contained behind. The only other comparable salt pan is the Bonneville Salt Flats south and west of the Great Salt Lake in Utah. That's a cool place! The "salt flats" there are so reliably and consistently flat that during dry weather, wheeled "race cars" used to compete in an effort to set land speed records, which continued into the mid-21st century. I doubted whether such races had ever taken place here in the Depression—it's not quite large enough.

Unfortunately, in 2034, just 12 short years after the completion of the Qattara Depression Project, a massive 7.1 earthquake destroyed the penstocks and release points and caused several large fissures along the length of the tunnel. The Project became unusable. It couldn't be repaired and was abandoned. The massive penstocks and tunnel are hugely popular tourist attractions, although Anta was very serious when she told me that they are *not* as popular as the Great Pyramids.

The best way to see the old Project and its vast salt pans now is by camel, and the tours start and end in El-Alamein.

Anta told me that the two ravaged bodies of photograph fame were discovered in the Qattara Depression, near the former Qattara Depression Project hydro-electric penstocks. She said that the only way to keep people away from the bodies was to shut down tours altogether in the area. Her father, Minister Abasi Chalthoum, didn't want to have to explain to the International World Order, the "IWO", why people were dying mysteriously in the Egyptian desert.

My research was interrupted by the chirping of my MEHD. Switching to the caller display I read a message from Anta. The ministry wanted to ask me a few questions in the morning.

When I realized how late it was, my next thought was, "What has Anta been doing for the last two hours?" With the interruption of my research, I realized how tired I was. I acknowledged Anta's message, then turned off the MEHD.

JANUARY 3, 2093—ANTA

Shift is a dork; but I can't help but smile, thinking how sweet he is! He clearly faked not knowing about my truck today. Why? I could tell he had a lot more experience with automobiles than he let on. Later though, as we discussed Egyptian history, he was way out of his league. I told him I was smarter than him, but he didn't seem to believe me. He just kept proving me right.

Of course, I have to think of the expedition, not of Shift. I'm concerned about our investigation. There's a large dust storm south of town that could prevent us from getting to the bodies. The weather forecast, as unreliable as ever, didn't even mention this storm; yet, there it is, right outside my window. It's not headed this way, yet. Maybe its south of where we're going—hopefully tomorrow.

Dad just sent me a message. He wants to talk to us in the morning. He's got some questions for Shift. I hope Shift is ready. Dad can be pretty abrasive when there's something urgent on his mind.

I sent a message to Shift, hoping he wouldn't sleep in again and miss the call. He responded right away. I wonder what he's doing up this late at night. Thinking again about my day with Shift, a smile spread from my heart to my head and finally to my lips. I need to sleep.

5

"How did you sleep Dr. Bader?"

"Excellent, Minister." That wasn't true. But if I couldn't lie to the Egyptian Minster of Health and Population, who could I lie to? I didn't think Minister Chalthoum even cared. I could see and hear him perfectly through the Holo, and he wasn't even looking at me—he was looking at Anta; probably trying to figure out if I beat her up, or worse, last night.

"Well, that's wonderful to hear," Minster Chalthoum mumbled as he looked down at something in his hand.

I didn't think he meant that. I had already learned that Minster Chalthoum was all business. He says only what needs to be said.

"Dr. Bader, I have a few questions. I hope you can answer them. As you know, we believe that the bodies found south of your location were infected with some kind of bacterial or biological agent. All of our people, from the scientists to the doctors to the clerks, believe that can be the only cause. Can you confirm whether this theory is plausible?"

"That's a great question Minister. Interestingly, from the point of view of biological agents—which is the reason I was hired after all—the vast salt marshes and saltpans of the Qattara Depression are likely to, at least in part, counteract any such agents in the area. I understand the bodies are located near the massive saltpan created by 12 years of salt water deposits from the Mediterranean Sea into the Depression through the Qattara Depression Project. Well, high concentrations of salt are lethal to bacteria."

I really wanted the Minister to think that I knew what I was talking about, so I broke out The Project.

He didn't look too impressed.

"Theoretically, though, it *is* possible," I continued. "Many dangerous biological agents have been known to survive extreme conditions, like the conditions in the Qattara Depression, for long periods of time. But most of those biologic agents are believed to have been eradicated nearly 40 years ago. The last to cause any concern was *Bacillus anthracis*, or Anthrax. Today, all biologic infections are easily controlled through simple antibiotic medications. Even *Bacillus anthracis*, if it were still around, is no longer a concern because it wasn't generally passed from human to human. In any event, the last known large-scale human outbreak of Anthrax was in 2001. There have been a few minor outbreaks since then, but nothing since 2051."

"Doctor, your answers may be factually correct, but you still haven't persuaded me that what you will find in those bodies could not possibly be biologic in origin."

"Minister, in the unlikely event the Health and Population Ministry's theory is correct, and the bodies are infected with some devastating agent of biologic origin, it'll be a real surprise. But that surprise may potentially give rise to a very dangerous situation."

"Why?" Minister Chalthoum asked. "What would make it so very dangerous?"

"There are no known biological agents which cause, or have ever caused such a disease process as depicted in the pictures of the two men. Typically, bacteria enter the body through breaks in the skin or through the nose and lungs. Early symptoms of Anthrax, for example—which often took up to a week to exhibit—included flu-like symptoms, followed by reddish-black sores on the skin or in the lymph nodes around the lungs. Hemorrhagic fever and death sometimes followed; but I've never studied, heard of, nor seen any body exhibiting characteristics similar to those exhibited in the two bodies. That's why I don't believe we'll find evidence of bacterial infection."

"Thank you Doctor. That response is more on point. In the event, however, that you do find bacterial agents at work, is there a danger that the infection could spread to the general population?"

"I don't think so. Again, I'll discuss Anthrax because it was the most recent bacterial threat our world faced. It's always been understood, even generations ago, that Anthrax isn't contagious in the general sense; that is, it can't be passed from person to person."

"So, you're saying that, if those bodies succumbed to Anthrax, or any other bacterial threat, it is unlikely that disease would be spread by personal contact with another infected human?"

"That's correct."

"Can one survive an Anthrax infection?" the Minister asked.

"Yes. Now. Prior to 2045, even without treatment, more than half of those infected with Anthrax survived."

"So what do you expect to find Doctor?" Minister Chalthoum asked, with a little too much derision only partially hidden underneath his controlled emotions.

"Well," I responded, "in the event we discover some form of biological agent at work out there in the desert, it will certainly be enlightening to learn, if possible, how the men became infected. *If there is some kind of biological agent out there, I want to know where it came from and how it survived in that area.* I believe we'll find some other cause of death, but I don't know what that will be at this time. As I've said, I've never seen a body in the condition of those bodies."

"Thank you Doctor. I appreciate your time. I understand that you are going to be making contact with Mr. Riyad Shafik this morning. Good luck. And good luck to you Anta."

"Thank you father."

Without further warning, Minister Chalthoum disconnected the Holo.

"Anta?" I paused mid-sentence, not knowing how to complete my sentence. "Uh, your dad doesn't mess around, does he?"

"No," she replied, "but I can tell he was impressed with your knowledge."

"Really? I'm pretty sure he thinks I'm full of crap. But if you think he's impressed, I guess that's good."

"It is. Let's go find Mr. Shafik."

JANUARY 4, 2093—SHIFT

Following our meeting with Minister Chalthoum, Anta and I got back in her old truck and headed back to the office of Mr. Shafik, arriving just before 10:00 AM local time. During the short drive, Anta commented on the potential onslaught from the aggressive sandstorm that looms just south of us and fills up the southern horizon as far as we can see in both directions. It's pretty freaky.

Mr. Shafik wasn't at the office, again. The overly-unexcited secretary whom we had met at the door yesterday informed us that he hadn't returned yet. He'd been expected two hours earlier. She was understandably concerned that Mr. Shafik was somewhere in that sandstorm, hunkered down waiting out the storm. Upon our request for further information as to his travels, she informed us that she was "not at liberty to say" but that we "may wish to inquire at the offices of the Tourism Board as to the permits taken out for Mr. Shafik's travels". We did wish to.

The office of the Tourism Board was located prominently in the center of town where every tourist to the area could reach it from any direction. The exterior of the building had a white-washed stucco finish, with large windows looking out into lush gardens around the outside. The gardens had several benches and picnic tables placed at varying intervals, interspersed with Lotus Flowers, "Birds of Paradise" and other colorful flowers. Inside, the wide-open space had several desks and kiosks with computer terminals and Holos full of information on all the different tourist attractions in the area.

A few attractive young men and women sat among the various information booths talking to tourists.

A bubbly young female staff member approached us as we entered the building.

"Can I assist you sir," she asked in accented English. She looked directly at me, batting her eyelids and smiling. Anta immediately stepped between us, holding out her hand for a shake, and then led the conversation, leaving me out completely. I was okay with that—it made me feel a little cool actually!

"Yes. Thank you," Anta said. "We're looking for travel permits taken in the name of Riyad Shafik." Anta appeared to be attempting to mimic the young secretary's flirtatious attitude, and was doing a pretty good job.

"Okay." The young lady tried to look around Anta, but Anta leaned sideways, cutting off her view.

Finally, the young lady gave up trying to look at me. "Let me look it up," she said. "While I'm doing so, may I ask your purpose in learning this information?"

"You may certainly ask," Anta replied, "but we won't be able to answer you."

Producing her government identification badge, Anta said, "We're searching for information to aid in a confidential government search. I can tell you no more except that neither Mr. Shafik nor this office is in any kind of trouble."

The obvious initial concern on the young woman's face visibly eased upon hearing that she wasn't in trouble. She then opened a digital file for us to peruse on a nearby table and we sat down. A review of the Board's records indicated that Mr. Riyad Shafik had traveled into the Depression south of town prior to government advisements against doing so.

Mr. Shafik's most recent permit indicated that he would be entering the Qattara Depression, traveling approximately 45 miles south of El-Alamein, by automotive travel rather than camel. He was supposed to be back by nightfall—yesterday. The young woman informed Anta that he had not checked in to the Board's computers last night, nor had any word been received from his party regarding their whereabouts.

We spent the next few minutes speaking with a supervisor at the Tourism Board and some local police officers who were lounging on a park bench outside in the garden. Slow crime day, I guess. Without telling them about the deaths in the Depression—the Health and Population Department forbid us from providing any information to any person, apart from Mr. Shafik, in regard to the deaths—we inquired about accident reports. None of the officers had knowledge of any. We were left without any choice—we would stick around and hope that Mr. Shafik returned soon.

Over lunch, Anta asked, "Have you given any more thought to what my father asked about this morning? Is it possible that these deaths may have been caused by some biological agent or disease?"

"Actually, I *have* given it thought, although until this morning's conversation with your dad, I had thought it highly unlikely. As I tried to explain this morning, biological infections, like Anthrax for example, were almost completely wiped out by the 2050s. And, based on everything I've studied, which is *a lot*, there have been few successful attempts to engineer or create biological weapons. The nerve gases created during the Cold War era in the second half of the 20th century, the last historical instance of which I'm aware, were later destroyed when the containers they were stored in began to deteriorate. The US government spent a lot of money constructing facilities to contain the agents during the destruction process and even paid for a major portion of the destruction of the Soviet arsenal. So, without biological weapons and without any substantive biological agents running amok, there's little to persuade me that pure biology is a possible cause of death. I still think we'll find some other cause of death. But I've been wrong before."

"*No!* You?" Anta exclaimed with a smile that lit up her face.

She was teasing me. That didn't take long.

"I think I agree Shift, but I'm not convinced we should wholly discount the possibility."

"Oh, I haven't discounted the possibility; but we need to get to those bodies, and fast. If we can't get to the bodies soon, and the bodies are actually decomposing rather than just sitting there after mutilation by some human or animal vandal, it's possible that the decomposition of the bodies will have continued far beyond the point of any meaningful observational evaluation. That will leave us with only the possibility of body property analysis."

"Agreed."

"Of course, assuming the bodies are decomposing, based upon what we observed in the photographs, the bodies could be dust, blown away by the wind, before we ever get a chance to see them. That sandstorm started about 20 hours ago, right? So I assume our chance of finding the bodies now is a little more remote in light of the shifting sand."

Anta nodded.

After lunch, we made our way to the beach. It was beautiful. After a nice, long stroll along the beach, looking at Mediterranean seashells and watching the few beachgoers, I turned my head toward Anta and said, "I need dinner. All that talk of biological diseases made me hungry."

"We just ate," Anta said with a smile.

"Your dad's paying. I could eat all day." I returned her smile.

JANUARY 4, 2093—ANTA

Over dinner I brought up my concerns again to Shift.

"I'm worried about what we're going to find in the desert," I said. "You seem pretty comfortable stating that those bodies weren't infected by some biological agent, but I'm not convinced. After lunch today, that uncomfortable feeling I told you about, you know, when I first saw the pictures—well, it's come back. I'm going to take precautions before we go looking for dead bodies, and I've got a good one."

"Oh, what's that?"

"You'll see. I'll bring them to your room a little later."

"Them?"

"Yes, one for each of us. You'll see. You should take a shower before I arrive." I had to turn away so he didn't see my smile. "By the way, I just exchanged messages with Mr. Shafik's office. He still hasn't returned to town."

"Great. I guess we won't be going out to look for anybody or any body, today."

JANUARY 4, 2093—SHIFT

After Anta and I had gone to our respective rooms at the Porto Marina Hotel, I showered as requested. Then I sat quietly, watching some local news on the wall Holo and thinking about our dinner conversation.

What is Anta up to? I wondered. *She thinks I didn't see her mischievous grin as she turned away.* While I contemplated on that, there was a knock at my door. I saw Anta through the peephole, and didn't want to keep her waiting, even though I was in my pajamas. So I opened the door. She quickly looked me up and down, grinned, and then, before I could invite her in, strode past me carrying a large box that looked awkward, but not heavy.

"What have you got there Anta?" I asked casually; although inside I was dying to know.

"Chem suits," she replied simply.

Since she wasn't offering anything more, I finally asked, "Why?"

Anta lifted two "suits" out of the box. They looked vaguely like something a firefighter or an astronaut would wear, but less bulky. She carefully laid each on the bed. She even took extra time to straighten out some creases. Then, finally, she answered my question.

"Dad made me bring these with us from Apion. Apparently, they were in some old government storage facilities. I'd never seen one until after our meeting at the airport, when dad gave me a little tutorial. They're actually called 'CBRN suits'. They're government-grade personal protective suits, intended to provide protection against direct contact with, and contamination from chemical, biological, radioactive or nuclear substances—CBRN."

"Of course," I said. "Now I remember seeing that box in the back of your truck. You tried to kill it with my suitcase yesterday."

Anta laughed.

"According to my dad, the suits were originally designed to be worn for long periods of time to allow the wearer to fight, and generally function, while under the threat of, or under actual chemical, biological, radioactive or nuclear attack. The civilian equivalent is, or was, the Hazmat suit."

"Ahhhhh, the Hazmat suit. I used to wear one of those when I walked to my friend's house as a kid. His street was pretty bad."

She laughed again—more of a giggle really—for too long. That needed to stop. If we don't remain professional, I could make a mistake.

Anta then spent some time teaching me the basic functions of the suit and providing general precautionary instructions in the event my suit or its attached breathing apparatus is breached. Anta *had* intended for us to wear these suits for a few hours only, while we investigated and bagged the bodies; but, after requiring me to remove my pajamas and put on something more appropriate for daytime activities, she helped me put it on. I didn't look at her as I changed my clothes, wondering whether she was watching me. After helping me put on the suit, she casually informed me that I am not allowed to take it off for any reason until she says so; not even to sleep, shower or pee. *She's so bossy*, I thought.

Thankfully, she also taught me how to use these specialized suits to poop and eat. She couldn't explain how it worked, but I marveled as my suit expanded and contracted by entering a code on the arm-band. The expansion process blew the suit up like a huge tent that would allow me to move around inside the suit. Once "inflated", there were pocket-like sections of the suit that would allow for the entrance and exit of items, like waste products, food, and other things that we might want to physically handle rather than just relying on the gloves. Those little pockets, Anta explained, would "decontaminate" objects before allowing them to enter the suit. I was impressed.

Anta's explanation as to why we get to wear the suits indefinitely had to do with the sandstorm, of course.

"Sandstorms," she explained, "are known to increase the spread of disease. Bacterial and viral spores are blown into the atmosphere by the storms."

"Ahhh," I replied, feigning ignorance. Of course, I knew that this was why the spread of illness from infectious diseases had dramatically decreased in northern Africa. The whole area now has better access to medicine than ever before. But the expansion of farms through the Sahara, and the resulting decrease in sandstorms and strong winds in general, has resulted in a massive decline in the spread of disease by wind.

"We're going to wear these suits now," Anta continued, "because the wind is forecasted to shift and drive across the desert where the possibly-diseased bodies rest, toward El-Alamein. I know the bodies are probably covered by sand now, and if something biologic infected them, it's probably not dangerous any longer; but we're not taking any chances. I wouldn't even be able to sleep tonight thinking that whatever may have infected those two men could be traveling on the wind in our direction."

"Okay. You sold me. I'll wear the tent-suit. I'm pretty sure we'll attract a lot of attention walking around tomorrow. Might want to keep our public appearances to a minimum. By the way, how will we know when it's safe to take them off?"

"The control on the arm of the suit has settings for safe air in all four conditions. If the light turns from green to yellow, we're entering marginally safe air. Normally, it will go immediately to red, meaning the air is contaminated and not breathable. When the process is reversed and the light returns to green, we know the air is safe again. But that doesn't mean there aren't spores around, stuck to things. So, no matter what, before we get out of our suits, we'll need to decontaminate."

"And do you have that worked out as well?"

"Of course," she replied.

And then she smiled again. She was *killing* me with her face, despite her efforts to keep me alive.

6

During the night, the sandstorm blasted our windows and kept me awake for a long time. I didn't care. It was awesome! By sunrise, the storm was over—or gone.

This morning, around 9:30, Anta and I had breakfast in our rooms, ordering only food that would still taste good after going through the chem suit's decontamination cycle, or was prepackaged, bottled or could be peeled, by us. Then we left the hotel still wearing our chem suits with their green blinking lights shining for the whole world to see. We probably looked ridiculous in the bright sunshine of this post-sandstorm morning, but we had to talk to Mr. Shafik.

Upon our arrival at his office, his stunned secretary rewarded us with the look of disbelief that I had anticipated. Her lower jaw hit the floor as she looked at us in our space suits. It was pretty funny, and I laughed. Anta hit me. Unfortunately, these suits don't provide much insulation from that kind of assault.

The secretary eventually picked her jaw up off the floor, dusted it off, and then used it to inform us that Mr. Shafik had arrived back in town early this morning, a couple hours after the storm had abated. He was being briefed at the El-Alamein Police Department in regard to "rumors of murder in the Depression". The cat was out of the bag, it would appear—but at least the locals thought those two guys were murdered, not infected by some crazy disease. That would probably be better anyway. And truth be told, we still don't know that they weren't murdered, or killed by a wild animal.

Of course, if the two men *had* been murdered, that would still create a media circus around here. I've never had a problem with the circus, but I've always preferred the kind with elephants and cotton candy, not the kind with questions firing out of the mouths of reporters like rounds from a machine gun. I'd experienced that kind of circus, back in 2084, when I was involved in the "discovery" of a buried Native American city in the desert of southeastern Utah, near the "Four Corners" area. The discovery was cool. The circus was not.

Violence, anywhere in the world, has become extremely rare over the past few decades, thanks to the work of the IWO and its political allies. And international conflicts are virtually non-existent now. Of course, theft, rape and murder still occur, along with the more petty offenses; but instances of all these crimes have been heavily reduced by police forces with nearly unlimited resources. Because countries no longer need to spend tax dollars on massive militaries, they focus their resources on controlling local crime. The reduction in crime, including in Egypt, has made nearly every case of murder a national, and sometimes international, headline. Then the circus comes to town—the bad kind of circus.

So, if these two men were murdered, and I hoped we could discount any other cause of death, then little El-Alamein will be in the headlines, and I might have a front seat.

When we arrived at the police station, again, to the perplexed looks of the locals, Mr. Shafik was just finishing his report to the police. I waited for him outside while Anta had a frank discussion with the Police Captain about keeping any information gleaned from Mr. Shafik confidential. She also told him that, pursuant to a direct order from the Ministry of Health and Population, he was not authorized to conduct any investigation into any matters divulged by Mr. Shafik. That likely didn't go over very well.

By the time Anta joined Mr. Shafik and me outside, I had confirmed that it was, indeed, Mr. Shafik who had taken the photographs of the two bodies; and that he knows where the bodies are located.

Mr. Shafik confirmed that he took the pictures on December 28, just two days before I was contacted by Minister Chalthoum. Soon after he arrived back in El-Alamein that same day, he sent the pictures to the Ministry of Health and Population. The pictures were taken during a tourist expedition he had led into the Qattara Depression. None of his clients observed the bodies as he led them away from the area after nearly stumbling over one of them. Mr. Shafik agreed to take us into the Depression to find the bodies.

Before Mr. Shafik answered any more questions, though, he begged us to tell him about our chem suits, which he had been examining since the moment I first approached him. I wanted to tell him a fantastic story about how the suits were a precaution against an army of biologically-created supermonsters, spreading disease and destruction throughout Egypt. But I didn't want to, nor was I permitted to ignite a probably-baseless hysteria. So, I lied.

I told Mr. Shafik that, several days ago, we had been asked to investigate what was believed to be an ancient biological weapon discovered east of Cairo. And, because we may have been exposed to some ancient bacteria, as a precaution to those we come in contact with now, we had to wear the suits. Anta backed up my story, filling in the fake details that I missed. I hoped that this story would squelch any thought he may have about why we had suits, but it didn't.

Mr. Shafik was enthralled with both the look and the functionality of the suits. He pleaded with us, like a giddy child, to show him how everything worked. Mr. Shafik's naivety was a pleasant diversion, and pretty funny. Since I didn't want to tell him why we were really wearing them, I spent the next several minutes showing him all the cool features. He laughed out loud when I showed him the poop chute in the back. I laughed a little myself, right along with him. His cheerfulness was infectious. I secretly hoped that was all that was infectious about him.

I concluded my demonstration of the suit's remarkable functionality. Mr. Shafik then began to relate a curious tale of what he called "extraordinary things" on his most recent trip, from which he had just returned.

He told us that, two days ago, he took a scientist from the University of Cairo, and his young daughter, into the Qattara Depression to collect salt. He didn't know what type of scientist Dr. Ghannam was, or why he needed the salt. But he saw some of the Doctor's notes that talked about how salt reacts with chemicals to store energy, "or something funny like that," he said.

Mr. Shafik explained that their ride into the Depression, by automobile, took no more than two hours. It was quick despite severe blowing winds and massive sand drifts across the highways. That same evening, when they were scheduled to return to El-Alamein, the doctor's young daughter was missing. They hadn't noticed her wander away and they thought she was probably lost in the storm.

Neither Mr. Shafik nor Dr. Ghannam had any luck contacting authorities in El-Alamein due to the sandstorm, so they spent the entire night and the next day (yesterday) searching for the girl. When they finally found her, after the storms had quieted down a bit, she led them to a cave. Mr. Shafik didn't know of any caves in the area, so he concluded that it must have been buried beneath sand for a long time. This seemed likely given Mr. Shafik's description of the uncharacteristically high number of sand storms over the past three weeks or so.

The young girl indicated that she had become lost in the storm and had waited in the cave until the storm died down. She was hungry and thirsty, but otherwise, no worse off than when they had last seen her the day before.

The cave, on the other hand, was quite a sight, according to Mr. Shafik. The men spent many hours exploring the various tunnels and caverns before returning to El-Alamein early this morning. Mr. Shafik minimally described the caves to us, but said he wanted to show us, rather than tell us what was inside. That bothered me because he was so excited about what they found. He wouldn't budge.

We spent nearly two hours with Mr. Shafik before he begged leave of our company in desperate need of sleep. We agreed to meet tomorrow at 6:00 AM to travel to the cave, and, hopefully, to retrieve, or at least analyze the two bodies identified in his photographs. He said they're "no more than 15 to 20 minutes from the caves, walking."

During an enjoyable dinner of decontaminated and pre-packaged food, in Anta's room, Anta raised the concern that had been on my mind since our discussion with Mr. Shafik.

"Do you think Mr. Shafik has been contaminated?" she asked. "If he is, do we have an obligation to tell him the truth about the suits, and maybe even supply him one for the return to the desert? He could be contaminating others."

"My thoughts exactly," I replied, as I tried to get more food into my suit through the decontamination pouch. "Let's think about it overnight and decide in the morning. My light's still green."

Our conversation then drifted into a discussion of why Mr. Shafik's client, Dr. Ghannam, needed salt specimens from the Qattara Depression. After dinner, Anta made a quick call to a friend in Cairo. Her friend said that Dr. Ghannam is headed to the moon in two days as part of Egypt's first attempt at colonization.

"So, why does he need salt?" I asked. "Are they running low up there? Perhaps the fries just aren't worth eating without salt."

"Shift!" Anta said with a laugh. "Are you hungry for fries? I'll have a large order sent up if you like."

"I know—I'm a little fixated on fries. They're awesome! Yeah, let's get some, even if they taste terrible after decontamination.

"You know, it might be simpler than that though," I continued, returning to the subject. "Maybe the colonists are simply trying to make an ocean and lack just one key ingredient for the salt water."

Anta laughed again.

"I guess Dr. Ghannam could have several reasons for needing salt for his trip to the moon," Anta said. "We really don't know anything, apart from Shafik's talk about energy storage."

"Well, actually, I *do* know a little bit," I replied, all joking aside. "But it won't quite get us to the issue of the salt, I don't think."

"Just in case you missed it in history class, even 30 years ago, many people thought space travel was a huge waste of time and money. Populating the moon, as it is now, was even more divisive. Of course, the 'moonies' finally won. Initially only scientists, astronauts, a few military types, and their families made the trip to the small moon station, but later, wealthier people began going.

"I'm sure you remember about 15 years ago, July 4th, 2076, 300 years after the date of the adoption of the American Declaration of Independence, and just 107 years after the United States' landing of Apollo 11 on the moon on July 20, 1969, the first moon colony was established. It was a pretty elaborate celebration, so you must have seen the footage."

"Yeah, I saw it, and I remember it. Typical Americans making a *huge* to-do about something that was only *pretty* cool." Anta grinned.

"Uh, yeah. Us crazy Americans. Anyway, that newly-inhabited portion of the moon was established as a United States colony. Some argued that it should be made a State. I didn't ever understand any of the main arguments for statehood; but there was one minor argument that made sense. The United States was down to 48 states with the departure of Texas and New Mexico in the early 2030s. Puerto Rico finally attained statehood in 2048. So, some people thought it would be cool to have 50 states again since the United States' flag still had 50 stars. That made sense, but it was pretty trivial. It never happened anyway. The United States still has only 49 states.

"But between 2076 and 2091, England, Portuguese-Brazil, Poland, Mexico, and Burmo-Thailand each established colonies on the moon. And, as you know well, the Egyptians are about to send people up there too."

"Yeah. According to my friend in Cairo, we're sending nearly 1000 people to the moon, including Dr. Ghannam," Anta said. "But what has any of that to do with salt?"

"I don't know. I just wanted to sound smart. Did it work?"

"A little," Anta said, smiling.

"But I know a way to find out about the salt, I think," I replied, as I walked over and turned on the internal Holo stuck to the wall in Anta's room. "There are a lot of people up there now—thousands of them. They're conducting tons of experiments that can't be conducted here. Lots of the technology we have now on Earth, like the wall units that produce such delicious meals for the lazy among us, was first developed on the moon. Something about low gravity not interfering with the experiments, or something like that. And salt is an essential nutrient and a pretty important part of some of those experiments, or so I'm told. Or, maybe there really is a salt shortage. I don't know. But I know a guy who can probably tell us."

"Well, let's get him then," Anta said. "Even though it probably has nothing to do with what we're out here for."

Using the holo, I contacted a colleague from the International World Science and Health Library in Geneva, Switzerland. Dr. Jeffry Undermane, a very large, jolly man, with at least three chins and an appetite the size of Anta's truck, was apparently asleep when we called. Whoops! Once we got into our scientific mode of inquiry we lost track of time and didn't realize how late it was. I felt bad for waking him, but he was eager, as always, to discuss science. I knew I could count on him. Every time I've needed information about chemistry or technology, he has jumped up and down (sometimes literally) in his zeal to educate me. That's just the way he is, sleep-deprived or not.

I quickly related Mr. Shafik's tale, and explained why we were wearing the chem suits. He was intrigued.

"Jeffry, what do you make of it? I mean, how, or why, might Dr. Ghannam use salt in relation to the storage or creation of energy?"

What I really wanted to know, but didn't believe Jeffry could tell me was, could there be any relationship between salt and the deaths of the two men in the desert? Is there any relationship at all, or are we fishing in a dry, salt-water pond?

"The answer is simple!" Jeffry replied. "Dr. Jafari Ghannam is a colleague of a good friend of mine in Cairo. He is on the cutting edge of this research, and has been for the past decade. His writings and research litter the scientific databases dedicated to chemistry and its applications to future scientific endeavors. Dr. Ghannam's reputation is outstanding in our field!"

"So what is he working on now?" I asked.

"Well, about eighty years ago, chemical researchers first learned how to store hydrogen in the form of methanol as part of a method for storing excess energy produced by wind and solar power plants. In layman's terms, salt is used in the formation of a catalyst which aids in the process of utilizing excess electricity to electrolyze water. The surface of the catalyst is coated with a thin film of basic salts, namely a mixture of lithium, potassium, and cesium acetate. Eventually, through a process that I won't try to explain, hydrogen can be stored as a liquid. The liquid hydrogen can then be released at a later time to power a fuel cell."

"*That* was layman's terms?" I asked. Jeffry either ignored, or was completely oblivious to the look of confusion on Anta's face, and probably mine as well. But I could read her face and it said, quite clearly, *What is this guy talking about?* Those were my sentiments exactly.

"Oh yes, I forget who I'm talking to. I'll go slower," he said.

"Thanks, I think."

"Salt makes a funny sizzling noise when it's thrown on electrolyzed water. Then the electrolyzed water goes crazy and can be scooped up and put into a big bucket. The stuff in the big bucket can be dumped into smaller buckets and used to make the lights go on. Was that better?"

"You obviously think I'm an idiot. But, thanks, that *was* better," I replied. "So, Dr. Ghannam could be using the salt to experiment in the storage of electricity, right?"

"Yes," Jeffry said. "But the dumbed-down Shift-sized version isn't quite accurate. I won't bother trying to explain it any better. The technology has been in use for decades, in one form or another; but not until the late 2040s was the technology used with any precision or effect. There may be some other purpose for the gathering of salt by Dr. Ghannam, but my belief is that he would be using this salt to continue that research."

"Doctor," Anta said, "we've recently received information that Egypt will be sending a group of scientists to the Lunar Space Port two days from now, and that Dr. Ghannam will be traveling with them. Could his research benefit the moon colonies?"

"Ahhhh, indeed. Now the pieces come together. I recently attended a seminar where we discussed difficulties the colonies are having with the storage of surplus electricity they are creating. They are having intermittent power outages on the moon. Now knowing that Dr. Ghannam is traveling to the moon makes it reasonable to believe that his salt specimens will be traveling to the moon with him. He will certainly be experimenting with catalysts needed to store energy at low gravity. That makes sense. I would be happy to make some inquiries if it will aid you in your quest."

"No thank you Jeffry," I replied quickly. "If we think of some reason this information may be useful to what we're doing, I'll call you again. Right now, I can't see any relationship between what we're trying to accomplish in El-Alamein and what Dr. Ghannam is going to do on the moon. And, I've had all the insults I can take for the time being. Perhaps it's nothing more interesting than coincidence. Thank you for taking the time to speak with us."

"Ahhh, both insulting you and educating you have been my pleasure Shift! And it was wonderful to meet you Ms. Anta! Even with your chem suit, your beauty will inspire my sleep this evening! Good night."

"Th-thank you Dr. Undermane," Anta stuttered. "You're very kind."

I repressed my laughter until the Holo closed, and then let it erupt. Anta was not nearly as amused as I was. She hit me in the shoulder, apparently to inform me that she wasn't thrilled about being in the large man's dreams tonight.

Before she physically pushed me out of her room for my behavior, Anta mentioned that her older brother, Hasani Chalthoum, would also be traveling with the lunar party on Egypt VIII. He is Egypt's Junior Ambassador to the IWO. Anta seemed very excited to hear and see his perspective of the moon through holo messaging tomorrow evening.

As I tried to fall asleep tonight, I became curious about Anta's brother's perspectives because I had gained knowledge that tied his expedition to mine—if only loosely. Anta's embarrassment was cute. Perhaps she would be in *my* dreams tonight too.

JANUARY 5, 2093—ANTA

Disgusting. Dr. Undermane just paid me the ultimate compliment, if I was a whore. I better not find myself in his dreams tonight. Plus, now my hand hurts. I hit Shift—hard—for thinking that was funny. He deserved it. He wouldn't shut up. When I shoved him out into the hall he looked like he was going to sulk. It's a good thing I didn't puncture his suit. That would have been terrible.

7

Takeoff: January 6, 2093, 1800 hours EET.

Destination: International Lunar Space Station, U.S. Moon Colony.

Operating time estimate until landing = 6 hours, 16 minutes

All systems operational and functioning within calculated parameters.

On board: Pilot; two co-pilots; 28 operations officers; 983 passengers (547 male, 436 female) including 173 youth under age 18.

Passenger List:

. . .

Dr. Jafari Ghannam (Cairo, Egypt)

Miss Shani Ghannam, age 7 (Cairo, Egypt)

Ambassador Hasani Chalthoum (Cairo, Egypt)

. . .

JANUARY 6, 2093—SHIFT

This morning, just after 6:00 AM, Anta and I met Mr. Shafik at his office to begin our journey into the Qattara Depression. Cue the epic music! On the way in we discussed whether or not to tell Mr. Shafik the truth. We agreed that until we know more about what we're facing, that would be foolish. It was bad enough to have to swear the police chief to secrecy. I couldn't imagine a *tour guide* keeping his mouth shut.

Our drive into the Depression, in Mr. Shafik's SUV, was without complication. Mr. Shafik continued to quiz us about the chem suits and we continued to redirect the conversation back to what Mr. Shafik discovered in the caves. Neither he nor we wanted to share more, so the conversation stalled eventually and we continued on in companionable silence.

Despite being so dry that the guts of the bugs hitting the windshield instantly dried and likely became permanently stuck to the glass, the Depression was a beautiful, serene place. There were high dunes and low, salty deadpans as far as we could see. Wisps of sand sprayed into the air from the crests of the dunes. Rugged and rocky hills and mountains shot into the sky on the horizon far in the distance. A few rocky outcroppings rose from the sand here and there like sentries guarding the land.

There was only a light breeze down in the gulfs between the dunes, where we drove. The clusters of insects—those that didn't become permanent elements of the windshield—swarmed like bees to an overturned can of Pepsi. The world and all living creatures therein, were a smorgasbord to these pests. Anta and I were wearing our chem suits so only Mr. Shafik had to endure the incessant buzzing, landing and biting of the various bugs. He didn't *seem* to mind, but certainly, he wasn't past feeling.

A short 90 minutes after we left El-Alamein, Mr. Shafik told us to start looking for a small outcropping of rust-colored sandstone in the shape of a snowman. He said the bodies were lying near the butt-end of that rocky snowman. I'd never considered a snowman to have a "butt". I wondered whether Mr. Shafik had ever *seen* a snowman.

Within 40 minutes of locating the sandstone snowman—and it really did look like a snowman—and Mr. Shafik's verification that this was, indeed, the location of the bodies, we gave up hope that the bodies would ever be found again. As we suspected, the huge sandstorms of days past had covered whatever was left of the bodies.

We left the snowman and headed toward the cave, on foot, as no road led that direction. Mr. Shafik told us, probably trying to lift our spirits, that we would be pleased with what we saw in the caves. I secretly hoped it was a juice stand. It was dry out there. And, even though it's January, I had sweat dripping down my back, forming a small oasis in my trousers.

In less than 20 minutes, we arrived at the entrance to the cave. Mr. Shafik opened his pack and produced handheld flashlights and headlamps for each of us, which we carefully donned. The headlamps barely fit over the head pieces of our suits with the straps fully extended. Then he led us to a small hole in the side of a rocky hill and got down on his hands and knees. We followed.

The cave entrance was very small, and made me glad my mom and sister forced me to eat healthy at home. Entrance to the cave required crawling on hands and knees for several meters. We carefully squeezed past jagged rocky protrusions while trying to avoid kneeling on the remnants of rocks that had broken from the entrance walls and now rested under the sand, quietly and secretly waiting to bruise and bloody our knees. Thankfully, our chem suits were durable and didn't rip open; plus, with the push of a button, the suits contracted and became rather form fitting in most places, so they didn't really restrain our progress.

Claustrophobia, on the other hand, was a real problem for one of us—and it wasn't one of the men. I literally pushed Anta through in front of me with my hand on a couple of occasions. Her rear end, inside the now tight and form-fitting suit, was . . . well, the situation was awkward, at least for me. But she didn't comment about me putting my hand on her, and what choice did I have? I wanted to get in and she was in my way. Eight or nine meters in, the cavern opened up into a large room with a few small openings around the outside walls.

We spent a bit of time exploring the surrounding rooms and tunnels, but their only significance to our investigation was their previously-unknown existence. In the large first room, though, we saw some amazing things! I was as giddy as Mr. Shafik had been when he told us about the cave yesterday. There wasn't a juice stand, but I literally clapped my hands as I looked around with my flashlight—and

I'm not proud of it now. But at that moment, looking at the remains of what appeared to be a very old human camp, I was like a child. In fact, I actually felt like Indiana Jones! I decided to tell Minister Chalthoum. He'd be . . . well, he probably wouldn't care.

During my childhood, I was fascinated with archeology and ancient civilizations, particularly civilizations from Persia and Africa. I spent hours watching two-dimensional adventure films on an old 46-inch television set my grandma owned. I explored and suffered, and conquered wild jungles and deserts right alongside Indiana Jones. I stormed the deserts and beaches of Nigeria with Sarah Scorefield, running from and fighting the Nigerian Tero regime of the late-2020s.

My friends and I used to act out brutal, action-packed scenes from the movies developed around these two fictional characters. Often, by the end of the day, one or more of us went home with a black eye or a bruised elbow or knee. The only aspect of our play that could have been more real would have been the use of real weapons. Thankfully, those were a bit difficult to come by; otherwise, my neighbors, Katie and Shanna, would have killed one of us with their undignified fighting styles.

So, there in that cave, with Anta and Mr. Shafik, I felt like I was actually living in a movie. It was awesome!

The large room of the cave was about 12 meters wide at its widest point, 15 or 16 meters long at its longest point, with a ceiling that varied in height between 5 and 10 meters. Anta seemed more comfortable in this space than in any other inside the cave. The floor was rocky in some places but sandy in others—the sand being as fine and soft as a bunny's tail. Although, candidly, I'd never felt a bunny's tail. But I suspected there were sharp rocks hiding beneath the sand waiting to stab the unsuspecting traveler tired enough to plop down for a rest. That wasn't going to be me, and I warned Anta as well.

On one side of the cave, against the wall in a sandy depression within the rock floor, was a small table of sorts. A meter-long slab of thin sandstone sat on top of a pile of smaller sandstone rocks. The table-top had various stains and scratches across the surface. The sandstone wall next to the table had 24 fairly-uniform scratches, like tally marks.

Adjacent to the table was a sandstone rock just tall enough to make a decent seat. It probably served as a stool based upon its dimensions and proximity to the table. On top of the table sat a rusted, scratched compass likely dating from the early to mid 1900s. Its design and functionality were clearly from long ago. Its arrow turned as the metal cuffs of my suit got close.

Underneath the compass was a dry, torn, and yellowed paper map detailing the northeastern corner of the African continent. It looked like an old pirate's map, including an "X" to "mark the spot". Alongside some typed words and symbols were handwritten and faded words and diagrams. They were so faded that we couldn't read them in this light, even with a flashlight. Mr. Shafik opined that the "X" probably marked the approximate spot of the cave. The town of El-Alamein was circled on the map to the north of the "X".

On another flat rock that looked like it could have served as a countertop or shelf, near the makeshift table, was an antique mess kit containing a small aluminum bowl, plate and cup, an aluminum fork missing one prong, a spoon, and a slightly bent, dull metal knife. Against another wall, not far from the small kitchen, was a bedroom of sorts. There was a small, ravaged blanket that looked more like a cat's ball of string than anything useful for keeping a body warm. It lay in a pile next to an equally thread-bare jacket bearing a small cross-like symbol on its lapel. Anta, seeing the symbol, gasped and breathed the word "swastika".

Hearing Anta's gasp, a skittish Mr. Shafik asked, "What is 'swastika'?"

"A swastika," I answered, "is an ancient symbol—an equilateral cross, with four arms bent at 90 degrees."

"Huh?" he interrupted.

I pointed at the symbol on the lapel, tracing my finger along the four bent arms.

"The swastika was used as a symbol by several ancient civilizations around the world including cultures in Turkey, India, Iran, Nepal, China, Japan, Korea and some European countries. A long time ago, it was widely used in Indian religions, specifically Hinduism, Buddhism, and Jainism, primarily as a tantric symbol that invokes *Lakshmi*—the Hindu goddess of wealth, prosperity and auspiciousness. Some smaller sects of those religions still use the swastika.

"Famously though, and the reason Anta was shocked at seeing it, the swastika was adopted as a symbol of the Nazi Party of Germany in 1920. The Nazis used the swastika as a symbol of the Aryan race. You've heard of the Nazi Party, right?"

"Yes, of course," he replied. "But I do not know much. I did not go to school."

"Well, between World War I and World War II, Adolf Hitler—the eventual Nazi leader—rose to power. In 1933, a right-facing 45 degree rotated swastika was incorporated into the flag of the Nazi Party, which was made the state flag of Germany during the Nazi era. As a result, the swastika became strongly associated with Nazism and related concepts like anti-Semitism, hatred, violence, death, and murder in many western countries."

"This is starting to ring a bell," Mr. Shafik said.

"Well, following World War II, the swastika was outlawed in Germany and many other countries if used as a symbol of Nazism. Prior to the creation of the IWO in 2048, many white nationalist and Neo-Nazi groups, like the Russian National Unity party and the Ku Klux Klan in the U.S. used stylized swastikas or similar symbols to signify their own brand and style of terror, hatred and bigotry. In the 2030s, if memory serves, a large terrorist group centered in Indonesia, with large pockets and cells in many places of the world, incorporated the swastika as a symbol of hatred against democracy. Those groups left burning swastika effigies at the sights of their terror, violence and murder all over the world.

"Since the rise of the IWO, the swastika has been banned as a symbol in all but religious connotations, with severe penalties for its use in acts of violence or hatred. In other words, even though the swastika was initially used as a symbol for good, peaceful things, it was made famous, beginning in the early 1900s as a symbol for hate. Its former beauty as a symbol is now almost-universally regarded as ugly and terrifying."

"Wow! One little mark could do such damage? It is hard to believe," Mr. Shafik replied.

"Believe it Mr. Shafik," Anta said. "The hate and evil that 'little mark' symbolized became the cause of the deaths of many of our countrymen and women, including some of my ancestors, and probably yours too. When we get back, you should look up the history of World War II and the wars that were fought outside your front door."

Mr. Shafik looked sheepishly at the ground, but, quickly regaining his composure, nearly shouted, "Look what else we found!" The excitement was back.

He led us to a backpack leaning against a wall in a dark corner of the cave. At one time, it probably held food and water. Now, it held only an empty canteen, a rusted, antiquated hunting knife, a small notepad and pencil, and a German Mauser M712! I immediately understood why he was so excited. That gun was awesome! I had to pick it up, despite Anta's warning against disturbing the artifacts. Whatever. I'm a man, and men can't keep their hands to themselves, right? So, I ignored her. I'm sure I dropped a notch or two in her esteem.

As I was ogling the rifle, I could see Anta quietly thumbing through the notepad—*disturbing the artifacts* I thought; but I didn't say it. I'm not that stupid. When it appeared she could no longer stand it, she called quietly for my attention while watching Mr. Shafik across the cave, presumably to make sure he wasn't paying attention.

"Shift. Shift! Look at this," she insisted, quietly.

As I approached her, I suddenly realized why she seemed so cautious. "That's a journal, isn't it?" I whispered, moving toward her while also looking toward Mr. Shafik to confirm that his attention was elsewhere.

"Yes. Look at the last entry." The writing was shaky, almost illegible, and in what appeared to be German. Because neither of us could read German, only one word stood out to us.

"... anthrax ..."

Anta and I both immediately looked down at our wrists. I don't know why we hadn't thought to do so earlier. The lights were green. The cave wasn't contaminated, or at least, that's what our chem suits led us to believe. If this place was dangerous, our suits were fooled. I silently prayed that it was as it seemed.

Anta placed the journal into a sealed bag and placed it in her pack. I gently put the rifle down where I found it. As Anta took pictures of all of the objects in the cavern, I walked back over to the kitchen area to see if there was anything more to see before we investigated the main attraction. As my headlamp passed over an area beneath the table, I saw a tiny glimmer coming from the sand. I bent down and ran my gloved fingers through the sand. As one handful of sand sifted through my fingers, a small metal vial appeared. Its cap was off and it was empty. I decided to keep it.

Because the Health and Population Ministry believes the condition of the bodies in the photographs have something to do with biologic miscreants, and the vial appears to be of the type which could have been used for such a purpose, I placed it in a personal airlock canister where it will remain until it can be analyzed.

Apart from the journal and the vial, we left everything in place for a subsequent exploration and documentary expedition. That wasn't the reason we were there.

The only remaining item in the cave—the main attraction—was a human body. That's why we were there! The body is the reason Mr. Shafik seemed to think we would be okay not finding the two bodies that he'd photographed. He was right. As soon as we saw the body, that failure was no longer quite as disappointing.

The cave person was obviously an adult male. It was approximately five feet, ten inches tall and still had skin which would have covered the ... uh ... "male regenerative organ". The left knee bone appeared to have been shattered at some point, and poorly healed; but otherwise, externally, it appeared to be in a similar state as those found by Mr. Shafik nine days ago.

One striking difference between this body and the bodies of the men Shafik found, however, was the condition of the organs and tissue underneath the skin. Shafik's bodies appeared to be dissolving or decaying from the inside, but the organs, or parts of them anyway, were still there. In the cave man, though, only the bones and skin remained. The skin was well-preserved, probably because of the tomb-like encasing of the cave prior to the recent sandstorms. But the inside organs and other tissue were gone. Completely. With me blocking Mr. Shafik's view, Anta placed skin and bone samples into sealed containers and placed them in her backpack.

After our return to El-Alamein and our hotel, we retired to our rooms for the night. I was shattered, and sweaty. I needed a shower, but this crazy suit only allowed me to sponge bathe. Not cool, but I did it.

Now I'm just sitting here, contemplating the fate of the cave man, waiting for Anta to call me over. We need to talk.

The guy in the cave probably entered the cave during one of the battles of World War II or some time shortly thereafter, and hunkered down. I'm fairly certain that there were sandstorms during part of the El-Alamein campaigns in 1942. Perhaps this dude got caught in a storm and, like Dr. Ghannam's daughter, hid in the cave to wait it out. But the cave is many miles from the battle zones of 1942. How he got here, and why, is a mystery. Anta is sending the notepad to her father for translation. That may solve the mystery.

Assuming the cave man was between 20 and 30 years old at the time he entered the cave—the age of a typical soldier during World War II—the body must be approximately 170-180 years old. Biologically, I guess it could take a few years for a body to decompose naturally when it's buried in a cave like that in the desert, but that decomposition would be complete, minus the bones. The decay of this guy's body, from the inside out, but leaving the skin still intact, shows that the natural decomposition process was altered somehow. I'm no biologist, nor a medical doctor, but even if I had knowledge in those areas, this would still freak me out.

It seems incredible to find this body, in this location, in this condition. There was no tissue from which to take a sample except for the bones and the skin. I now have a sample of both, along with the metal vial, sitting in my case ready to be analyzed as soon as my machine tells me it's ready.

Now, finally, I'm beginning to believe that the two men in the desert may actually have died as a result of some biological disease, rather than murder or accident. Whatever caused the three bodies to dissolve from the inside is unknown, obviously, but it can't be good. That one word—"anthrax"—is getting under my skin—only figuratively, I hope. But the solid green light on my armband is a good sign, I think.

I wish I could say that there could be no trouble from this. I'd love to argue that if some disease killed the cave man, it was so long ago that the disease is dead, and no longer a threat, since our chem suits didn't warn us of any danger. Unfortunately, the two men Mr. Shafik found in the desert within walking distance of the cave weren't entombed with the cave man. At least, I'm *fairly* certain that two 170-year-old men could not be unearthed from the cave and then wander the desert. No; I'm pretty sure that Mr. Shafik found the bodies of men who found the cave some time over the past few weeks, after the cave was unearthed by the storms.

They may have been infected at that time, and then succumbed to the disease soon thereafter. That's an unpleasant thought. Also, it would be much better if they contracted the disease by touching the body than if the disease is spread by airborne transmission. If it's airborne, then Mr. Shafik may be infected, along with Dr. Ghannam and his daughter. This is still speculation, of course. Unless and until Mr. Shafik shows signs of some kind of illness, we can't be sure how the disease, if any, is even transmitted. The two men may have touched the body. Maybe they took a bite—some people are crazy like that. It may not be an airborne pathogen at all. That's my hope. Anta says the red lights on our suits should have blinked if there was something in the air.

Earlier today, when we'd looked at the body, I saw the worried expression on her face through her face plate. I could tell she was having thoughts similar to mine, despite the apparent safety of the air around us. When she glanced at me, I shook my head slightly to tell her not to speak her thoughts. Her features relaxed slightly. Her expression changed to one of determination, letting me know she understood my message and that we would discuss it later. I'm looking forward to that discussion.

I wish that we'd found the other bodies to see if we could determine how long they'd been dead. Without confirmation that the deaths were caused by the same factors as the body in the cave, we don't have much useful information; at least not much that's useful in determining what real precautions should be taken at this point, if any.

During a quiet conference with Anta outside the cave, as we trudged through the deep sand back to Mr. Shafik's SUV, we decided to request that the Qattara Depression, along with El-Alamein and any cities or towns downwind of any of the recent sandstorms should be quarantined—at least until we determine what caused the bodies to be in such a state. While walking, Anta made the request to her father via the satellite uplink on her watch. Anta hasn't called me over to talk yet, so maybe her father hasn't responded.

JANUARY 6, 2093—ANTA

Dad is pissed! But thankfully not at us. He's just mad about the situation. I asked him to quarantine the Qattara Depression and El-Alamein. He went ballistic. His voice raised a couple of octaves. It would have been funny—although I wouldn't have dared to laugh out loud—if the situation weren't so dire.

I explained what we'd found, and he began to calm down; but he wanted to know how long this quarantine would have to last. I think his problem with this is that he can't see how to keep it a secret from the IWO. He doesn't want mass hysteria. I get that. Not my problem though. I don't get paid the big bucks. In answer to his question about how long the quarantine would have to last, I told him there was no way to know—so indefinitely. He was not pleased.

Dad authorized us to place Mr. Shafik into quarantine as a precaution. I arranged for that, attempting to spread as little information as possible. Mr. Shafik understood and agreed to keep quiet.

When Shift first suggested that we request a quarantine, he had to remind me what it meant. I'd forgotten because it's a term and a process so seldom used. The word "quarantine" means, at least when used in circumstances like these, to separate and restrict the movement of healthy persons who may have been exposed to a communicable disease to see if they become ill. The word comes from the Italian "quaranta", meaning forty, which is the number of days seagoing ships were required to be isolated at sea before passengers and crew could go ashore during the Black Death epidemic in the mid-1300s. If we have to quarantine El-Alamein for 40 days, dad will not be able to keep it a secret.

After our trip out into the desert, while waiting for my Holo with Hasani, mom and dad, which is in a couple hours, Shift and I talked about what we found in the desert. Well, mostly I talked. Shift listened. We didn't want to have the conversation in front of Mr. Shafik. Just common courtesy really.

"It's probably historically important that the items located in these previously-unknown caves had remained buried for years," I said, while Shift nodded his head in agreement. "Mr. Shafik, a guide who takes tour groups regularly into the area, didn't know anything about them."

"Yeah, I'm sure that's meaningful," Shift replied.

"One thing is certain, Shift—I'm scared. I've never seen anything like that body, and I've seen many things that I can't talk about. I've certainly never seen a dead body with the skin still intact, and only bones on the inside. It was disgusting." Again, Shift was nodding his head.

"Have you?" I asked. Shift moved his head side to side silently.

"What's most interesting to me," I continued, "is that the desert bodies and the cave body appeared at nearly the same time, in nearly the same place, after a three-week period of repeated sand storms. In my short 34 years of life, I've only seen four or five sandstorms. I remember stories dad used to tell us when we were children, about great sandstorms, which were much more common when he was a child.

"But this current period of extended sandstorms is abnormal. It's probably the only reason the cave was unburied."

"Maybe it should be covered back up," Shift finally said, with a tone that showed he wasn't joking.

"You're probably right," I replied. "I'm afraid of what may have been unearthed by the wind. I'm glad we had on our chem suits, but I'm worried about Shafik and all the people here in El-Alamein. I'm concerned for Shafik's client and his daughter too. They've probably already left Earth on Egypt VIII, headed for the Egyptian moon colony."

"Well, hopefully he and his daughter are okay. And, hopefully, your brother is okay too," Shift said.

"If only we had been out there and found this stuff yesterday," I continued, starting to feel a little preachy. "I would have made sure that Dr. Ghannam and his daughter were not on that ship. Instead, we just have to pray that they weren't exposed to anything."

After our conversation, Shift said that he still isn't fully convinced that there's any further danger. But he certainly seems more convinced. It's rather obvious that all three men died from some disease, but Shift is hopeful that the disease isn't communicable by air. Me too. The journal we found may be telling, and I can't wait to get it translated. I hope dad's got that process going already.

I'm excited to talk with Hasani in a bit, but neither I, nor dad, will be sharing with him the details we've uncovered so far. We all agree that it's better to not incite panic about something that may turn out to be strictly isolated and now harmless.

8

Ambassador Hasani Chalthoum (aboard Egypt VIII)
Anta Chalthoum (El-Alamein)
Minister Abasi Chalthoum and Mrs. Mariam Chalthoum (Cairo)

"Hello mother and father; Anta!" Ambassador Hasani Chalthoum said, his excitement palpable even through the holos.

"Hello son," Mariam, his mother, replied, excited to see her son.

"Hello son," replied Minister Abasi Chalthoum.

"Hi Hasani. I'm so excited!" Anta exclaimed. "Tell us what you see. Is the moon beautiful?"

"Yes, it's wonderful! We're about half an hour from landing, but I can see everything very clearly through the windows. I'll move out of the way while we talk so you can see what I'm seeing, but I'll describe it for you too, since my view will be much clearer. And, since I've been reading so much about this for the past few weeks, I'll try to explain how things operate, if I can."

"WOW!" Anta said, loudly, as she looked past her brother out the windows of Egypt VIII. "Look at that! It's amazing! Sorry, go on."

"Ha ha, that's alright; it *is* amazing!" Hasani replied. "The surface of the moon is light, but not as light as we see it from Earth at night.

It's more of a dull gray light. I can see craters and hills, all in various shades of gray. What's *really* amazing is seeing the distinct line where the sunlight stops hitting the surface. You can see it on the left side of the hologram. It's just like when we look at the moon from Earth, or look at the edge of a shadow, but it is so much more distinct and so much bigger from here. I read that the sharpness of the shadow edge is a result of having no atmosphere.

"All those bright lights you can see are the Encapsulation Shells that cover each colony and the other outposts. The smaller Shells, I've been told, are laboratories, factories, farms, vacation spots, and that kind of thing. But the six big ones are those covering each of the colonies. We're going to land at the very biggest one, which was the first one built. It's the United States' shell which also houses the International Lunar Space Station. We'll be staying there for a few months while Egypt's encapsulation shell is completed. In fact, I've been told that the darker spot just to the left of the United States shell is where construction is underway."

Mariam, wide-eyed, said, "Hasani, this is amazing! We've seen the pictures, of course, but this is beyond words! How are they lit?"

"Well, as I understand it, there are hundreds of luminescent energy cores embedded into the shell walls that give off light 24 hours a day. They're never shut off. I don't know why that is, but I understand it makes it difficult for some to sleep. I don't know when we're going to sleep—if there's a period of time designated as "night" when we all sleep. I'm sure I'll find that out."

Abasi added, mechanically, "Yes, I've been told that there is a general time when most people sleep. The energy cores remain on at all times because it takes a great deal of energy to start them up and, as you may have heard, the colonies are having a difficult time storing excess energy that is produced. So, when they shut down the cores, they have difficulty restarting them—its more energy-efficient just to keep them on. You may have already met Dr. Jafari Ghannam, from Cairo. He and his family are on board with you. He has been assigned to help facilitate the development of some kind of energy storage system that may help alleviate the problem with restarting the energy cores. Then, maybe you can sleep in the dark."

"That's great news! No, I haven't met Dr. Ghannam. There are nearly a thousand people on board and the flight isn't very long. I'm sure I'll meet him soon."

. . . mumbling . . . unidentified noises . . .

"Don't go out of your way to find him, son. He's going to be very busy and I don't want my son to disturb that," Abasi said. But Anta knew what he meant: *Stay away from him and his family. They may be contagious.*

"I agree Hasani," Anta added. "Just do your thing. I think it would be more interesting to meet other people, not a scientist from your home town."

"Ok. If I meet him I meet him. Anyway, you can also see all the lines running between the Shells—those are the tubes. I can't recall their actual name, but people travel through them to get from one shell to another. Some of them require walking, but others have a seat of some kind that floats as it travels through the tubes. They're supposed to be really fast. As we get closer, I can see different colors inside the Shells. I know there are grasses and plants and different colored buildings, and water, so those are probably the colors I'm seeing, but I can't make out shapes very well yet.

"I'm envious brother!" Anta said, after seeing that the Moon wasn't gray and flat, like so many pictures she'd seen.

"I'm sure you are," Hasani replied with a smile, "but maybe you'll still get the chance to see this place in person. The next ship leaving from Egypt will be in a couple of years, I think. You should apply for entrance. You'll probably have a good chance having a wonderful, talented, handsome brother like me. Plus, you've got dad as a fall back."

"Very funny son," Abasi said, without even a hint of a smile.

Anta, on the other hand, smiled wide and proud as she replied, "Oh yes, how could I possibly be rejected with a humble servant like you for a brother?"

"Agreed!" Hasani exclaimed. "Well, the crew is announcing that we need to shut down communications while we make our way down to the surface. I don't know when I'll have another free minute to talk, but I'll contact you as soon as I can. I've been told that, because of my . . . ahem . . . position, I'll have access to all the different data ports and information available here, so I'll be able to give you a good run-down of what goes on and how people live, and how the various governments function here. I'm excited! I love you! Signing off."

"Goodbye son. I love you!" Mariam looked sad to see her son go after such a short time.

"Goodbye son. Signing off," Abasi stated matter-of-factly.

"Bye brother. Let's talk soon." Anta really was sad to see her brother go. She was very close to Hasani, being only two years apart in age. They shared interests, hobbies, friends, and, when they were little, a bedroom. Even as they grew into adults, they talked several times a week. Being apart from Hasani, even though it had only been a few days, made Anta feel like crying. She didn't.

9

We returned to our hotel in El-Alamein late last night. Anta talked with her family, which was probably very nice, while I spent an equally-enjoyable night scanning the epidermis and bone specimens collected at the site and analyzing the data output from a Bio-Pen. I'd cleaned up the joint in anticipation of Anta's arrival following her com. I hoped it smelled okay—I'm a guy after all.

"This is pretty slick," I said as I opened the door to let Anta in, holding the Bio-Pen out for her to see. "I've used one of these before, but only in a test-run in Colorado a couple of years ago. I've never had any need for analyzing potential biological threats before now."

"How does it work?" Anta asked.

"I don't really know, but the literature says that the Bio-Pen was originally developed at the Ben Gurion University in Israel during the 2010s," I answered, looking at Anta for any reaction. When she didn't immediately speak, I continued lecturing.

"The current version of the Bio-Pen—the version I'm using—is a field tool capable of performing on-the-spot 'analysis and identification of encountered suspect materials', according to the literature in the box. It uses fiber optic technology—developed 100 years ago or so—along with some kind of adaptation of the equally-antiquated ELISA, or enzyme-linked immunosorbent assay, which is a similar immunological technique from the same time period. The Bio-Pen's functionality and abilities are supposed to be the best there is at detecting known biological agents in a short time span."

Anta cocked her head to one side, with a "really?" expression on her face and I became a little self-conscious. Okay, I felt stupid. We'd been through this before—where she played dumb, yet all-the-while knew exactly what I was talking about, and maybe even knew more than me. But she didn't stop me, so I continued.

"I guess the technology could be better, had there been any reason to continue to develop it. But biowarfare and bioterrorism haven't been an international concern since the 2050s." I was on a roll again, in my best lecturer mode.

"Plus, there haven't been any bad biological outbreaks in the past 40 years, as you know. So, this technology represents some of the best field analysis technology our world has produced, albeit rather outdated in comparison to lab technology. It certainly appears to do the job though."

When I looked at Anta again, she was smiling. "Good work Professor Bader," she said with obvious sarcasm. "What have you found?"

"Uhhhh, well, it's quite interesting really. I left the machine testing all night and . . . well . . ."

"Shift, what is it?" Anta asked, now with some concern in her voice.

When I told her, she looked a bit smug, although no "I told you so" ever came out of her mouth.

"Amazingly, the Bio-Pen has identified an agent very similar to *bacillus anthracis*; yet, it appears to contain some elements not previously known or identified. Traces of the same agent exist in that metal vial we took from the cave. The cave man's journal may have actually been right. I can't believe it's anthrax-ish."

"I'll call dad," Anta said quietly. "Why didn't our suits pick it up?"

"I was wondering the same thing. Maybe whatever it is in there that I can't identify renders the agent undetectable, since the agent is unknown."

JANUARY 7, 2093—HOLO CONFERENCE

"Hello father. We have news," Anta said.

"Excellent. I can't wait to hear it," Minister Chalthoum replied with about as little conviction as humanly possible.

"Doctor Bader spent the evening conducting tests on skin and bone tissue samples taken from the cave. He also analyzed the small vial I told you about. His conclusions after overnight testing are very interesting, and could be very bad; but I'll let him tell you about it, if that's okay."

"Sure. Good morning Doctor Bader. What can you tell me?" Minister Chalthoum asked.

"Good morning Minister," Shift replied. "You will recall that we previously discussed the possibility of a biological cause for the condition of the men in the desert? I wasn't convinced that it was possible given the scarcity of any such disease over the past few decades. Well, the man in the cave, as you know, looked very much like the men in the photographs. So, we've made an assumption that whatever caused the death of the men in the desert also caused the death of the cave man. Because the cave man looks like he was isolated in that cave for generations, while the desert men appear to be from our modern time, I think we can rule out murder or accident.

"In fact, my testing seems to confirm the existence, in both the cave man and the vial, of an agent very similar to *bacillus anthracis*, or, Anthrax; yet, the results reveal the existence of certain elements not known to exist in Anthrax, or anywhere really—they look man-made. My testing can't confirm what those elements are at this point. So, with the possibility of a biological cause for their deaths, a bit of historical perspective may be warranted, if you'll indulge me."

"Doctor, I'm not in the habit of saying 'I told you so', so I won't," Minister Chalthoum said with a completely straight face.

"Was that a joke?" Shift whispered to Anta.

A moment later, Shift responded, with slight hesitation, "Right. Thank you? Anyway, as I mentioned a few days ago, prior to 2051, there were three recognized forms of human anthrax: Cutaneous,

Gastrointestinal and Inhalation. But all three forms of Anthrax are believed to have been eradicated through IWO-mandated controls on the use and ingestion of animal products a few decades ago."

"Could this be Anthrax then?" the Minister asked.

"Well, maybe. But unless the desert men touched or ate the cave man, this could only really be inhalation anthrax. Inhalation anthrax occurred when anthrax spores were inhaled. The spores traveled through the air and into the body, and then to the lymph nodes near the lungs. The spores produced toxins that caused severe breathing problems and shock. Inhalation Anthrax was very difficult to treat and was often lethal. So, the answer is 'maybe'. The men are dead, and inhalation anthrax did cause death once upon a time."

"Is it treatable, if that's what we face here?" Minister Chalthoum asked.

"Historically, yes," Shift replied. "Several different antibiotics existed during the first part of this century that were effective against anthrax. But, the early symptoms were often confused with respiratory or gastrointestinal diseases; and once the obvious symptoms occurred, it was usually too late to counteract the destructive effects of the anthrax toxins."

"Is that what this is, Dr. Bader?"

"I don't know Minister. I haven't found any record of reported inhalation anthrax-related illness since 2023. And, as I just mentioned, the last known episode of anthrax, in any form, was 2051, and it was believed to be cutaneous anthrax.

"So, with that in mind, and me eating 'humble pie' as they say, I think it's safe to assume that what we have here is some form of communicable anthrax, but just what form is still unknown based upon those unknown elements.

"I'm going to send the results to a lab at the University of Colorado for further exploration. We don't know, yet, whether this agent is communicable by air, like inhalation anthrax, or only by physical contact with the disease, like cutaneous anthrax, or a combination of the two."

"How will we know Doctor Bader?" the Minister asked, now with more concern in his voice. "If, as you say, this *bacillus anthracis* contains unknown elements, how can we, or you, determine what precautions to take?"

"That's a hard question Minister," Shift replied, with equal concern. "*Bacillus anthracis* was never considered transmissible from person to person, and rarely, if ever, caused secondary infections in others, like secondhand smoke from cigarettes. While inhalation anthrax could be blown on the wind, so to speak, it wasn't as if a diseased person could blow or cough or sneeze on you and give you the disease."

"What Shift is saying, father, is that without more information, we won't be able to tell if this particular strain of *bacillus anthracis* was spread from the cave man to the desert men via the wind, via physical contact, or via some form of blood transmission, or something else," Anta said. "But we do know that the little red lights on our armbands never went off when we were in the cave."

"That's interesting," the Minister said.

"Yes, interesting," Shift said. "But not too strange really, and certainly not too comforting. It's possible that the suits didn't detect the Anthrax-like agent because whatever it is that is combined with the known agent is still unknown. Perhaps the suit's functionality was hindered as a result of finding something unknown. The technology is somewhat primitive, if I understood Anta earlier."

"Yes, they are primitive. And, they have not been updated with any new information, or so I've been told."

"To answer your earlier question Minister," Shift said, "what we can do is begin observations of people who may have come into contact with wind-borne spores, beginning with Mr. Shafik. Minister, if there is any possibility that this disease may be spread on the wind, we've got to close down this whole area. What is the status of the quarantine we requested yesterday?"

The Minister replied, with some urgency, "The request was denied pending further investigation. I now believe that was a mistake, even though your suits did not detect a problem. Having this information in hand, I will renew the request and I'm positive we can accomplish that by nightfall. Considering the evidence you have supplied, it could be a grievous error to not provide this information to those authorities to whom the original request was made. Please pardon me. I am going to sign off and renew the requests. Please stay where you are. I have further questions, but time seems to be of the essence. I will get back to you very soon."

"Thank you father," Anta said.

10

We're waiting for Minister Chalthoum to get back to us. I'm starving. We didn't eat breakfast this morning. I guess this Anthrax stuff is more important, and I'm feeling like a real arse for not giving this possibility real credence in the first place, not that it would have changed anything.

I'm really worried that the desert men's deaths were caused by the same agent, and contracted either through handling the cave body or from being within the wind zone of any spores that may have been released from the cave body over the past three weeks. I've got to find a way to figure this out. We'll probably have to go back out into the desert to look for more death.

Minister Chalthoum is contacting us, this conversation could be interesting.

"Welcome back Minister," I said.

"Hi dad," Anta said.

"Thank you Doctor Bader. Hello again Anta. I've good news. Authorities are presently coordinating emergency plans and will soon begin the process of setting up a quarantine boundary around El-Alamein and the Depression, as you previously requested. Nobody arrives and nobody leaves—including the two of you, unfortunately. But I will search for a way to get you out. We have to be sure, however, that you have not contracted any illness which you may spread outside the quarantine. You understand that, right Anta?"

Anta looked wary, and nervous, but replied, "Yes. I understand. We'll be fine with our chem suits."

"That's good. Doctor Bader, what will you be looking for to determine whether *bacillus anthracis* has spread to the human population? And what can we have our people inside the quarantine zone look for?"

"That question isn't nearly as difficult to answer as some of your others Minister. Of course, my answer will be based upon information we have from historical sources. Remember that we haven't seen a biological outbreak of any significance in over 40 years, and this strain of anthrax contains additional unknown elements. So, what we could have expected to see then, and what we may expect to see now, may not be the same; but I hope that they are similar. That would certainly make this easier.

"So, we need to be looking for what appears to be ordinary flu-like symptoms. In the case of a large-scale anthrax outbreak, which we could, hypothetically, see here, it would be likely that within 24–36 hours after the outbreak, some small percentage of individuals, like those with compromised immune systems, or those who have been exposed to a large dose of the organism due to proximity to the release point, will become ill with some of the classical symptoms and signs like fever, cough and shortness of breath. Thereafter, the greater population will begin experiencing the same symptoms. If there are more than a few hospitalizations with these symptoms, we'll know we're in trouble. So, we need to be ready with treatment, if possible."

"Can it actually be treated Doctor?" the Minister asked.

"Well, remember that we're probably dealing with some mutated or evolved form of *bacillus anthracis*, of which we know very little at this point. *Bacillus anthracis* in its prior constitutions was easily treatable with suitable antibiotics. We can only hope that modern antibiotics will be as effective."

"Indeed," Minister Chalthoum replied. "I will have my team begin assembling the information necessary to acquire such antibiotics after you send me data as to the composition of such medication, if you can."

Minster Chalthoum's whole persona had changed over the past hour. It was remarkable! I had been mildly afraid of him prior to this conversation, but now he seemed humble and appeared to be both capable and willing to rely on me for advice.

"I will, certainly," I replied. "In fact, I can find that and send it while we're talking."

"Excellent. Thank you. May I ask a few more questions of you Doctor, if you're not too busy?"

"Absolutely," I replied. *If I'm not too busy*? Of course I was busy. I was busy with *this*. What happened to his bravado and his machismo? The guy was breaking down. I wondered if Anta had ever seen this side of her dad.

"Thank you Doctor. If you have a theory, I'd be very interested to know from where this may have come. From where it originated, I mean—apart from the cave."

"That, I don't know. But the notepad Anta sent you could answer that question. But while we're waiting for that to be translated, I think that you and Anta should both understand what I know. Perhaps, together, we can think through this and come up with some solutions to future problems, and maybe even figure out the source. I assume you still want to keep this under wraps for a while?"

"Yes. That is what my superiors tell me. They don't even want the IWO to know for fear of leaks, which could lead to hysteria, particularly here, in Egypt. But once the quarantine is in place, there will really be nothing to keep the IWO from learning of the situation."

"Okay. Let me start from the beginning. Historically, nearly all classical biological diseases began with animals, the only notable exception being smallpox. So, with any biological outbreak, it was nearly always true that animals became ill either simultaneously with, or even earlier than humans. There have been hundreds, or even thousands of instances of biological or viral outbreaks throughout our history, most of which followed that pattern.

"Many of these outbreaks have caused death, and *any* of them, if merged with another disease, could theoretically create some kind of super-illness. That may be a possibility here, but the additional elements I discovered didn't show up in the data register. While Anthrax has never been considered transmissible between *humans*, when fused or amalgamated with any other communicable respiratory disease, it could potentially become very dangerous due to the ease of transmissibility of the disease. Certain transmissible respiratory illnesses have already destroyed whole populations, albeit many, many years ago. The theoretic combination of any such disease with Anthrax could be a very bad thing."

"Can you give me an example of what you're talking about?" the Minister asked.

"Sure. Smallpox, which first showed up around 10,000 BC I think, killed something like 400,000 Europeans per year near the end of the 18th century. It was responsible for a third of all blindness. Smallpox was responsible for an estimated three hundred to five hundred *million* deaths during the twentieth century. Thankfully, the World Health Organization certified the total eradication of smallpox in 1979.

"The Bubonic Plague, believed to be the cause of the "Black Death" in Europe during the fourteenth century, was another one. It killed 50 million people in the Roman Empire alone beginning in the sixth century. It killed another twenty-five million people, in Europe centuries later. The Bubonic Plague came around a third time in the mid-nineteenth century killing another 12 or 13 million people."

"Should I continue Minister?"

"Yes. This is fascinating. Thank you for asking."

"There was an unusually deadly H1N1 flu pandemic between 1918 and 1920. It was believed to have infected 500 million people across the world, including remote Pacific islands and the Arctic. It killed between fifty and a hundred million people.

"There were also a few smaller-scale epidemics more recently— SARS, MERS, Ebola, to name a few—that scared people pretty bad but didn't end up doing near as much damage as their predecessors.

"As you can see, biological diseases, and viral diseases for that matter, are nothing to take lightly, even though we've come a long way in preventing and treating them. That's why the quarantine is so important. Hopefully, if anything happens, the quarantine will stop the spread of the disease before it gets out of hand."

"Could this be some kind of attack, from a man-made agent?" Minister Chalthoum asked. "It seems so unlikely given the world's political climate, but maybe. What do you think Doctor?"

"Well, the weaponization of biological agents has never been a real threat."

"What do you mean?" the Minister asked.

"What I mean is that, while biological agents have been weaponized, they haven't resulted in near as much damage as non-weaponized strains of the same agents. Several known agents were, at one time or another, considered suitable for weaponization, including *Bacillus anthracis*. Theoretically, some combination of agents could morph into a deadly biological agent to be used in war. But that has rarely been accomplished.

"The agent in the cave man, however, although resembling *Bacillus anthracis*, is clearly something more. There may have been a natural morphing of the disease or some kind of adaptation of the classical biological agent; or, possibly, the intentional modification of it. So, like many other questions, that's something we can't really know without further testing and/or the notes in that notepad."

"How can we know," the Minister asked, "or when will we know, whether this disease is going to become a problem for us? I can't begin to tell you how worried I am about this."

"As I said before, we're looking for classic flu-like symptoms; coughing, fever, headaches, breathing problems. If we see an unusual amount of hospitalizations with these symptoms in the next few days, we'll know we've got a real problem. If we see anything like that in Mr. Shafik, I'll begin to get worried."

"I see. What do you propose we do at this point Doctor?

"You've already started. First, get the antibiotics I requested. Second, keep the quarantine up until we have something more to go by. And third, get that journal translated, quickly. Anta and I will begin earnest communication with others in our field to try to figure this out."

"Father?" Anta said with an obvious attempt to control her emotion.

"Yes dear?"

"I love you. Please tell mother that I love her too."

"I will Anta. I love you also. I'm so proud of you. Keep your head up. You and Doctor Bader are doing wonderful things that could end up saving many lives. Thank you. And, thank you Doctor Bader."

"My pleasure, Minister. We'll contact you again as soon as we have more information."

With the holo ended, Anta turned to face me, laid her head on my shoulder and broke down. She cried for several long minutes, but not in that deep sobbing way that people cry when they've lost a loved one. Her cries were those born of sorrow over what may be—not what is. I was hopeful that "what may be" would never come to pass.

For a moment after Anta laid her head on my shoulder, I didn't know what to do with my hands and they hung limply at my sides. I argued with myself for a few seconds about the correct action to take, and finally concluded that it was ok to comfort her; so I wrapped my arms around her shoulders and patted her on the back in a "fatherly" way.

"Anta." I spoke softly. "In the event any spores traveled from the cave body into the immediate vicinity, then the government-created quarantine zone should act to contain any contagion to people already in the wind zone north of the Qattara Depression, unless and until the wind changes direction." Then I thought to myself, *I hope that we put on Anta's chem suits before any exposure ourselves.* The day of our arrival in El-Alamein was a calm day—a break between storms—so we might be okay. Time will tell.

"While I was waiting for you to call your father earlier, I considered whether there was any way Mr. Shafik could take us back out into the Depression tomorrow. I called him to talk. While we were talking, he had a coughing spell, which he passed off as too much dust in his lungs. I hope that's all it amounts to. The next few days will tell I guess. Anyway, he's received a nebule pulmonary injection. He confirmed that he's keeping this all quiet. So that's good."

"Good," Anta replied.

JANUARY 7, 2093
EGYPT VIII SPACE LOG

Takeoff: January 6, 2093, 1800 hours EET.

Acquired Destination: International Lunar Space Station, United States Moon Colony.

Operating Time: 6 hours, 17 minutes

Arrival time: 0517 LT (Lunar Time)

Status: All systems operative and functional within calculated parameters throughout voyage.

Personnel/Passenger anomalies:

Dr. Jafari Ghannam (Cairo, Egypt): mild cough. Attempted treatment with nebule pulmonary injection, no recovery prior to disembarkation.

Miss Shani Ghannam, age 7 (Cairo, Egypt): mild cough. Attempted treatment with nebule pulmonary injection, no recovery prior to disembarkation.

Ms. Schent Wasom (Asyut, Egypt): injury to left index finger, broken glass from cracked water container. Cleaned, bandaged.

Ms. Alexi Streven (Houston, Texas, United States of America): headache. Treated with Ibuprofine, recovered prior to disembarkation.

11

Sheesh Dad, it's the middle of the night.

Dad's communication contains the following information from the Egypt Health and Population Ministry Computer Databank, dated today:

Following data received from agent Anta Chalthoum, on the ground in El-Alamein, quarantine is in effect for El-Alamein and 40 kilometers north thereof; also 20 kilometers east, west and south of the outer border of the Qattara Depression beginning at 2230, January 7, 2093 and continuing indefinitely. No person without authorization may pass through quarantine zone until quarantine restrictions are lifted.

Restrictions have been communicated to all requisite personnel inside and out of the quarantine zone, including international officials within the IWO responsible for the safety of its member citizens.

Good to know. Shift will be pleased. I'll tell him in the morning. He'll probably make some joke that I don't understand, in his dorky, scientific language. And I'll laugh because I'm such a nice girl.

I guess Dad's goal of keeping this a secret didn't work out. The IWO knows. That's probably for the best.

JANUARY 8, 2093—SHIFT

Mr. Shafik, despite his continued coughing this morning, assured us that he was fine. He gave us directions to help us maneuver in the Qattara Depression again. We were trying, without much hope, to find the two bodies. No luck. The trip wasn't wasted though. We found the body of a gazelle in a little grove of *Acacia raddiana*. Performing the role I'm being heartily paid for, I cut open the body, from the sternum all the way down. The smell that had so rudely accosted us when we found the body grew a thousand fold. I nearly passed out, seriously, despite the odor dampening capabilities of our Chem suits.

The inside of the gazelle's body, just like the three human bodies, had begun to dissolve, for lack of a better word, from the inside out. Unlike the human cave body, though, the gazelle still had most of its internal organs, albeit in various states of decay. It clearly died within the past couple of days. It still had dark, wet blood throughout the inside of the body cavity that looked like oil in the bright sunshine. More blood stained its fur around small holes that looked like bite marks, probably from other hungry animals. Great. The smell, of course, was seriously nasty.

"I have a bag for that," Anta offered as I removed a specimen from what I think was an intestine. I placed the specimen in the small, clear, plastic, resealable specimen bag she held open.

"Are you my lab assistant now?" I replied as calmly as I could while trying not to breathe in the overwhelming odor.

"You only have two hands." She chuckled as she opened another bag for me. We continued this way until we had gathered organ, skin, bone and hair specimens and stashed them inside the pockets of our suits.

"How can you handle the smell?" I questioned, a bit sarcastically.

"It's my Egyptian iron stomach; blood of the Pharaohs, you know. That, and the Vaseline I just rubbed under my nose," she added with a wink and a smile.

"Does that really work? Give me some."

The flies and other bugs gathering to aid in their God-given role of spreading crap around the Earth were awful. Before long, Anta could no longer repress a gag. I glanced over at her and watched her as she tried to keep her breakfast where it belonged. I silently thanked her. I didn't want her to get me started. How would we even clean up puke inside our chem suits?

With specimens stored away, we moved to the shady side of a nearby dune and sat. Anta closed her eyes and leaned back against the dune while I retrieved the specimens and my Bio-Pen. Anta opened her eyes and started to sit forward, saying she needed to help. I could see she was still struggling with her stomach and told her to relax while I ran the first analyses. Since the Bio-Pen had already analyzed the cave body specimen, which took several hours, it would take much, much less time this time around if the gazelle turned out to contain the same disease.

"I won't let you miss out on anything," I offered in conclusion. Then, "I guess the Vaseline reached its limit?" She rolled her eyes and moaned.

Upon data analysis of the gazelle specimens with my Bio-Pen, I found quantities of the same biological agent found in the cave body. I let out a frustrated "Cripes!"

Without moving or opening her eyes, Anta said, "The gazelle died from the same thing, didn't it?"

"Yes," I continued in frustration. "There's nothing else around here, or on the body, that shows death from anything else as a possibility. The bite marks are too small to have caused death. They're only flesh wounds, probably received after the animal died. So, the gazelle died from the same cause as the cave man and the other two men."

The pattern was disturbing.

Unfortunately, or fortunately depending on one's perspective, after returning from the desert this afternoon, Anta and I went straight to our hotel rooms. We were locked down as a result of the quarantine that *we* requested, so there wasn't any place else to go.

"I've just sent my findings to the University of Colorado Biological Research Department head, my friend, Dr. John Silitzer," I explained to Anta while we waited for our dinner. "He assured me that this information is now his top priority. Having gone to college with this guy, I know he's smart, about as smart as they come; but he's also a little unreliable, like a horny college frat boy on a Friday night. He better not screw this up. I hope to hear from him by morning with information about what this agent is, how it might be transmitted, and what can be done about it. I'm considering who else to tell, in case John falls asleep on the job."

"That's a little harsh isn't it? You say he is your friend and you talk about him like that." Anta was clearly amused.

"Of course, you're right. But this is too important and too urgent for him to mess it up."

While Anta and I were enjoying a lovely meal of . . . something unidentifiable from the processors on the wall, we were com'd by Mr. Shafik. He stated that his cough has taken a turn for the worse and the pulmonary injection hasn't done a thing. According to his doctors, that treatment works to stop coughing, for nearly every person, in nearly every instance of coughing, from nearly every cause. So, this is something different. Doctors from the local hospital are running tests even though he's still confined to the quarantine cell. I decided that I would check on him in the morning—by holo, not in person.

I have a very bad feeling about this. I'm beginning to wonder whether the money is worth it after all. Plus, this food is disgusting. The processor units are supposed to give us a "speedy, nutritious and delicious meal when we don't have time to prepare one or go out", according to the literature. I don't know how they work—probably never will—but one thing is certain, the food is *not* delicious—well, not usually. I'm glad we haven't fallen, as a society, to a level where home-cooked meals are forgotten in the wake of the fast, processed, sterile, and cardboard-tasting meals of the wall unit.

"You know Mr. Shafik may be putting more people at risk of catching this." A statement. "Don't we have an obligation to tell his caregivers what we suspect?" I asked Anta after ending the com with Mr. Shafik.

"Shift, you know we can't say anything yet. It's unfortunate, but we have to stay focused on the task at hand. My father would call it collateral damage. But he's quarantined anyway. His caregivers are wearing masks and washing regularly. What more can be done?"

After a few moments, I asked, seriously, "By the way, do you think maybe those guys in the desert died from eating food from a wall unit? Maybe we should have the hospital check to see where Mr. Shafik has been eating."

My comment was so off-the-wall that, despite the seriousness of the situation, Anta started to laugh, choking momentarily on her last bite of food. That got me laughing too. I laughed so hard that my stomach hurt. When we both settled down enough that she could finally catch her breath, Anta said, accusingly, "That wasn't a nice thing to say." We both started laughing again and couldn't stop for several minutes.

Finally, again serious, Anta asked, "Did you tell your sister about the quarantine?" Anta knew I was struggling with our decision to keep the details out of the media and Arilee could accidentally leak the information as easily as anyone else. It really goes against my instincts to keep things this important from Arilee, since she's the only family I've got. Anta was testing me.

Anta looked right into my eyes as I responded, certainly wanting to determine if I would tell her the truth. I looked right back at her and said, "She doesn't know about the quarantine. She doesn't even know I'm in El-Alamein."

Anta seemed surprised by my directness.

"Before we left Apion," I continued, "I told her that we'd be traveling into a remote part of the Sahara Desert, where communications are not always reliable. She questioned that because I told her before I left Colorado that I have the latest coms technology and should be able to overcome any local anomalies."

"What about now," Anta asked. "How do you explain to her what you're wearing?"

"I haven't talked to her through the holo since we put the suits on. Again, I've made the excuse about the unreliability of communications. She seems to believe me—probably because she can tell my voice isn't very clear, talking through this Chem suit."

"So you lied to her?" Anta asked.

"Yes. I told her we couldn't use the holos due to the remoteness of the area where we're working. And it's killing me. I haven't lied to my sister since we were kids and I accidentally ripped the arm off her stuffed bunny."

Anta's eyes opened wider at this last remark. She looked away briefly, then back at me. I could see the sympathy in her expression, or maybe it was the reflection from the table lamp off her visor.

"I hope this doesn't damage your relationship. From everything you've said, your sister seems like a wonderful person and she doesn't deserve to be hurt. We need to get out of here so you can reassure her honestly."

"As soon as I can, I'll tell her everything," I replied.

JANUARY 8, 2093, 0818 LT
INTERNATIONAL LUNAR SPACE STATION, U.S. MOON COLONY
MEDICAL TREATMENT FACILITY LOG

Treating Physician: Dr. Feter Slomanson, MD, PhD

Patient: Dr. Jafari Ghannam (Cairo, Egypt).

Subject Complaint: severe coughing, headache, bloody sputum and stool.

Analysis:

According to Dr. Ghannam, he and his daughter began to cough, and became somewhat lethargic aboard Egypt VIII on its voyage to this Station. During the approximate 6-hour duration, his condition, and that of his daughter, became progressively worse until this morning, around 0600 LT, he began to have diarrhea, containing blood. He now presents for evaluation. Such complaints are rarely seen in combination, but are not entirely unheard of.

Dr. Ghannam was given a nebule pulmonary injection onboard Egypt VIII, which did little to arrest his coughing attacks. Before admittance here, he was given a second injection along with a combination of Ibuprofine (for pain) and Respiritol (for coughing/ breathing). Neither seems to have effectively reduced his symptoms or condition. This is the more-peculiar aspect of this illness. These medications prove effective in greater than 99.98 % of patients with similar ailments. I have uploaded test data, including urine and blood samples and arranged for a telecom conference with Dr. Yurgi Shevchuk at MIT-Medicine in Boston at 1300 LT tomorrow.

Treating Physician: Dr. Feter Slomanson, MD, PhD
Patient: Miss Shani Ghannam (Cairo, Egypt).
Subject Complaint: severe coughing, headache, bloody sputum and stool.
Analysis: See notes for Dr. Jafari Ghannam, Shani's father.

12

Treating Physician: Dr. Feter Slomanson, MD, PhD

Patient(s): Dr. Jafari Ghannam (Cairo, Egypt) and Shani Ghannam (Cairo, Egypt).

Subject Complaint: severe coughing, fever, headache, bloody sputum and stool, and now, severe pain throughout the patients' entire bodies, interior.

Analysis:

Scans show mild deterioration of muscle and other tissue, whole body. I have just concluded a lengthy telecom with Dr. Yurgi Shevchuk, in the presence of Dr. Ghannam and his daughter (at Dr. Ghannam's insistence). The news is not good. Dr. Shevchuk ran every conceivable test in his attempt to discover the cause of the symptoms, the origin of the illness, and what may be accomplished to arrest the symptoms and return the patients to baseline. His information reveals that the illness is caused by a mutated form of the biological agent *Bacillus anthracis*. His data sources revealed that this mutation has never before been documented in any patient, anywhere in the world, nor has an infection from the common form of *Bacillus anthracis* been reported, in any location or person, in more than 40 years. Because the patients arrived with symptomology aboard Egypt VIII, it can be assumed that this strain of *Bacillus anthracis* was received by contagion from Earth, not from persons on the moon.

We have learned that Dr. Ghannam and his daughter made an expedition into the desert in Egypt prior to boarding Egypt VIII. A holo conference is being arranged for later today. Based on information received from the Egyptian Minister of Health and Population, Dr. Shevchuk hopes to locate a tour guide and a researcher in Egypt who may have knowledge about this infection, and have them join us on the call. Dr. Ghannam has a lot to tell us, but we'll wait until the holo conference.

JANUARY 9, 2093, 1330 EET—SHIFT

This morning Anta and I contacted Mr. Shafik at the hospital by holo. We've decided to stay indoors to avoid what we believe would be an onslaught of questions, or worse, by the locals. They know they are quarantined, but they may not know why—yet. Their communications with outside the area are being blocked by some technology beyond my understanding, and so are most of ours. If we go outside, in our chem suits, we're likely to be mobbed. I'm not ready to deal with that.

Strangely, looking out the windows, the people in the streets appear to be going on with their lives, believing, I guess, that this is temporary and will be over soon, and that all their questions will soon be answered. There's no chaos like I expected. Our world has certainly come a long way from the days when mass protests and rioting broke out whenever a perceived injustice occurred, even to a stranger. Whether the distance we've traveled is good or bad, I'm not sure; but in any event, the people here are handling this quarantine peacefully.

Anyway, Mr. Shafik is now experiencing severe coughing and headaches, which we can clearly observe while speaking over the holo. He explained that his entire body feels as though it is being "struck by a million sledge hammers from the inside". He has also been coughing up blood, remnants of which we can see on his hospital gown. His doctors can't explain the cause and are unable to treat it, but are "doing everything they can".

I had a short conversation with Mr. Shafik's doctors to discuss the possibility of Anthrax. The head doctor, though seemingly doubting my theory, has assured me that he will utilize all channels of communication at his disposal, which currently isn't much, in an attempt to verify my theory and, if confirmed, locate any medicines or other treatment protocols for Anthrax. He is admittedly uncertain whether any such medication, beyond what they currently have, still exists. I told him, confidentially, that Anthrax medicines have been ordered. Minister Chalthoum told us that such medications have to be produced, as no stock is kept on hand anywhere in the world. That sucks.

The doctor told us that Mr. Shafik's body scans this morning reveal deterioration of his muscle and organ tissue. He likened it to an incredibly rapid aging process, as if Mr. Shafik was an old man, and getting much older by the minute.

Shortly after our Holo with Mr. Shafik and his doctor, while choking down some pre-buttered toast and scrambled eggs from the wall unit, I received a holo com from MIT Boston. Anta was with me and equally perplexed.

"Hello, this is Doctor Bader."

"Good morning Doctor Bader, my name is Yurgi Shevchuk. I am a doctor and research professor at MIT-Medicine in Boston, Massachusetts. I must apologize for contacting you like this, without warning, but what I need to discuss with you is urgent."

"Okay. This is my colleague Doctor Anta Chalthoum, from Cairo. May she sit in on this com?"

"Certainly. Good morning Doctor Chalthoum."

"Good morning."

Doctor Shevchuk continued: "I located you in a somewhat roundabout way. I believe you know of Dr. Ghannam and his daughter, who undertook an exploration of sorts near your location several days ago. They are currently hospitalized at the Medical Treatment Facility of the International Lunar Space Station. I was contacted by Dr. Slomanson at that facility regarding an interesting medical condition being suffered by Dr. Ghannam and his daughter. Dr. Ghannam provided me with the name of an Egyptian tour guide in El-Alamein. When I attempted to contact the tour guide, a Mr. Shafik, my call was re-routed to a Minister Chalthoum in Cairo who, I presume, is related to you, Doctor Chalthoum. Minister Chalthoum provided me with your name and arranged for my call to get through the communications quarantine in El-Alamein."

"Well," I replied, "that's a lot of work. The reason for your com, I suppose, has to do with an untreatable form of *Bacillus anthracis*, doesn't it?"

"Yes, it does. Let me introduce you to Dr. Feter Slomanson, the treating doctor at the lunar facility. He is with Dr. Ghannam and his daughter, Shani, right now."

"Good morning Dr. Slomanson, Dr. Ghannam, Shani. I should com my friend, Dr. John Silitzer, Department head at the University of Colorado Biological Research Department. Just a moment."

As we waited for John to come on, hoping he wouldn't be asleep or in his pajamas at this hour, I reflected on my initial impressions of the people on the com. Dr. Slomanson and Dr. Shevchuk were both impeccably dressed, and probably in their late 60s or early 70s. Dr. Ghannam and his daughter both looked sick, like Mr. Shafik, and that was frightening, but expected. Anta was hot. I mean, Anta looked very presentable this morning, in her elegant chem suit. I, on the other hand, looked wrinkled in my chem suit; and, just as John looked when he picked up the holo com—old jeans and a t-shirt—very fitting for a man of science. I'm sure we made quite an impression.

More introductions were made and we began a discussion of the situation in earnest. Dr. Ghannam provided a detailed history of his trip to the Qattara Depression—interrupted by regular fits of coughing and obvious pain—some of which Anta and I already knew, but was news to the others.

Five days ago, January 4, 2093, Doctor Ghannam and his daughter traveled with Mr. Shafik into the Qattara Depression south of El-Alamein. Their purpose was to gather salt specimens for use in scientific experimentation on the moon. He didn't go into any explanation of those experiments since it wasn't pertinent to our discussion. He then provided a short version of Shani's disappearance and the cave discovery.

Dr. Ghannam then said, in a heavy, but clear Egyptian accent: "In the caves, we discovered a human body which appeared to be very old, along with many ancient-looking artifacts. The body itself appeared fairly well-preserved on the exterior, but was completely hollow on the interior, apart from bones. There were no organs or other tissue. It was strange to see skin on the body, but otherwise, just a skeleton. Due to the bizarre and somewhat frightening state of the body, we did not touch it, nor get too close. It worried me. Our guide informed me that he would report both the cave discovery and the body to officials upon our return to El-Alamein. I thereafter put the body out of my mind while I focused on the arduous task of finalizing preparations for our journey to the moon.

"My daughter, Shani, who is seven years old, expressed to me last night that, while she was in the cave by herself, with no light, she stumbled in the dark. She didn't know what she had stumbled over, and couldn't see it, but reached out to feel it. It felt, in her words, 'cold and kind of hard, but not like a rock' and her hand entered a 'hole' in the object that had other 'hard things sticking out, like branches on a tree', again in her words.

"One of those 'branches' scratched my daughter's hand; but she explained that she didn't tell me about it because it didn't hurt very badly. She's very brave, you see. There was nothing in that cave that could have fit her description except the body, with holes in the torso and bones in the interior. So, it must have been the body that my daughter stumbled over, touched, and from which she thereafter received a scratch."

"Doctor Bader, Doctor Chalthoum, based upon your observations, is there anything else about that cave and its occupant that may help us in our research?" Doctor Shevchuk asked, his face contorted as though he were trying to piece together a jigsaw puzzle.

"Yes, there is," I replied. "We also found a small metal vial, approximately two inches long, which contained traces of *Bacillus anthracis*, along with some elements that we couldn't identify. Dr. Silitzer, do you have anything to add?"

"Unfortunately, we have also been unable to identify those elements to date," Dr. Silitzer replied.

"Ahhh," Doctor Shevchuk said quietly. "That matches our research into the disease found in the blood of Dr. Ghannam and Shani. With that information, it seems apparent that Dr. Ghannam and Shani contracted the illness while in that cave. What about the tour guide? How is his health?"

"Unfortunately, it isn't good," I said. "He is experiencing the same symptoms as the Ghannams. His doctor told us this morning that his organs and muscle tissue are deteriorating. He said Mr. Shafik's insides look like a very old man's, but they didn't look that way 24 hours ago.

"And another thing: Our sources here in Egypt inform us that there is no treatment for Anthrax currently but that a lab in Egypt is trying to produce it. I'm not so sure it will be effective once produced."

"I agree," Dr. Shevchuk replied. "The Ghannams have each received antibiotics which should have stopped, or at least slowed the disease processes. It has been ineffective. The rate at which our patients seem to be deteriorating may preclude any chance to even offer treatment. I'm sorry that you had to hear that Dr. Ghannam."

Dr. Ghannam, wary, but not defeated, stated, "I would rather know now, in order to prepare myself and my daughter for the reality of death. Thank you for not keeping this a secret."

"Dr. Slomanson," Dr. Shevchuk asked, "will you please place your patients into an isolation chamber? Unfortunately, because our usual methods of treating the mild illnesses that still remain within the human population have not been effective in their treatment, and because this illness is obviously something never before encountered, and contagious, that appears to be the best course of action at the present. I believe it would also be wise to locate everyone with whom the Ghannams have been in physical contact over the past few days. They should each be placed into isolation for testing and analysis."

Dr. Slomanson, now understanding the ramifications of what was occurring, and clearly seeing the threat, said, with urgency, "Yes! I will get on that right now. Nurse Chow," he called over his shoulder, "please escort Dr. Ghannam and his daughter to the isolation chambers. Dr. Ghannam, I will be back with you shortly, after we conclude this com. I am so sorry for this. Please forgive me for what we must do."

To this, Dr. Ghannam, with tears in his eyes and a voice choked with emotion, replied, "Do not worry for this small inconvenience. I understand. Shani and I will pray for the health of all, and for the strength of you and your colleagues while you search for your answers. Thank you for what you have done. Thank you to each of you. Goodbye."

Shani began to cry as two nurses took her hands and began to pull her away from the group, with her father close behind. "Daddy, where are we going?"

"We're going to a private room—one for each of us. But I will be very close by."

Sensing the tension in the nurses pulling on her arms, Shani cried out, "Where are we going? Daddy! [coughing] Daaa-dddy! Don't let them take me away, please! Please daddy! [coughing]."

"Be still darling," Dr. Ghannam said quietly to his daughter as they left the room. "Everything is going to be okay. I love you very much Shani."

Shani screamed. The rest of us watched in silence as the Ghannams left our view.

With tears of her own as she watched the nurses over the holo remove Dr. Ghannam and Shani from the room, Anta choked, "What is going on? What does all of this mean?"

"I don't know, Dr. Chalthoum," Dr. Shevchuk replied. "I know that is difficult to hear, but I really don't know. Does everyone have a little more time to talk with me? I need more to go on than what I have."

For the next 90 minutes, we discussed John's and Dr. Shevchuk's theories. We discussed their respective findings, including Mr. Shafik's condition, the Ghannams' condition, and what we have learned about *Bacillus anthracis*. I didn't like what I heard.

I also explained what I know about World War II and the two Battles for El-Alamein, given that the body in the cave appears to have been involved in one of those skirmishes in some way. John theorized that the person in the cave may have been transporting the vial, which contained *Bacillus anthracis*, or some mutated form of the disease, when he entered the cave. Perhaps he got lost, or trapped in the cave somehow. Eventually, after the cave had been closed off to the world, probably by sand, the vial was opened and the man in the cave was exposed. Dr. Shevchuk reasoned that, if John's theory is correct, then we may expect that Dr. Ghannam, Shani, and Mr. Shafik will all die in the same way. And, perhaps thousands more people in and around El-Alamein. Again, a translation of the notepad we found in the cave could be very useful.

Anta may have saved our lives by procuring and insisting that we wear chem suits, but we won't know for a few more days. We need to get out of El-Alamein, but to leave would be irresponsible. We can't accomplish any more here though. Dr. Shevchuk and John and their respective teams will be handling the situation now, informing the proper authorities, spreading the word to the various health organizations around the world and in the lunar colonies, and to the IWO. The release I'm feeling as that burden is lifted from me is tremendous.

John is going to have his people set up some kind of communication system for invitees' eyes only to share data. Within hours, or perhaps minutes, the artificial quarantine zone boundaries here will be much more difficult to bypass. Anta is currently working on an 'escape' plan for the moment we determine that we have not been infected. I hope she comes through for us. I'm sure she will. Now we need to call daddy.

JANUARY 9, 2093, 1015 EET
EXCERPT FROM A NEWS STORY PUBLISHED IN THE "ENCIG"
(EL-ALAMEIN NEWSCORP INFORMATION GUIDE)

In what has, until now, appeared to be only fable and myth, it appears that El-Alamein has been visited by some pestilence, just as ancient Egypt was visited by the Biblical 10 plagues at the time of Moses. While not as severe as the Bible would lead us to believe at the time of Moses, El-Alamein's "plague" has sent at least 141 individuals to local hospitals in the past 24 hours with coughing, fever and headaches.

An anonymous Health Ministry official warns that, although such illnesses have been largely contained in the past, this particular illness is not responding to now-universal medications and treatment. It is presently unknown what the illness is or where it came from, but the Health Ministry official has indicated that, for now, it appears to be just another common illness that will run its course in due time.

JANUARY 9, 2093, 1630 EET
EXCERPT FROM A NEWS STORY PUBLISHED IN THE "ENCIG"
(EL-ALAMEIN NEWSCORP INFORMATION GUIDE)

In an update to our story published this morning, over the past six hours, more than 850 more individuals have presented to El-Alamein hospitals complaining of headaches, fever and coughing. Earlier admittees have not responded to common treatment protocols, but instead, appear to be getting worse, with some displaying bloody phlegm and stool.

Health Ministry officials now warn people to stay indoors as the illness appears to be communicable.

13

Anta and I continue to wear our chem suits, day and night. I haven't taken a shower for days. We put them on January 4th, in the evening. If we were exposed to *Bacillus anthracis*, it would have been before that. So, it's been over five days and although we are both sick at heart, neither of us feels physically ill. We might be safe.

Earlier this evening, Anta had arranged for us to be aboard a private government jet leaving El-Alamein very early tomorrow morning. Even though commercial jets have been grounded for a couple of days, some private jets were still getting out. Not anymore. Our flight was just cancelled following reports by the local news that hundreds of people are experiencing the same symptoms Mr. Shafik initially suffered. So, we're stuck, even though we're probably free of contamination. So, what now?

After telling me we weren't going to be able to leave the city, Anta said, "You know, nobody in this town, apart from Mr. Shafik, has ever been near those caves. Mr. Shafik couldn't have coughed or sneezed on so many people in the short time between when he started showing symptoms and now. He probably hasn't been in physical contact with more than a dozen people. So how are all of these people getting sick, and so quickly?" Anta was quite calm, considering that her plan to get us out of El-Alamein had just crumbled.

"Well, a biological outbreak is occurring, obviously."

"But how did it get here, and how are so many people catching it?" Anta asked. "You said Anthrax isn't communicable between people."

"Well, the *traditional* forms of Anthrax weren't communicable between people, but this isn't traditional Anthrax. We already know that. There may be something in the concoction that makes it communicable. I don't know yet.

"But I do know this: the vial we found in the cave obviously contained some mutated form of Anthrax, likely inhalation anthrax. The cave man opened the vial and caught it. You and Shafik both said that this area has suffered through three weeks of sandstorms, which, at some point within that time span, unburied the cave. The stuff was locked up in that cave for 150 years, and somehow survived. Then, after the storms, the desert men caught it. Then Shafik and the Ghannams caught it."

"But all of them went into the cave," Anta said. "The townspeople here haven't been near those caves."

"Right. And since the vial itself hasn't been released from its air-proof canister at any point since we first found it in the cave, its presence in El-Alamein can't be the source of the illness. Plus, remember the gazelle? There's no way it crawled into the cave either."

"So are you and I safe?" Anta asked.

"I think we might be, but I can't be sure yet. Both Shafik and the Ghannams first began coughing approximately four days after likely exposure. Apart from any possible spread of the bacteria by Shafik, the bacteria likely arrived in El-Alamein on the last day of the sandstorms, just after you made me put on this crazy chem suit. But, if that's the case, the other bodies and the body of the gazelle were exposed many days prior to the last day of the sandstorm.

"I've been looking at local weather charts and databases. It looks like the wind, throughout most of the duration of the storms, was blowing from the northeast, which likely kept the spores from traveling into any population centers. But during the last 18 hours or so of the storms, the wind changed direction and pushed the sand,

and probably the spores, into El-Alamein. So, it seems to me that the bacteria can be, and has been spread by wind.

"At this point though, I don't know whether it's communicable between people. All of these people were downwind from the caves for up to 18 hours. But because the wind is no longer blowing this direction, or at all really, I imagine we'll find out whether it's communicable if people continue to get sick over the next few days."

"Makes sense," Anta said.

"I'm hoping that, even though the casualties in El-Alamein will be in the thousands, maybe it can be contained here. Of course, since I don't know much about the lunar stations and populations of the moon, I don't know what precautions have been taken there, or whether they'll be effective."

"Yeah, I don't know either," Anta said.

"In any event," I continued, "I've shared my hypothesis with the database John set up. Looking through the notes there, it appears Dr. Shevchuk has invited several other doctors and biologists in the lunar colonies and on Earth to participate in this database. Unfortunately, none of them have posted any additional information. Maybe that's a good sign."

Anta looked skeptical.

"Anyway, based on my timeline, we're probably safe as long as we continue to wear the suits until we're out of here."

"We have to be safe," Anta whispered. "We have to beat this thing!" she exclaimed with more determination. "I'll contact dad again and work on a plan to get us out of here. Are you going to tell your sister what's going on?"

"Not yet. Besides, if I call her now, she'll probably hear in my voice that something's wrong."

"I'm sorry Shift," she whispered and placed a gloved hand on my shoulder. It was a nice gesture and actually made me feel a little better.

JANUARY 9, 2093—ANTA

It appears that Shift and I have done all we can in El-Alamein. Our only goal now is to get out of here, but I'm being cautious because we don't know, yet, whether we're contaminated. We're probably fine if Shift's estimates are correct. At least, Shift is *looking* pretty fine today! It's my fault that we're stuck here. But how was I to know that hundreds of people would get sick so quickly and that the flight dad helped arrange would be cancelled as a result?

Shift's theory about how El-Alamein became sick fits with everything we know. If he's right, and the wind of the sandstorms carried the spores from the cave into the city, then even though the city is on lock-down, if we get any more major wind storms, the disease will spread. Thankfully, we've felt very little breeze, of any kind, since the end of the last windstorm. That's probably the only reason there aren't any reported illnesses outside El-Alamein and the lunar station.

I haven't prayed to Allah or to any other God since I was a little girl, until now. Some people don't believe in Allah, or God; yet, despite my own reservations on the subject, now seems to be a good time to exercise a bit of faith. I can't rid my mind of the look in Shani's eyes, her scream, and the tremor in the voice of her father as they told us goodbye and were escorted out of the room earlier today.

That little girl's reaction was heartbreaking and I felt a tremendous weight press down on me. But the love her father showed to her was simply amazing. I'd like to think my father would act the same way, throwing his arms around me, hugging me, and validating my feelings. I have cried a lot today—more than ever in my life—and I wish dad was here to hold me.

14

The mutated form of Bacillus anthracis, now dubbed "Anthrax E" by Dr. John Silitzer ("E" for Egypt), has spread throughout El-Alamein. Containment procedures appear to have halted its spread into outlying areas, although approximately 3200 persons are reportedly exposed to date. Each individual presents with varying degrees of fever, coughing, sputum, blood, and pain. Because the people are getting sick at varying times, it seems probable that the disease is spread both through the air and via human-to-human contact, as the common cold is spread.

Moreover, Mr. Riyad Shafik, now known as "Patient Three" ("Patient One" is Miss Shani Ghannam, "Patient two" is her father Dr. Jafari Ghannam, both presently isolated at the International Lunar Space Station) appears near death. Imaging shows organ- and vessel-liquifaction, whole body. Stabilization procedures are ineffective, currently, and Patient Three's physicians hold out no hope of survival. No medical procedure or medication has slowed the spread of the disease within Patient Three's body.

As reported yesterday by Dr. Slomanson of the International Lunar Space Station, via this database, only Patients One and Two present with any features of this illness on the moon. Patients One and Two were isolated within hours after their arrival at the Space Station, along with others known to have been in close physical proximity to them. Because there is little air movement, and indeed, no wind to affect the spread of the disease on the moon, I remain cautiously hopeful that there was no contamination prior to isolation.

JANUARY 10, 2093—SHIFT

"Mr. Shafik has died," Anta mumbled through her tears as she walked into my hotel room. Her head was down and her posture was that of one carrying a heavy burden. It broke my heart.

Anta and I haven't left our adjoining hotel rooms for a while now. We're using the connecting door between our rooms to meet now rather than going out into the hallway. Each time I have looked into her eyes over the past few hours, the sorrow she displays causes my throat to constrict. But even in her sorrow, she has shown strength beyond comprehension. Everything she says, and everything she does is geared toward the safety of human lives, including ours. She's awesome!

The epidemic, now known as Anthrax E, has swept through El-Alamein like a crazed swarm of Africanized killer bees. It's scary—and this is coming from someone who has studied plagues in significant depth. Reports and data from Doctors Shevchuk and Silitzer, along with reports from the Lunar Space Station, indicate a probable gestation time of approximately 80-110 hours.

Physicians here in El-Alamein theorize that coughing may be the main causal instrument of the spread of Anthrax E. Of course, several of the infected people have said that they haven't been exposed to any coughing in the last four or five days. That's the most awful news of all because it means that the infection, as we previously supposed, must have been carried here on the wind. Thankfully, there still hasn't been any wind more than a slight breeze in the area since the last day of the storms, apart from small afternoon breezes from the Mediterranean Sea southward, away from any human population.

Of course, we're still stuck in El-Alamein and it's driving me nuts. Doctors Shevchuk and Silitzer have begun research into possible causes, cures and vaccines. No word on any success yet.

"He was a good dude, wasn't he?" I asked, mostly to myself as Anta sat down on the bed next to me. "I don't know whether he had family or friends. I don't even know whether he had a dog or anybody to look after the dog if he had one. Nobody's leaving their houses in this town anyway, so the dog wouldn't fare so well even if somebody were supposed to watch out for him. Poor dog."

Anta lifted her head and looked at me, giving me a funny look. Then she said, "The doctor said that Mr. Shafik's organs began to liquefy and Mr. Shafik lost consciousness shortly thereafter. I don't know if it would do any good to go to the hospital to take a look though. I think we have enough tissue samples and it will just make me sad."

"I guess his body will end up looking like the cave man and the gazelle soon." That thought crushed me, but I didn't say it. "I need to work out."

"That's kind of insensitive, isn't it Shift?" Anta asked, looking perplexed by my attitude.

"Yeah, I'm sorry," I replied.

Unlike Anta, I'm resolved to be an unsympathetic arse about this whole mess. If I allow myself to feel sorrow for every person who dies from this thing, I'm going to go under myself. After watching little Shani break down yesterday, which broke my heart, I've determined that I'm going to have to harden myself.

Minister Chalthoum didn't hire me for my sympathies or my tears; he hired me to figure out why a couple of dudes died out in the sand dunes. So, I've got to treat this like a job, not like the whole of the human race is in peril here. I'll let Anta be the warm, kind, sympathetic person. I'll be the jerk. Plus, we're probably not all in peril. Like every other disease in the course of human history, this one's likely to go down after a few people, or maybe a few thousand people die.

"Did we needlessly expose him to harm by having him take us to the caves?" Anta wondered aloud. "Of course, we couldn't have found them alone, and, judging by the way this epidemic has spread through El-Alamein, it seems like he would've been exposed anyway."

That lessens my guilt, I thought, *but doesn't eliminate it*. Oh yeah, I forgot, I'm not going to feel guilt. This is a scientific mission and nothing more. *Do not get attached to people Shift.*

15

Anthrax E has not been contained in the moon colonies. The International Lunar Space Station is reporting two new cases of bacterial infection. One case is the intake nurse at the Medical Treatment Facility; the other is a young child who, according to reports, associated with Patient One onboard Egypt VIII. Both patients have been isolated and an extensive interagency search is underway for any other persons showing any symptoms of the disease. I understand the search is confined to the United States Moon Colony as no person from aboard Egypt VIII logged into or out of the Lunar Portal System since the arrival of Egypt VIII. There's probably a good chance others who were in contact with persons from Egypt VIII [/did/] travel through the portals, but I'll let the experts up there figure out what to do.

Patient One and Patient Two have died following the liquifaction of their internal organs.

JANUARY 11, 2093—SHIFT

I just read a post to the Anthrax E database. It says that no passenger or staff aboard Egypt VIII has logged into or out of the Lunar Portal System on the Moon. What does that mean? Well, Dr. Silitzer has the same question. He wants to know, as I do, by what methods and means Anthrax E could be spread through the lunar colonies. I'm going to present my findings to the group soon—actually, now. They're calling.

"Hi Shift," Doctor Silitzer said.

"Hey John. Good afternoon Dr. Shevchuk."

"Where's Dr. Chalthoum? Is she joining us?"

"Yeah, she's busy for a minute. Would you like me to knock on her bathroom door and ask her if she's finished peeing?"

"That's nice Shift. Why don't you just tell us what you've learned?"

"Okay. Here's the scoop. The Lunar Portal System, apparently, is a series of interconnected glass-like tubes connecting the various colonies and outposts within the inhabited sector of the Moon. Actually, why is it that I'm telling you about this instead of someone from NASA or from the moon?"

"There is a great deal going on within the moon colonies Dr. Bader," replied the ever-formal Dr. Shevchuk. "NASA and the colonies need to focus on the crisis that is at their door. As you know, Dr. Silitzer and I have been heavily engaged in research of Anthrax E itself. That's why *you* got this assignment. Was the burden too great for you Doctor?" The twinkle in Dr. Shevchuk's eye told me that he might not be quite as serious as I thought. We may have a closet jokester on our hands.

"Right. I'll stop complaining." I wasn't complaining anyway, really. I just wanted to know whether someone else might be better able to read and interpret stuff on the internet than I am. That's all I did here.

"Anyway, there are approximately 750 miles of cylindrical 'tubes' floating several feet off the surface of the moon. Both human and product movement, as well as the sharing of data occurs through these tubes. Through migration of the tubes with the various Encapsulation Shells, a person can travel through the tubes without having to wear any PPE, uh, Personal Protective Equipment, or travel outside the regulated atmosphere of the Encapsulation Shells. In other words, the tubes carry stuff—people, things, and information.

"Lunar Encapsulation Shells cover nearly all outposts in the inhabited sector of the Moon. With only a few exceptions, the Shells maintain atmospheric pressure within a defined space. There are currently six large main Shells, one each for the United States, England, Portuguese-Brazil, Poland, Mexico and Burmo-Thailand, with another under construction by the Egyptian government. There are also 46 smaller Shells covering various outposts used for science, exploration, vacations, etc.

Crap. "Gentlemen, I need to go, literally. I don't know what did it, but my insides are feeling quite . . . mushy right now. Must be something I ate. Talk to you later . . ."

Okay. That was intense. Feeling good now. I need to ask Anta if something we ate might have done that to me. We ate something "Egyptian" last night from our wall units. It smelled good at the time, but now—a little less pleasant.

16

"Hold on John, let me get Shift over here. He had quite a night."

"Anta, are you laughing?" Doctor Silitzer asked, with a little smirk rounding out the corners of his mouth.

"I'm trying very hard not to. Shift was convinced, last night, that he had Anthrax E. He was scared shitless—literally. Now look whose laughing. Okay, that was profane—I'm sorry.

"Shift and I had a nice meal last night, but the meat was seasoned with an ingredient that causes an allergic reaction in a very, very small percentage of people—mostly just the weak. Okay, don't tell him I said that—I'm kidding. The reaction causes quite severe diarrhea. I reminded him that diarrhea isn't one of the symptoms of Anthrax E, but that it *is* a symptom of eating this particular meal. I'm not sure I convinced him. He's lying in his room, probably praying, or reading the Bible. I mean it—he was practically delirious with fear. Let me get him. We'll call you back."

Thirty minutes later, after Shift took a sponge bath in his chem suit, which he probably REALLY needed if the smell of diarrhea inside the suit was anything like it was when he released it from the suit's refuse compartment—or "poop chute" as he calls it—we called Dr. Silitzer back. I tried, and it took a great deal of self control, to not tease Shift through the bathroom door during his "bath".

Shift started talking the instant the connection was secure.

"*Don't even say it John.* I know I'm crazy. I know I'm a wimp. But this isn't funny, so shut it."

"Dude, I was only going to ask if everything came out alright in the end." Doctor Silitzer broke up. He laughed for several seconds—even wiped away a tear that was running down his now splotchy, red face. It was funny, but not that funny.

"I'll tell you what's going to come out in the end, John . . ." I had to cut Shift off before these two children said something stupid. I mean, more stupid.

"Gentlemen, if we could get back to the *crappy* business at hand, that would be wonderful." *Good one Anta.* Now they're both laughing. "Seriously, Dr. Silitzer, what do we need to be talking about?"

"Yeah, right, let me just gather myself here. I can't stop. It just keeps *coming out.*" That really did it. Shift actually fell off the chair laughing. It's too bad I have to be the grown up around here.

"Seriously Anta, you're such a party *pooper.*" Shift got a kick in the ribs for that one. If he hadn't been on the floor laughing, it would only have been his shin.

"Goodbye gentlemen; and I use that term very loosely."

"Just like Shift's bowels, eh? No wait, don't walk away Anta, I really do have something to tell you two. I'm done *running* at the mouth." Shift actually crawled away to catch his breath. I've not seen anyone laugh like these two clowns in a long time. I guess they needed to blow off some steam, because poop jokes really shouldn't be that funny to grown men.

"Let me know when you're finished guys. I'll just sit here and wait. Don't even say it . . ."

It felt like an eternity, but finally, both Shift and John calmed down. I like these guys, but the timing is a little off. I'm going to forgive them because of the stress that we're all under right now. Finally, John got serious, although I could tell that he was really fighting his emotions. Shift, on the other hand, giggled like a school boy for the next few minutes.

"Okay, I think I'm done, unlike Shift. Okay, that was out of line. I'm really finished with the jokes. This is actually serious. I don't know if you've been paying attention to the boards, but there's a new report from the moon.

"The moon colonies report, on a regular basis, any and all irregular events that might have some bearing on the other colonies. For instance, any illness or injury is reported in the International Interagency Assembly Database, or "IIAD". So, of course, they are currently keeping close tabs on Anthrax E in that database. The current news is that, as of yesterday, the United States colony is reporting 15 cases of Anthrax E. I'm sure that's increased by now. As of yesterday, no other colony was reporting any illness.

"On January 9th, the IIA began requiring that any person, with any medical symptom, other than a physical injury, be contained in some kind of quarantine booth. The IIA also halted all movement, both of product and person, through the portals. So, wherever a person was located, as of January 9, that is where the person will stay, indefinitely. Probably a very good idea. All of this seems to be working, except that the illness is in the United States Shell already. The IIA is hopeful that it will stay there, of course.

"The last item of business is that the IIA has shut down all Earth-Moon communications except for the IIA database, to which our Anthrax E database is connected. I think that means that no private communications are allowed with the moon. Even most governmental agencies won't be able to contact the moon. So, Anta, you won't be speaking with your brother any time soon. I'm sorry about that, but it's not my call. I'm just the bearer of the news.

"I guess I'm not too surprised," I said. "My brother is pretty resourceful, though, and he may just find a way to get a message to me and my parents anyway."

"Well, that would be nice. I hope so. That's all I've got for you. Try to enjoy the rest of your day. Oh, wait, Dr. Shevchuk also wanted me to strongly encourage you two to get out of there and meet with us in the United States. I don't know where yet, but he's working on that. Try to get home Shift, and bring Anta with you. I'm out, just like last night's dinner!"

With that last crack, John shut the com before Shift could retort, leaving Shift to giggle while I glared at him.

It would be nice if Shift could call his sister to tell her he's trying to get home, but with the coms blackout, that won't happen. Maybe by the time John gets it arranged, the blackout will be lifted. Yeah, right.

**JANUARY 12, 2093, 0600 EET
EXCERPT FROM A NEWS STORY PUBLISHED IN THE "CNCIG"
(CAIRO NEWSCORP INFORMATION GUIDE)**

As of 0600 hours today, nearly 7900 people are reported to be infected with "Anthrax E" in El-Alamein. 59 are confirmed dead of the same, including Mr. Riyad Shafik, believed to have been an original carrier of the disease. There are no reported cases outside the city limits, likely the result of a government quarantine put into effect on January 7. That quarantine, which is still in effect, includes all areas of El-Alamein and the Qattara Depression and extends at least 20 kilometers in all directions.

Additionally, the International Lunar Space Station in the United States Moon Colony reports similar infections, although in a rare instance of concealment by the IWO, and its Lunar arm, the IIA, the number of infected and the number of casualties, if any, have not been disclosed.

17

I began to cry tonight as I thought of what was occurring and what was likely yet to come. My heart hurt and my lungs burned. The sensation was overpowering. I've known sorrow in my life, but this was incomparable. The tears dripped down my face, and I couldn't make them stop until Shift knocked on my door about 15 minutes later.

Before opening the door, I wiped away my tears the best I could; but I'm sure Shift could see that I had been crying. When he first looked at me, I noticed a slight twisting downward of the corners of his mouth, and his eyes softened as he appeared to share my pain and grief. He didn't say anything, but I was touched that he cared. I wanted him to hug me, but the suits prevent that kind of contact.

After a few seconds of silence, Shift came in and sat down on one of the soft chairs near the small table in the corner. He sighed as he stared into the blackness outside my window. It looked like he was also fighting his emotions.

We know, having talked with the doctors at the local hospital, and having regular coms with Doctors Shevchuk and Silitzer, that there isn't any available treatment for Anthrax E, or even the old-fashioned Anthrax. But the world doesn't seem to know that—yet. Each hour brings hundreds more to the doors of clinics and hospitals where no treatment is helping ease pain or slow the disease.

As we sat in silence, each trying to deal with the pain that was enveloping our hearts and minds, our reverie was suddenly broken by a dull popping sound, like corn kernels in a popper, coming from the window. Shift and I both rushed to the window, which we now keep draped, nearly tripping over each other on the way. I got there first.

"I'll get the lights," Shift grumbled.

"Thanks," I replied cheerfully.

Once Shift turned out the lights, he rejoined me at the window. He peered over my shoulder as I opened the drapes a bit more for him to see out. Outside, the half-moon cast pockets of light through partly-cloudy skies. Out on the water of the Mediterranean Sea, many stories below our hotel room window, it looked like a small boat was attempting to pass through the blockade that was set up on the water when the quarantine was initiated. As we peered through the moon-lit, but shadowed night, we saw several small bursts of light on the water, followed seconds later by more dull thuds.

"Was that a gun?" I asked.

"Sure sounded like it," Shift replied.

"It looks like someone is trying to get past the blockade out there," I said.

"And they're being shot at?"

"Or, maybe the runners are doing the shooting," I replied.

Just then one of the small boats exploded in a ball of flames. Shift stiffened behind me.

After a few seconds, in which both of us were lost in thought, Shift said quietly, "You know that could present a problem for us if we try to leave. Have you and your father come up with any ideas?"

"We're working on it," I replied gloomily.

We watched for a few more minutes, and, not seeing any further action, backed away from the window. I shut the drapes, walked over to the wall unit and ordered some hot chocolate.

"You want anything Shift," I asked.

"Some water please."

I returned to the small table where Shift was sitting and set a glass of ice water on the table. "Thank you," he said, looking at it.

"We're going to get out of here Shift," I said, feigning conviction.

"I know. But nobody out there is."

I looked down at my lap and began to cry again.

We'd heard the latest reports about the quarantine, indicating there is no infection outside the city apart from the lunar colonies. I certainly didn't want to be stuck here, but I was grateful for government officials who had done their best—I think—to contain the spread of Anthrax E to the boundaries of El-Alamein. It seemed to be working. Maybe my parents would be safe. With Hasani in very real danger, I hoped mom and dad, at least, could survive this.

After several minutes of silence, I asked, "Have you thought about the rate, or the potential rate of the spread of this thing?"

"Yes."

"And?"

"Well, the population of permanent residents here is about 29,000, right?"

I nodded, adding, "And foreign travelers likely account for another 8,000-10,000 at this time of year."

"Okay. So, Mr. Shafik first showed symptoms only five days ago from Anthrax E likely contracted just three days before that. He then died three days later, on January 10—or six days after probable contamination. Does all of that make sense so far? I mean, do my estimates seem correct so far?"

"Yes," I replied. "Go on."

"Okay, so Dr. Ghannam and his daughter both died a day later. If that timeline follows, and no cure or vaccine is found or created in a reasonable time, each person who has contracted the disease, or who will in the future, will likely be dead within six to seven days of first exposure. It seems possible that every person in this town will be dead within a week to 10 days—including us if we can't get out of here."

"I don't know what to say to that Shift," I said. "What a burden to have this knowledge. I think . . . well, this sucks! Innocent lives are being sacrificed in El-Alamein because of the quarantine—a quarantine that we initiated.

"I get it though. I know the purpose is to prevent, if it's even possible, a greater calamity. But more than 35,000 people will probably die in El-Alamein. Some of them might have been able to escape untouched. But I guess it's impossible to know which of those that escaped would have actually been healthy, and which would have exposed so many other people. I guess it's better this way."

"I think so," Shift replied.

Ultimately, even if Shift and I die, it's better that we die than that we expose countless other people to Anthrax E, who would then expose others. The end result of that selfishness could be greater death and destruction than this world has ever known. We're both feeling healthy though, and we've had on our suits for eight days now. We're likely going to survive, at least for now.

"So, I've attempted to contact Hasani several times over the past couple of days, but it appears that John was correct," I said, intentionally changing the subject. "All communication channels, at least the ones that I can use, seem to have been shut down."

"That sucks. I'm sorry Anta," Shift said.

"Oh, Dad just com'd," I said, looking down at my wrist.

"What does he say?"

"The journal from the cave has been translated. Dad sent me the translated digital book."

"Open it!"

Shift is as excited as I am. This could solve the mystery of how Anthrax E got here.

My Dear Anta,

The notebook you sent us was indeed a diary. The poor man who wrote it died in misery and pain. Here are key excerpts. The parts we left out are just more of the same.

Love,

Your father

7. NOV. 1942

I'm safe, for now. Oh, how I miss Hanne and the children. The sounds of war outside the cave have stopped, but I hear a wind howling that is as frightening as the bombs of yesterday.

It's very cold in here, but I dare not light the wood scattered across the floor in case the enemy might be lurking outside. Or the smoke may suffocate me.

I don't know why anybody would be looking for me, but I'm too scared to tempt fate.

I feel a desperate urge to leave this shelter provided by a compassionate God, but cannot for fear that I may not make it back on my ailing knee. It pains me greatly and appears to be infected.

9. NOV. 1942

Why has God forsaken me, in my most desperate hour? The sand blown on the winds has shut the cave's mouth. I am trapped! I cannot dig my way out, although I have tried. Through the sand I hear the continued wail of the great storm. It is probably piling sand on top of sand, burying me deeper and deeper in this cave of sorrow. It may become my tomb.

Thankfully I still have light and food and water. But they will not last long.

13. NOV. 1942

The infection in my knee has spread into my hips. I can feel the burning and smell the stench day and night. I cannot walk.

The cave entrance remains closed and I have no strength to search for another way out. I have no strength to dig myself out.

God has abandoned me as retribution for my acquiescence to the depraved plan of destruction laid before me by Herr Himmler. His cursed plan to test a new weapon among the poor inhabitants of this desert, and his damnable pressure to make me an accomplice, has left me feeling as vile and despicable as Himmler himself.

15. NOV. 1942

My food is gone. A small pool of water has formed near the former opening to my prison. It must be raining outside. Or perhaps it rained days ago. Nevertheless, the water only prolongs my certain death.

Oh, that I had refused to help in this awful plan! But if I had, my dear wife and children would already be dead at the hands of that wicked man.

22. NOV. 1942

I have been 15 days in this cave. The agony of infection, although barely endurable at best, is a mere trifle compared to the agony of emotion that has plagued me since I arrived in this place to fight in this unholy war.

The little bit of wood in the cave ran out days ago. The water is nearly gone, but could last for several days yet. I've stored as much as my mess kit and canteen will hold for use when the pool runs dry. But I'm starving.

Whatever is sealed up in this small vial could end this suffering. Or, would it prolong or increase my misery? I am afraid to find out.

26. NOV. 1942

I have nothing to sustain my life but a little water. I will never see Hanne and the children again. What have I done? The despair is destroying my soul, and the excruciating pain of infection has now consumed my body. I cannot move except to the table to mark my days. Nor do I have anywhere to go.

I have opened the vial. Let it destroy me as punishment for my sins.

30. NOV. 1942

I am a dead man. My insides churn and move of their own volition. It feels as though millions of tiny insects move within me, devouring me, like a plague. Blood seeps from my nose and mouth and every cough sends spasms of pain throughout my devastated body. Himmler's Anthrax has killed me.

This is the price I pay for my sin. God have mercy on my soul.

"Oh Shift. That poor man." I choked out the words and started to cry again. All my earlier emotion returning, magnified by the knowledge of the pain these people in El Alamein are going through.

"Yeah," Shift said as he reached across the table and rested his gloved hand on mine. There was little else to say.

18

As of a couple of days ago, the United States colony thought they had contained Anthrax E to the medical facilities, but they were wrong. 17 more cases were reported on January 11. All of those people were placed in containment, but it didn't work. Today, the United States colony is reporting an additional 264 cases of Anthrax E!

But it gets worse. Other colonies on the moon now report illness. Only the Burmo-Thailand Shell and the Mexican Shell are still clear. Containment facilities in the United States shell are full and all the colonies are implementing safety procedures and no-travel restrictions. It looks like they aren't working.

Here in El-Alamein, it's estimated that over 11,000 people are infected and more than 200 have died. And that's the estimate from two days ago. We're not receiving any more local reports, but I'm sure today is much, much worse.

"So the only colony not affected, or so it appears, is Mexico?" Anta asked, sitting on the couch in my hotel room.

"That's what they say. There's over a thousand people sick or dead now up there."

It still seemed strange to be wearing this chem suit. What should have been the most ordinary scene was anything but ordinary. Anta sat on the couch with her legs crossed and her hands in her lap, while I worked on my tablet at the table. Ordinary, except that we were both cocooned in silver-colored body armor looking at each other through plasteel face plates.

Anta continued, her voice pensive, "Because travel restrictions were put into place several days ago, and all the other colonies are experiencing illness, do you think it's possible that the Mexican colony may actually stay clean? That would be great for them, I guess, except, what happens when everyone else is dead? There's no way the IIA or the IWO is going to allow Mexico to come home. And there's no way, at least not for a very long time, that the IIA or IWO is going to let any ship leave Earth for the moon."

"I'm sure you're right," I replied. "Dr. Shevchuk isn't any closer to a vaccine or cure. He desperately wants us to go to Boston, and bring our physical samples with us. John just got there today, along with a couple other specialists of some kind. Shevchuk thinks that the actual samples we have would be more helpful than the data and transfigured samples that we previously sent him. I'm sure he's right."

"Where are they anyway?"

"In some kind of bunker outside Boston somewhere. They won't tell me where they are until we've escaped from this place."

"Why?" Anta asked.

"They're trying to keep it a secret, I guess, probably to keep people away from wherever they are. If word got out that they're working on a cure or a vaccine, there could be a potential rush on the medications or information before it's ready for official release."

"That makes sense, but most people don't seem to think this is much of a threat, do they?"

"Seems that way," I replied. "Since nearly every problem like this has been easily contained—at least during the lifetimes of the majority of humans on Earth now—and have never posed much of a world-wide threat, people don't seem too worried."

"Well, I am. We need to get to Boston."

JANUARY 15, 2093—ANTA

Ignorance is NOT bliss; at best it's just a short-term denial of reality. We're in the dark regarding what's happening all around us here in El-Alamein, but that ignorance doesn't comfort me. Even dad has no idea what's happening here.

What we see, of course, is quite telling. For the past several days, Shift and I have spent significant time watching out the windows, looking at the town below. We don't have much else going on.

The flow of people has dried up. There are no people on the streets or in the air. No more gunshots in the night. No sounds of people in the hotel. Shift "moved in" with me. We're both just a little more comfortable having another living—and healthy—person nearby.

Our door is locked and we've put furniture in front of it just in case some crazed person decides to try to break in. I know that's a pretty unrealistic fear at this point—but that's what always happens in the horror movies.

When you're bored, depressed, and on edge, like we are, your imagination can play tricks on you—like thinking you're in a horror movie. We're alone, left to decide whether we should venture outside and risk near-certain death, or wait in our hotel room and hope to fend off the oncoming wave of monsters. At least, that's what it feels like.

Shift is getting a little pissy though, so we're not having much fun in our little movie. I'm thinking of kicking him out.

Thankfully, our room's wall unit continues to function, providing us with a never-ending supply of what Shift calls "wall-crap". He hates the food, but I don't think it's that bad. At least we're not starving.

It seems obvious, though, that if the people who maintain the units have stopped doing so, because they're all sick in bed or worse, then the machines will eventually break down or run out of whatever it is that supplies our nutritional needs. Of course, the demand for the food and drink is probably down to two—Shift and I. This hotel has over 4000 rooms. If the units installed in each room are meant to work for hundreds, or thousands of uses before maintenance is required, then, assuming we can ever leave this room, and can remove the probably-deceased occupants of other rooms without becoming infected, we should have plenty of food and water for many years to come. But I don't want to stay here to find out, especially if Shift can't get past his funk. Plus, we don't have that much canned air.

JANUARY 15, 2093—SHIFT

The combined lunar colonies have reported more than 2300 infected, with more than 800 of those resulting in death—so far. And the deaths, although not detailed in the database, can't be pretty. I don't know how they get rid of bodies up there; or who's doing it?

Who is brave enough to touch them or even go near them? Probably nobody. The bodies are probably piling up in the medical facilities while the bodies of the dead outside the facilities likely lie where they fall.

Anta has just finished speaking with her father. I can see that her eyes are red, so she's been crying again. This has got to be difficult for them.

"Want to hear the stats?" I asked as Anta sat down next to me on the bed.

"Sure."

"Okay. From what John tells me, the total lunar population is 14,502, with approximately 2,900 of those stationed in the Mexican colony, either permanently or temporarily due to the restriction on transportation. And, Mexico has just applied for authority to transfer all of them back to Earth."

Anta nodded, though her eyes unmistakably changed from sorrow to fear.

Seeing the fear rise in her expression, and having felt it myself while talking with John earlier, I hastily added, "But the IWO hasn't given them permission yet. Selfishly, Anta, I hope they never get to come home."

"I feel the same way Shift. And I feel terrible about that."

19

"Did you hear that Anta?" I whispered.

"Yeah, what was it?" Anta walked over to the window and looked down toward the deserted street below. "It sounded like a motorcycle, didn't it?"

I joined her at the window, but looked up instead. "Look!"

Since the quarantine was established, we'd heard very little automotive noise.

"I think that plane has the IWO logo on the side. Can you tell?" Anta asked, squinting into the sun to our right.

"Yeah, I think you're right. If the IWO has started physical surveillance of this place, maybe we'll get out of here soon."

Anta's father told us yesterday that the IWO has taken control of the situation and no branch of the Egyptian government has any influence on what transpires here now.

"Well, if we can verify that it's the IWO, I say we go up to the roof to see if we can make contact. Dad told the IWO we're here, but they may not believe we're still safe and healthy. I guess we've got to show them. What do you think?"

I'd learned that this type of question from Anta was merely an attempt to humor me. She'd go up on that roof no matter what I said.

"Yeah, let's go. Wait, it's leaving," I said, pointing to the sky.

The plane headed away from the city. We both stood there for several minutes, in silence, wondering if it would come back. It didn't. They probably saw no sign of life and turned around. Finally, we both wandered away from the window and resumed what we had been doing.

Logically, Anta and I are the only people still alive in this town, unless some fortunate soul locked him or herself inside some kind of bomb shelter before the outbreak. Interestingly, we haven't seen any animals either, except for the birds. There are no dogs frolicking, no cats running amok at night. No animals foraging through the trash.

But there *are* birds—lots of them. Maybe birds, at least, are immune to Anthrax E. If so, that will have to be taken into consideration for both potential immunities and potential spread of the disease. Birds seem to be the most likely means—apart from wind—of carrying the disease outside the quarantine zone. If they are immune, might they still be carriers? That would suck.

"I think we need to figure out a contingency plan just in case the IWO doesn't believe we're still alive, and doesn't send another plane back to check on us," I said, my thoughts becoming words.

"Yeah, I've got a plan, and we probably need to act on it now," Anta replied, with her usual air of confidence, which she may have been putting on for my sake. But that's good, because we're running out of compressed oxygen cubes. We haven't talked about it, but we both know that we've got to get out of here within the next couple of days or we'll run out of air, risking probable contamination ourselves. Contamination equals death.

"So, what's the plan dude?"

"Can't I at least be a *dudette*?" replied Anta sternly. I was speechless for a few moments, until Anta began to laugh and said, "Close your mouth. You look silly."

I did and she continued seriously, "If we haven't been rescued by the IWO by tomorrow evening, which seems almost certain, we're driving out of here, through the desert, *dude*. At the latest, we've got to be out of here in the next couple of days or we'll run out of air."

"Yeah, but how do we get out without taking Anthrax E with us, or getting shot? What's your plan for that?" I asked.

Then she told me. We're planning our evacuation route now. In addition to the chem suits Anta brought with us, she also brought a ton of high-level Glutaraldehyde sterilant spray used to disinfect medical instruments in hospitals and operating rooms. She believes that, with a high enough dose of the sterilant, we should be able to kill any microbes or spores attached to our chem suits, our gear, and her truck before we remove the suits, thus protecting ourselves from Anthrax E infection. She's got this whole plan figured out, and a specific order for it all. She's so cool!

JANUARY 20, 2093—SHIFT

Reports are in from the moon. 85% of the United States colony is infected, along with more than 1000 people in the Polish colony, over 1600 in the German colony, more than 1200 in the Portuguese-Brazil colony, and over 1000 people in the Burmo-Thailand colony. Most people have not lived more than 98 hours after first exhibiting signs of infection. Mexico is still infection-free, but it's been denied permission to return to Earth—twice.

A little while ago, I was reading a press release on the Net, with today's date, but no author taking credit for the information. It said:

The IWO has been hiding a serious crisis taking place within the moon colonies. A disease, previously-unknown, and now dubbed "Anthrax E" has devastated the population of the lunar colonies. Thousands are dead and hope for the survival of others is slim at best. The disease has no cure and there is no vaccine. Every person who has contracted the disease thus far is dead or is expected to die. There is no treatment.

All communication with the moon (except for security channels) and all travel to and from the moon has ceased. This secret of the IWO certainly places all of us at risk. Who knows what this malady really is? Who knows what this outbreak really means for the survival of our planet? Where did the disease come from and are we at risk?

We call upon the IWO to . . .

But just as I began the third paragraph, the article disappeared, right before my eyes, like some creepy, digital magic trick. The IWO probably didn't authorize that article and got rid of it. I wonder how many people read it first. I wonder whose head is being chopped off for the posting.

Anta hasn't been successful in her "official" attempt to get us out of here, and we haven't seen or heard any air traffic today. So, we're leaving, within minutes, both for our survival and possibly for the survival of this world. If we survive, awesome! If we can't get out of here alive, then I'm pretty sure that this great planet is screwed. I'm not overly confident in the quarantine, since the people patrolling the borders will have one heck of a time containing the wind should it rise again.

"Shift!" Anta called through the open door to the bathroom, where I was attempting to shave inside my expanded suit. "Dad is hailing you. Get in here! Oh, he isn't on the line—it's just a message."

"What does it say?" I asked as I hesitated, then hurried across the room, my chem suit rustling as I moved. Anta's dad has been communicating with us like this for a few days. I think he may be worried about actually telling us anything. Instead, he just passes on information, usually authored by others. We know he wants us to get out of here, and I know Anta has told him of our plan to leave today.

"Let's read it," Anta replied, as she typed in my password to access the secure documents on my MEHD.

Final conclusions and resolutions reached following Ministry meeting held on January 20, 2093, scribed by Aloli Baz:

The following conclusions and resolutions have been reached with regard to the El-Alamein situation, and have been cleared and approved by the IWO:

Beginning at 0600 hours, tomorrow, which is January 21, 2093, El-Alamein will be searched, house to house and building to building, to locate any survivor of Anthrax E. Any living individual(s) located will be scanned to determine his or her health status. Upon scanning, the inspector will either aid the individual in hastening death or remove the individual from the city, depending upon whether the individual is contaminated. Animals will not be inspected as time is of the essence. 1,200 inspectors will be assigned this task. All inspectors will be outfitted with CBRN suits to prevent infection.

The search will conclude promptly at 1600 hours that day and all inspectors and healthy survivors will have one hour to report to the east quarantine checkpoint for departure. No further time for inspection will be permitted based upon an incoming storm front projected to arrive on January 22. Thus, inspectors will be expected to act in haste.

Upon check-in at the east quarantine checkpoint, all survivors and inspectors will be cleansed and placed into individual mobile holding blocks for examination for seven days. All precautions will be taken to ensure that no such individual is allowed to leave his or her block. All necessary comforts will be provided to all held individuals.

At 1800 hours on January 21, rigid HMP Foam (high-density, microcellular polyurethane foam) will be applied, via application guns mounted on low-speed, high-altitude hovercraft. The entire city will be sealed with such foam. Applicators will be expected to ensure, using high-resolution satellite radiography, that every inch of the city and the Qattara Depression, to the edge of the quarantine zone on all sides, is completely enclosed.

The goal of these measures is to seal Anthrax E within its current location to ensure the safety and survival of the human race.

The current quarantine and isolation will remain in effect indefinitely. Following the HMP application, a no flyover zone will be enforced for 1 mile above the tallest building in the city. This additional measure will be in force indefinitely.

"Holy crap! I'm glad we're getting out of here now!" I said.

"Yeah. We don't have time to sit in confinement for seven days. Shevchuk needs your samples now." Anta spoke so matter-of-factly that I was confident she had no doubts about her plan for escape.

That's good, because we're out of here. I wonder if they'll find any survivors.

20

Yesterday at 6:30 PM, near twilight, Anta and I braved the elements and the sick air outside the hotel. Hauling our gear down the stairs to avoid potential dead people on the elevator, we loaded her truck with all of the provisions it could carry. It took us several trips. We had to make sure we had enough food and water to last several days in the desert, just in case our plans for escape failed. We probably loaded two weeks worth—which we hoped was overkill. We wondered if someone would see us, so we used caution at first. But we didn't see any movement, anywhere.

We traveled south into the Qattara Depression along the pot-holed Al Betrol Road. The air was still and the moon was bright—not exactly the best cover for our escape, but it meant we could keep the headlights off until we left the city limits and some distance beyond. We didn't see a single person though, living or dead, after we left the city.

In fact, even before we left the city, we only saw two bodies, maybe 60 meters away. They were far enough away, at the entrance to an alley near a bakery, that we couldn't tell what condition the bodies were in. But they were lying on the ground, either dead or very near to it. With a bit of shame, we drove right past. If they were alive, we reasoned, they would be found by the inspectors only a few hours later. We would not have been able to help them anyway.

Approximately five hours after we passed the city limit on the south, driving through the barren Qattara Depression, we neared the junction of the Al Wahat Al Baharia Road. 15-20 minutes before we would have actually reached the junction, Anta turned off the headlights and slowed our speed. She believed a quarantine checkpoint would probably be located at that junction because there are so few roads out here.

"This old truck is a noisy bugger," she complained. "We can't afford to have anybody at the quarantine border hear us coming." The land between us and the junction was completely flat. Our headlights wouldn't have helped us stay hidden for long. She stopped the truck and turned off the engine.

We exited the truck and searched for any sign of a checkpoint in the distance. The bright moon, our only source of light, reflected off the sand like lamplight at night on fresh snow. The sand was a fascinating shade of turquoise blue. There wasn't a single sound reaching our ears. Even the insects had gone to bed. It was other-worldly, and peaceful.

"I don't see any sign of life," Anta said.

A few moments later, though, I saw specks of light in the distance, at two points—one to the left and one to the right.

"I see the lights," Anta said quietly before I could point them out to her.

"Yeah, one in each direction. They look like they're a couple miles away."

"More like five miles. Things look closer in the desert than they really are."

"Do you think those are quarantine checkpoints?" I asked.

"Yes, along the Al Wahat Al Baharia Road, as we had suspected," Anta replied.

If she was correct, then those two checkpoints would restrict travel out of the Qattara Depression on any surface road. Of course, we didn't intend to ever reach that junction. Using satellite-fed pinpoints on my watch, I located an old dirt road heading south just behind us.

Anta's old truck seemed reliable, but the whole desert in that area was deep sand—presently glowing a beautiful blue. I was concerned that the dirt road may be impassable. But we didn't have any other option.

Turning that noisy truck around, we began to look for the road. Several minutes later, in the dark with no headlights, we finally found a small, raised section of dirt road heading south off the highway. It was lined with rocks making it look, on that otherworldly night, like the backbone of a giant, blue lizard. While the lizard spine running along the west side of the road was likely meant to keep the sand off the dirt road, several sections were covered over anyway. It made travel slow and difficult, even with the truck's wheels engaged into "four wheel drive".

After driving a few miles down the old sandy road, sometimes on hard-packed dirt and sometime across drifts, we stopped again, this time to cleanse ourselves and our gear. We hadn't yet left the quarantine zone and prudently, Anta decided that it would be incredibly stupid to travel any closer to civilization without first destroying any Anthrax E spores on our chem suits, vehicle and possessions. Plus, we eventually had to get out of the suits before we met any people.

The truth is that, even after sterilizing everything in our possession, we still risked personal contamination just by virtue of our location very near the south-eastern edge of the Qattara Depression. The risk, of course, seemed minimal since the winds had not traveled south-east since we discovered Anthrax E. Nor had we heard any reports of illness to the east or south of El-Alamein—and Anta had asked her father that very question before we left El-Alamein. So, we were—well, Anta at least was—fairly confident that, in our present location, the only risk of infection was from our own stuff. So, we sterilized everything inside and out of the truck—our gear, the provisions and our suits. Well, not inside our suits. That would have been stupid.

Then we drove 20 miles farther down the road and sterilized everything again. Then we traveled another 20 miles and repeated the process. That's right, three times. Then, with great trepidation, we removed our chem suits and left them in the desert to be swallowed up by the foam application that was to commence shortly.

Finally, after nearly two hours of steady, but slow and difficult travel on that old dirt road, we came to the Al Wahat Al Baharia Road, but this time nearly 60 miles south of what we believed was the quarantine checkpoint we'd seen earlier. From there, a right turn and a quick 45 minutes later, we arrived in the small town of Bawiti, just before 3:00 AM.

Anta pulled up to the back of a small motel and turned off the engine.

"Wait in the car," she said. "I'll check in, then come and get you. They shouldn't ask questions if I'm alone and pay with cash."

Since authorities were supposedly going door to door in El-Alamein, we assumed that they would be looking for us, thinking that we might still be alive. If, or *when* they didn't find us, dead or alive, they may have become suspicious. We didn't want them to know where we'd gone.

"Why do *I* have to wait in the car?" I asked, with a smile.

"Oh, you're much too handsome to be a local," Anta replied, smiling. "We don't want to raise suspicion, do we?" Her smile was tired but mischievous.

A few minutes later, she returned and pointed to a dusty-looking cottage behind the main building. We grabbed our bags and hurried across the hard-packed ground to the small building where we crashed for the remainder of the night.

After an amazing, hot shower and relieving myself on a real, flushing, porcelain toilet, I laid down on the couch, across the room from Anta and the bed, with no chem suit. Just before I fell asleep, I caught Anta looking at me. Her hair was wet from her shower, and she was wearing a tight t-shirt and gym shorts. She was cute. I smiled. She smiled back. Thankfully, I didn't have long to ruminate on the issue of her sleepwear as I fell asleep almost immediately, and slept soundly.

JANUARY 21, 2093, 3:45 AM—ANTA

That shower was amazing! It's been 17 days since we put on the chem suits. Sponge baths do a pretty crappy job of keeping a girl clean. Plus, you can't wash your hair without real shampoo and water. Shift's hair is short, so he didn't look so bad tonight when we left our suits in the desert; but he had to be disgusted by *my* appearance. I certainly was. He didn't say anything though. I wonder what the motel clerk thought of me when we showed up here a little while ago. I was stinking up the joint.

Shift just crawled into bed—literally. This isn't the first time we've slept in the same room together—we've always been in separate beds—but it's the first time sleeping in the same room without the chem suits. He's wearing some long, thin, cotton sleeping pants but no shirt. The dude—to borrow his apparent term of endearment—looks good! His six foot frame is quite muscular, which I wouldn't have thought given the clothes I've seen him in. He's pretty tan too, with dark blue eyes and very short, light brown hair. He's no supermodel; he just looks like he cares about himself.

His tan skin is a little surprising considering he came to Egypt from Colorado, in the winter, where there's snow, *and*, we've spent the last 17 days covered from head to toe. Maybe it's just the natural color of his skin. It's nice, whatever its source.

When Shift looked at me tonight, just before he closed his eyes, I couldn't help but notice his kind face. It's the face I first saw at the airport in Apion. Lately though, it's been hard to see as we've struggled with our reality.

But despite the turmoil, just being with him has kept my spirits up. When he smiles, however seldom lately, it makes me feel like things are going to work out okay. When he sighs, I feel like I should slow down and enjoy life a little more. When he cries—which I've only seen a couple of times—like during our Holo conference with Dr. Ghannam and his daughter Shani, when they took them away for isolation—I feel like my heart will stop beating.

Phew! I've got to stop thinking about Shift this way, and I've got to stop looking at him. There's nothing I can do. He's my colleague. He's not married though. I wonder if he has a girlfriend. Why haven't I asked? *Ahhh, stop it Anta! Go to sleep!*

21

When we left the motel this morning, the small town of Bawiti was buzzing with life—life as I imagined existing a hundred years ago. There were merchants on the streets in little kiosks selling necklaces, dishes and meat with flies circling hungrily. There were camels for rent, although anybody renting one would have to go south away from the Depression—probably not too good for business lately. The buildings were, for the most part, run-down; but they had a mystic charm, like in that old cartoon "Aladdin" with the blue genie from the lamp that sang and danced. We saw a few automobiles, but only one hovercar.

The breeze was calm but noticeable, and coming from the West! A wind from that direction, blowing across the Depression, would send Anthrax E right into Apion and Cairo. But the palm trees were only gently swaying in that breeze, and, I hoped, El-Alamein and the Depression were already covered in foam.

Just down the block from our motel, kids were playing at a small park, just like any small-town playground you would find in the United States. Swings were swinging, the sun glittered off a short metal slide, and it looked like a game of "tag" was underway. It was peaceful, and a bit surreal. It was hard to believe that we had just been surrounded by death—and a very gruesome death at that—concerned for our lives, and anxious that we would never be able to leave El-Alamein; and yet, there, in a place so close to all that carnage, life continued to move at a leisurely pace, seemingly unconcerned with anything else going on in the world. There was no sign that the people had any concern for their health, despite the deadly bacteria wreaking havoc less than 300 miles away. The press had been adequately constrained.

We reluctantly left the peaceful town of Bawiti, headed for the closest international airport not located in Cairo. There are relatively few major roads in Egypt's deserts. A direct route to Cairo from Bawiti would take us back past the quarantine checkpoints. While we weren't necessarily concerned that the guards there would know anything about us, we didn't want to take the chance. So, we had a long drive ahead of us. There's an international airport in the city of Asyut, 560 miles away. In Anta's old truck, and on those dilapidated roads, at times covered with sand, it took us over nine hours to get to Asyut, but we were on our way. Our destination—Boston, Massachusetts.

En route to Asyut, Anta sent an encrypted com to her dad to report our whereabouts and to ask him to arrange passage for us to Boston. Then, just before we arrived in Asyut this evening, Anta received another communication from her dad describing what actually occurred in El-Alamein today.

"Read it out loud," she said as I took her datapad and began scanning it.

"It's in Arabic, but I'll try."

Anta gave me a look that said, *I know you read Arabic, so cut it out!*

"Okay. Your old man says, '1,200 inspectors were dispatched to El-Alamein, just as planned, and began their search at precisely 6:00 AM, as scheduled. During the next 10 hours, approximately 70% of the city was searched. In that time, only seven survivors were located, five of which were . . . I think the word is "sick". Of those five, four agreed to humane dispatch, and the other was dispatched without her consent.'

"Dispatched?" Anta questioned out loud.

"Were they just shot in the head?" I asked.

"Oh, I hope not," Anta replied.

I continued. "'The two other survivors showed no signs or symptoms of any contagion, both tested positive for infection. They were both female—a 37-year-old woman and her 13-year-old daughter. They were discovered in their home. They had not taken any precautions to keep the plague out of their home. They had been breathing normally, eating normally, sleeping normally. The only precaution they had taken as to their own safety was to stay indoors. The two healthy survivors and 1,199 inspectors all checked in by the designated time. One inspector failed to check in and was likely buried in the foam with any other person who may have survived the plague.'

"That's all it says," I concluded.

"They only searched 70 percent of the city. That means they needed more inspectors or more time. What if there were others?" Anta asked, her voice a little tremulous.

"I suppose finding only two uninfected people out of that 70 percent of the city means that they likely wouldn't have found any others in the remaining 30 percent," I replied.

"You're probably right," Anta said. "They might not have even found us, except that we would have been looking for them too, not hiding out in the hotel."

"It's a good thing we'll never have to know. I wonder if that mother and daughter are immune or just lucky. They tested positive, but aren't sick."

"I'm sure we'll find out," Anta said.

Through some brief coms with Minister Chalthoum, we learned that there have been no alerts about us; so we didn't know whether the authorities in charge of the search in El-Alamein realized that we weren't there, or whether they even cared. Our tickets granted us passage on a flight to Boston and nobody at the airport stopped us or even gave us a second look.

22

We landed in Boston yesterday afternoon, just before dusk. Our flight was without incident. I was pretty worried that our flight would be stopped just before take-off and that somebody would come on the plane, drag us off, and haul us to some containment facility, there to remove our heads and limbs as punishment for our crimes. But that didn't happen.

During the flight, I couldn't stop thinking about how, just a few hours earlier, Shift and I were worried that we may not live to see another day. But when we landed in Boston, there was no indication that anybody even knew about the problems in El-Alamein. A news program playing on the holos at the terminal had no ongoing coverage of the situation, which was contrary to what I'd come to expect in times of crisis. In fact, there wasn't even a blip about El-Alamein in the 45 minutes we watched. Instead, the news coverage had stories about a basketball game between the revered Boston Celtics and the Honolulu Waves (Boston got creamed, not that I care), an aviation trade show in South Boston, and a fairly-interesting editorial on the Second Boston Tea Party of 2032, which I didn't get to finish watching.

We were met at the airport in Boston by Dr. John Silitzer. He seemed thrilled to see us, with a big smile and warm hug for Shift, and two-handed hand-shake for me. It seemed he was holding back on a hug he wanted to give me too. Perhaps in time.

"Hey John, can I call my sister," Shift asked as we headed toward the exits.

"Better now than when we get to our destination," John replied. "In fact, try not to mention any details of our plans, just in case your call is monitored."

"Are my calls being monitored?" Shift asked, nervously.

"Not that I know of. But better safe than sorry, as they say."

Shift wandered away as he dialed. When he returned a few minutes later, he was in a good mood.

"Looks like that went well," John said.

"Everything's fine in their world. I told her I would be out of touch again for a while. She's not happy about it, but she's glad I'm in the States instead of overseas. And, it was great to talk to my nieces again."

After our brief reunion at the airport, we headed off. From the Logan-Bush International Airport in Boston, we traveled east along the Massachusetts Turnpike Air Corridor, flying in a new 2092 Chevrolet Fluxor. Sure, we have hovercraft of various types back home, and nearly every family owns one, but there's clearly more affluence in the United States. According to my studies, that's been the case for almost 200 years. This craft was beautiful and the ride was incredibly smooth. After all that time in my truck over the past couple of days, it felt like we were drifting lazily along on a cloud, or, at least, a very nice mattress on wheels.

We followed the Massachusetts Turnpike Air Corridor for about 70 minutes at a very rapid pace relative to the speed of my truck—through the urban center of Boston and then through its vast suburbs—and then turned northwest. Our route took us through a very dark, heavily-forested countryside unlike anything I've seen before. The trees and undergrowth were so thick that my visibility was limited to perhaps 80-100 meters in any given direction, and it was dark.

Deep, undisturbed snow covered nearly everything, but little sparkles reflecting off the smooth surface of the snow told me that there was a moon out somewhere. I saw very little animal life, but one young deer looked at us from under the trees just off the side of the road. The dark green pine trees still had their needles, with a scattering around the base of each tree; but other trees, the names of which I'm uncertain, were mostly bare, their fallen leaves hidden under the beautiful twinkling snow.

I understand that autumn here is spectacular, but that season has long since passed. I wish it'd been lighter outside as we drove through the forest. I'd love to see this place in the daylight, especially the snow, which I've only experienced a handful of times during my travels. Even though the sights were beautiful, albeit dark and mostly in shades of gray at this time of night, I had a strange feeling of helplessness as we traveled through the forest—a feeling as though I could get lost and never get out. I think getting lost here wouldn't be so bad but for the cold and the possible starvation. Okay, those two things are pretty bad.

After a while, with our speed slowed due to the twisting and turning of the roads on which we were then traveling, we continued northwest for another few minutes to the southern shore of a large lake. Even with the moon out and few clouds in the sky, because of the dense forest between us and the water, I could just barely make out the silver ripples of the water made by the breeze as it swept across the lake from the North.

I couldn't see the edges of the lake, but I imagined it was frozen and I daydreamed of skating on the lake, in the moon-lit night, holding Shift's hand. Thankfully, my limited view of the lake disappeared for a moment as we rounded a corner and I was able to stop that train of thought. Despite the limited view, which came and went for the next several minutes, the lake was beautiful, like everything else I'd seen in Massachusetts so far.

Soon, we were off the "beaten path" on what appeared to be a seldom-used, but paved, back-country road. This narrow road had been cleared of snow. The snow banks on either side of the road were nearly five feet high and would have completely blocked our view of the lake had we not been hovering close to a foot off the surface of the road. Many years ago, I'd read an article about some young children in Bosnia who had dug a massive snow cave in a snow bank like these and had died when it collapsed on them. That memory still didn't detract from the beauty of it all. Perhaps it should have. Maybe I'm sick in the head.

About 15 minutes later, we stopped in a small clearing near the side of the road and exited the Fluxor. The air smelled wonderful and clean. But the cold and humidity, to which I'm wholly unaccustomed, pressed in on me and drove into my skin like thousands of needles, causing me to begin shivering within minutes despite the winter clothing that John had given me.

John told us that we'd need to carry our belongings, but that the trail was short and the snow wasn't deep. Still, the trek was difficult, even with John and Shift carrying some of my gear.

Not long after leaving the Fluxor, walking on a narrow trail with deep snow banks piled high on both sides, which gave the sensation of being in a cave—a cold cave— we approached a small, two-story cabin that appeared to be well-maintained—at least on the outside. Suddenly, I heard more than felt a thump on my lower back and turned around to see Shift and John, each with arms raised in a defensive position. I reached around to my back and felt the wet, cold remains of a snowball. Rushing at Shift, I tackled him to the ground and rubbed snow in his face while he laughed and tried—pretty lamely—to push me off of him.

After a few seconds, I realized, and I think Shift did too, the awkwardness of the situation. We work together; thousands of lives have just been lost that we couldn't prevent despite our efforts; and we were rolling around in the snow like children. The freedom and joy of the moment, so different from the last two and a half weeks of our lives, was over as quickly as it had begun.

Our new silence allowed the soft sounds of John's laughter to carry across the snow drifts to where we lay. Looking at John, I could see the mistake I had made. Shift didn't throw that snowball.

Keeping his back toward John, Shift motioned for me to stay quiet, surreptitiously packed his own snowball, and with a quick turn heaved the snowball at John catching him on his left cheek. In his surprise, John fell back into a snow bank and lay there, stunned. We both laughed at his shocked silence as Shift walked over to help John to his feet. Shift turned toward me, with a look that said he was a hero and I was the rescued princess. As I gazed at these two good friends I felt a warmth deep inside that took away the night chill.

Quickly putting ourselves back together and picking up our gear, we continued toward the cabin. It had a massive wrap-around porch devoid of any patio furniture—obviously—its winter after all. The windows were all shuttered and no outside lights broke the night's darkness. John remotely unlocked the front door—I heard the quiet click of at least three locks—and we entered a faintly-lit room modestly furnished as if it were just a hunting cabin.

I knew, of course, that this was no ordinary cabin since John had explained to us that we would be going to a "top-secret underground military installation". After the front door was closed and locked behind us, John—again remotely—caused the nearby staircase to rise from its bottom on hinges that couldn't be seen from our position, but which likely connected the various pieces of this hidden passageway on the underside of the staircase. Underneath the stairs, which ordinarily gave access to the second floor, was a second staircase, metal, which descended into the ground beneath the cabin.

John led us down four flights of stairs to an isolation or decontamination chamber of some kind. We stepped into the chamber and the doors closed behind us with a hiss. The air inside was sucked away and was replaced by fresher air, tainted with a light lemon scent.

Within moments, the door to the interior of the hidden basement opened. We stepped into an open, bright foyer furnished with soft, padded chairs and lamps, like a cozy living room. Almost immediately, two men rounded the corner and we were heartily welcomed by Dr. Shevchuk and another doctor. Even though we'd never met, I instantly felt a connection with Dr. Shevchuk. He was a grandfatherly figure, perhaps 70 or 75 years old, with short, dark, but graying hair and a prominent bald spot in the middle on top. His voice was soft and kind, and he hugged me as if we'd known each other all of our lives.

Even though I thought his first concern would be to get a hold of Shift's samples, he seemed genuinely concerned that we were fed and rested. He reached out and gently grasped my elbow and led us out of the foyer and into an adjoining mess hall where steaming spaghetti, crispy garlic bread, cooked vegetables and some kind of juice were waiting for us. I loved him instantly!

After proper introductions to some of the others here in the bunker, we ate a hearty home-cooked meal for the first time in weeks. And we told our story of escape. While everyone seemed genuinely interested, Dr. Shevchuk was enthralled with the story, asking dozens of questions along the way.

After our meal, we moved to a recreation room to discuss the doctors' progress so far. This large room had a card table and a small movie screen against one wall. Although obviously not from our generation, it could surely provide adequate viewing of 2D films, if there are any around. There were couches and tables, magazines from decades ago, and even a record player with a stack of old 45 vinyl records standing on a shelf nearby. We sat, happily, in this bunker among the relics of generations past. I secretly hoped the research equipment these guys were using was a little more modern.

Shift and I were told a little about our location, but there's a lot of secrecy surrounding this area and we'll probably never know the whole truth. That's okay. We *were* told that this particular facility was built during the "Cold War" of the late 20th century when there was a "substantial threat of nuclear war with the former Soviet Union". The lab was built as both a safety bunker and an underground laboratory.

After some time, I was stifling a yawn, not too successfully it seems, when Dr. Shevchuk apologized and promised a full tour of the facility in the morning after we'd had some rest. We retired to two adjoining rooms at the end of a long, well-lit hallway. Our luggage had already been placed for us.

My room looked identical to Shift's, complete with white walls, short, dark brown carpet, a low ceiling with a ceiling fan, a chair and small wooden desk, a single bed with crisp sheets pulled tight, military style, a simple lamp on a small table next to the bed, and a chest of drawers with a mirror on top. Clearly, nobody was looking to impress when they furnished these rooms. And probably no female had a hand in it either. I'll live. Thankfully, there were separate male and female bathrooms and shower facilities just down the hall.

As I closed the door behind me, ready to sleep off the weariness of our travels, I began to get a now-familiar feeling of discomfort. *Was I really safe now? Was this bunker going to protect me in the way the chem suit had?* I was truly alone for the first time in many days. After a few agonizing minutes alone in my room, I walked over to Shift's room and quietly knocked on his door. Even though I was painfully tired, I wouldn't be able to sleep.

"Come in," Shift called.

"Hey," I said as I walked in. "I can't sleep; can we talk?"

"Sure, what do you want to talk about?"

"The Cold War," I replied.

"Really?" Shift asked, surprise obvious in his voice. "Why?"

"Actually, what I really want to know is why this bunker exists and whether we're actually safe here. From what I've seen, and the life I've lived to this point, it seems secure, and so unnecessary." I thought this line of questioning might lead to some comfort. Or, it might be so boring that it put me to sleep. Either way, I figured I'd get the rest my body sorely needed.

"Well, then you haven't lived long enough," Shift said, smiling. "There was a period of time in our world—during the Cold War— when bunkers like this were thought to be the most promising method for ensuring the survival of the human race."

"In what way?"

"Sit down, this could take a while."

I did, then said, "I'm ready."

"Alright, here we go," Shift began. "The Cold War was a very long, drawn-out period of political and military tension between the United States and NATO on one side and the Soviet Union, now 'Russia' and some adjoining countries, and its allies in the Warsaw Pact on the other side. The Cold War . . ."

Shift's explanation, occasionally interrupted by my questions, went on and on. It was actually fascinating. But ultimately, not much of it was relevant to our situation. I was primarily concerned with our safety here. Finally, we got to something that related to our current situation.

". . . so, the Cold War eventually expanded throughout the world as the superpowers provided financial and military help to poorer countries, particularly countries in South and Central AM. The expansion of the conflict into Central and South AM sparked a few small crises there as well, like the Cuban Missile Crisis of 1962 when the U.S.S.R. supplied Cuba with a huge nuclear arsenal pointed directly at the U.S."

"So that's why bunkers like this were built then—to provide some protection against missiles coming from Cuba?" I asked.

"That's right," Shift replied. "Nuclear missiles, *and* the subsequent fallout from the explosions."

"So, what's up with Cuba?" I asked. "They're still communist. Why is that?"

"Well, first of all, until a few decades ago, communism wasn't unusual. Many countries of the world once practiced communism. But Cuba, specifically, has been governed by one form of communism or another since the early 1900s, long before the Cuban Missile Crisis. Although Cuba opened its borders to tourism in the early years of this century to see if it could benefit from an influx of capital, that was a short-lived experiment because they nationalized all of the foreign investment and went back to their old ways.

"Because Cuba alone continues to practice communism, it is the only country still suffering from widespread poverty and a myriad of other problems despite significant modernization funded by foreign capital. Cuba continues to decline invitations to democratize and unite with the IWO, for reasons that are beyond my knowledge."

"It's because they're crazy," John said from the doorway.

I hadn't heard the door open.

"Yeah, maybe," Shift said. "At the very least, their leaders continue to make poor choices and the people are the ones suffering."

"Crazy," John repeated.

"Come in dude," Shift said. "Eavesdropping, huh?"

"It's what I do," John replied smiling as he jumped onto the bed and sprawled out. "It's a good thing y'all have your clothes on."

Ignoring that comment, Shift continued: "Anyway, following the Cuban Missile Crisis, in the early 1970s, the two sides of the Cold War began talks meant to create a more stable and predictable international system. But in 1983, tension arose again when the U.S.S.R., or some faction of the government, shot down a Korean plane. So, the United States increased diplomatic, military, and economic pressure on the Soviet Union at a time when the Soviets were already suffering from economic stagnation.

"In the mid-1980s, a new Soviet leader—Mikhail Gorbachev—introduced reforms that eventually led to mostly-peaceful revolutions in several then-communist countries. Even the Communist Party of the Soviet Union lost control and was banned following a coup attempt in 1991. That led to the formal dissolution of the U.S.S.R. in December 1991 and the collapse of many other Communist regimes.

"President Ronald Reagan, then president of the United States, was influential in that process," Shift added.

"That's the movie star Ronald Reagan?" I asked.

"Yeah, Ronald Reagan was a popular president, at least partially because of his motion picture background. Anyway, President Reagan is famous for telling the Soviet leader, publicly, 'Mr. Gorbachev, tear down this wall!' He was referring to the Berlin Wall which was demolished by the citizens of East and West Germany following the collapse of the USSR. After that, the United States remained as the world's only superpower. Of course, communism was still alive and well in a few countries, including China and Cuba."

"So, when and why did communism finally end for everybody except Cuba?" I asked.

"Well, by the 2060s, the world's political and geo-political climate was generally stable and peaceful; a condition which had never before existed in the recorded history of the Earth, unless one considers the Biblical representation of the Garden of Eden historically accurate.

"Ooooh, tell her about the Middle East and terrorism," John interjected with a smile.

"What about terrorism in the Middle East?" I questioned as Shift turned his attention to John and glared.

"Different subject, different solution," Shift summarized as he refocused on me and continued.

"In 2048, the International World Order ("IWO") was created as a successor to the failed United Nations. The IWO was initially governed by freely-elected representatives from each participating nation. Those representatives served limited terms, with fixed minimal pay, and worked to "create harmony between and among the nations of the world", according to its charter.

"Nowadays, while highly powerful, even having some limited control over the militaries of the participating nations, the IWO hasn't been granted control over industry, local government, or numerous other country-specific operations. But, even though the IWO isn't sovereign, its real power is in its acceptance by governments globally as a dominant force for peace and harmony, notwithstanding a few minor, mostly-trivial exceptions where participating nations have attempted to assert greater control over the process than legally entitled.

"Here's the interesting part, which finally answers your question about Cuba and communism," Shift said. "A country's acceptance into the IWO was gained only after its designation, by the IWO, as a free democracy. By 2051, if I recall correctly, about seventy-five percent of the world's countries had been designated as "free democracies", with the remainder—apart from Cuba—continuing with some form of socialism or other form of government, like in the Middle East. By 2055, only Cuba remained communist."

"What's so great about it?" I asked. "It seems like, if everybody wanted to get away from communism, it couldn't have been that great, right?"

"Communism's core tenets seemed appealing to many people for a long time. But those tenets were never really successfully put into practice. Communism's ultimate goal, throughout time, seemed to be the perfection of a classless, moneyless, and stateless social order structured upon common ownership of production, as well as a social, political and economic ideology aimed at the establishment of social order," Shift said.

"That never really worked out though—anywhere, did it?" John asked, rubbing his eyes in an apparent attempt to stay awake.

"No, not really," Shift replied. "In reality, Cuba, just like many other communistic societies throughout history, maintained a familial dictatorship throughout the majority of the twentieth and twenty-first centuries. As a result, Cuba, while not necessarily poor, still falls way behind international standards in medicine, education and wealth. And, as of today, Cuba still hasn't applied for, nor been granted the international designation of "free democracy".

"Like I said—they're crazy," John laughed.

"Yeah, they pretty much do what they want, even when the IWO threatens them with sanctions and even though the Cuban citizens, for the most part, want to join the IWO," Shift replied.

"So, there's your answer Anta," John said. "Communism was over, everywhere but Cuba, about 40 years ago."

"That's why I didn't know much about it," I mused. "I wasn't even alive when all of that went down."

"The scary part though," Shift added, "is that Cuba's government really *does* do whatever it wants. It may not have been in the news in Egypt, but a few years ago, two Cuban cops shot down a teenager who they thought was being belligerent—that's it. They killed the kid for talking trash. He didn't even break any law. Do you remember that John?"

"Yeah, it was big news," John replied. "It seems like the cops just got a slap on the wrist for it too. And even though the IWO tried to step in, it had no authority and Cuba didn't listen. If that had happened here, in the U.S., the cops would have been hung, figuratively of course."

"And there's probably plenty of other examples," Shift said. "In fact, just the fact that they don't ever attend IWO conferences tells us what they think about cooperation and obeying international laws."

I was a little surprised by what I'd been hearing about Cuba.

"What would happen if some great calamity, like a hurricane or earthquake ever hit Cuba?" I asked. "I'm sure Cuba's government would seek international assistance then, wouldn't they? But they don't think they have to play by the rules the rest of us play by. They're not crazy, John. They're selfish. Or maybe it's the same thing.

"So, what was John saying about terrorism and the Middle East?"

"You sure you want to get into this?" Shift asked.

At my nod, he continued, "Bottom line is that some Middle Eastern states supported global terrorism into the mid-21st century. A massive military effort in the 2050s, sponsored by the IWO and supported by most world governments, appears to have eliminated the threat as the countries joined the IWO. There hasn't been a recorded case of terrorism in over 30 years."

"That's good," I said, yawning.

I went to bed feeling more secure in the knowledge that this bunker had been built to withstand a nuclear attack and nuclear fallout. If everything is still operable, it should easily prevent an invasion by Anthrax E.

23

Today, we explored this bunker, with John as our guide—at least the parts to which we've been given clearance. There are tons of rooms and tunnels, all underground, most of which look like they haven't been used for decades, which is apparently the case. We were told that this bunker hasn't been used in nearly 50 years, and was opened again for this purpose only. That seems logical given what Anta and I talked about last night.

The rooms we currently occupy include a decent-sized kitchen and dining hall, restroom facilities, a recreation room, separate sleeping quarters for each person and a *huge* laboratory and computer compound. There are 14 people here including Anta and I, 12 of which have special jobs to do in order to maintain the systems or find a cure for Anthrax E. Anta and I, though, don't have much to do yet.

While here, which could be a long time, we're completely sealed off—from the inside—against any nuclear, biological, chemical or radioactive threat—hopefully including Anthrax E. That's what the guys tell me anyway. Of course, we're also sealed off from physical contact with the remainder of the human race—which is both frightening and reassuring. Mainly, it makes me sad. I miss my nieces—badly.

JANUARY 23, 2093, 0845 HOURS EET
HOLOGRAPHIC CONFERENCE
Ambassador Hasani Chalthoum (United States Moon Colony)
Anta Chalthoum (near Boston)
Minister Abasi Chalthoum and Mrs. Mariam Chalthoum (Cairo)

"Hi, I have very little time to talk, this is a restricted channel and I'm illegally operating outside the confines of this system." Hasani was abrupt, and kept looking over his shoulder. "I could be shot for this, metaphorically—I think—so excuse my lack of formalities, and just listen."

"Why are you wearing a space suit? Sorry. Go on son. Are you alright?" Abasi Chalthoum asked, feeling and feeding off the urgency in his son's voice and mannerisms.

"Well, I'm alive, and I'm not sick, yet. But I could easily be. I've been hiding out in my personal quarters, but I'm feeling claustrophobic and mentally suffering a great deal.

"As soon as we started hearing that people outside the medical facilities were sick, I put on a space suit—the kind used to go outside the regulated atmosphere of the shells. Once I had it on, I went around to some of the vacant residences and gathered eighteen more oxygen tanks. People were staring at me, so I felt pretty dumb. But I'm alive and breathing clean air. That's probably the only reason I'm alive. I'm sure I stink too, but there isn't really anybody around to complain about it."

Hasani paused, thinking. "Dad, thank you for being so hard on us when we were kids, about being safe and planning ahead. In these conditions, it's made me think in terms of survival. That training is why I'm alive. Nobody here has any idea how to stop this disease from spreading. Of course, there aren't many people left alive and healthy to solve the problem. Nobody goes outside their residences. Nobody goes to work. Nobody goes to the grocery. People are dying everywhere. But the worst part is the mass hysteria, which is dying down now of course, as people realize their fate.

"Other people started putting on space suits, like me, but they're still dying. So I guess they put on the suits too late or something. Or maybe the suits aren't working and I'm still in trouble. I don't know.

"Anyway, the people here are, or were, of the highest caliber and have the brightest minds, and would seem to be the most sensible people to deal with in a crisis, but they aren't. Scholars, scientists, mathematicians, and nearly all other rational-thinking people here have gone nuts.

"I can't describe the state of panic properly, but hovers have crashed into buildings, alarms are going off all over the place, and windows are smashed. Over in one of the other colonies, I can't tell which one, I can see fires burning and the shell is filling up with smoke. Anyone still alive over there will probably suffocate anyway. Of course, now, there aren't many people left to panic. I don't know the numbers of casualties, but based upon what I can see out my windows, it's catastrophic."

Taking only a short breath, and looking around as a scream pierced the other-wise calm room, he continued: "But what I need to tell you is this. I have a friend in the Mexican consulate on Earth. All communications are restricted here, but, as with this communication, I've been breaking the rules. My friend just told me that Mexico intends to secretly contravene IWO orders and launch a ship from the moon to return home some time very soon."

Mariam gasped.

Anta, without thinking, replied, "That could be very bad Hasani."

"Go on son," Abasi said, clearly needing to hear more.

"Yeah, I've heard that Mexico has something like 3,000 people in their colony, but their biggest ship only holds about 2,500 safely. My friend indicates that they intend to cram everyone on board and get out of here before the infection spreads to their colony. I guess I would try to do the same thing though. I feel like I can't go to the IIA with this information for fear of punishment, and maybe stripping of my position. But if I'm going to get sick anyway, and because so many lives are potentially at stake, I should go to the IIA anyway, shouldn't I?"

"Son," Abasi replied, a little panicky and strangely out of character, "don't risk it yet. Let me try to get the message through first. And, if there is any way for you to avoid contamination, do it."

Anta began to panic too as another scream and a loud siren added to the confusion around her brother on the Holo. Feeling that panic creep into her psyche, Anta stated, but only barely above a whisper, "Hasani, Anthrax E has wiped out all of El-Alamein. My colleague, Shift, and I were two of only four people still alive in the city before our escape. Everyone who contracts that disease is going to die. There's no cure or vaccine, yet. We have friends who are hoping to accomplish that, but it seems that it may be too late for you and everybody else there. Although I wouldn't normally recommend breaching protocol, I suggest you look for a way out. Find a way to escape while you're still healthy and get to an isolated pod somewhere that has food, air and water to sustain you for a long time. That may be your only hope. Can you attempt to do that now and contact us in a couple hours?"

"Unofficially," Abasi said, with his usual authoritative voice returning, "I endorse your sister's suggestion. You must do what you can to survive."

"Okay, I'm going to try it. If I get out, I'll try to contact you again within a few hours. Be ready. If I fail to contact you soon, it's probably because I didn't make it and I won't be able to contact you again. But I will try. I love you mother and father. I love you Anta. I need to go, I hear voices coming this way."

The Holo closed abruptly.

24

"Ladies and Gentlemen, the news from the moon today is not good," Dr. Shevchuk began as John handed out a sheet of paper to everyone present. "A post to the IIA database identifies a rumor that Mexico may attempt to launch from the moon and return to Earth, despite the IIA's and IWO's explicit instructions to the contrary. The post is a strong warning to Mexico that launching from the moon will result in extrication from the IWO and probable imprisonment for those in charge."

Shift and Anta looked at each other. Anta's face showed the relief that both she and Shift felt.

"What does that mean for us?" asked Mrs. Chrissy Houghton, a short and stocky, but pretty maintenance staff worker from Massachusetts. She directed her question to Dr. Shevchuk, but it was John who answered.

"What it means," John replied, "is that if they launch, even if they believe they've taken every precaution, they may still bring Anthrax E back to Earth. As you know, it's believed that the only infection on Earth presently has been contained under foam in El-Alamein. Mexico's return to Earth, if it occurs, might result in a new outbreak here, which would be very bad, obviously."

"Is it possible that somebody in the Mexican colony could have Anthrax E, but not know it yet?" Mrs. Houghton asked.

"Possibly," John replied. "Most people have died within 98 hours of first showing signs of illness; but there have been a few cases, early on while they were still being tracked, where the people showed more minor symptoms for several days before their bodies launched into full-blown Anthrax E symptomatology. In each case, the initial symptoms just appeared to be minor colds. The longest recorded time from first symptom reporting to death was 191 hours, or nearly eight days."

"Well, when were the tubes closed down?" Shift asked, beginning to do the math in his head.

"January 9th, I think," Anta replied.

"So," Shift continued, "that means that anybody who entered the Mexican colony on January 9th, after leaving the U.S. colony, and was infected, would likely have first begun showing signs of illness by January 14th. Even if that person was one of the few individuals whose body reacted differently at first, and didn't begin to show Anthrax E-type symptoms for several days, we're still talking about nine days, now, from when he or she would have first begun to show any illness. That's a long time. It seems like the Mexican colony is probably safe after all."

"There's a problem with your theory though, Shift," John began, carefully. "I think it's important for the group to know about Hasani, even though you wanted to keep it a secret."

"Go ahead," Anta said, with equal caution.

"You told me that your brother, Hasani, thought he could get out of the U.S. shell and enter a smaller shell without going through the tubes, didn't you?"

"Well, that's not exactly what I said," Anta replied. "Hasani didn't say he could do it, but he didn't say he couldn't either."

John, gaining more steam, said, "If he *did* leave the U.S. shell and enter another shell without using the tubes, couldn't others do the same? Isn't it possible that some frightened person, already infected, but not knowing it, could have left any of the major shells and entered the Mexican colony without using the tubes?"

"I think you're right, John," Shift answered. "When I was looking into the function of the lunar tubes, back when we were still stuck in El-Alamein, and I had to stop our conversation because I had that, er, problem, I didn't get to finish telling you what I had learned."

"Oh yeah, your 'problem'. Shift had bad diarrhea everybody," John announced. Seeing Shift's glare, he added innocently. "What? We're all friends here."

"Thank you John, but now maybe we're not such good friends." John and Anta, who knew Shift well, could tell that he was clearly joking. A look around the room showed that the others were a little concerned with Shift's remark. He didn't try to correct it.

"Anyway, the tubes can be shut off at each end so that one Colony can control who comes and goes. The restriction on travel though, was a universal 'pulling of the plug' so to speak on whatever electronic technology allows for the opening and closing of the gates on the *tubes*. But that 'pulling of the plug' did not operate to permanently and completely shut off the ports leading to the *outside*.

"Once the tubes were built, the outside ports were no longer used for travel between any of the colonies. They were then only used to travel outside and to the unconnected shells. That would have been how Hasani got out and to another shell, if he made it. So, it's possible that someone could have left an infected colony by an outside port and somehow gained entrance to the Mexican colony through one of its outside ports. Granted, the person would have had to have been one of the last infected, and then believed that he was healthy, and then would have had to convince someone in the Mexican colony to help him gain access through one of the outside ports. There's a lot of 'ifs' in there, but that could happen, theoretically."

"But the shells all had records of who was there when the tubes were closed down," John said.

"Not necessarily," Shift replied, "because this theoretical person would have snuck in. So there wouldn't be a record of his entering the Mexican shell. Nobody would know he was there unless and until he got sick. Then, if he happened to be one of those that had delayed symptoms, or it looked like he just had a cold, then the time period for showing symptoms could be much longer than my estimates of a few minutes ago."

"Maybe the person was healthy but his space suit was covered in Anthrax E," Mrs. Houghton said.

"Remember Chrissy, that we're talking about a hypothetical situation here," John said. "We don't know if this even happened. But if it did, Anthrax E, a living organism, would not have survived outside the regulated shells. It needs oxygen just like every other living thing. Any bacteria on any hypothetical person's space suit would die once it left a shell. So, if someone did sneak into the Mexican shell from the outside, the spread of Anthrax E could only occur if the person was already infected."

Dr. Shevchuk, looking eager to get back to work, said, "This is an interesting theory gentlemen, and I would like the two of you to continue your debate and present me with your conclusions so that I can pass it along to the IWO. In the meantime, unless anybody else has something to bring up to the group, like a breakthrough in finding an antidote," he said with an inflection in his voice that made it a question, "let's adjourn for today. I believe we can all agree that our results here so far have not been good enough. In the event the plague returns to Earth, we will have a mess on our hands unless we can find an antidote, and it appears that no other research group has done any better over the past two weeks. So, let's get back at it. Thank you all for your hard work."

"Wait!" Mrs. Houghton interjected quickly. "Where did this rumor come from?"

"We think it originated in Canada," John replied. "But we can't be sure."

Again, Shift and Anta shared a knowing look. Anta's father had gotten the news out there, without divulging from where the news originated.

With nothing left to ask or to be said, they all filed out in twos and threes, talking quietly.

25

"Shift, I haven't heard from Hasani. It's been more than 16 hours since we last spoke to him."

"Hasani appears to be very resourceful."

"I'm afraid that I won't ever see or hear from him again." This time when Shift placed his hand on my shoulder, I felt the reassuring warmth of it. I'll try not to worry about Hasani and give him more time to contact us.

At our daily staff meeting this morning, Dr. Shevchuk, with the usual sparkle in his eyes, but somewhat more distant now, immediately deferred to John. Every time I look into Shevchuk's eyes, I feel like a child hearing a bedtime story from a wise old grandfather, even though I never knew either of my grandfathers. I like to hear him talk too. But John had the honors this time. He handed out a press release purportedly from Canada, dated today, author unknown.

Through a highly unfortunate series of events, which are not yet fully understood, a deadly biological agent was released within the United States Moon Colony at the International Lunar Space Station on January 7, 2093. The communicable agent, dubbed "Anthrax E", is now known to have reached the moon aboard Egypt VIII, and, within a matter of days, began to spread through the lunar population with terrible velocity.

Contagion appears to be through the transmission of bacteria via coughing and sneezing, like a common cold. Based upon evidence to date, Anthrax E has a gestation period of approximately eight days from initial infection to death of the host.

Pursuant to recent, but certainly out-dated reports, more than 9,500 out of the total 14,502 persons within the lunar colonies are infected with Anthrax E, 6,400 of which are now deceased as a result. The Mexican colony, housing over 2,900 persons, is reported to be illness-free.

Unfortunately, Earth has not been unaffected. Sources that have asked to remain unnamed indicate that Anthrax E was first 'discovered', accidentally, by one of Egypt's most reputable engineers and his tour guide within the Qattara Depression west of Cairo, Egypt. The bacteria spread quickly through the city of El-Alamein; but, through the actions of local and international police forces, a quarantine and isolation process was established which has purportedly held Anthrax E at bay on Earth by burying everyone in El Alamein in hardening foam, possibly killing hundreds, if not thousands of people.

There have been, to date, no reported cases of Anthrax E outside of El-Alamein, Egypt and the moon. Although medical and bacterial investigators are confident that the outbreak has been contained, it appears that every person within El-Alamein is dead. According to sources, two persons were removed from the isolation zone prior to the application of rigid HMP Foam over the entire zone three days ago. It is presently unknown who these persons are, why they were removed or where they have gone. Two individuals, rumored to have been sent to El-Alamein to investigate Anthrax E, and who are believed to have been in contact with local governmental officers throughout the ordeal, were believed to have been alive just before the foam application. Those two individuals were not located for rescue and have not been accounted for.

In other words, they think we're dead. Minister Chalthoum has not dispelled that belief. Soon enough, people will learn that we're here, but for now, I'm comfortable with my status as a dead man.

26

Over the past two days, there have been dozens of apparently leaked reports just like the one John handed to us two days ago from Canada, although the Canadian one was the first. In every instance, the reports have been pulled off the Net, probably by IWO authorities, within minutes of their posting. So, even though at least some people seem to know what's going on, at least on a basic level, the reality is that very few people have likely read any of the leaked reports and thus, very few people understand what is actually going on.

Instead, what appear to be governmentally-prepared reports about illness on the moon and in El-Alamein are all over the news. Those reports minimize the spread of the illness and attribute it to a flu-like bacteria that has hospitalized a few people and that most people are recovering from. I suspect that even the people who have read the leaked reports probably suspect they are just the rantings of crazy conspiracy theorists.

We only get the leaked reports in the bunker because someone here set up a continuously running search and download feature on our computers days ago, keyed on words like "Anthrax E", "El Alamein", "moon colony" and "disease".

JANUARY 26, 2093
STAFF MEETING
HIDDEN BUNKER NEAR BOSTON

"Good evening folks. Let's get started. We have much to talk about." The usual sparkle in Dr. Shevchuk's eyes was missing.

"The latest posting to the IIA database is from the IWO on Earth. It contains a request, to any person still alive on the moon, to provide a status update from the colonies. The only response to that plea was from the Mexican colony, apparently still alive and well. The Mexican colony reports that they observe no movement, and have received no communication from any other colony over the past 24 hours. The Burmo-Thailand shell is burning inside. Mexico believes there may be a breach in that shell within hours as a result. Mexico again requested authority to return home."

"Those poor people," remarked the typically emotional Chrissy Houghton, with fresh tears in her eyes.

"What did the IWO say to Mexico's request this time?" Shift asked.

"Well, interestingly, the IWO asked Mexico to attach all of its internal data links and medical record links to the database for inspection by IWO medical personnel. Apparently, due to the time that has elapsed since the outbreak, the IWO thinks the Mexican colony might be safe, but I'm not so sure, based upon our discussion and your presentation a couple of days ago."

"I agree," John said. "I think it's a very bad idea; but at the same time, don't we, as humans, have a responsibility to them?"

"I don't think we do," Anta replied, gravely. "The whole human race could be in danger. Can we risk that to save the lives of 3,000 people?"

"Well," Dr. Shevchuk replied, "the decision, thankfully, isn't ours to make, although I have discussed the issue at length with my colleagues at the IWO."

"What's their response?" John asked.

"They agree with me on that. And I agree with Anta. But, again, the decision isn't so simple. After the Mexican colony loaded their medical data, the IWO identified one potential infection and ordered the immediate quarantine and testing of that individual. Mexico complied and loaded the new test data to the database. The IWO checked it out and cleared the individual. The results showed a common cold."

"But that isn't necessarily accurate, is it Doctor?" Shift asked. "I can see it in the way you look right now. You have doubts, don't you? He could be our theoretical escapee."

"Yes. I have grave doubts, about the tests, about the diagnosis, about the rationality of any attempt to bring them home; and, I really hope your theory is incorrect. I have expressed those doubts, in depth, and with passion to my colleagues; and we've spoken at length about your theory. This time, they don't agree. The IWO has cleared Mexico to return to Earth."

"That's crazy!" Anta shouted, as commotion broke out among the remainder of the group. Dr. Shevchuk allowed everyone to rant for a few moments, until the commotion quieted down.

Dr. Shevchuk continued, "It may, indeed, be crazy Anta. Our task now, is to continue to perform our analysis and testing and find a cure as quickly as possible. Or, even better, we need a vaccination. For now, however, while we continue our work, let us each pray, individually, to any Deity in which we may believe, that Mexico's ship, Gortari II, and its passengers are free of Anthrax E."

JANUARY 26, 2093
ENTRY IN THE ANTHRAX E DATABASE
DR. YURGI SHEVCHUK

Shift and Anta arrived here at our research facility five days ago. They brought with them the physical tissue samples from the deceased individuals in the Qattara desert.

Additionally, we have arranged for two individuals (Mrs. Neirioui Safar and her daughter Suvan Safar) who were rescued from El-Alamein some days ago to be delivered to our location. It is my understanding that they have been held, and are continuing to be held in containment blocks to prevent accidental contamination. Those blocks will be delivered to our facility within 16 hours.

Based upon significant research of the transfigured specimens from those two individuals, and based upon test results of the specimens brought by Shift and Anta, it appears that a vaccine may be possible, although testing of live tissue from the El-Alamein subjects will be necessary to confirm such possibilities.

They may be immune."

27

For the past two days—at the International Weather Service, North American headquarters in Miami, Florida—North AM Office Director Marcus Dorian and his team had been watching Hurricane Miguel with interest as it built and strengthened. On this day, Marcus watched Hurricane Miguel approach the Caribbean islands from the southeast with sustained winds of approximately 120 mph. Marcus was pleased that the storm, finally, had stopped growing and was now maintaining its current strength. In fact, the storm was unlikely to cause much damage or destruction on land. It was late in the hurricane season. Marcus was anxious to see this one come to an end so he could close the office and leave on his annual end-of-season vacation. This time, he was heading to Brazil at the request of friends.

Marcus' staff frequently teased him about his solo travels. He had friends in various places around the world, they knew, but he never talked about them.

Despite their good-natured ribbing, Marcus was proud of the team he had put together in the North AM office, especially the climatological section, which was his specialty. He didn't think of himself as a people person; he was much better working with technology. But his team realized that he cared and they worked exceptionally well together.

Marcus enjoyed watching them animatedly discussing their latest observations as they raced off together to grab a bite to eat before the next reporting deadline. They were a family, and he loved them like a family since he didn't have one of his own.

The climatological team liked Marcus too. He was funny, optimistic, and caring. He had way too much intelligence for any one person, but was deferential to the opinions and conclusions of his colleagues. But most of all, the team appreciated Marcus' ability to market their office as the place to demonstrate the newest weather technology. Each of them considered Marcus an integral part of their hoped-for ability to rise within the ranks of the scientific community.

Thanks to the "storm chasers" of the 1980's and 90's—and the weather scientists who converted the storm chasers' raw data into theories about weather patterns—over the past several decades, scientists had begun to develop the ability to calm the ugly and destructive power of hurricanes and tsunamis. Some people thought science should be able to completely control the weather, but that had never happened—yet. Marcus truly believed that the day would come when mankind would be able to end both drought on one extreme and severe storms on the other. That day had not arrived, but science was clearly heading in that direction.

Marcus had volunteered his climatological team to test a new process last year, based upon similar older and primarily ineffective models, called, simply, "wind dispersion and diffusion" or "WDD". WDD amounted to dropping a sophisticated explosive into the eye of a storm and detonating it at a predetermined time and altitude. A successful detonation was predicted to reduce wind speeds by as much as 30-40 mph, which could conceivably lower a storm one full category or reduce a CAT 1 storm to a tropical storm. The physical effect of WDD was to break up the storm by dispersing and distributing its winds across a broader geography.

Marcus' peers outside the office thought his offer to test WDD was professional suicide. But Marcus, often a bit too optimistic, saw incredible upside, and his team supported his decision. Their first attempt to calm a storm was a year ago in December. It appeared to be a success. After dropping and detonating an explosive in the eye, the wind speed spiraled from 110 mph to 84 mph in a matter of minutes. Of course, the skeptics claimed that the hurricane was breaking up anyway. A second storm also broke up, with the same effect. Marcus and his team were convinced, and they were able to convince Congress, and the IWO, to fund the remainder of the season. Unfortunately, that was the last hurricane of the season.

This season had been the real test and the team tried to establish some protocols regarding timing and effect. With each hurricane they varied the protocols, monitored the results, and reported back to the scientific community that kept them funded. Their success was now being monitored in Hawaii and Australia. It was really working! Now, the whole team agreed that if hurricane Miguel stayed at CAT 3, they should be able to drop it to a CAT 1, or better, just before it hit land.

Within hours of the team's decision to employ WDD on Hurricane Miguel, the storm chose its course, heading west toward the Florida Keys to enter the Gulf, with likely landfall somewhere in Mexico. Marcus and the Director of the Mexican Weather Service in Mexico City discussed options with the Meteorological arm of the IWO, including the possibility and appropriate timing to apply WDD. A plan was put into place and Marcus and his team began to assemble the members of the deployment team who would carry out deployment of WDD the next afternoon.

Lin Zheng, Marcus' chief of staff, approached Marcus following his announcement that WDD would be employed the following afternoon.

"Marcus," Lin began, "have you heard about that disease that's killing everyone on the moon?"

"I've heard rumors. Why?" Marcus asked casually.

"Did you know that a ship from the Mexican colony is heading back to Earth tomorrow?"

"No." Marcus appeared confused. "Is there something significant about that event that I should be aware of Lin?"

"Well," she replied, "I'm not sure exactly. But I have some thoughts. I've made an assumption that the Mexican ship will be landing at the airbase in Verida, Mexico. Under that assumption, it might pass through Miguel on its approach across the Gulf of Mexico. If it approaches Mexico tomorrow afternoon, then our deployment of WDD may interfere with the ship's landing procedures, or worse. I don't have any concrete facts—just these thoughts."

"That's interesting Lin," Marcus said. "Will you please do some research and try to determine whether there could be any complications? Based upon all of the data, tomorrow afternoon is the time we need to deploy WDD, if we're going to. Let's see if there are any conflicts or complications with our strategy."

After Lin walked away, Marcus quickly com'd an acquaintance at the IWO's South AM office in Brazil. When a voice answered on the other end of the line, Marcus asked, "Sir, did you know that Gortari II is headed straight through our hurricane? What happens if we deploy WDD at the same time? I've got someone working on that possible scenario now."

"Interesting," the voice replied. "Keep your schedule in place. Let me know what you learn."

28

Investigation of live tissue samples from the two living subjects from El-Alamein confirms the probability that a vaccine may be manufactured from their tissue samples. The subjects are infected with the mutated form of Bacillus anthracis (Anthrax E), but have not developed symptoms. Based upon their location in El-Alamein, they were likely exposed to the bacteria some time between January 9th and January 21st. Thus, at the very least, the bacteria have been within their bodies for five to six days. In all reported and recorded cases to date, in which the infection date is fairly certain, only a few people have gone more than five days before showing symptoms. Additionally, most medical records indicate death within approximately 99 hours after first presenting with symptoms. There are some notable exceptions however.

In addition to the live samples brought by Shift and Anta, as recovered from the deceased desert men and the vial, we have now extracted live Anthrax E from our subjects' tissue for further testing.

It can be assumed that our subjects are immune, but it cannot be ruled out that they may be an exception to the general rule. We will continue to test and monitor them.

29

"Good morning everyone!" Marcus said, loudly. Marcus Dorian's team was used to his early morning excitement. But this morning, Lin's questions had been circulating for a while and they were eager for some answers.

Lin had spent the remainder of the afternoon researching whether Gortari II's approach into Mexico and the deployment of WDD would coincide and if they did, what that might mean. She was eager for the spotlight. After initial thoughts, Marcus let a beaming Lin present her research.

"Hi everyone," Lin began. "As you know by now—since you're all so nosy—Gortari II is scheduled to land in Verida, Mexico this afternoon around 4:20 PM Central Time. Our scheduled deployment of WDD is set for 4:00 PM Central today over the Gulf of Mexico. Gortari II's approach will be right through the projected path of Hurricane Miguel."

"So what does that mean?" Marcus asked.

"Well, I can't really see anything wrong with it," Lin replied. "But I'm a little nervous about it. My research tells me that, even if we didn't deploy WDD, Gortari II has the ability to fly right through a CAT II storm without any difficulty. And, as you know, Miguel's wind speeds are under 110 mph. So, as long as we don't deploy the WDD within the short time that Gortari is passing through the hurricane, we should be okay. But that possibility of mis-timing the detonation is a concern. We wouldn't want to detonate too close to the time Gortari II passes through."

"And what is the estimated time that Gortari II will pass through the hurricane?" Marcus asked.

"Gortari II should pass through the eye, or what's left of it, about 4:15 PM. So, with our scheduled deployment at 4:00, the destructive blasts should be long over and the remaining winds should be, based upon our experience to date, no stronger than 80-90 mph. Assuming our timing is on, Gortari II should cruise right through that storm and land safely in Verida."

"Excellent Lin, thank you," Marcus said.

Marcus assigned Lin to continue to monitor the flight path of the ship and watch to confirm at what altitude and time it would pass within the storm's affected zone. Marcus continued to monitor Miguel's wind speeds and checked in periodically with Lin. During the next few hours, all of Lin's observations and estimates stayed on track. The WDD would be deployed at 4:00 PM Central Time and Gortari II would easily pass through the remains of the storm 10-15 minutes later.

"Sir," Marcus said into his com, "it looks like the deployment of WDD will occur about 15 minutes before Gortari II enters the hurricane's airspace. But I'm a little nervous about it. If our timing is off, we could end up detonating too close to the pass-through, and that could be very bad for the ship and the people on board. It would be easy to let this one go. We don't anticipate much damage from the storm on land anyway."

"Thank you for your report Marcus," the Brazilian replied. "The detonation will remain on schedule."

"I understand."

At 4:00 PM Central Time, Marcus gave the word to the team already in the air, and the airteam successfully deployed WDD over the gulf. The eye of the storm virtually stopped in its tracks. Over the next several minutes, the hurricane-force winds began to break up, and began their ultimate distribution over a wide geographical area, predicted to range from Central Mexico and Belize in the south to the Gulf states and beyond to the North.

As the team once again monitored and celebrated the successful deployment of WDD, Gortari II passed over the Gulf on its approach to Verida. The detonation had been on time, and the ship was safe.

But the small team's celebration halted in an instant as they watched the monitors in horror, along with millions of people around the world, as Gortari II was struck by a projectile which breached the outer hull of the ship. At the speed the ship was moving, it disintegrated almost instantly. The heavier portions of the hull continued primarily forward into the gulf. Debris, including portions of the ship and its contents, were caught up in the dispersing winds of hurricane Miguel and were spread across a wide geographical area. The smallest and lightest materials were propelled by the wind in every direction as they dropped to the Earth.

Marcus left the room as his team stared in shock and horror at the monitors. He lifted his arm and punched a few numbers into his watch.

"Sir?" Marcus said moments later when the com picked up. "What happened?"

"An accident Marcus." Then the com disconnected.

30

"What the —!" John Silitzer shouted. He watched, along with the others in the bunker, as Gortari II was blown from the sky. Nobody else said a word. After his initial outburst, even John sat quietly, watching the Holo.

After several long moments, Dr. Shevchuk finally whispered, "Let's get back to work ... please." Nobody moved for several more minutes.

JANUARY 27, 2093, EVENING—SHIFT

Today, just after 5:12 PM our time, Cuba launched a Stimpled Missile at Gortari II during its descent to Earth. We watched it decimate the ship, live! Unfortunately, the missile was fired after Gortari II had already entered Earth's atmosphere and just as Gortari II flew through a defused hurricane. The resulting explosion and trajectory through the dispersing winds of the hurricane caused pieces of the ship and likely pieces of the bodies of nearly 3,000 people to be propelled all over North, Central and South AM, including the Atlantic Islands and the Caribbean. What a disaster!

Because millions of people were watching Gortari's return live, including the IWO and local governments around the world, the governmental backlash was immediate and tremendous. Immediate sanctions were issued against Cuba, just hours ago, and no trade with Cuba or travel between Cuba and other nations will be permitted in the foreseeable future.

Cuba has defended its decision with the argument that, even though the Mexican colony had been cleared of infectious disease by the IWO, the possibility that even one person aboard the ship could be infected was too great to risk allowing the ship to land on Earth, especially given the proximity of Mexico to Cuba. Frankly, I can't argue with that logic, but Cuba's unilateral decision to shoot down the ship, and the timing of that event were terrible.

The ultimate consequence of the IWO's decision to allow the departure of Gortari II from the moon, and the consequence of Cuba's decision to destroy the ship so close to its landing in Mexico remains a question. Time will tell. It's possible that there actually was no disease on board. I hope so. But dang-it Cuba—with your backward, stubborn communistic ways. All of that stuff Anta and I discussed last week actually seems relevant now.

31

During our staff meeting today, John handed each of us a copy of a recent news article, dated today, from NBC. It's interesting that John likes to give us paper, rather than just electronically sending these articles and information to our MEHDs. We each have one now. We use them to communicate with each other from various parts of the bunker, and we use them, personally, to communicate with our families, even though that communication is supposed to be hush-hush. Anyway, back to the article:

The fallout, both literally and figuratively, of Cuba's decision to destroy Gortari II upon its descent to the Mexican Space Administration Base in Verida, Mexico has been gruesome, swift and decisive. The IWO, fearing retaliation against Cuba by its member states, immediately initiated sanctions against Cuba, including an air and sea military blockade outside the territorial boundaries of Cuba and forbidding the entrance to or departure from the island nation, except for non-citizens wishing to leave to return to their homes. These individuals will be given until January 30 at midnight to arrange for, and take leave of the island.

Despite the IWO's sanctions, Cuban officials report thousands of death threats to persons at all levels of government. Many such threats are reported to have originated within Cuba's borders. Cuban peace officers and military agencies have been activated for increased security, particularly around the Cuban shorelines and air bases.

We have heard that one Cuban official, speaking on condition of absolute anonymity, blamed others outside Cuba for the decision to destroy the Mexican ship. During the interview, allegedly, a masked man or woman approached the official, shot him in the head, and then fled. Whether it was a random act of violence or otherwise, is presently unknown. The shooter has not yet been apprehended.

Sparking the international wrath against the Cuban government is the death of at least 2,921 Mexican nationals and 31 foreign citizens who had initially been quarantined within Mexico's lunar colony and not allowed to leave. This scale of mass murder has not been seen anywhere on Earth in decades.

The IWO, while contemplating various measures for discipline, has failed, as far as the Mexican government is concerned, to implement the one policy which needs to be implemented now—a counter-attack. According to an anonymous source within Mexico's State Ministry, many members of Mexico's bureaucracy and citizenry have called for an immediate counter-attack including missile strikes by the IWO upon Cuban military bases and governmental offices. So far, the IWO has not commented on any such calls for action.

In addition to the devastation of thousands of families, many homes and gardens from New Jersey to the eastern coast of the Brazils have been littered with spacecraft debris and body parts from the Mexican ship as a result of its flight through the winds of hurricane Miguel, which had just been diffused using a modern, and suddenly-controversial process known as "wind dispersion and diffusion" or "WDD".

This catastrophe is not only alarming in its scope, but also in revealing the potential for destruction by one lone rogue country.

This reporter expects to see increased calls for counter-attack. Of course, it should be expected that increased measures will be implemented against Cuba to force them to apply for admittance to the IWO so that the destructive weapons within its borders may be removed and placed within the control of the Central Weapons System Agency of the IWO.

There you have it—Cuba is in big trouble. They've been very naughty. But I'm intrigued by the mention of an anonymous official who was shot. He apparently blamed others for this mess. It will be interesting to see what comes of that, if anything. It is entirely likely, however, that the man or woman was just afraid. It's human nature to look for a scapegoat.

While we sat there reading the NBC story, John handed us each another document. This one was a print-out directly from the IIA database, dated today:

International Interagency Assembly database
January 28, 2093
Outpost 17 log post (1241 LT)
Be advised:

HELP ME!!! I may be the only person left alive on the moon.

My name is Dr. Jonas Sampson. I am an astrophysicist currently located in a shell roughly 6.5 lunar miles from the

Poland colony. I have been here since January 2, 2093. I was posted here to take atmospheric measurements of . . .well, none of that matters now.

I received word of the Anthrax E (I think that's what it's called) outbreak many days ago and was advised to remain where I am. I was then told that I couldn't leave. All travel between the colonies through the tubes was restricted. My shell is not attached to the tubes. I got here via rover. It still sits outside.

I haven't heard from anybody in the colonies in two days. At that time, I received a message, via handheld transmitter, from a colleague in the Portuguese-Brazil shell. She told me that she was sick and nearly everybody she knew was already dead. She told me to stay here and that my only chance of survival was to get to the Mexican colony, where nobody had contracted the disease, or to stay where I am.

I've been trying to contact colleagues in the Mexican colony for that past three days. I've also attempted contact with Mexico's Emergency Systems and Operations Division. Nobody answers. Nobody responds. Plus, I watched a shuttle leave yesterday.

I just figured out how to hack into this system. I've never used it before. I don't know how to access prior posts. I don't know whether Mexico has been compromised or whether anybody is even there anymore. I also don't know whether this message will be received by anyone.

Thankfully, my food, water and oxygen processors continue to operate. I'm worried that they may cease at some point, however, since this shell wasn't meant to be used long term. I don't even know enough about the machines to service them.

Somebody please respond.

IWO log post (1247 LT):
Be Advised:

Dr. Sampson, it is with great pleasure, and great concern, that we receive your log post. We respond to your post from the Kennedy Space Center in Florida. We have not received any communication from the moon in nearly 40 hours. Unfortunately, Mexico has left the moon. The nation was authorized to return to Earth two days ago by the IWO. Departure occurred yesterday. Upon descent to Earth, Gortari II was destroyed by a missile fired from Cuba. There were no survivors.

It is unknown whether there are others in like circumstances on the moon. We have not been hailed by any lunar colony apart from Mexico in many days, and we have had no contact with any smaller shells via this system. We do not have access to local communication channels, but we hope that you do.

We are currently analyzing possible escape plans to facilitate your return to Earth. This analysis has been underway since yesterday, contingent upon learning whether there were any survivors; but no plan has been finalized.

Be advised that there are 23 other outposts similar to the one in which you are located—a total of 24 shells not connected to the tube system. Of those 24 outposts, present data indicates that 19 are outfitted with life support systems, including food, water, waste and oxygen systems. At last report from the IIA, several days ago, at least 12 of them were, or may still be occupied. It is unknown whether any of those outposts still contain living humans or whether more than 12 may now contain humans. It is advisable that you not enter any of those shells without first contacting its inhabitant(s), if any.

Prior to entering any shell, it is incumbent upon you to first learn when the current occupant arrived at the shell, whether he or she has left that shell or had any visitors and whether, in the past 144 hours, the current occupant has experienced any coughing, bloody stool, bloody phlegm, aches and pains, headache, fever, or any other physical symptom associated with a common cold or worse. The attached document will provide detailed instructions about how to proceed prior to entering any new shell.

Furthermore, you will also find, attached to this post, a set of instructions to help you navigate this log system. Remember that communication with other shells that may hold survivors not already logged into this system will be up to you. Lastly, you will also find, attached, a file containing systems instructions for maintaining all devices currently supplying life support.

Please contact us at short intervals with your progress. This system is monitored continuously.

This Sampson guy has got to be terrified. He just learned that everybody is dead, Mexico is gone, and they're all dead, and that he may be alone on the moon.

There's an old book I read a long time ago as a teenager called *The Martian*. It was about a guy who was left alone on Mars. His crew, believing he was dead, and in peril themselves, made a hasty retreat from the surface and left him there. He wasn't dead though, and he had to learn how to live for a long time, alone, until he was rescued.

Dr. Sampson, even if he is alone, won't have to go through any of the struggles that "The Martian" had to endure. Sampson has all the life support provisions necessary to sustain him indefinitely. He's "lucky", some might say, but I wonder whether he feels the same way. What he doesn't know, yet, is that Anta's brother, Hasani, was also told to find a shell. He may be alive out there somewhere, and if so, there might be others too. God speed to them all!

32

Our Egyptian friends, Mrs. Neirioui Safar and Suvan Safar, continue in their health. Upon their arrival here on January 26th, tissue samples from their bodies, although already infected, were intentionally contaminated with a second dose of Anthrax E recovered from the gazelle specimens brought here by Shift and Anta. Those specimens have not shown signs of decay or illness.

The date of the Safar's original exposure to Anthrax E in El-Alamein was at least nine or ten days ago. Based upon the timelines recorded among those previously infected with Anthrax E, it appears, rather conclusively, that they are immune. We will begin work with their DNA to try to replicate such immunity in order to develop, if possible, a vaccine for Anthrax E.

JANUARY 31, 2093—SHIFT

Anta and I have now been in the 'secret lair' of our devoted scientist friends for 10 days. In that time, we've only been allowed to leave once, just before Gortari II was shot down. We sat by the lake outside to ponder life and breathe the fresh air. Anta was, and still is, going crazy being locked up in here. Now, her growing fear of some kind of problem resulting from the Mexican ship's destruction has made her determined to see the world outside again. Perhaps we'll be able to.

I'm glad we went outside when we did. It's beautiful here. The deep snow that day covered the ground and several small animals scampered past us through the trees, not realizing the danger we aggressive and terrible humans posed to their well-being. We saw deer, rabbits and squirrels. We even saw a skunk, even though that unfortunate animal has been on the Endangered Species list for nearly 20 years. I would've happily smelled that skunk too, if I'd known then that I may not get to go outside again for a long, long time.

I miss my nieces, and Arilee too. I haven't seen them in person in a month now. They're doing okay. I see them every few days on the Holo. Diamond is still doing well in school and she and Cedar are both having fun with their friends.

Seeing them on the Holo today, playing in the snow in their yard, reminded me of my own childhood, which seems far away right now. After dad died, when Arilee and I were very young, mom, sad and directionless, moved us and our meager belongings to Denver, Colorado where she'd grown up and where her mother still lived. We moved in with grandma.

My childhood was normal, I suppose, albeit without a father. I went to school, both in person and through Holographic Education Displays, or "HEDs" at home. I played street games with my friends, participated in four-dimensional holographic projection movies in our entertainment parlor, raced drift bikes, played basketball and soccer, played virtgames, and took piano lessons from an irritable woman on our street named Helena. Man, I miss Helena too. Arilee and I were very close, like siblings should be. Those were pretty good days. I'm a little worried that Diamond and Cedar won't get to live and love life like Arilee and I did.

33

FEBRUARY 1, 2093—SHIFT

John just gave us a news article, dated today, from NBC. This stuff is getting real crazy.

This morning, in a disastrous follow-up to last weeks' destruction of Gortari II, Cuban ground and air fire killed at least 6,044 people and injured at least 185 more. Cuban officials argue that the attack was provoked by Mexican outlaws as they stormed toward Cuba, en mass, by boat.

Sources in Mexico indicate that approximately 6,000 Mexican citizens, acting independent of the Mexican government, attempted to attack Cuba in order to avenge the loss of their bothers and sisters who died when Cuba shot down Mexican Gortari II on its approach to Earth from the Lunar Colonies. IWO sources indicate that 48 members of the IWO Peace Corps were killed as they attempted to interfere with the Mexican citizens' attempted attack on Cuba.

While both the IWO and Cuba have declined to release any further detail of the Cuban attack on Gortari II, speculation is rampant, with various sources indicating that persons aboard Gortari II may have contracted the now-infamous

"Anthrax E" which appears to have wiped out all personnel in the other lunar colonies.

In other news, the Cuban Police Agency has declined to speculate on the 'anonymous Cuban official', who was allegedly shot in the head while giving a news interview shortly after the destruction of Gortari II, or on the whereabouts of the alleged attacker. To date, there is no positive proof that the event occurred.

FEBRUARY 2, 2093
STAFF MEETING
HIDDEN BUNKER NEAR BOSTON

"That's nuts, man!" shouted Dr. Andrew Jones, a biological researcher from New York.

"Indeed, Andrew." Dr. Shevchuk was also having difficulty containing his emotions.

"What's nuts?" Anta asked as she and Shift entered the room for the afternoon staff meeting.

"CNN and the IWO," Dr. Shevchuk said, "are both reporting today that Hospital Herrera Llerandi in Guatemala City believes one of its patients has contracted Anthrax E."

"How did it happen?" Shift asked, quietly.

"Apparently an 84-year-old gentleman presented at Hospital Herrera Llerandi with complaints of coughing and bloody mucus. He said he'd picked up what he believed was a bloody human finger that landed in his yard on January 27; and now he's sick."

"That's right after Gortari II was shot down, right?" Chrissy Houghton asked.

"Yes," Dr. Shevchuk replied. "Police in Guatemala City found the subject finger and, following a DNA test, determined that the finger belonged to one of the passengers aboard Gortari II."

"Do we have a copy of those test results, or any transfigured specimen from the finger?" Dr. Jones asked.

"Both have been promised. I expect to have them within 12 hours."

FEBRUARY 2, 2093
ENTRY IN THE ANTHRAX E DATABASE
DR. YURGI SHEVCHUK

The Safars continue in their health. Infected, but not symptomatic tissue samples from their bodies, intentionally re-contaminated on January 26, still show no signs of decomposition seven days later. Our efforts to develop a vaccine or cure for Anthrax E from the Safars' DNA continues, but I feel we are no closer to our goal.

Communications with the various research institutions around the globe who are working on this matter simultaneously reveal no progress greater than our own.

FEBRUARY 3, 2093—ANTA

Yesterday, we learned that some guy in Guatemala caught Anthrax E after he picked up a bloody finger he found in his yard. Who would do that? That's disgusting. Anyway, it doesn't matter now. Today, hospitals and clinics in San Pedro Sula, Honduras, Trujillo, Honduras, Colon, Panama, San Andres Island, Mexico, and Fort Lauderdale, United States of America have each reported Anthrax E infections.

The story, in each case, is just like the guy in Guatemala. Each of them came into contact with human body parts from Gortari II. That means that someone aboard Gortari II was infected with Anthrax E prior to leaving the lunar colonies.

Shift came to my room earlier today, visibly upset, angry even. His eyes were lit up like a cartoon character who had just been thwarted in his evil plan to rule the Earth. I could have warmed my hot cocoa on his forehead.

"How the hell could the IWO not know someone on Gortari II was infected?" He practically shouted the question. "If this hadn't been kept a secret for so long, more of the world would have known of the potential problem with a ship from the moon exploding above the

Earth. Maybe Cuba wouldn't have shot it down. At the least, the IWO could have quickly and easily warned people not to touch debris or body parts from the ship."

"Do you think that would have made a difference?" I wondered aloud.

"Those idiots thought they had this all under control." Shift continued to rant as though I wasn't in the room. "Nothing Shevchuk said meant crap to them. Now we could all be screwed.

"The IWO has ordered that all infected people, and everybody they've been in contact with over the past six days, has to be isolated. There's something like 434 people in quarantine so far. That's not going to work. They tried that on the moon and they're all dead. It's too late for that now."

"Shift, can you calm down a bit, so we can talk this through," I said. Shift wasn't listening.

"Someone on that ship was infected before they left the moon," Shift continued. "And that person had to have known he was infected. The only way to really spread the disease from person to person is through coughing or sneezing. The guy had to have been coughing."

"I know," I said, quietly.

Shift finally looked at me as though he had just noticed my presence. Now that I knew I had his attention I continued. "So, does this sound right? The person coughed on the ship. Several people were probably contaminated while on Gortari II, but their bodies never had a chance to deteriorate before being blown apart over the Gulf. Then, in the days after the explosion, people began to find and handle various body parts and became infected. Finally, over the past few days, those people became sick. Now it will spread."

"Yes. That's how it must have happened. How can you be so calm and reasonable about this?" Shift asked.

"Shift, we can't do anything about what already happened. We can only move forward, knowing what we know and dealing with it the best way we can."

"I'm more worried that we haven't heard from Hasani," I continued. "I keep up the hope that he might still be alive. He knew how to keep himself safe. Maybe he made it to an outer shell. In any event, our world is in serious trouble now, unless we can do better at containment than the moon did—which I seriously doubt."

"You think so? Idiots."

"Who?"

"The IWO, of course." Shift seemed to collapse within himself, frustrated. "We had a lengthy discussion about this very scenario a few days ago and then Shevchuk presented the theory to the IWO before Gortari II ever left the moon. They knew this could happen. They *knew* it! Why didn't anybody pay attention? Why didn't the sick person say or do something if he knew he was ill. He just got on the ship before it left for home. How irresponsible and selfish does a person have to be to do that, especially someone on the moon who has already seen everybody die?

"What's worse is that Cuba decided to blast Gortari II out of the sky right before it landed!" Again, the shouting. "Whatever moron made that choice clearly had no idea what they were doing. Shoot them down earlier and every piece of that ship and every person on board would have fried up entering the atmosphere. Instead, Anthrax E is all over the place now and will spread. There's no way we can stop it. We're all going to die—including my sister and her kids, and your parents Anta!"

"Shift, I get it. You're mad. Come over here and sit down. Let me get you a drink."

"I don't want a drink. I want to hit something. What can I hit?" Shift asked.

Typical male.

"Go down to the gym then. Knock a punching bag senseless. When you're finished, come back and let's talk about this. We need to help figure out how to solve this problem, and yelling, especially at me, isn't going to help."

Silence . . . then, "I'm sorry Anta."

Those three simple words, coupled with the clear remorse in his voice, made everything better—at least for me. Shift is my friend. His emotions are right. I'm mad too. He'll be okay, but we've got to stay calm.

"Shift, go work out. Come back when you're done. I'll be waiting for you."

"Thanks. I will."

34

I'm feeling much more like myself today. After yesterday's outburst at Anta, for which I profusely apologized after my workout and a Pepsi, Anta and I are back on good terms—I think.

After an additional 16 cases of Anthrax E were identified in Central AM and the Caribbean islands in the last few hours, the IWO just ordered the "immediate halt of the distribution of all goods internationally." Plus, all countries have been ordered to secure their borders. Now, no travel is allowed, worldwide, outside a person's country of residence. The IWO has mandated that all persons currently in foreign countries must remain where they are currently located. Within the United States, all individual states have been ordered to secure their borders too. That *totally* worked on the moon—I'm *sure* it'll work here too. Idiots.

Many days too late, the IWO has finally updated its digital site with information concerning Anthrax E and its symptoms. Also too late, the IWO has ordered that any person believing that he or she might be infected is ordered to rush off to a hospital immediately, avoiding contact with everybody. How's that going to work?

Anybody finding any body part or material believed to be from Gortari II has to "remain at a distance of no less than 20 meters from the object or body part and should inform local authorities of the discovery immediately." Again, probably too late. The IWO should have issued that order three seconds after Gortari II blew up.

Following our staff meeting today, John asked me what I thought about the travel ban. Even though it hasn't been my primary area of study, my education has offered me plenty of opportunities to learn history, in all of its various facets.

"It's crazy. None of this is going to work," I said, responding to his question. "The travel ban is going to be impossible to enforce. We already saw it fail on the moon, in a place where the primary way to get from point A to point B was completely closed and inaccessible. But beyond that, only once or twice in our world's history has a ban on travel, or a restriction on the movement of people been successful. And even when travel restrictions have worked, they haven't lasted."

Others gathered around. When it comes to history, I'm the best we've got in this little sanctuary. Sad really.

"Well, when *has* a travel ban worked, and what made it successful?" Anta asked. "Or, why don't they work?"

I think Anta likes to hear me talk. She always gets me into these long discussions and I'm pretty sure she doesn't even care what I say.

"Is this actually interesting to any of you," I asked, puzzled about why anybody would care.

"Yeah man," John replied. "I want to know how safe my family and friends are. If this isn't going to work, I've got to know; well, we've all got to know. What do we tell our families to keep them safe, if it's even possible?"

"Okay, got it," I said. "But this might be incredibly boring. I hope you've all got some caffeine."

John held up his steaming mug of coffee to prove he was ready. Nobody else had anything to drink. But they looked interested.

"Well, historically, especially in Europe and Asia, international borders were almost-always secured militarily, sometimes even with towering walls and other physical fortifications. Most of those fortifications and restrictive measures were partially effective, at least for a while, but none of them, at least none of which I'm aware, were able to fully restrict the movement of people. People who are desperate to get somewhere usually find a way. That's always been the case and it won't change now. Humans are quite resourceful.

"Here's a great example. The 5,500-mile-long Great Wall of China was a series of walled fortifications constructed over time by several of the Chinese ruling dynasties, between about 470 B.C. and 1600 A.D. The adjoined structures were built as defensive fortifications to repel invasions by the Huns, the Manchus, and other raiders and invaders. The wall wasn't very successful though as the different invading groups successfully breached the wall on several occasions throughout the centuries. This was despite the wall's massive length, width, and height, and despite the military presence in place much of the time to provide even greater fortification. In other words, not even a massive wall kept people out of China.

"During the second century, the Romans built a 73-mile-long wall called 'Hadrian's Wall'. It ran from east to west just south of the current Scotland-England border, and marked the northern edge of the Roman Empire. There are a couple of different theories as to its purpose including restricting movement between northern Britain and southern Britain without the payment of customs and keeping the barbaric and warring ancestors of the modern-day Scots—the "Picts"—out of the Roman Empire. Or at the least, the wall was meant to prevent the Picts from bringing horses and other heavy military equipment into the Roman Empire with them. Even though the wall was heavily fortified by Rome's awesome, powerful military, the Picts successfully breached the wall on numerous occasions. Again, not even a huge wall could do the job.

"Shall I continue? Jones, you look like you're nodding off." Dr. Jones was definitely falling asleep.

"Ha ha ha . . . no. I'm not Shift—just resting my eyes . . . and my neck . . . and my brain. Okay, I was dozing, but not from boredom. This is interesting. Keep going."

"Alright, but I'm watching you. If you fall asleep, I'm gonna start throwing things, starting with John's coffee. So, in the early 1900s, the

'Maginot Line', which was originally built by the French as an attempt to ward off future hostile takeover attempts by the Germans, was utilized as a defensive fortification by the French and then the Germans during World War II. The Maginot Line was a series of trenches and underground fortresses, along with above-ground fortifications and arms battlements. Its success, albeit short-lived, was notable. Of course, the Germans overpowered the French along the Line and then the Americans later overpowered the Germans along the Line. The Maginot Line, like nearly all stationary defenses before and after it, didn't really work out either.

"During World War II, the Germans attempted to restrict the movement of the Jews and other minority groups within Germany and its conquests; and tried to keep people from fleeing its borders. Through the use of Secret Police, informants, and the German military, Jews and others had very little freedom of movement and ultimately, millions of people who could not flee were killed. The Holocaust—I'm sure you're all familiar with it. There were, of course, thousands of escapees from Germany's borders; thus, that particular system, while devastating to human life, ultimately couldn't prevent all movement.

"Probably the greatest and most-successful attempt to restrict movement was the 'Berlin Wall'. Following World War II, the Allied powers divided the 'spoils' of war. The 'spoils' included the whole country of Germany. By 1949, Germany had been divided into Soviet-controlled East Germany and a democratic West Germany. The same east-west division took place inside Germany's capital city, Berlin. Since the city of Berlin was situated entirely within the Soviet-occupied zone, West Berlin became what was called an 'island of democracy' within Communist East Germany.

"Shortly after the division, economic conditions in Communist East Germany became so poor that many people living in East Berlin wanted to escape the repressive living conditions. So, they packed their bags and headed to West Berlin. Although some of them would be stopped on their way, hundreds of thousands of others made it across the border, and tons of them never went back. Many of those who escaped were young, trained professionals. By 1961, East Germany had already lost 2.5 million people and desperately needed to stop the mass exodus."

"I thought you said this was one of the most-successful attempts to restrict movement." John's voice sounded serious, but I know that smartass too well. "Doesn't sound too successful if two and half million people got through. I hope we can do better than that this time around."

"Thanks John. Let me continue please. How's Jones doing over there? Ahhh, asleep. I guess I'll let him off the hook."

"Anyway," I continued, "getting a little bit anxious, Soviet-controlled East Germany decided to build a 'wall' to prevent its citizens from crossing the border into West Germany."

"Hmmmm." Anta made a noise that clearly exposed the skepticism that the whole group appeared to share.

"Yes, that's right; the old wall idea rears its head again; but this time, it was serious business. During the night of August 12th, 1961, crews tore up streets that entered into West Berlin, dug holes to put up concrete posts, and strung barbed wire all across the border between East and West Berlin. Telephone wires between East and West Berlin were also cut. No longer could East Berliners easily cross the border for any reason. Approximately 60,000 commuters were suddenly unable to enter West Berlin for well-paying jobs. Families and friends were no longer able to cross the border to meet their loved ones. Whichever side of the border one went to sleep on during the night of August 12, 1961, they were stuck on for the next 28 years. Is that any better John?"

"Yes; please continue," John said. "But don't even try to convince us that barbed wire kept people out of West Berlin for 28 years."

"Thank you for that observation," I said. "No, barbed wire didn't do the job. It was just the beginning. A real wall was soon built. Then, over the years, the Berlin Wall underwent several further, more-formidable transformations. It stretched over a hundred miles. It ran not only through the center of Berlin, but also wrapped all the way around West Berlin, entirely cutting West Berlin off from the rest of East Germany.

"Eventually, the Wall included a 300-foot No-Man's-Land, an additional inner wall, soldiers patrolling with dogs, anti-vehicle trenches, electric fences, colossal light systems, watchtowers, bunkers, and minefields. The East Germans even raked the ground along the wall so that any footprints would be obvious. That's dedication, eh?"

"Sheesh." Now John seemed impressed. "That probably would have been my job. I rake a mean plot, man."

"I'm sure you do. While the restrictions in place to keep East Berliners in East Berlin were highly oppressive and probably represented the most effective restrictive system ever enforced in the world, hundreds of people *still* 'breached' the wall and 'escaped' into West Berlin and freedom, mostly by digging under the wall. So, even this massive, 28-year undertaking—with raked dirt, John—couldn't wholly prevent the movement of the people it intended to restrict."

"Shift, all of these examples are super old. Hasn't anybody been more successful recently?" Anta asked.

"Well, there hasn't been any need recently, but there are other slightly-more-modern attempts at restriction.

"In southeast Asia, seemingly-endless conflicts between North and South Korea throughout the 20th century resulted in the creation of a 'demilitarized zone' in 1953. The demilitarized zone was a two and a half mile wide buffer zone running east to west between North and South Korea. It was created following the signing of an Armistice Agreement that officially ended the Korean War which had started three years earlier. More than three million people were killed in that war.

"Although called a 'demilitarized zone', the area was actually the most heavily-fortified military zone in the world well into the 21st century. During the existence of the Zone, no person was allowed to travel through it into the adjoining country without special permission. A few people were allowed to move back and forth for certain work assignments, but the general populace couldn't.

"Following the signing of the "Korean Peace Treaty of 2028", the Zone was abolished and anybody, from either side, could finally move freely throughout the Korean peninsula, after more than 70 years. But even though the demilitarized zone was pretty effective, it still failed to prevent people from both sides, both military and civilian, from periodic encroachments into and through the zone."

"During the late 20th and early 21st centuries, the United States' border with Mexico was patrolled by the United States Border Patrol, a more modern version of the 'Mounted Watchmen' of the United States Immigration Service that began operations in the early 1900s. A fence was built from the Pacific Ocean south of San Diego, eastward, most of the way to the Gulf of Mexico. Its original purpose was to keep 'illegal aliens'—Mexicans and others lacking legal permission to enter the United States—from crossing into the states of Texas, New Mexico, Arizona and California.

"Following the infamous September 11, 2001 terrorist attacks on New York and Washington D.C., the Border Patrol's purpose began to include the detection and prevention of terrorist movement through Mexico and into the United States. Between 2021 and 2025, the United States constructed a 25-foot-high wall along vast expanses of the border. Despite the United States' tremendous, expensive efforts to restrict the movement of 'illegal' immigrants into the country, over the years, hundreds of thousands, or perhaps millions of Mexicans and others crossed the border. They went under the wall in underground tunnels, sometimes over a mile long. They came over the fence, over the wall, through breaches in the fence and wall, and hidden in the backs of trucks and buses. Obviously, this attempt to stop people was pretty lousy as well."

"In 2031, Brazil was divided in two through a relatively peaceful, democratic vote of the people. Some of you probably remember this. I understand it was a pretty big deal, even here in the U.S. The southern portion of the country at that time had a significant German population, both linguistically and culturally. The northern three fourths was largely Portuguese mixed with the poorer indigenous groups. Of course, many of the people on both sides of the divide, but particularly in the north were displeased with the division.

"Thousands of people from the north attempted to cross into the wealthier German-Brazil without authority to do so; and, as had occurred between Mexico and the United States years earlier, and also between East and West Berlin 70 years earlier, a 'wall' was built to keep the citizens of each country on its own side. That wall—jokingly called the "Jungle Bungle"—was torn down less than six years later in 2037 as an eyesore and a near-complete failure. Of course, the North—Portuguese-Brazil—has come a long way since then, as demonstrated by its funding and construction of a lunar colony."

"It seems like the restrictions were getting harder to manage as time progressed," John said, quizzically.

"Yeah, it was getting harder. Probably has something to do with the growth in population and technology. The more advanced we become as a species, the better our means and methods of transportation, and the more of us there are to try to contain, the harder it seems to get.

"The most recent *major* attempt to restrict the movement of people happened in 2033, after Texas 'peacefully' ceded from the United States, closely followed by New Mexico. I say 'peaceful' only because there was no military struggle. Politically, the cessation of these two states was a huge battle, as I'm sure some of you can attest.

"Both former states became independent nations, as we have today. After the initial break with the United States, their respective borders were patrolled by their newly-formed militaries for two primary reasons—fear of reprisals from angry United States' citizens who perceived the action as, frankly, a slap in the face, and to prevent the exit of disenfranchised Texans and New Mexicans from the newly-formed republics."

"So the U.S. built a huge wall along the Mexican border in 2025, and then, eight years later Texas and New Mexico weren't even part of the states?" Anta asked. "What happened to the wall along their borders?"

"It's still there, but not patrolled. Just like with most other national borders in the world, walled or not, people move fairly freely through them."

"I've been down there and seen the wall, but it was in Arizona," John said. "It was pretty impressive. And, even with the way I look, they still let me through into Mexico."

"That's shocking," Dr. Jones said sleepily.

"Ahhh, you're awake," I said. "And just in time to insult John. Perfect!"

"Anyway, the patrolling of the New Mexican and Texan borders was generally unsuccessful too, and hundreds of thousands of Texans and New Mexicans ultimately made their way back into the United States. Soon, largely due to the regulation of, and favorable increase in economic conditions globally, movement between the republics of Texas, New Mexico and the United States became simple, much like movement between Canada and the United States had been traditionally.

"Of course, there have been hundreds, if not thousands of smaller attempts to restrict the movement of people throughout history, but none of them really worked out either. So, even in times when travel was more difficult, the cost of travel more expensive, the means of travel less flexible, and when there were fewer people to control, regulations and attempts to control people's movement never really worked out."

"If what you're saying is true," Anta said, "and I don't doubt it, then now, when travel isn't so limited as it used to be, it sounds like this travel ban isn't going to work . . . at all."

"Surely not," I replied. "If I wanted to leave here, assuming I could get past Yurgi's security system, all I'd have to do is get in a hovercar, leave the road and travel until I didn't want to travel any more or my battery ran out—but then I could just get back on a main road and charge it. There aren't any militarily-enforced border restrictions anywhere in the world except the current quarantine around El-Alamein and the recent militarily-controlled shores of Cuba. And there aren't any effective operating stationary boundaries at any national border. So, I could go where I please. What's to stop me?"

"And no government will be successful if they attempt to militarily enforce a border restriction, will they?" John stated as much as asked.

"I don't see how that could possibly work," I replied.

"I guess the IWO is simply hoping that we'll all thoughtfully and lovingly consider the well-being of our neighbors, and in love and peace, surrender to the tasty epidemic that's about to turn our insides to soup." John's sarcasm was evident. "Rather than try to escape the coming smorgasbord, and thereby potentially spread the disease to neighboring towns, we'll all just sit here and die. Sounds good to me."

"Riiiight." I drew out the word to show my agreement with John's sarcastic point of view. "That's what we'll all do. I'm no expert on human history . . . oh wait, I am an expert on human history. Thus, I predict, with near-certainty, that this attempt will fail, as did nearly every other attempt in our history."

"Maybe people will just obey the travel ban, even though they can't be forced to," Mrs. Houghton said, without conviction.

"I don't think so," I replied. "We talked before about how Anta and I left El-Alamein. Consider how easy that was. El-Alamein was the only militarily-enforced movement restriction in the world at the time. We just got in an old—but awesome—pick-up truck and drove away. The quarantine around El-Alamein, while pretty inefficient obviously, may have been the most efficient border restriction any government could hope to enforce; yet, it couldn't keep us in. It couldn't keep two people inside one small town. What's worse, we didn't even have a hover. We were on existing, albeit forgotten roads, and they still couldn't keep us in. Nobody even saw us leave."

"It makes me wonder, and not for the first time, how many others got out of El-Alamein," Anta said. "Since there haven't been any reported illnesses anywhere over there outside El-Alamein, if anybody else got out, we're very fortunate that they hadn't been contaminated yet."

"I agree," I said. "But I've also wondered if the people of El-Alamein, because they were left in the dark about what was going on, didn't really try to escape for the most part. Maybe most people just sat there and took it. There have been so few diseases threatening the general population during most of our lifetimes. They may not have been too worried."

"But that won't happen now because the whole world knows what is going on, more or less," Anta said.

"Well then, how does the IWO or any other government hope to make people stay home?" Mrs. Houghton, as usual, was on the verge of tears, her emotions bubbling to the surface again, probably as she thought about her children out in the world.

"I don't know," I replied, with as much empathy as I could express. "Regardless of what measures are taken to enforce the restrictions, people will still flee diseased and dying towns. There's nothing to stop them, and human nature requires that we attempt to preserve our lives—that's just how we're built. Just like Anta and I did. That means that Anthrax E will not be contained or stopped without a vaccine. Nothing else will work, unless, by some miracle, it just dies out."

Dr. Shevchuk, seeming determined to build hope among his now-family exclaimed loudly enough to wake Dr. Jones, who had fallen back to sleep, "Ladies and Gentlemen, if the only way to stop the spread of Anthrax E is to develop a vaccine, then let's get back to work. Enough of this doom and gloom. Let's make sure that people will live."

"Here, here," Dr. Jones replied as he leapt to his feet and jogged out of the room toward his lab. The nap did him some good. I'm glad we let him sleep.

35

Dad and I talked today about what precautions he and mom might be able to take to avoid contagion in the event Anthrax E is not contained in the western hemisphere, which seems likely. Shift told me that in the United States, following a 2001 anthrax bioterrorism attack, the United States Department of Homeland Security advised families to use duct tape and plastic drop cloths around windows and doors to seal out chemical or biologic agents. It didn't take long before people began to realize what a naïve idea that was.

Shift also said that during several zoonotic outbreaks in the early 2000s, many people, particularly from the Asian continent, began wearing surgical masks in public places in an attempt to prevent accidental contagion. That might be a little better idea; but neither of those two options is going to prevent the spread of Anthrax E, and my parents won't be using either option.

Instead, when news reaches them that people in Egypt and neighboring countries might be infected, they're going to leave home and travel out into the desert, with provisions to last as long as possible. They're going to begin stockpiling provisions now. They don't know where to go, though dad will begin searching. They're pretty pessimistic about their chances of survival if Anthrax E gets back to Egypt. I don't blame them. I want to go home, but dad forbids it. I'm an adult, damnit, but he's still my dad. I'll obey him on this one. Plus,

I don't think they'd let me out of here—unless I cried maybe? These doctors are a little soft after all.

Shift and the others here think *we're* safe, at least for now. We've been sealed inside the facility for a long time and we'll stay here indefinitely. The air locks won't be opened from the inside and we've been assured that they can't be breached from the outside. In fact, Dr. Shevchuk has assured us that only high-ranking government leaders even know about this bunker.

According to one gentleman with whom Dr. Shevchuk has been corresponding, there are a few other bunkers very similar to this one around the United States. Most of them are smaller than ours, and most of them aren't being used for research. Shevchuk's source claims that governmental leaders and other "important" people have already been shut inside those other bunkers as part of a "Continuation of Government" policy that's been in place since the invention of ICBMs, or InterContinental Ballistic Missiles, "just in case"; but he doesn't know how many people. At a minimum, it would include the President and his family, the Vice-President, their security teams, Cabinet members and Leaders of the House and Senate, spread out in the various bunkers and able to communicate with each other to coordinate government responses to emergencies like this one.

There are 14 people here, including Shift and I. When we first arrived, there was one other guy here, but he left the day after we arrived; and he hasn't returned. What was his name? Candor? Canter? Maybe Canton. I don't know why that's important. I met him only briefly and I don't remember what I was told about him. He was a big man, though, perhaps six and a half feet tall. And strong. He had dark eyes and dark hair.

He was a very handsome man and I felt a strong attraction to him, a strange magnetism, even though I knew nothing about him. I think he felt something too from the attention he paid to me. The way he looked at me as he shook my hand made a shiver run down my spine into my toes. Thinking about that brief encounter now and his penetrating gaze still gives me goose bumps. I'll probably never see the guy again, but I've thought about him a few times since then. All I can remember about his departure was that he had some kind of conflict with the others here just before we arrived.

Anyway, Dad's been searching for information concerning the moon colonies, looking for Hasani. He's not finding anything. John and Mike, a computer guy here, monitor the IIA database every day, checking the continuously running routines, sometimes several times a day. They've been doing that for a couple of weeks now. The last report from the moon came on January 28, seven days ago. That report contained the desperate words of one man named Sampson. There's been no word from anybody else. I don't know if Hasani ever made it to a remote outpost, like Sampson did. How could he still be alive?

36

FEBRUARY 5, 2093—SHIFT

John just handed us two papers to begin our afternoon staff meeting today, which started a little late due to a minor problem in the lab. Apparently, a sealed test tube containing an uninfected human tissue sample fell and shattered. Sheesh—it's a good thing it only had an uninfected sample. Otherwise, we'd all be dead within a few days. I hope they're a little more careful in there from now on.

Anyway, the first article was from CNN today. The second was another print-out from the IIA database, also dated today, which contained incredible news!

CNN/IWO News article, February 5, 2093

An additional 41 cases of Anthrax E have been reported throughout Central AM and the Caribbean islands. IWO orders halting all travel and requiring the isolation of any sick persons remain in place.

International Interagency Assembly database
February 5, 2093
Outpost 18 log post (1650 LT)
Be advised:

Hello Kennedy Space Center. This is Dr. Jonas Sampson. I have spent the last eight days searching for survivors. My travel has been difficult due to mechanical problems occurring in the airlock system of my Rover. Over the past eight days, however, I have attempted contact, contacted, and visited each of the independent, unconnected shells. 11 of the shells contained humans, but only five people were alive. 18 people were dead. One of five alive was sick and, with great sorrow, I declined to enter her shell. She was unable to move on her own and was aware that she would not live long. The survivors' names, colony origin, Earth citizenship, and location of discovery are as follows:

Dr. Thomas Bird
United States Moon Colony—Reno, Nevada—Outpost 18

Mrs. Misty Bird
United States Moon Colony—Reno, Nevada—Outpost 18

Ambassador Hasani Chalthoum
United States Moon Colony—Cairo, Egypt—Outpost 21

Dr. Jerad Beaudoin
Poland Lunar Colony—Gorges, France—Outpost 4

Dr. Bird is a physician and has thoroughly scanned and examined each of us. He has determined that all five of us are in perfect health; free, not only of Anthrax E contamination, but also of any other viral or bacterial contamination.

Dr. Bird and his wife Misty were vacationing at Outpost 18 when the outbreak first began. Some days later, Dr. Bird's colleague informed them, for the first time, of the outbreak and warned them to remain where they were as no cure or vaccine was available and everyone who contracted Anthrax E was going to die. Thus, with great sorrow, and (in his eyes) in violation of his Hippocratic Oath, Dr. Bird and his wife remained where they were. I and the others have attempted to allay his guilt.

Ambassador Chalthoum, of Egypt, reports that his father and sister were somehow involved in the discovery and initial research of Anthrax E in Egypt. He knows very little, however, about what has occurred because the communications center in his shell was malfunctioning. The Ambassador last spoke to his family on January 23 and he thereafter sought shelter outside the connected lunar facilities. He traveled to Outpost 21 via Rover and has remained there, without communication, since that time.

Dr. Jerad Beaudoin, a shuttle pilot and aeronautical engineer, was found in Outpost 4, which has six small, separate, insulated shells, each within approximately 25 meters of each other. Three of the other shells housed deceased individuals upon my arrival. The four shells had been in communication with each other for several days as the others began to get sick and then die. While they had some knowledge of Anthrax E when they first entered the shells to conduct research of some type, they were not aware of the deadly results of contracting the illness or that they may have been infected. Dr. Beaudoin believes that one or more of the others must have contracted the illness prior to their arrival at the Outpost, but then, because each of them was isolated in different shells when the symptoms first appeared, he was not exposed. Dr. Beaudoin is very weak and malnourished. His shell did not have a food processing unit, but instead, had old stores of food, mainly canned food, from many years ago, most of which he was unable to open. There was water, but he had used nearly all of it by the time I arrived. He appears to be recovering nicely at this time.

We are currently located in Outpost 18, where the Birds were vacationing, as it is the largest and has plenty of room and entertainment. It is a vacation outpost which can sleep up to 30 people at a time. Thus, because only the Birds were here, we assume that the life support systems will last a long time. If those machines break down, we'll be able to move our quarters to other posts that held no people at the time of the outbreak or thereafter.

The others have read your prior update and are aware of our dire circumstances. We are, of course, hopeful that a plan is underway to take us home. We grieve, along with you, at the desperate state of affairs on Earth and here on the moon. Please advise.

IWO log post (1719 LT):
Be Advised:

Dr. Sampson, again, it is with great pleasure that we receive this contact from you! Having not heard from you for several days, we assumed we would not again have the pleasure. We are currently attempting to make contact with relatives of the individuals housed with you. We will update you upon our contact with those individuals.

Be advised that, as of today, at least 50 people in Central AM and the Caribbean are infected with Anthrax E as a result of the destruction of Gortari II, and the spread of the disease resulting therefrom. It has been confirmed that, although

Mexico was authorized to return to Earth, having been given a clean bill of health for each individual reported to be on board, there was an error. At least one person must have been contaminated, and that contamination spread. Body parts from several people have been found in various communities throughout Central AM. Containment procedures are underway, and all available government resources have been, and are, being utilized to contain the spread of Anthrax E on Earth. Thus, no further plans have been developed to bring you home.

We will keep you updated. Please do the same.

37

Hasani is alive! And he isn't sick! I received word late yesterday. Mom and dad now know too. I can't believe it!

Unfortunately, he has no way to come home, nor do I think it'd be wise for him to do so if there was a way. People all over Central AM are getting sick. I still hope the ocean will keep the disease confined to the west. Unfortunately, there's no way to know whether that's true, and if not, for how long the east will be safe. Will birds carry the disease across the seas? Will massive storms—hurricanes, tsunamis and tornadoes—send Anthrax E into the atmosphere only to fall later in new lands?

Within a few weeks, there may not be a safe landing zone anywhere on Earth. I'm being pessimistic, but I saw the devastation of El-Alamein first hand. I know what this plague can do, and I know that, at least for now, there's no way to protect anybody who is exposed to it. Hasani is safer on the moon.

FEBRUARY 7, 2093, 1030 HOURS EST
HOLOGRAPHIC CONFERENCE

Ambassador Hasani Chalthoum (at Lunar Outpost 18)
Anta Chalthoum (near Boston)
Minister Abasi Chalthoum and Mrs. Mariam Chalthoum (Cairo)

"Hi Family!" Hasani nearly shouted as his family came on the Holo.

Mariam and Abasi talked over each other in their excitement.

Abasi, throwing his usual demeanor to the side, nearly shouted back, "Hi son! I'm so grateful that you're alive!"

"I can't believe it! I can't believe it!" Mariam began to cry almost immediately upon seeing her son's face on the Holo.

Anta, in a poor attempt to control her own emotions, stated simply, "Hasani, we've missed you." Then her tears began to fall as well.

"I can't believe I'm able to talk to you again!" Hasani cried. "I was sure that the last time we talked would be the very last time. Nobody was getting out. Nobody had any knowledge of how to escape Anthrax E. Thank you for your advice. It kept me alive!"

"Well," Abasi replied, "the advice, along with your wonderful mind and the glorious will of Allah kept you alive. We don't know everything that has happened to the people on the moon, but we understand that you may be one of just five individuals who have not been exposed to Anthrax E. Is that correct?"

"Yes, as far as we know. I'm with four other survivors. We're in Outpost 18. It's a vacation shell several kilometers from the nearest major colony or shell. Dr. Jonas Sampson, the gentleman who found me and the others, has searched all of the small outposts like this one, looking for survivors. We're the only people he found alive and healthy. I guess it's possible that there might still be life in the colonies, but given what we've learned over the past few hours through the IIA database, it seems doubtful. Plus, even if there was a chance that someone was still alive, none of us are brave enough—or perhaps it's stupid enough—to go looking. We wouldn't even know what to do if we found someone alive. They may be infected and not even know it. How would we isolate them while we waited? Where would we put them? How would we transport them?" Hasani's voice grew more sullen with each question he asked aloud.

"Hasani," Anta replied, "you don't have to explain why you won't, or can't go looking for survivors. I understand completely. I've seen the complete devastation Anthrax E leaves in its wake. Nobody survives. Don't feel guilt. The chance of you finding a survivor is slim, and if you did, the chance of that survivor infecting you all is great. There's no heroism in suicide, especially when nobody will be saved by your work. Stay where you are."

"I agree son," Abasi added, in a marked return of his usual air of authority. "Stay where you are. I have been talking to my colleagues at the IWO. They assure me that they are looking for a way to get you home, but, as I'm sure you know, Anthrax E has spread. When the Mexican ship that left the moon was shot down, it rained this horrible disease from the sky, and Central AM is being swept up in the flood. It may not be long before all of North AM and South AM are consumed by the plague. Of course, your sister is okay. She is in a bunker on the east coast of North AM. Not even your mother and I know where she is. But she assures us that the plague cannot reach her."

Anta, feeling somewhat shameful at her relative safety, humbly said, "This is true, but I'm so worried for the safety of the rest of you. In any event, Hasani, I don't think your arrival here on Earth would be something to really look forward to. It's probably good that the IWO can't get you home yet—that it believes it has more pressing matters is understandable. Of course, the people working here in this bunker are trying, desperately, to find a cure or a vaccine. They think they're getting closer. Just three days ago, Dr. Shevchuk told us that dead cells can be modulated to repel Anthrax E bacteria. They haven't figured out how to make live cells do the same thing, but seem quite optimistic that they're on the right track. There are many other doctors and scientists around the world also working on a cure or vaccine; but I understand Dr. Shevchuk is likely the closest at this point."

"That's good," Hasani replied. "Mother, how are *you*?"

"I'm fine," Mariam replied. "But I am dreadfully frightened right now for your circumstances. I know you are a grown man, but you are still my son. Be careful Hasani. I want you to come home to me when this is all over. May Allah have mercy and grant my prayers!"

Anta, remembering, asked, "Wasn't there a shell on fire? What happened to that?"

"Oh, that was bad! It basically blew up! We're a long way from it here at this outpost, but yesterday we heard the explosion and saw smoke and debris shoot up into the air. Although I'd really like to go over there, it's probably a bad idea."

"Wow!" Anta replied. "That would have been amazing to see! But sad too. What if someone was still alive in there when it blew up?"

"Yeah, I've tried not to think about that. While we watched, it appeared that everything that wasn't tied down floated away into space. It will fall again somewhere though—hopefully not on top of us."

"Yes," Anta mused. "With the low gravity on the Moon, anything that was shot up with any velocity would probably not come back down for a while and not in the same place. That would be strange to see."

Abasi, looking as though something was weighing on his mind, said, "Son, we will contact you again, hopefully with better news. Please help the others. It is your duty as an Ambassador to the lunar colonies to help those with you survive."

"I understand father. I will do my best. Anta, good luck."

"I love you Hasani!" replied Anta and their mother, at nearly the same time, as if it had been orchestrated.

"I love you too—all of you!"

38

"My friends," Dr. Shevchuk began, "yesterday's reports indicate that Anthrax E is spreading quickly through dozens of cities and towns throughout Central AM. At least 294 cases have been confirmed in the 12 days since the explosion of Gortari II.

"I have been informed that several people will be joining us here in our little underground sanctuary. The U.S. Government is in the process of selecting people to hide away in bunkers like ours to 'ensure the survival of the fittest' in the event Anthrax E overwhelms our society." Dr. Shevchuk raised both hands and used two fingers on each hand to indicate a quotation, even as he rolled his eyes.

"I understand other national governments are doing the same. I don't know who is making the decision as to who will join us, but it's my understanding that the general public has not been made aware of the relocations of these 'important' people or the use of these bunkers for safety. What I do know is that the IWO isn't in control of this process, which is interesting."

"That is interesting," Shift said. "Why would the IWO back off from this when their hands are in practically everything else?"

"I don't know that Shift," Dr. Shevchuk replied. "Perhaps they are too busy worrying about other things."

"This is crazy!" Dr. Andrew Jones said, getting a little testy. "You can't just pick who survives. We can't play God, can we?"

"It doesn't sound like we have any choice in this," Anta replied.

"Yeah, you don't have to worry because everyone in your family is alive and safe," Dr. Jones said. His comment sounded much more insulting and harsh than he meant for it to sound.

Anta's revulsion was palpable and her voice trembled as she responded. "Don't you dare accuse me of being apathetic! I saw my countrymen and women die before you even knew there was a problem! I've lived for weeks in fear for my brother's safety and have shed more tears than can be counted as I've grieved for the *lack* of safety of my parents! Don't you dare!" Anta was shaking now and it took all of her self-control to refrain from raising her arm and swinging at Dr. Jones.

Shift, having been on the receiving end of one of Anta's punches, when she wasn't angry, wrapped an arm around Anta's shoulders and turned her away from Dr. Jones and toward the restroom.

Dr. Jones' face became ghostly white and he stammered, trying to think of something appropriate to say. Finally, he squeaked out, "that's not what I . . . Anta . . . I'm sorry. That's not what I meant. I'm sorry."

"Friends," Dr. Shevchuk said consolingly, "we all have emotions, and can't be expected to hold them in in times of crisis. Let's just try to be careful about what we say. Let me continue. Anta, can you hear me? I want you to be part of this."

"Yeah, I'm here. I don't know what came over me. Please continue Dr. Shevchuk." Anta's words seemed to show she was over it, but her emotions were boiling. She, like everyone else, was experiencing a form and quantity of stress not previously known to most of them.

"We've been told to expect an additional 12 people, bringing the total to 26 in the next few days. We can't support many more than that, at least not for very long. I've been told that a few bunkers in the United States, Russia and China can hold as many as 100-120 people, but that the majority of bunkers around the world have the capability of holding no more than 10-15 people long term. It would be interesting to learn how many people are stowed away, or will be stowed away in bunkers within the next few days worldwide, but I doubt if we'll ever know."

"Is anybody digging more holes or building more bunkers?" Shift asked.

"I don't know that. It seems like that would be an advisable thing to do, particularly in the Eastern Hemisphere where there is no imminent danger. But I have not been privy to any conversations on that topic."

"How do we know the people coming here won't be contaminated?" asked Mr. Javier Franco, a cook and maintenance staff member from Massachusetts.

"That's a great question Javier. I'm told that each person, prior to entering the bunker, will be screened for any trace of Anthrax E. Additionally, extra provisions will be brought in, after screening, to ensure that we can stay in here for many, many months if necessary. Of course, I hope that isn't necessary. And, each person will be thoroughly decontaminated in the decontamination chamber, which should kill any spores that may be attached to their bodies or belongings."

"What about our families?" Shift asked, emotion crumpling up his face like a used dishrag. "Is there anything we can do for them?"

"No. I'm sorry," Dr. Shevchuk replied, clearly sharing the concern and sorrow of his friends. "There is nothing we can do for them. If you need to leave us Shift, or any of you for that matter, I will understand, although I would hate to lose you. When the doors are opened for our guests, each of you will be given the option to leave, but you won't be able to come back. Think about that, and pray about it if you're so inclined. While you may not be able to save your families, if the disease spreads, you can be with them at least. But know this, each person here—including you Javier," Shevchuk said with a warm smile, "has served a good purpose and is needed. Our best chance of survival, as a race, is to continue the good work that each of us is doing here. The more of us who survive the better."

"Can we at least tell our families, finally, what is going on?" Javier was tense, and agitated.

"I have been given strict orders to contain the spread of information from the bunker. But Javier, I'm not your father, your boss, nor your King. I can't force you to obey rules that I understand to be very difficult. Plus, any decision about whether to stay or go should be made with your family."

Mike Petrovsky, a computer scientist and good friend of Dr. Shevchuk's, who was usually silent during the group's daily staff meetings, finally spoke up. Looking knowingly at Dr. Shevchuk, he said, "As each of you knows, I have kept a very close eye on your communications with the outside world over the past weeks. I didn't want to, but it's been one of my responsibilities. You've all handled the responsibility of silence awesomely, apart from a few slip ups where I looked the other way and pretended not to notice! But, if for some reason the communication ports aren't monitored, say between 10:00 and 11:00 tonight, what could I possibly do about such a computer malfunction?" Mike's eye had a little twinkle as he winked, looking around the room into each person's eyes.

The small group of people assembled in the room understood his meaning, every last one of them.

After a moment's silence while people contemplated Mike's words, Dr. Shevchuk continued. "What I say next is classified information. And by classified, I mean that it does not leave this room, not even tonight between 10:00 and 11:00. Am I clear?" Receiving a few nods, but no comments as he looked around the room, Dr. Shevchuk continued, "On my direction, but against orders given to me from my superiors, Mike has been attempting to locate information on the spread of Anthrax E from government sources which, uncharacteristically, have remained cautious and silent on this issue. He has been attempting to hack into classified web centers and databases. We need to know more about what's happening out there if we are to be able to help effectively. My sources are providing only the basic information and it is not enough."

"What don't we know Doctor?" Shift asked.

"Well, that's a good question Shift. But it's hard to know exactly what it is we should know, but don't. I would *like* to know more than just the number of people infected. We aren't being told their symptoms or how long they're living after contagion. We don't have access to medical records from a single one of the infected individuals except Dr. Ghannam and his daughter. The only data we have about the manifestations of the disease are from yours and Anta's Egyptian samples and from the limited data entered into the IIA database early on, right after Dr. Ghannam and his daughter passed away."

"Why is the IWO being so secretive about this? Don't they want people to be prepared, and maybe live after all?" This time Anta asked the poignant questions.

"That's easy," John replied, "they're a bunch of crooked, greedy, secretive politicians." After a pause for effect, and smiling, John continued. "I'm kidding. I'm sure it's because they don't want to cause panic in the streets."

"You know, that's not necessarily inaccurate John," Shift replied. "It wasn't that long ago that governments were so secretive that their citizens had no faith or trust in their so-called 'leaders'. We all know that, right? John, you just articulated the centuries-old mindset of most of the world." Several people nodded in agreement.

"Until recently, even in the United States, the Justice Department and the Department of Homeland Security, and several other agencies—all operated by the Federal Government and funded by tax dollars—had assumed so much authority that they even began to detain and spy on their own citizens."

"But that mistrust of government isn't exactly the current sentiment in our world now, is it?" Mike asked.

"No, it's not really. Things seem to have changed a lot. About 90 years ago, a U.S. District Court Judge said that 'democracies die behind closed doors.' Over time, that kind of attitude slowly spread. During the 2030s and 2040s there was a radical redistribution of governmental power in the United States and then other countries of the world. It was that attitude of mistrust that eventually led to the creation of the

IWO in 2048. Since that time, it seems as though world governments, particularly the IWO, have maintained a fairly transparent existence; or so I thought."

"Well," Mike replied, "I think the IWO is probably hiding a lot more than you, or any of us, think. I haven't learned anything that the media hasn't already divulged, yet. There are some serious firewalls in place keeping me out of all the medical information. So someone's trying to keep secrets. But don't worry, I'll get in."

FEBRUARY 9, 2093—LATE—SHIFT

I just got off the Holo with Arilee. She wants me to stay. I'm the only family she and the girls have left and she wants the Bader legacy to continue. I cried when I heard her say that. She cried with me. She wants to live and she wants her girls to live. But, she wants me to help solve this crisis even more. She correctly pointed out that I can't save her and her girls by being with them. Their only chance of surviving is a cure or a vaccine; and here, I can help with that. How can she be so logical and reasonable while I'm so torn up inside?

39

Mike found a little information early this morning that hadn't been provided to the public. It isn't very useful, but it's something. Apparently, our leaders now know that Anthrax E is spread by wind, as well as by person-to-person contact, and perhaps, even by contact with infected animals. That's not news to me, but it would certainly be interesting for the general populace to learn. Somebody even found out about the gazelle we found in the Depression. I didn't tell anyone except Yurgi and John. Anta says the same. What else don't we know? Is there someone out there, in the IWO or elsewhere, who is keeping secrets? And if so, why?

Latest reports are that at least 1100 people have contracted Anthrax E in Central AM. The Brazils have each reported the probable presence of Anthrax E too. What's worse, at least to my family, is that there are at least seven cases in Ft. Lauderdale, Florida.

There are several reports of looting and vandalism in Central AM and South AM, but so far, the United States has avoided that crap. I've never understood what causes people to vandalize their own neighborhoods when something they perceive to be negative happens somewhere far, far away. What did that ever accomplish? Thankfully, until the last few days, we haven't had such idiotic displays of emotion too often in recent years.

In other news, all 12 of our new guests have arrived. We have in our presence such notables as Mr. Threet "Street" Kimball of NFL football fame and Ms. Shylene Aristorma of international street dance fame. I'm thrilled to be in their presence and wholly understand the decision to list such celebrities among the "important" people in our society. Yes, that's sarcasm.

More importantly, we've been joined by four more medical professionals along with a virologist, a bacteriologist, two university professors (math and computer science), an archeologist, and one member of the CIA, who, I'm informed, is here due to his "knowledge of governmental functions and operations on both national and international levels". Goodie. I hope this guy doesn't try to take over operations here. Shevchuk's doing a bangup job.

There are a couple of people of note among our group, and I'm not talking about "Street" Kimball and Ms. Aristorma. Those two will have to earn my respect. I'm talking about Dr. Angel Robertson, a biological researcher from New York and Dr. Steve Porter, an archeologist from Nevada. These two are both renowned for their contributions to their respective fields.

Dr. Robertson, a young, tough, silky-haired brunette is one of the leading researchers in what some people now call "supernatural" genetics. I don't understand all that entails exactly. But her published research leads one to believe that there are various genetic mutations within our society that cause, or may cause a person to exhibit physical capabilities beyond what was traditionally thought to be the limit of human ability.

Dr. Porter is a popular archeologist whose research and knowledge are highly sought after, worldwide, to aid film producers in their attempts to accurately portray the past through film. Plus, I've worked with the guy on a couple of occasions. He's a stud!

FEBRUARY 13, 2093—SHIFT

More than 1,900 people have contracted Anthrax E now in the Americas. Many of them have already died. New cases are popping up all over South and Central AM. In the United States, cases have been reported in Florida, Alabama, Louisiana, South Carolina and Georgia. So far, no cases have been diagnosed in the Eastern Hemisphere, which is good.

Just four days ago, I sat in a staff meeting with my friends and complained, along with everybody else, that the government, uncharacteristically, seemed to be hiding information, or at the least, wasn't being completely transparent in regard to Anthrax E. Well today, President Leroy Daniels, President of the United States, openly talked about Anthrax E. He seemed sad, but he didn't cry. Daniels is a tough sucker. While the news was grim, it was a relief to know that the United States government, at least, is attempting to inform the public about the dire realities we face. Perhaps our elected leaders were just waiting for the appropriate time, to avoid chaos and confirm reports. In any event, I'm not sure I trust the IWO, but perhaps our United States government is okay after all.

The President said:

My fellow Americans, and those of you outside our borders who have access to this e-cast, we are presently facing a terrible epidemic, the size and character of which have not been seen in many lifetimes.

Anthrax E is wreaking havoc in parts of Central AM and South AM. It is also within our borders, specifically in the southern states. We have been warned, by medical and scientific personnel, that, left uncontained, Anthrax E has the potential to cause the death of a major portion of our society, as has recently occurred in El-Alamein, Egypt and the lunar colonies.

The IWO has issued a warning, and I want to reiterate that warning: do not cross the borders of the state in which you currently find yourself. Do not cross any international borders. Do not leave your home if you feel sick, are coughing, or have a headache. Instead, summon your local medical response team and do as you're instructed.

I want to go further, however, to educate you about this grave danger, as I have recently been educated. Anthrax E is spread through contact and by air—through coughing and sneezing and the various other means by which a common cold is spread. It is also probable, as is believed to have occurred in El-Alamein, that Anthrax E is spread upon the wind.

Federal response teams, part of our National Security Agency, are presently being stationed in all major metropolitan areas within the United States. Countries around the world are acting similarly. From those metropolitan locations, local teams will set up in smaller communities. The job of these women and men will be to locate, educate and quarantine those who are believed to have been in contact with infected individuals, and to isolate those who are confirmed to be infected with Anthrax E. Summon your local response team immediately, via direct dial to 911, if you believe that you, or someone you know, is infected. While containment procedures may seem harsh, in the event you or your loved ones are infected, it behooves you, as a citizen of this great nation and our world, to help protect your neighbors, and to help protect our civilization. Thus, if you are infected, because there is currently no cure for the disease, you [/must/] help us stop its spread. You [/must/] voluntarily give up your freedoms so that others may live.

Do not riot and loot, as we are learning has occurred and is occurring in other countries. There is no good that can come of it. Instead, love your neighbors. It would be wise, however, to stock up on basic supplies and necessities. Our stores and shops are full. There is plenty for everyone. Service your water and air support machines to ensure they will last as long as necessary.

Rest assured, my friends and fellow citizens, that your government, the IWO, and governmental and private research facilities all across the globe are working day and night in an attempt to produce a cure and/or a vaccine for Anthrax E. One of the greatest research teams of our generation is located right here in our country, in Massachusetts. I have been informed that this team, along with several other teams around the world, is getting closer. They are working 24 hours a day, tirelessly, in an attempt to protect us. Pray for them. Pray for their success. Pray for the health of your neighbors, for strangers, and for yourself. It is not selfish. We need the blessings of the Almighty to overcome our current difficulties.

May God bless you. May God bless our country and our friends throughout the world.

FEBRUARY 15, 2093
ENTRY IN THE ANTHRAX E DATABASE
DR. YURGI SHEVCHUK

The Safars, and the tissue samples taken from their bodies and intentionally re-contaminated on January 26, still show no sign of decomposition. Our work with the subjects' DNA continues, but still we have had little success in creating a vaccine or cure for Anthrax E. Our previous finding that certain dead human cells could be modulated to repel Anthrax E bacteria has not yet been replicated in live tissue.

Young Suvan seems to be thriving in this environment. Her tissue samples have been very strong.

Communications with the various research institutions around the globe who are working on this matter simultaneously still reveal no progress greater than our own.

40

"Anta!" Shift practically yelled at me from the other end of the hallway. "Hold up!"

"What's up dude?" Yeah, I've started to use "dude" a little. It's catchy.

"*Dude?*" Shift questioned.

"Yes Shift, Dude."

"Okay. Come to the cafeteria with me. I feel like we haven't talked for weeks." He didn't have to ask twice. I'd go anywhere with this guy.

As we walked toward the cafeteria, to eat another gourmet meal from the hands of the great Javier, Shift asked, "Have you heard the latest infected counts?"

"No, not for the last couple of days. Why?"

"They're really getting bad. I knew those travel restrictions wouldn't do crap."

"Yes, Shift, you knew. What's got you so excited?"

"Well, it's not a good excitement. Estimates are over 15,000 now outside the United States!" Shift's voice had an edgy, raspy quality, like he was trying to control his emotions. "Here, there are over 1,300. It's already spread to 18 states and Texas. That's getting way too close to Colorado. What am I going to do?"

Ahhhh, that's the reason he's so excited. His family.

"Shift, just call them. Talk to Arilee openly. Screw the rules. Isn't there some place safe they can go? Doesn't Colorado have all kinds of open space and deserts and mountain caves? There's got to be someplace they can hide."

"Yeah, I have a place. It's a cabin they can go to, pretty remote. They've been there tons of times and the girls love it! We've already talked about them going there."

"Well, don't stand here. I'll save some food for you. Go call them. GO!"

FEBRUARY 23, 2093—ANTA

Crap. There's no stopping Anthrax E. It does what it wants to whoever it wants. Shevchuk and his colleagues are franticly working to develop a vaccine, but in the meantime, people are dying everywhere. Life outside the compound appears awful.

While the official news reports haven't really talked about it much, there are rumors on some of the satellite channels that small riots, vandalism and looting are occurring in several southern cities in the United States. Shift and I talked about the idiots that do that kind of thing. I agree with him. Why destroy your neighbor's shop just because you might die of something that your neighbor has nothing to do with?

It's estimated, as of this morning, that there are over 31,000 people infected or dead from Anthrax E in the western hemisphere, including at least 2,800 in the United States. Those numbers don't include as many as 40,000 already dead in El-Alamein or the approximately 14,500 dead in the lunar colonies. 85,000 deaths, or near-deaths, in only 50 days since Mr. Shafik, Dr. Ghannam, and his daughter entered the cave! That's a pretty fast-moving epidemic, I think.

I realize that I've been pretty pessimistic lately. But, with the current population of our world estimated at approximately 10.45 billion, and with the current rate of infection increasing exponentially, unless a vaccine is created soon, our world could succumb to this plague within a matter of months. Scary.

At night, when I'm lying in bed trying to fall asleep, I think of Hasani, lonely, up there on the moon. He's safe for now, but has no hope of returning home any time soon, or maybe ever. I think of mom and dad, also safe for now, but constantly worrying about what they will do if, or when, Anthrax E shows up in the east.

Inevitably, I think about Shift. I even think about his family. I've seen them on the Holos a couple of times and I even talked once with his sister, Arilee. Shift says they are very close, and have been since childhood. They seem to be.

Arilee is beautiful! She has a gorgeous smile that stretches all the way across her face when she talks to Shift about her daughters. Her light skin is perfect and her straight blond hair has these amazing natural highlights. Her voice, calm and soft, even under stress, is mesmerizing. Of course, she's thin and petite too. And her kids are just as beautiful. They look like smaller versions of their mom.

And Arilee is smart. Everything she says is logical and well-reasoned. She's kind and deferential. It's no wonder Shift talks so highly of her. Shift told me that her husband died in a hover accident just after their second daughter was born. How tragic that must have been.

When Shift talks to his family, I can see the soft, kind side of him that he hides here at the bunker. Even though I know he's afraid, just like I am, he hides it well. He's a strong man.

Others here in the compound don't hide their fear so easily. I can hear several of my companions weeping at night, both men and women, old and young. They cry for their families and friends, and they cry for themselves. I don't hold it against them. I understand the fear and the sorrow. Mom taught me to be compassionate toward others and their suffering, even when it appears weak and useless. I'm trying to do that.

FEBRUARY 23, 2093—SHIFT

"Hi Arilee," I said, wearily.

"Hey Shift. Sorry the girls aren't awake. I put them to bed a little while ago."

"That's okay. I actually wanted to talk to you privately anyway."

"What is it Shift?" Arilee asked, with concern in her voice.

"Remember we talked about going to my cabin a few days ago? Well, it's time to go."

"I knew this was coming Shift. We're ready. We can leave first thing in the morning."

"Can you leave before light?" I asked, anxiously. "I think you should get out of Boulder while nobody can see you. I don't want you to be followed. And yes, I know I'm acting a little paranoid."

"I think that's a good idea, not paranoid," Arilee replied. "I'll wake the kids up in a few hours and we'll leave."

"The sooner you leave the better I'll feel about it."

Our cabin sits in a small clearing among tall aspen and pine; almost ten acres of lush forest on a remote hillside seventy miles outside Boulder. Year-round, it is hidden from view and most-easily accessed by hovercraft along a narrow, winding, mostly overgrown trail. Running through the clearing near the cabin is a small stream full of beautiful, but mostly small fish. I have stocked the cabin over the years with the basic necessities to live, fish and hunt for several weeks. I've always considered the cabin my "escape from civilization". Now, Arilee has stocked the cabin over the past couple of days, at my request, with the additional provisions she may need to outlive Anthrax E in the inevitable event it comes to town.

Anthrax E, according to reports, has now spread to every state east of Colorado. Clearly, the IWO's travel restrictions have done nothing to stop the spread of the disease, and probably very little to even slow its progression.

As of today, there are still no reports of Anthrax E outside the American continents and Caribbean islands, the lunar colonies and El-Alamein. This is fortunate, but I don't have much hope that the rest of the world will remain safe. One hurricane ripping through the Caribbean, or one rogue traveler could be the cause of devastation anywhere and everywhere else in the world.

"Do you have everything you need?" I asked.

"I think so."

"How did the girls take the news when you told them you would be leaving soon?"

"They think it's great. They love the cabin. I love the cabin. But we've never been there without you. I hope all the electronics are working, and the fireplace."

"Actually, maybe you shouldn't light a fire. I don't think you should have smoke coming from the roof giving away your location. You should probably just run the heaters."

"Okay. I will. I'm scared, Shift."

"I know. Me too. My friends here are working so hard and are getting close to a solution to this mess," I lied. "Just get to the cabin. Stay out of sight. Keep the doors and windows locked and only use the repurposed air from the wall machines. Don't go outside for anything. If you can do all of that, perhaps you'll stay safe until Dr. Shevchuk finds a cure or a vaccine."

"How is your friend, Anta, and her parents? And how is her brother?" Arilee asked.

"They're all okay for now. Anta is as scared for them as I am for you though."

"You're lucky to have her Shift," Arilee said. "Don't go ruining that relationship like you have with every other woman in your life."

"What are you talking about?" I objected jokingly. Arilee knew that I'd only had one serious relationship, and that one ended badly. "Anyway, she's my colleague, not my girlfriend. It'll be hard to 'lose' her until all of this is over."

"Good. I love you, Shift. You're the greatest brother I could have ever asked for."

"You too Arilee. I mean you're the best *sister* I could have asked for," I corrected as Arilee chuckled quietly. "Tell the girls I love and miss them."

Anthrax E rages around us and above us on the surface. We're protected here. I don't believe my sister will be so lucky, nor do I necessarily consider myself to be lucky because I'm here, without her and her daughters. It's too late for me to leave now. We made our choice. Now I have to live with that choice while my beautiful nieces are in peril of dying without me by their side to comfort them. What kind of uncle am I?

41

It is with grave sorrow and a newfound terror that I write this article on behalf of my colleagues in Washington D.C. Every state of the United States except Hawaii, every province of Canada, and every country in the western hemisphere has now reported cases of Anthrax E. Latest official reports indicate that over 92,000 people have been diagnosed with Anthrax E in North AM alone. Reported estimates for Central AM and South AM are well over 800,000.

The danger has spread, however. Unconfirmed reports from a remote Russian outpost in far northeastern Russia indicate the possible existence of Anthrax E there. A man checked himself into a local clinic with symptoms of Anthrax E and has been isolated, but fear prevails in that small community.

Furthermore, there are unconfirmed reports of Anthrax E infections in the Kelvin Islands off the eastern coast of the United States. Authorities in the Kelvins report that no craft has landed on the islands, either by air or by sea, since the IWO first warned against international travel. IWO authorities speculate (if the report is true), based upon a few cases of Anthrax E confirmed in seagulls, that Anthrax E may have been delivered by birds to the Kelvin Islands. The gulls, reports say, may be carriers, but do not appear to succumb to the disease.

The relative peace felt in the Eastern Hemisphere may not last. May God have mercy.

MARCH 4, 2093
STAFF MEETING
HIDDEN BUNKER NEAR BOSTON

"Please get us started Mike."

Dr. Yurgi Shevchuk had largely, by this time, handed over the reigns to others to discuss various aspects of life both within and outside the bunker.

"Thanks Yurgi. As you all know, accurate statistics are getting hard to come by. Right now, estimates of infection in Central and South AM are in the 1.2 to 1.5 million range. Canada reported this morning at least 28,000 cases. A couple of days ago, Mexico reported more than 69,000 cases. Texas and New Mexico haven't been reporting, but we can assume they are in the thousands as well. The United States now has at least 70,000 cases, with several thousand of those in the state of Puerto Rico, but stretching from coast to coast. These numbers are staggering, but probably low."

"'Reported' cases," Mike continued, "only include people who are actually reporting to a medical facility or contacting a response agency. Those that get sick and never leave home or make a call aren't being reported. That is likely a significant number of additional people."

"Andrew, what have you learned about how the disease is spreading?" Dr. Shevchuk asked. "Is there any way to stop it?"

Dr. Andrew Jones replied, "Some of the animal conservation movements, those that are still functioning, particularly in the western states and Canada, are reporting that all kinds of animals are succumbing to the infection. The exceptions are seabirds, saltwater fish and other marine animals, including marine mammals. Apparently, none of those animals are sick at all. But we know that several seagulls have been tested and found to carry the disease, but they aren't getting sick. That's not a comforting thought, at least not to me."

"Why is that? Anta asked. "What makes the sea creatures and the birds immune, if that's what it is?"

"There's a theory, but it hasn't been vigorously tested, probably because nobody is too keen on getting near sick animals. I think it makes perfect sense though. As we know, Anthrax E is an airborne pathogen. It's spread by both wind and through contact with infected objects or persons on which the pathogen has landed. When a person coughs or sneezes, tiny fluid particles containing Anthrax E are spread through the air. Or, when the wind blows, the bacteria spread.

"Marine animals have no exposure to airborne pathogens unless they leave the water. Obviously, that will happen, but since the majority of marine animals stay under water most of the time, and only come up sporadically, they are likely to be safe. Plus, high concentrations of salt are lethal to bacteria."

"Does that theory give us any hope as to ways in which the spread of Anthrax E may be stopped?" Anta asked. "I mean, can salt be used to kill the disease in some way?"

"Well, there may be a way, but nobody has figured it out yet. It's not like we can just stand in salt water and be saved. We can't throw salt into the wind and hope that it kills the bacteria heading our way. Whether salt can be used in some kind of injection that could kill Anthrax E in the bloodstream seems highly doubtful. So, I think the answer to both of your questions is 'No', unfortunately; but it hasn't been ruled out as a possibility. I think one of the teams in Europe is doing some experimentation with salt."

"Charles, is there any truth to the rumors that seagulls are carrying Anthrax E to the islands or that Anthrax E has been found in Russia?" Dr. Shevchuk preferred to call Mr. Charles "Lucky" Rabene, a CIA agent from Washington D.C., by his given name. "Lucky" hated it, but kept it to himself when addressed by Dr. Shevchuk. Dr. Shevchuk had made Lucky feel welcome, even though some of the others in the compound had looked upon his inclusion as a way for the government to keep track of, and regulate what the scientists were doing.

Lucky had tried, largely in vain, to persuade everybody that he was there, not on assignment, but as one of a few lucky agents chosen by lottery to be included. That was the truth. Lucky had no real contact with any government entity, particularly since the United States government had ceased to function in any regular sort of way. Plus, Dr. Shevchuk had given him an important assignment—to monitor rumors and look deep into those rumors to ascertain their truth—something Lucky was very, very good at. His nickname—"Lucky"—stemmed from his colleagues' belief that he had to be lucky. There was no other way to explain how often he was able to successfully complete difficult tasks for the CIA.

"Well," Lucky replied, "It does seem true that the seagulls aren't getting sick. I don't think that's just a rumor. As for the Kelvin Islands, yes, the news is accurate. According to my sources, which I believe to be wholly reliable, there are at least 16 confirmed cases. There are also two confirmed cases in Bermuda. As for the Russians, there are now four confirmed cases in a small fishing village in the remote northeast corner of Russia, across the Bering Strait from Alaska."

"Does anybody have any idea how Anthrax E got across the Bering Strait?" Shift was puzzled by this. "I mean, even if seagulls or other birds carried the disease across the Strait, it seems unlikely that birds would be flying that far north this early in the year. But maybe I'm wrong."

Everybody looked at Lucky. "It is absolutely accurate that Anthrax E has arrived in Russia. How it got there is still a mystery, but there are theories. This is what I know, and it's somewhat complex. I'll go slowly to make sure I get the details correct.

"The first confirmed case of Anthrax E in *Alaska*—a fisherman by trade—was on February 27. That infected person was identified in a native village 70 miles east of Anchorage—over 700 miles from the Bering Strait. The first case of Anthrax E in *Russia* was confirmed on February 28, one day later. As you all know, international travel has been restricted and both U.S. and Russian transportation officials confirm that no boat or flying vessel has landed anywhere near the Russian coast in that area.

"So, one theory is that the sick fisherman, who frequently fished in the waters of the Bering Strait, but who had been restricted to shore fishing since the travel restrictions went into place, continued fishing from the shore and may have contracted Anthrax E from seabirds. That's possible, but it doesn't explain why he checked himself into a clinic 70 miles inland. A more likely theory is that someone actually crossed through the Bering Strait Tunnel on an earlier date—earlier than February 27—carrying Anthrax E with him or her, and infected others as he went. It seems farfetched given the difficulty of getting through the Tunnel even under ideal conditions and without the travel restrictions."

"Why would that be difficult Charles?" Dr. Shevchuk asked.

"Well, I was talking to Shift about this a little while ago. Maybe he'd be a better person to answer that. He seems to know just about everything." Lucky was genuinely complimenting Shift, and Shift smiled as he began.

"I don't know everything, but I do know it would be difficult to get through the Bering Strait Tunnel on foot, under any condition.

"The tunnel is actually a series of four big adjacent tunnels, each 60 feet wide and 75 miles long, give or take.

"Initially, back in 2034 or 2035, two tunnels were built to house electric trains and 18-wheel trucks. Sometime around 2045 or so, two additional tunnels were completed for the magnetic levitation trains and an airless Maglev Tube transportation system stretching from Washington DC to Berlin, with speeds upwards of 1,800 miles per hour. I've been on that—and it's awesome!

"Additional smaller tubes or tunnels were constructed to house water, oil, gas and electrical lines. Anyone who has been paying attention knows that this system of tunnels has been extremely successful at bridging the gap, literally and figuratively, between North AM and Asia.

"The reason it would be hard to get through the tunnels, now, is that the Port Authorities have been monitoring both sides for weeks, and, according to Lucky's research, no vehicular travel, including the trains, has gotten through. Foot travel is not allowed in the Tunnels, and never has been. Plus, any person walking through on foot would certainly have been apprehended. And, the tunnels are 75 miles long—quite a walk, especially if someone is feeling ill. I guess a bicycle might work though.

"So, yeah, it would be difficult for someone carrying Anthrax E to get through the tunnels; but, I don't think it would be impossible. I'm sure that the employees of the Port Authority are as scared as everyone else. There's a very real possibility that some of those employees have gone home to be with their families, like many of us would like to do. The other possibility, of course, is avian transfer. I don't think the Port Authority would be very successful at keeping the seagulls out of Russia, but that's really not my area of expertise."

"Well, that's interesting information, but not our problem at the moment. Does anybody else have anything they would like to add this afternoon? No. Okay, let's get back to work." Dr. Shevchuk closed the meeting.

42

MARCH 6, 2093
EXCERPT FROM A NEW RUSSIAN FEDERATION NEWS AGENCY
ARTICLE

Local authorities in Stansk, Siberia have located the body of a man believed to have violated IWO, American and Russian orders prohibiting international travel. The man, presently unidentified, was not local to Stansk. Several sources have indicated that they saw this man many days ago on the street outside the local police department building.

Upon inspection, the man's body was found without any papers or other identifying information. The only inference of his origin is a college sweatshirt on his body from Montana State University. His body has been confirmed infected with Anthrax E, and has deteriorated in alarming fashion.

MARCH 6, 2093—SHIFT

Holy crap! Lucky just told us that at least 13 people are infected in Stansk, Siberia. Stansk has been quarantined. Russian and IWO military personnel are organizing to contain the plague in the area around Stansk, just like they did in El-Alamein! The IWO plans to apply the same HMP Foam across the entire city, sealing everybody and everything inside, alive or dead. They want to contain Anthrax E in that area, and try to keep it from spreading any further into Asia. I guess it says a lot about the impact this plague is having on us when I say their actions make sense to me, even though they'll be killing hundreds, or maybe thousands of *uninfected* people in the process.

In fact, my biggest concern is that if Lucky was able to learn about the plan to apply the foam, even though he's trained in how to find information, there's no way that he's the only person who knows. Someone is going to get out of Stansk before they apply the foam.

MARCH 9, 2093—SHIFT

Cases of Anthrax E in North AM are now in the hundreds of thousands. We haven't heard what happened with the foam in Stansk. I intend to ask Lucky if he has any news yet. It's killing Anta right now, not knowing whether Anthrax E is in Asia.

The doctors and researchers here and around the world are using tissue samples, or transfigured samples, taken from the Safars in their attempt to determine and locate whatever it is that causes the immunity. The Safars, by the way, appear to be perfectly comfortable with this whole thing. The limitations imposed upon them by the isolation don't seem to bother them at all. They want to help. Mrs. Safar never sleeps, or so it seems. She is always ready and available for Yurgi when she's needed for further testing and interviews. Hopefully their willingness to help will pay off soon and we'll get some real results.

43

"I want to see just one news report from America, Anta. Just one." Anta and I have had a hard time getting together to talk lately, except over dinner occasionally. There's no time. Everybody is helping with research and tests that run all day, every day. We take turns sleeping and eating so that there are always people up to keep the research moving along. Human survival is on the line. But when we *do* talk, I feel like I'm with an old friend—someone who really gets me and understands my emotions. I feel so comfortable with Anta.

Tonight's meal: I'm not sure. I *think* we're eating beef in some kind of pasta. I know its pasta, but beef, I'm not so sure. Fresh food is running low. Soon we'll be stuck with the food processors and I'm sure Javier will be pissed. Me too.

"Are there any cable channels still broadcasting live from the U.S.?" Anta had to know the answer already, but she humored me. We all watched the Holos during our short time off, even if just for a few minutes.

"No. Everything's coming from Europe, Asia or Africa," I replied.

Just one week ago, media outlets in Canada and the United States were broadcasting that infections and deaths in the United States and Canada were in the hundreds of thousands. Those same media outlets are no longer reporting. Only sitcom reruns are airing, and they suck. Of course, media outlets from the eastern hemisphere are continually talking about events as they unfold over here. I don't know where they're getting their information unless there are still news sources alive here. I'm sure that some news men and women are still alive, but they're just not going to work. If I were on the outside, I wouldn't leave the cabin where my sister and her kids are still hunkered down and safe.

"I haven't been watching lately. Is there anything on besides the foreign news? I mean, is there *any* entertainment happening?" Anta asked.

"Not really. Every once in a while I pop onto a foreign channel that's showing some infomercial or lame talk show, but mostly, it's just the news. And the news sucks."

"I'm sure," Anta said. "What's the latest on the foam thing in Russia?" We hadn't talked about this in a long time, surprisingly. There's been nothing to talk about. There haven't been any news stories about Stansk. I don't know why, but I'm sure it has to do with avoiding panic, like always. Until today.

"Actually, I wanted to talk to you about that. There's finally news. I saw it just before I came in to eat."

"What is it?" Anta asked quietly. She looked both excited and worried. After what I had to say, she wouldn't be excited any longer.

"The media in Europe are saying that it failed. There are reports today of new outbreaks all over Russia and Mongolia."

"Huh."

That's not exactly the response I expected, but Anta isn't one to go overboard with her emotions.

"It gets worse," I said. "Several other Pacific Islands are now reporting outbreaks. For now though, Europe, South Asia and Australia are still safe, but that probably won't last. I'm sorry Anta."

"Shift, you don't need to worry about my emotions. You've got your own to worry about. How are your sister and the girls?"

"They're good. They're still safe, tucked away in the cabin." I really hoped that was true.

"That's great." Anta tried to act excited, but she was clearly not thinking about my family right now.

"How are your parents?" I asked. "I guess you'll be talking to them soon about leaving home?"

"Yeah, probably tonight," Anta said.

"How is Hasani? Have you heard from him recently?"

"No. I don't know what he's up to. We can't talk on the Holos so I only get the news John or Mike give me from the IIA boards, which is very little. I don't know what they're doing up there, but they're all still alive and healthy, as of a couple of days ago."

Anta paused. "How is this all going to end, Shift?"

"I think you know Anta. It will probably end very poorly, but I think Yurgi is making progress. That's what I hear anyway."

Thankfully, some of the people who were assigned to our bunker continue to have contact, albeit sparse, with the government agencies that sent them. It appears that the United States hasn't crumbled, yet; although most governmental functions have ceased since most people refuse to show up for work. While we don't have a realistic headcount, it's safe to assume that there are so many infected or dead, that it's only a matter of time, and maybe not much time, before there are very few people left on the outside.

I don't see any way the currently-infection-free continents and countries around the world are going to stay that way. Our only hope is for a vaccine. The good doctors here are still working on it, and despite what I said to Anta, they haven't given us much to hope for recently.

44

There's news from the moon! In our meeting this afternoon, John gave us all a printout from the IIA database.

International Interagency Assembly database
March 19, 2093
Outpost 18 log post (1230 LT)
Be advised:

Hello Kennedy Space Center. This is Dr. Jonas Sampson.

We haven't received a transmission from you in many days. Are you still there? Is there anybody by whom this message will be received? I certainly hope so. Last we heard, Anthrax E was spreading rapidly in the Americas but hadn't yet progressed into the Eastern Hemisphere. What's the latest?

Here, all is as well as can be expected for five stranded lunar colonists. Our resources are plentiful and we don't lack entertainment—if movies, music and books are considered entertainment. I've just sent a request through this system, asking any researchers currently working on a vaccine for Anthrax E, who are currently accessing this message board, to send me data and transfigured tissue samples so that we too can begin to work on finding a vaccine.

Doctors Bird, Beaudoin and myself, although not specifically trained in the areas likely necessary to help much, hope that we can be of assistance while we have nothing else to do but wait. I haven't received any response from any researchers yet. Again, I ask for such data so that we can help, if possible.

Or, maybe we can do something else to help; but I don't know what.

Please respond.

IWO log post (1432 LT):
Be Advised:

Dr. Sampson and others. It is with sorrow that I inform you that the Kennedy Space Center is no longer active. No personnel are presently on the premises. I am communicating with you from the IWO station in Hamburg, Germany. The destruction left in the wake of Anthrax E in Florida and throughout the Americas is so prolific that entire sections of the governments of those countries have ceased active duties. It is with great concern and guilt that I inform you that it is unlikely that you will be returning home any time soon, or, indeed, that you have any home to return to in some cases.

Of course, you are not forgotten. I am pleased to hear that you are well. Continue the course. We will be in touch.

Unauthorized log post (1925 LT):
Be advised:

Dr. Sampson, this is Dr. Yurgi Shevchuk. I am responding from a location near Boston, Massachusetts. I am not presently authorized to speak with you through this system, but, for reasons explained herein, I have chosen to do so, and I doubt greatly that I will be rebuked or disciplined for this post. Nor do I care if I am.

I have with me several doctors and scientists from numerous disciplines. We are working diligently to find a cure, or a vaccine, for Anthrax E. Our team was the first to begin such research. We have two live persons who we believe are immune. It is from them that we have obtained tissue samples with which to work.

We also have in our presence Dr. Anta Chalthoum, whose brother is with you on the moon; but you probably already know that. She sends her regards and is pleased, as I am, for your lives and for your desire to assist us in our laborious task.

I am sending data and samples now. While I don't know what you may be able to do to assist us, and even though our testing and data is supposed to be confidential, I see, at this point, that there is harm only in preventing others from seeking to create a vaccine. Currently, Anthrax E threatens to destroy the whole human population. As a result, any secrecy in this research is preposterous.

I will not direct your course of work, but have included our research logs thus far. It seems more prudent, due to our current frustrations, to have you begin your work from whatever process and thoughts you may have, which, ultimately, may prove the key to finding or creating a vaccine. The research and samples I am sending will contain data on the little success that we have had, so that you will not need to duplicate that work. Please keep us apprised of your work so that we may duplicate any successes you achieve. Our team is large and equipped to work through all angles and avenues.

God bless you in your endeavors.

45

"What happened? What's going on?" I was desperate for answers and Arilee, as usual, kept her head on straight. That's one of the things people love about her!

"Early this morning, while it was still dark, I woke up to the sound of the cabin's front door closing—you know that whooshing sound it makes when it is sealing?"

"*What?*"

"Shift, let me tell you the story," Arilee said.

"Okay, okay. Sorry. Go on."

"I was scared," she continued, "so I unlocked the gun safe and grabbed that little gun you had me learn to use when we were younger. As I crept down the stairs from the second floor, nearly peeing myself, I saw three silhouettes creeping toward me on the stairs. They didn't see me until I flipped on the lights with my gun pointed at the one in the front.

"I asked them who they were. They gave me first names and said they were only trying to find a place to hide, away from the chaos and hysteria in Boulder. I told them that they couldn't stay."

"Did you tell them about the kids?"

"Of course not. Even though they seemed peaceful and nice, I'm no idiot."

"Were they young or old? What did they do when you told them to leave?"

"Shift, seriously, let me tell the story."

"Okay. Tell me what happened."

"They were probably all in their mid to late thirties; but no, I didn't ask. When I asked them to leave, with my gun still pointed at them, they didn't hesitate any longer. They asked my forgiveness and promised they wouldn't come back. They said they'd find a different cabin."

"Arilee, there aren't any other cabins close by. You know that, right?" I asked.

"Yes, I know that, and they must have found that out too."

"What do you mean?"

"Well, about seven or eight minutes later, while I was sitting on the couch waiting for the sun to rise, and considering how they could've accessed and breached the locks, the door opened again and I felt this terrible pain in my left shoulder. They shot me."

"I'll kill them Arilee! Where are they? I'll kill 'em!"

"Calm down. No you won't. How will you even get here? Shut up and just listen to me. I'm obviously fine, right?"

"Okay, go on. I'm trying," I said. Arilee actually did look fine. She wasn't even grimacing from pain. Maybe she was okay.

"So, after I felt the pain in my shoulder, those same guys came rushing through the open door holding guns. I was stuck. I couldn't hide. But I was determined to save the girls. So I dropped to the floor. Shift, you would have loved it! I was like a superhero, seeing my own moves in slow motion as I rolled behind the couch, shooting right at them! I hit two of them before I felt a shot pass through my shoe."

Arilee held up her shoe to show me where a bullet had passed through the sole of her shoe.

"I couldn't get my foot behind the couch in time. But I'm okay, it completely missed my foot! Get that look off your face. I'm fine, unlike those bastards.

"The third man ran away, while the other two tried to crawl toward the door. I didn't know whether I was safe or not, and I didn't initially see the lone standing man race back through the door, so I kept firing toward the front door where the moaning and crying was coming from. Finally, the sounds of men in pain died off. I crept over to the front door. They were both dead, Shift. I killed them, right there in your family room. Now I don't know what to do."

"What about the girls?"

"They woke up during the first interruption, but stayed quiet until I returned to them. Before I settled on the couch to watch the sun rise, we discussed the possibility of being discovered and they acted exactly as we had agreed. After the men left I warned the girls that the men might return and that they were to stay upstairs no matter what happened." Arilee began to sob, but quietly, as though the emotional pain was too great to let out all at once. "They locked themselves in the hidden room and would have left the cabin through the escape tunnel if I didn't get back to them within a half hour. That was the deal."

I was stunned into silence for a few moments. The strength Arilee was showing amazed me; and I've known her all my life. But there was nothing I could do, and I didn't know what she could do either; so I finally said, "It's going to be okay. They attacked your family and your home—well, my home. You protected your daughters. You kept everyone safe. You *are* a superhero, and you didn't do anything wrong. You know that, right?"

"Yes."

Arilee told me that, after the room grew quiet, she first checked on the girls, avoiding physical contact, then she put on some rubber gloves and a mask and dragged both men out into the yard and away from the cabin; but they were too heavy to take any further. She knew she couldn't spend the time outside that it would take to bury them. She can't call the police either—they likely wouldn't respond, or even answer the call. Plus, if someone *did* show up to investigate, that person might be infected with the plague that's devastating the entirety of the western hemisphere right now.

"I'm afraid Shift, and now I'm not just afraid of Anthrax E."

"I know. Me too."

My biggest fear, now that Arilee has used very simple home medical kits to clean and bandage her gunshot wound, is that one of those men might have been contagious already, or that Anthrax E may have been in the air that breached the cabin when the door was opened. They said they had come from Boulder. Arilee's last contact with anyone in Boulder, several days ago, informed her that Boulder is largely contaminated, and many people had been fleeing to the mountains.

"What should I do now, Shift?"

I didn't know. What could she do but wait to see if she will die like everybody else. And if she dies, so do her girls.

"You wait," I said. "Be vigilant, especially at night. You'll have to decide if you need to quarantine yourself from Diamond and Cedar. But if you do that, you may scare them more than they are now. I don't know which is worse. If I was you, I would stay with them Arilee, watch for symptoms . . . and pray. Pray like you've never prayed before. If you're contaminated, they will be too before long, no matter what you do."

Then we talked, in depth, about the early signs of infection. We didn't make a decision about what to do if the infection had entered the cabin. I didn't want to think about it unless I had to; although I'm sure I won't be able to *stop* thinking about it for the next five days. I want so desperately to be with them. Even now, I can't stop the tears flowing from my eyes and the lump in my throat that threatens to cut off my air. I haven't been so frightened since the day Anta and I left El-Alamein.

46

"Who would want to kill your sister?" I asked.

"I don't know," Shift replied.

"I'm so sorry Shift," I said. Then, after a moment, I continued. "I guess we'll never know who they were, if she killed two of them and the other took off. It's not like she can go out and hunt the guy."

"Nor would she anyway," Shift said. "So, what did you guys talk about this morning while I was on with Arilee?"

"Oh, it was awful," I said. "We were discussing the fate of the world, as usual. Most of us talked a little about our families. Somebody mentioned how we may be the only family each other has left in a few weeks. People talked about how their families were already dead or sick. It was so sad and depressing."

"Did you talk about your family?" Shift asked.

"I was asked. But I only said a little. I mentioned how Hasani was doing, and that my parents were trying to get ready. But not much else. I was a little ashamed, knowing that my whole family was still alive, and that nobody else in the room could say the same thing.

"Andrew and Javier both read something from their wives. The pain in their voices and in their eyes was almost unbearable. I broke down and Andrew actually put his arm around *me* for comfort, when he was the one in need of comfort. I'm so ashamed of that Shift."

"I'm sorry Anta. I wish I had been there."

"We recorded the whole meeting, as usual, if you want to hear what people said."

"Maybe I could just listen to Javier and Andrew," Shift said. "Can you find them for me?"

I pulled out my MEHD, found the file and pushed play.

I searched until I heard the voice and saw the image of Dr. Andrew Jones on the screen.

"Okay, this is from the journal of my wife, Lauren Jones, dated March 15. She says:

Andy is safe; at least he was four days ago when I last talked with him. His place in some secluded bunker—a place that's secret even from me—probably assures his safety long past the point in time when our children and I pass on.

Over the last few days, news channels here on Long Island have, one-by-one, stopped reporting. We're no longer in communication, through any means, with any of our friends or neighbors. Just two days ago, Stephanie (our next door neighbor) called to tell me that her four-year-old son had a fever. She was desperately afraid. I wanted to console her and tell her everything was going to be alright, but I knew that would be a lie; so, instead, I just listened to her grieve. It was heartbreaking.

I'm sure that our time is coming too. Even though we've remained indoors for the past 9 days, and schools were shut down two weeks ago as a precaution, there doesn't seem to be any way to prevent the spread of Anthrax E. Andy can't help me. He prays for us, as I do for him.

Each night, before I tuck Jordan and Jacoby into bed, I pray with them that the Lord will keep us safe and will keep daddy safe. At 6 and 3 years old, they seem to be aware that something isn't right, but I haven't had the heart to tell them that our days are numbered and we're all going to die. Jordan was happy to be out of school initially, but now she misses her friends and doesn't understand why she can't go play with them. Jacoby wants to go outside for a walk so badly that he cries. What can I do?

Each night for the past week, I've laid next to my children at night until they fall asleep, then I curl up on the floor, under a blanket, and cry until I finally fall asleep. I'm so lonely and so sad. I miss Andy. I miss my friends, many of whom are probably sick or dead.

I looked at Shift as Andrew finished speaking. There were tears in his eyes.

"Do you still want to hear Javier?" I asked.

"Yes, thank you," he said.

I moved forward in the file until Javier Franco's face appeared on the screen. His face was drawn and tear-streaked, even before he began to speak. It was evident that this was a hard thing.

"This was written by my wife, 'Archie', on March 19."

I can't handle this anymore. I'm afraid of the boogie man, that isn't even a man, which is creeping down our street and through our town. But now the boogie man is in my home. All three of my children are sick. Elisha cries uncontrollably while sweat pours from her face. She is in the early stages compared to Nia and Brum. Both of them started with fevers three days ago. They cry out in pain all day and all night. Nothing can take away their pain. Nothing even dulls their pain.

Little Elisha is next and I can't go through this with my baby. I have failed as a mom. I can't protect them. The worst part is that I don't feel sick, yet. Maybe that's good because I can care for them, but to what end? If their fate is like the fate of so many of our friends and all of our family in Florida, they'll be dead within a few short days.

I pray to God and to the Virgin Mary that my sins are forgiven so I can see my babies in Heaven when my time comes. Javier, my lover and protector, has been away from home so long. I pray to God that he is safe. It was a blessing when the call came for him to leave and take his assignment in the bunker. While his absence is terrible, I wouldn't change it, even though my children miss him so. He cannot help us here.

To my children, who, during their worst times, call out for Papa, I am an insufficient substitute. My strength is gone, although I am healthy. The heartbreaking wailing and suffering of my children has worn me thin. I will die soon, and when I do, I think it will be a wonderful day."

"What will become of us Anta?" Shift asked through painful tears and a hitch in his voice.

I reached out and touched his hand. I had no words to say to comfort him, just as I had had no words of comfort for anybody else that morning.

47

Arilee and Diamond are both sick. Cedar has not begun to cough, but she doesn't look well. This is the beginning of the end for my sister and her family.

Shift's nieces, Diamond and Cedar both passed on a little while ago. Shift and I were on the holo with them when they passed. It was heart wrenching. Arilee is on death's door. He didn't want to turn off the com while she was still alive, but she insisted. She made him promise to go back to work so that we might be able to save someone.

After I shut off the com, Shift sank to the floor. I tried to help him get up, but he said his desire to live left with them. So I won't let him be alone.

I've now been sitting beside him for several hours. I don't know whether he appreciates it, but each time he begins to cry anew, I wrap my arms around him and pull him close. During a short break in his mourning, he told me how lonely he felt and that it was beginning to consume him.

"I just said goodbye to my sister, Anta. Forever. I'll never see her girls again. They were so beautiful. They never did anything wrong. How can life be this way? How can God allow good people to die in such a terrible way, leaving their loved ones to mourn, without any knowledge of when such a fate will befall the rest of us?"

I didn't speak, but just held him tighter. I don't imagine that any of us will survive this plague. Without a vaccine, which hasn't been developed yet despite the tremendous efforts of our friends, we will all die.

Thankfully, I believe that life continues after we die, and that we can be together again after this life. While my faith is being tested now, I hope that it will remain strong enough to carry me through this time. But I didn't want to talk to Shift about that. He needed to grieve. I couldn't imagine anything I said would actually be of comfort. It's going to have to come from within himself. I sighed as a tear dropped from my cheek onto his shoulder.

Just before we hung up the com with Arilee, she asked Shift to read the story of Job in the Bible. She pled with Shift to be like Job and stay strong in faith to ensure that their lives together as a family would continue, whenever it happened that God called him home. She begged Shift to keep the faith for his nieces, who adored him.

I couldn't speak and wanted to leave them in privacy as I listened to these two siblings grieve together and talk of such spiritual things. But Shift held tightly to my hand. After a few minutes of silence, Arilee seemed to understand that Shift was struggling. She told him that she loved him and that she would continue to pray for all of us.

I hope that Shift understood her faith and strength and will be able to feed from it in time. Arilee was an amazing woman.

APRIL 6, 2093—ANTA

Shift is still despondent, but doesn't appear suicidal. He's taking the death of his family very hard. I'm trying to understand it. I think I will be equally devastated when my brother and parents die.

I've been by his side, except for his trips to the toilet, for better than 40 hours now. Last night we fell asleep sitting on the couch in the common area with my arm around him and his head on my shoulder. It was nice, but when I woke up, I had to hurry away to freshen up and brush my teeth. Funny how we adapt to our conditions, like wearing a chem suit for days without worrying about bad breath or body odor. That was hard to get used to, but by the time we left El Alamein it didn't even cross my mind. Now, I couldn't go more than a day without taking a shower. And I know Shift is aware of his appearance and grooming when I'm nearby. He's normally so careful about the impression he's making on me that I can tell this is really killing him.

We've talked a little, about his sister, and about her daughters. I don't ask questions, but I haven't stopped him from talking. It appears therapeutic. I'll let Shift talk as long as he wants to, and about whatever subject may concern him. Ultimately, I'll probably call upon him to perform the same service in the near future.

The longer I sit with him, the greater love I feel for him—as my friend and my brother. I think this is what Shift referred to a few hours ago as a "Christ-like love". I don't know what that is, but I know that right now, I would do anything to take away his pain, if I could.

Anthrax E is spreading further into Asia, with noted infections throughout Russia, Mongolia, China and the Baltics. It won't be long before the infection spreads into Europe and then the Middle East. It probably already has. Mom and Dad are fully aware of this, unlike many others they encounter. Apparently, many people in Mom's circle of associates and Dad's political associations deny the risk that's on their doorstep. Many refuse to take precautions that may save their lives. Perhaps they're in denial or perhaps they know there is nothing to be done.

Mom and Dad have been searching, so far in vain, for a place to take refuge from the oncoming "storm" as Dad calls it. Although they continue to search, they're not so deluded as to think that, even if they find refuge, they will live long. They have, more or less, resigned themselves to their fate. Dad tried to lighten the mood of our last com by suggesting that maybe they should go bury themselves in a cave in the desert; I've never heard him use sarcasm to make a point and I know it hurt him to say it. They have chem suits, like Shift and I wore, but they can't survive in those for long. They need a more permanent solution. Dad said that, if they can't find a permanent solution, they may not even wear them just to prolong the inevitable.

It may be weeks, or it may be months, but without a vaccine, Mom and Dad will die. Unlike Shift and his sister and nieces, we at least have time to prepare ourselves for this probability. Hasani understands it well too. While we may never see each other again in the flesh, when death finally comes, and it almost surely won't be long now, we won't be taken by surprise. We'll be ready—I hope. But on the chance that grief strikes me like it has Shift, I'll call on him to be my support, as I am trying to be his.

The people in the bunker here have had much less contact with any governmental leaders over the past few days. The IWO continues, at least until two days ago (the last we heard from them) to function as a world governing body; but other local governments and agencies, including the United States federal government, haven't contacted us in the last few days. Our days as a human race are numbered—I can feel it.

48

APRIL 8, 2093—DR. STEVEN PORTER

I haven't heard from the family in several days. It is terrible. I know that everybody is losing loved ones. Shift's family just died a few days ago. It's greatly affecting him and it's torture to watch his suffering. I don't know whether my good wife is alive or dead, or whether my children are safe—although I doubt very much that there's any hope for them.

It seems unnatural that I, along with my friends here, must sit and watch our world crumble and our families and friends perish by means of some unholy disease unleashed upon mankind. My prayers that they may live—and that I may see them again—may yet be answered; although if they are now gone to rest with their maker, I will grieve, but not lose faith. The Lord is good, and his reasons and purposes are just, whatever we may think of them.

I intend to continue to attempt to contact my family until I have confirmation of their death or their continued life. In the meantime, I grieve with my friends for their losses.

49

Over the past week, Anta has been my rock. What a wonderful human being. I'm not sure I've forgiven God for taking my family from me, but I do thank him daily for putting Anta in my path.

At this afternoon's staff meeting, John handed us each a copy of an op-ed piece published in Germany's "Free People's News Corp. Press", dated April 10, 2093.

Anthrax E, that highly-contagious and deadly bacteria, which softly arose from the desert sands of El-Alamein, yet came crashing down from the killing moon, has continued its steady advance through the nations of Asia. It has now begun its relentless decent upon Europe. There are none who can avoid the putrid ramifications of this apocalyptic pandemic. As came to pass with our ancestors of old, this new 'bubonic plague' has attacked, and will devour our civilization.

The ancestors of our great German race, who suffered and died by the hands of the impious Adolf Hitler 150 years ago, fought themselves free from the 'better life' prophesized by the Führer. That unholy man preached the cleansing of European society of those he deemed undesirable. Yet, our noble ancestors finally came to understand, far too late, that the destruction of one societal element would lead to the destruction of the whole. It is now manifest that the evil minds of the early twentieth century could not understand, or, at the least, refused to comprehend, the significant ramifications of the development of biological weapons, as Anthrax E must surely be.

Historical documents, contemporary researchers, and generations of politicians want us to believe that, during the great battles of World War II, Nazi Germany, at the behest of Führer Hitler, forbade the development of biological weapons due to some immense horror from his own past. That Hitler, the fanatical, delusional, evil and self-proclaimed savior of the Aryan race would experience apprehension at the thought of the destruction of living souls, by whatever means, is beyond comprehension. Yet, the leaders of grand nations of the world today continue to spoon this revolting propaganda down our throats. While there has been, from time to time, historical evidence which sheds light on the true nature of the biological weapons research programs in Europe and America during World War II, the truth has remained hidden behind deceptions and secrets meant to keep us, the sheep, in order.

The truth, which should not be kept secret, and which will now be known unless the publishers of this news outlet are censored by the IWO, is that Germany did, indeed, have an extensive biological research program dedicated to the complete annihilation of several political and religious factions throughout the world. During the early 1940s, high-ranking puppets of the Nazi regime, including scientists and medical "professionals", began clandestine research into the development and use of biological weaponry. Concurrently, the British were also experimenting with biological agents aimed at thwarting the German war machine. Bacillus anthracis, the etiologic agent of anthrax, was heavily studied and transformed, by both the British and the Germans, for future use against the 'enemy'.

While the whole truth may not ever be revealed, it [/IS/] known by those of us who have spent our lives exposing hidden truths, that have been covered up by our governments, and informing the world thereof, that the Germans ultimately developed an abominable strain of Anthrax to be utilized along their hoped-for, but ultimately unrealized path to world domination. Not even the Italian or Japanese militaristic regimes, which, along with Germany comprised the strongest corners of the Axis power, understood the ramifications of sitting idly by, watching this development unfold.

Clearly, some form of [/Bacillus anthracis/] was released in the Egyptian desert. Our leaders, and their puppet media have claimed that such release was 'accidental' and that Anthrax E was discovered in a 'hidden', 'unknown' cave during a sand storm. The truth, my friends and allies in our fight against governmental tyranny, is that our leaders, those to whom we have given our blind and ignorant respect and trust, have intentionally released against us the very agents that our ancestors fought so hard to defeat 150 years ago.

To be clear, we, the human citizens of this vast world, have been intentionally infected by our government! While it is foolish to believe that our leaders knew the ultimate outcome of this plague—the death of the entire human race—it would likewise be foolish to believe that they did not intend for many people to die.

The cleansing of our world has been occurring since the first human awoke to a sunrise on this world. Tyrannical leaders and oppressors have sought, throughout all ages, beginning with the creation of our world and the dominance asserted by

Cain over Abel, to lead through fear, and to destroy life as a means to that end. This is no different. Do not believe that we live in a safe and sophisticated world, and that the IWO labors on your behalf. The IWO and all of its political affiliates want power and control. They want to rule you. They want you to serve them.

Indeed, you are a slave already; but you can throw off those shackles and be free now. The truth is out. You, the individual, are not required to be bound by their laws and their restrictions. You, the individual, have been pushed far beyond what is natural and moral. [/YOU/], the individual, have the right to stand up and demand the release of the vaccine that your government developed long before the 'accidental' release of Anthrax E upon our world!

The vaccine exists! Even now, your 'leaders', and those deemed worthy to continue to live in this world, are hunkered down in bunkers receiving vaccines. They are safe. Do not rest, satisfied that you may, yourself, be safe from Anthrax E. You are not. You are going to die from the horrible madness intentionally released upon our world unless we rise up together and demand, through whatever means necessary, that our governments release the vaccine to the public. Fight with me! Live with me! Or die trying!

WOW! Are you kidding me!

APRIL 11, 2093—SHIFT

"Could that actually be true John?" I asked. "I'm just so pissed off about it!"

The op-ed article John gave us yesterday had been consuming my thoughts for several hours. I wouldn't even talk to anybody about it for some time.

"Shift, of course it's not true," Anta replied, before John had a chance to speak. "John knows that. Everybody here knows that. There's no cure out there."

"I know it's a lie man. And you should be pissed," John said. John and Anta were both taking this much better than I was.

Within minutes of its publishing yesterday, John and Mike saw the article popping up all over the internet, on thousands of websites. Within an hour of its release, the websites that were republishing the story began to be shut down, probably by the IWO, or whatever is left of it. Today Mike has found over 6,000 websites with that same article published. He's also found nearly a dozen similar conspiracy theories. I suspect that, over the next few days, hundreds, or maybe thousands of similar stories and conspiracies will sweep across the internet.

"Seriously though, do people really think that some government agency, somewhere, intentionally released the plague, all the while having a vaccine to prevent the total annihilation of our species?" I asked. "Do they *really* believe that? It's asinine!"

"People believe a lot of things Shift," John replied, "but that doesn't necessarily make them true."

"If they knew what we know, John, they wouldn't believe it. I mean, we found the stupid thing. We walked and talked with the first infected people. We walked in the damn caves. We held the vial and saw the stuff left by the German soldier when he died from that very disease 150 years ago. I held his gun, man. I read the dude's bloody journal. It was authentic!"

"Hey, I believe you," John said calmly. "I don't think any government, apart from Nazi Germany's government, of course, wanted this to happen. And I know there's no cure, obviously."

"Well, let's not be too hasty guys."

John, Anta and I all turned to see Dr. Angel Robertson standing in the doorway to the lounge.

"What do you mean Angel?" John asked.

"Maybe Anthrax E wasn't released intentionally, but can we be sure there isn't a cure somewhere? If the Germans developed the thing in the 1940s, and I have no reason to doubt that, isn't it possible they also developed a cure or an immunization?"

"I doubt it," I said. "It was the 1940s. Wartime. The Nazis wanted to take over the world. Hitler wasn't necessarily a forward-thinker."

"Even if he wasn't," Angel said, "he also wasn't the mastermind behind much of the evil that occurred during that time. There were others—smarter than he. Perhaps they had something. Perhaps they didn't. But I don't want to discount the idea that there may be a cure out there."

"So, you're saying that the Nazis may have had a cure, but it's been hidden somewhere, or by someone for 150 years, just in case the plague was released at some point?" Anta asked.

"I'm saying that the Nazis may have had a cure or vaccine. And, if they did, it, or its formulation could still be around somewhere. That's all. I certainly don't think anybody intentionally released Anthrax E at this point in time. I'm sure it was lost to the world and then accidentally released a few months ago. But maybe we should go digging and see if we can come up with information about an existing cure."

"Okay Angel, I'm with you on this," John said.

Anta and I both looked at John. I was a little surprised. But hey, if there could be a cure out there, I won't stand in the way of a search. I just don't think they'll find anything.

Even though I felt a bit better after our conversation, I still couldn't relax. Anthrax E and I have walked hand-in-hand for months. Plus, Anta and I have been in this bunker for weeks while the smartest minds of our generation attempt to find a cure or create a vaccine. If there could ever be a vaccine, these are the people who will find it. There's just no way a cure or a vaccine already exists! I can't fathom how any scientist from the 1940s could do something we cannot, unless by accident.

APRIL 11, 2093—LATER-SHIFT

Okay, I've calmed down a little. Anta brought me a bag of Lay's and a Pepsi. I'm feeling better. I love those chips.

Anyway, there's no cover-up. If there was, that conspiracy would've started in the 1940s, with some illogical plan to come to fruition in the 2090s long after the death of everyone involved. That's stupid.

But I've come around to the idea that, even though Anthrax E was accidentally released a few months ago, there may still be a cure, or the ingredients and plan for one, somewhere on Earth. But, the scientists working here in our bunker are the best in the world. If they can't find a vaccine, who else could, and when did they do it?

In any event, I think that article, and all articles like it, that continue to pop up on the net are going to wreak havoc on the already-fragile existence of the people in any place Anthrax E hasn't yet spread its ugly, ugly wings. I expect to see people, who have become so desperate to survive, risk the end of their lives a few days early for the chance to live. People are going to kill each other over this. The people who started these rumors are idiots.

APRIL 12, 2093
IWO PROCLAMATION

> *Let it be known: the IWO wholly refutes the alleged conspiracies now being propagated by agitated and scared individuals in our society. Do not believe the stories. There is no truth to the theory that your government intentionally unleashed the plague that is now ravishing our brothers and sisters in all quarters of the world.*

> *While no vaccine is currently available, as has been stated from this venue multiple times in the past, dozens of facilities and teams, employing the brightest minds, have been organized throughout the world, working to find or create such a vaccine. When it is discovered, or created, it will be freely distributed to the masses.*

Please be calm and rational. This conspiracy theory is no different from those of the past which have been generated to promote fear and stir up hostility. Do not be led down that path. Let us strengthen one another and resolve to spend whatever days we may have left on this Earth making peace and loving our neighbors.

50

"Aaggghhh, what is that? I think I'm going to be sick!" Dr. Steven Porter yelled to nobody in particular, gagging as he rushed out of his sleeping quarters.

Dr. Porter's quarters were located in the same hall as several others on his research team. His pleading question, just after 6:00 in the morning, was left unanswered for several moments until the curious, sleepy faces of the people on his shift began to peek from the doors of the sleeping quarters nearby.

"What do you mean, Steve?" Shift asked urgently. "Are you sick?" The desperation in Shift's voice was palpable. Several people who had peeked out from their doors in response to the commotion, closed those same doors until only a sliver remained.

"No, I'm not sick," Dr. Porter replied, "but I might be sick. The smell is awful!"

"Are you sure you're healthy?" This time it was Anta, clearly worried, like everyone else, that Dr. Porter might be ill.

"I'm fine," Dr. Porter said, exasperated. "I'm not sick, I swear. Can't you smell it? It's coming from my room."

As his friends realized that he was fine, but merely smelling something foul, they opened their doors and tentatively entered the hallway. Shift, being closest to the action, smelled it first. "Oh, dude, what did you do in there? Is there a dead animal in there or is it just your feet?"

Dr. Porter smiled a little, as several other people began to snicker. "No *dude*, it's neither. It smells like your business from last night is leaking its odor into my room. Don't you flush?"

Now the snickers became laughter. People were gathering closer to Dr. Porter's door. The smell was definitely something closer to feces.

"Anta, go check out the men's room," Shift said, with a twinkle in his eye, thinking Anta would never do it.

"Okay." Then she did. In less than four seconds, she rushed back out gagging. "Shift! Learn to flush the crapper!"

"Right. I'll try to remember." Shift enjoyed Anta's reaction as much as everyone else did.

The next several minutes were spent trying to figure out the source of the smell. They took turns running into the bathroom looking for the source. Nobody lasted more than 15 seconds before running back out, choking back vomit or eyes stinging with tears. Every time another person ran out, laughter would break out again. After a few minutes of this, others from different work shifts began to gather in response to the commotion. Finally, Mr. Carón Blanchard, the bunker's ventilation specialist and electrical engineer arrived, to the loud applause and eager faces of 13 of his associates.

"Carón! Dude, you've gotta check this out. Worst. Smell. Ever." Laughter erupted again. Shift had a way of making people laugh. People loved him. His sense of humor and the way he said things just made people comfortable. But not even Shift's words made Carón comfortable about entering the men's room.

Finally, with a lot of persuasion from those in the hall, and a gentle shove from Shift on the back, he plugged his nose and went in. Four seconds later, he was back, face pale, with tears in his eyes. "Let me get a mask." More laughter. It wasn't even that funny, but people were in a good mood.

Carón soon returned carrying a face mask and some aerosol air freshener. With a serious look of determination, he bravely faced the stench emanating from the men's restroom. In the hallway, people speculated about whether Mr. Blanchard would ever return, and if so, whether he would be disfigured or 10 pounds lighter from vomiting. People were having a good time until Anta finally spoke up. "He's been in there 10 minutes already. Someone should go check on him."

As Shift, who had been volunteered by everyone, was about to go in, Carón returned. Shift let out his breath with obvious relief.

"Ladies and gentlemen, and Shift," Carón announced, "what we have here is a case of the ventilation system gone bad. I can fix it though."

Someone in the back shouted, "You're the man Carón!"

"Thank you, thank you. The problem is that it will take some time. The ventilation system allows our smells, from the kitchen and the restrooms, along with the carbon dioxide we expel when we breathe, to leave the bunker and escape at the surface. The odors and gases are treated just before they're let out above so that the smells don't draw attention to our location. But deep down here, the smells are just as we made them."

"Do you have to go outside?" Anta asked seriously.

"No. I shouldn't have to go outside, thankfully, but if we hadn't caught this now, we'd all be suffocating within a couple of days, or worse. The ventilation system keeps us alive by expelling particulates without allowing anything, no matter how microscopic, back in. It keeps us safe from Anthrax E, if it's working right. So, thank you to whoever caught this."

Dr. Porter received several pats on the back while he contemplated where he would sleep for the next few days.

51

It's time for our daily meeting. These are pretty gloomy affairs and nobody likes to sit here anymore. John stood up, looking pale and glum, just like the rest of us.

"Anthrax E has now spread throughout the world," he began. "There are few places remaining where it hasn't been reported. A few of the more desolate and remote locations around the globe appear to have been spared, for now; but that won't last. We all know it."

Indeed, the wind seems to have carried Anthrax E beyond the borders and lines drawn in the sand by our militaries and police forces. Of course, there's nobody policing those lines anyway. Anthrax E doesn't respect such arbitrary boundaries. This pandemic respects no thing and no person.

John continued, with no energy and what seemed to be the last of his breath, "The last worldwide estimate of infection, many days ago, was 2.1 billion, approximately one-fifth of the world's total population, with an estimated 1.4 billion of those people already dead."

Mom and Dad told me yesterday that the disease had spread to Egypt. They haven't found a safe zone or place to hide. While they aren't currently sick, they have no idea if they've been exposed, nor do they expect to be free from exposure anyway. They traveled out into the desert many days ago, but haven't found shelter apart from the hovercraft in which they travelled.

Dr. Shevchuk, in an attempt to bring us back and help us continue on our path, stated, with a little zeal, but not quite enough to make us celebrate, that there is hope. "My friends, we have just had a breakthrough. We've passed a critical junction in our experimentation and are now in a position to test one potential vaccine on live animals. Testing on animals was outlawed, worldwide, over 30 years ago, but I don't think anyone will mind now."

"Yurgi," Shift probed, "that means someone will need to go outside the bunker to gather some animals, right? Or do you have some little creatures hidden under your bed that we don't know about?" There was a little laughter, briefly.

"Yes, Shift. Someone will need to go outside. We will need to trap live animals. A dead animal obviously does us less good. Plus, the live animal must not be infected already. Here, outside this bunker, miles and miles away from civilization, we may just be lucky enough to find such animals. Unfortunately, I didn't think far enough ahead to gather animals weeks ago while the plague was still far away. I just didn't think . . ."

Dr. Shevchuk bowed his head.

"Hey, none of us thought that far ahead," John said, trying to comfort his mentor.

"Who do you propose to send?" Dr. Angel Robertson asked, a little too excitedly.

"I don't know. We need to decide that, and soon. Any proposals about how we go about that decision? Or, do we have any volunteers?"

"I'll go."

Threet "Street" Kimball raised his hand above his head, just like we learned in school! What a guy! He didn't hesitate. I've liked the man for a while now. While he was rich and talented and famous in the real world, he's been kind and helpful and sympathetic here in the bunker. Perhaps without the prospect of American football to define him, he's been searching for something meaningful by which to earn his right to live.

"Thank you Mr. Kimball. We'll need another volunteer," Yurgi said. "Let's all think about it for a while."

52

Just one day after I learned that my parents were still safe, the hope has been taken away from me. Mom and Dad have both become infected. Each will be dead within the week. I'm having trouble . . .

"Anta! Are you okay?" I dropped my food tray and ran toward Anta as she staggered and fell toward the wall. I had been watching her from across the small room where we were both taking a needed rest from our labors. I'd been having a hard time keeping my eyes off of her recently and it was a little disturbing. She's my friend and my colleague. But she's also been my constant companion over the last three and a half months. This time, I was glad I was watching.

"Anta! Somebody help me please!"

Dr. Thia Treggor, a radiation oncologist from Utah, had run over toward Anta just after I did. Together, we lifted Anta and took her down the hall, only about 40 paces, to her room and laid her on the bed. Thia left to get Dr. Marilyn Swenson, and a glass of water, while I tried to talk to my friend.

"Anta, can you hear me?" Her eyes were closed and her breathing was shallow. I must have sounded desperate. Desperation clouded my mind.

Thia arrived with a glass of water, and splashed some onto Anta's face. It worked, just like in the movies! Marilyn walked in right after.

"Shift! Oh, you're here. Thanks."

She was awake, but that was pretty lame after what she had just put me through.

"Anta, what happened?" I asked.

"I'm not sure, but I guess I just fainted."

"Do you feel okay?" Marilyn asked.

"Yes. I'm fine. Thank you."

Anta laid her head back on the pillow as I propped it up behind her. "Mom and Dad are sick. They just . . ." Anta's voice trailed off as she began to cry. Tears fell from her eyes and dropped onto her tank top. I wanted to wipe them away, but thought that might be too personal. I understood the pain.

Thia and Marilyn excused themselves from the room, Thia closing the door behind her. Sitting beside Anta's bed, I placed my hand on her left arm and stayed still. She cried. After a few moments, she placed her right hand on top of mine. We sat that way for a long time.

Finally, after her tears were spent, Anta apologized. "Shift, I'm sorry. I'm sorry."

"For what?" I asked, surprised.

"For crying like that. I knew they would die. *They* knew they would die. We've known it for weeks. I thought I was ready. They haven't even passed and I can't control myself. I'm sorry you had to see that."

"Anta, after what you've done for me, I'd be a real arse if I couldn't be here for you. You're my closest friend Anta. I'll sit by you until you tell me to leave, which I hope you won't do for a long time."

"Then thank you Shift. That means more to me than you can imagine."

Anta's eyes were puffy and red, but the tears had stopped. We talked for a while then, about her parents, and how they were coping. We talked about Hasani too.

"Hasani's still fine, but I don't think he'll ever leave. He'll die on the moon, with the rest of them, with little to do, nothing to see, nobody to love, and loneliness as his best friend. But at least he won't suffer physically from disease like the rest of us will."

Anta's grief is profound, which is a little disconcerting given that her parents are still alive. I guess she knows their days are numbered. They'll be dead within a few days, and she knows what that means as well as anybody. Anta knows what her parents' last days will be like. Perhaps that's the cause of her tremendous grief. It doesn't matter to me why she's sad. I'll sit by her, like she did for me, until I've worn out my welcome.

There's news of import to *our* current situation. Street Kimball and Lucky Rabene are headed outside today to find and trap animals. Apparently, Street was an avid hunter in his former life—of quarterbacks and animals. Lucky has pretty good skill with weapons as well, or so he told us. Hopefully they can trap animals and not kill them. Street's a big dude, and Lucky doesn't appear too gentle.

Their task is to proceed through a series of very specific directions to the locations of animals recently seen through the surveillance system, and which will also lead them away from any potential human contact. Additionally, they'll be fitted with chem suits very similar to the ones Anta and I wore in El-Alamein. Once they return, they and the animals will be separately isolated for many days, with numerous tests undertaken during that time, before they'll be able to fully rejoin us. They both say they're ready for all of that. Good for them!

Assuming they've accomplished their task, we expect Street and Lucky to come back by nightfall. In order to gather the required animal specimens, Lucky Rabene is currently teaching Street how to utilize a long-range stun-gun apparatus that will demobilize the prey, but not kill it. Nice. Leave it to the CIA.

APRIL 18, 2093—ANTA

Mom and Dad are still alive, but very near death. We said "goodbye" last night for the last time, while they were still coherent enough to talk. Ahhh, it's killing me.

Just when I think I've cried my last tear, they start up again. I feel so helpless, because I am. I don't look forward to telling Hasani, but I need to get the message to him, perhaps through Dr. Shevchuk on the IIA boards.

Anyway, Shift has been sending me cute little messages on my MEHD from around the compound. He's getting people to say something nice to me, or about me, and then sending them. I didn't think he was a romantic. Of course, he's probably not being romantic intentionally. He just lost his family too. We work together. He's not thinking about me that way. *Is he?* No. I doubt it. But it's romantic anyway and it's very nice.

53

"... hey, I knew I could do it!"

"Yeah Mike, you told us. You're the man!" Shift's mood was surprisingly light, just like nearly everybody else in the room. Dr. Shevchuk's testing on the animals brought back by Street and Lucky was going well. Dr. Shevchuk had already announced some of the results of his testing, earlier in the meeting. The affect was nearly instantaneous. There were smiles on mouths that hadn't turned upward in many, many days. Eyes that were drooping with sorrow and grief finally had a sparkle.

"Man, I knew I could get through. This is going to change everything! Well, not everything, but at least we can see it now." Mike had been trying for weeks to access security camera uplinks from USCAN in the hope that the group would be able to see what was really happening around the world. USCAN encryption codes, and the way to break through them, had been elusive—until now.

"So Mike, tell us how this works." Dr. Porter was a great archeologist and fine friend, but he was far from knowledgeable in the ways of electronics. He was one of those guys in school who didn't take his head out of the books—the paper kind, not the digital kind. What he lacked in the way of real-world knowledge though, he certainly made up for in the realm of very old, crumbling civilizations, which wasn't all that useful at the moment.

"Well, the Uniform Security Camera and Navigation system, or "USCAN", was originally built, and primarily maintained by the United States Department of Homeland Security starting in the late 2020s or something like that. After that, similar systems were developed and used all over the world. The original purpose, or so we've all been told, was to help police forces and the Department maintain both security and traffic flow in major cities."

"I have a feeling you don't believe that was the real purpose of USCAN," Shift remarked, with a smile.

"No. I don't." Mike returned the smile. "Prior to USCAN's inception, throughout the 1990s, lots of cities around the U.S. had a similar, but much more rudimentary system which was used, at first, to reduce traffic violations by monitoring and photographing traffic patterns at intersections. Nearly everybody finally came around to the idea that those cameras were probably unconstitutional. Then that system wasn't used anymore, or so we've been told.

"Anyway, as most of you probably know, since it was such a big deal in all of our history classes as kids, like a whole chapter or something, on September 11, 2001, some crazy terrorists hijacked four planes and flew them, one plane each, into the Pentagon in Washington D.C., each tower of the World Trade Center in New York City, and the fourth, into a field. Not long after that, like within weeks, the Department of Homeland Security was created as an agency of the United States federal government."

"What do you mean, 'they flew it into a field'? Why would a terrorist fly his plane into a field?" Shylene Aristorma asked.

"Well, apparently, when the terrorists tried to take over the plane, several of the passengers attacked the terrorists in the cockpit and forced the plane down. They think it was meant for Washington, D.C.; perhaps the capital or the White House. Some of the other passengers called loved ones on cell phones and sent video footage of the incident before they crashed. Everyone on board died."

"Amazing!"

"Yup. Anyway, between 2001 and 2027, governments, particularly in the U.S. and Europe, increased the watch on global terrorist organizations dramatically and tried to reduce the flow of information out of the country and into the hands of terrorists. At first, Americans didn't have a problem with that because they were all feeling pretty vulnerable. So, most people didn't really object to the increased intrusion into their personal lives; but over time, those intrusions became a menace. By 2027, however, Americans, and really, people all over the world, had grown so accustomed to the intrusion on their privacy that USCAN was initiated virtually undetected."

"So, USCAN kind of snuck up on us, eh?" asked Dr. Manford Stevens, a bacteriologist from Leduc, Alberta, Canada.

"Well, it snuck up on *us*—as in the United States; not on you, ya Hoser." This got laughs all around. Even Dr. Stevens. Of course, by now, he was used to the ribbing as the only Canadian in the group.

"Anyway, Americans, *from the U.S.*, and then later, people all over the world, finally realized, beginning in about 2031, that USCAN's real purpose wasn't to maintain security and traffic flow, but to watch people and track their comings and goings. By 2035 or so, in every major American city and most smaller cities, a person walking along one city block could be photographed by as many as five or six cameras. Any person could be monitored and tracked at nearly any time except when in his or her own home and a few private businesses.

"This violation of privacy finally led to massive conflicts in the streets between police forces and demonstrators. By 2037, the United States Supreme Court ruled that USCAN was an unconstitutional invasion of privacy and that it had to be shut down. It was, we're told. And in order to prevent terrorists and hackers from using the system to do bad things, all connections, which were fully wireless at that time, were disconnected, leaving the cameras in place without function. Similar events occurred all over the world, leaving very few systems operational."

"How do you know all of this?" John asked.

"I read, man. I read it weeks ago when I started trying to get in."

"Oh, reading; that's smart." John was grinning and others joined him.

"Are you finished … ? Okay. In 2068, 20 years after the IWO was created, a different form of USCAN was brought back on line for use in broadcasting news bulletins and information directly from the IWO. You've all seen it, on all the streets where those big Holos broadcast the news and show the game. The IWO preferred this method of broadcasting over the internet because it wasn't subject to transmission interference by the broad usage of the bandwidth by the masses of people connected to the internet.

"USCAN's cameras were connected to central holographic displays. The reason you can be in one city and see one news program delivered from the IWO, and someone else can be in another city at the same time, seeing a different story is because the cameras' and the Holos' connectivity to satellite placement applications determine what news might be most important to any particular region and then broadcast news tailored to those individual locations.

"Now, 25 years later, I, and maybe others if they're as awesome as me, have figured out a way to use the cameras as they were originally intended—to watch the people." The fake evil grin on his face, and the menacing laugh, like an evil mad scientist, brought the group to laughter again. It *really* was a different kind of meeting.

"So, what's it good for then?" Shift asked.

"We're able to see, with a few virtual swipes, almost any place in the United States or around the world! I can use USCAN right now, and see, on the Holo, exactly what is happening in Rome, or Calcutta, or Jamaica, or even Leduc, Canada, if I felt like it." Dr. Stevens laughed with the rest—a pretty good-natured fellow really.

APRIL 20, 2093—SHIFT

After our staff meeting today, Mike and I, and a few others who were scheduled for breaks, walked down the long hall from the conference room to the computer lab. The lab was full of Holos. But it also had older computer monitors and old computer terminals that took up whole sections of the space under desks. They were all dark. Instead, Mike was using newer computer terminals that sat nicely on one square inch of a desk, only two inches high. Mike had also furnished "his" space, as he called it, with a couch and a matching loveseat from the break room. I've never asked him what he used those for. I seriously doubt he watches movies or plays the virtgames in here.

What we saw on the Holos was a little shocking. Each one depicted a three-dimensional scene from somewhere in the world—live.

"How long has this been going on?" I asked. We expected there would be riots and vandalism after the conspiracy theories that had been circulating for days now. It was bound to occur. But we never expected to see the violence that was now displayed before us. Through the security camera linkups, we saw whole cities and towns around the world in flames, although mostly in Europe and Australia. It made sense. There were a lot more people alive in those places when the conspiracy first began its terrible circulation. Dead people don't start fires.

"Several days I guess." Mike's reply was a little too nonchalant.

But the violence and chaos wasn't restricted to those continents.

"Look at that one," Dr. Steve Porter said, pointing to a holo just off to the left of the center of Mike's command chair. "That's just over in Boston, right?"

On that monitor, we could see part of Boston and an adjacent suburb, less than 100 miles outside our bunker. It looked like looting and rioting were fairly widespread at one point, but probably died off a few days ago since so many people were sick or already dead.

"Yeah, I know," Mike replied. "I've been watching that one pretty closely. It makes me nervous." Mike was clearly more concerned with what was happening close to home than he was with the majority of the violence and destruction in front of us.

Even though only a few buildings were on fire in Boston, particularly in the government section of the city, large portions of the city were littered with broken windows and blowing trash, rotting food, broken electronics, and even clothes.

"It's kind-of surprising to see people still walking in the streets," I remarked. "They don't look so good though, do they?"

"Nah," Mike replied. "It's like they have nowhere to go and nothing to do, but they can't just lie down and die."

"They look like zombies! All drooling and bumping into things." Every one of us in the room turned to look at Dr. Angel Robertson, who had just come in. She was literally bouncing on the balls of her feet, with apparent excitement. She looked and sounded like an evil villain who couldn't wait to get her hands on all of those people and turn them to the dark side.

"Dude," John said, "you're a little sick, you know." Dr. Robertson didn't acknowledge the rebuke. There was a gleam in her eyes, but she didn't say anything else.

John was right, it was a bit inappropriate. But Angel was right too. The people were just wandering around, like zombies, although we knew they weren't. They were just sick.

There were also bodies on the ground, thousands of them, all apparently dead.

"Man, the stink out there must be awful with all those dead bodies," Dr. Porter said, with wonder. "I wonder what they're all doing outside instead of in their homes—the dead ones and the live ones."

"Strange," I replied. "Maybe the conspiracy theories from last week brought them out. Perhaps they thought they could get some free stuff from the mall. But they were already sick, or soon became sick, so they had no strength to return home."

Mike zoomed in on a few of the bodies. One of them had a bullet hole in his forehead!

"Holy Crap! That dude was shot!" I don't know who said it. I was staring at the monitor in horror, like everybody else. Murders are so foreign nowadays that something like that would have made headline news all around the globe.

"Yeah, I've seen a few others like him too. It's crazy," Mike replied.

"Look at that one!" Dr. Steve Porter said, pointing to a spot on the screen about 50 feet farther up the street from the murder victim. "Look how he's all sprawled out."

Mike zoomed in on the person in question and several people gasped.

"It's a she and she looks like she's been beaten . . ." someone in the group said.

"And molested!" another said.

Mike became sullen and quickly changed the zoom, turning the camera to focus on another street.

"I've seen enough," Dr. Porter said as he turned to leave. Then he turned back to the group.

"It really is remarkable," Dr. Porter said. "While death is at our very door, from something we can't control, even more carnage is raining down upon those not dead from Anthrax E—from their fellow humans. Are people really being shot and mutilated by strangers?"

"Why?" I asked, to nobody in particular. "They can't be fighting over food or clothes. Maybe it's just insanity caused by the fear of death."

"Who knows?" Mike said. "But I'm glad I'm in here." Several others nodded their heads and mumbled agreement.

As the group slowly dispersed in silence, I thought, again, about our world. My heart ached looking at the death of so many people out there, especially the apparent murder and molestation. Just thinking about what it must have been like out there, or what it is probably still like, makes my skin crawl. And it's world-wide! Several of the people who just left this room, who had held their heads high and laughed at the jokes in our meeting only a few minutes ago, had tears streaming down their faces as they walked away in silence. I'm having a hard time myself.

I believe I'm a good person, but how would I act in the same situation? I sit here in safety, watching my fellow beings destroy each other, and it's easy for me to judge them harshly. But would I really be different?

It's probably only hours or days, at most, before Anthrax E destroys those people out there anyway. Perhaps, for some, death by human hands is, or would be more welcome than the four or five days of suffering and pain that awaits them if they survive their neighbors in the street. It's a crazy, messed-up world.

54

I'm not a religious nut, nor am I as faithful as I should be. I guess I'm somewhere in the middle—good but not great. But I went to a Christian church-like meeting this afternoon with some of the others, held in the conference room. I wanted a little peace and solace after what we saw on Mike's holos this morning.

I've been to these meetings before, but this one was different. Instead of a bland speech or lecture by someone in the group, quoting scripture that warns us to repent of our sins and pray more, several people read short selections of recent speeches given by Christian leaders around the world.

Each person who contributed to the meeting read something from a Christian leader who had influenced his or her own life. It was quite good. There was definitely a spirit of camaraderie and hope in the room. As I understand it, leaders of most of the major religions have already made, or are now making declarations to their followers.

Since this was a Christian service, I didn't get to hear what non-Christian leaders were saying. I'm sure those speeches exist too.

There were a few that inspired me.

Dr. Juan Gamez, a viral neurologist from Mexico City played a portion of a speech by Pope Andrew II dated yesterday, April 19. Of course, since the Pope is from Honduras, his speech was in Spanish.

Dr. Gamez translated for us after we watched the Pope's holographic image kneel before a crucifix and cross himself before speaking.

My fellow beings under God, with a lack of alacrity or clarity, yet a desire to inspire, I speak to you from my humble sanctuary under St. Peter's Basilica in Rome.

The Bible has warned of this time and we are now seeing a fulfillment of prophecy, which is both wonderful and frightening to behold. These times are considerable based upon the depth and breadth of the current calamity which disrupts and destroys our society. Of course, we recognize that this time is one of great sorrow and anguish for all, but that it need be necessarily more sorrowful for those who are wicked and are, and will, die in their sin. Conversely, upon leaving this life, great joy and peace may be had by those who have no sin to hide from God.

In Revelations, the Lord declared that the fearful, and unbelieving, and the abominable, and murderers, and whoremongers, and sorcerers, and idolaters, and the liars, shall have their part in the lake which burneth with fire and brimstone: which is the second death; but Matthew declared, gloriously, that the righteous shall have life eternal! Oh then, how great need have we to repent and turn to God that we may have eternal life!

Let us, His church, not fear God's wrath. Let us look forward to His eternal glory. Be at peace, but be mindful of your sins. The end is nigh for many of God's children.

Dr. Manford Stevens, from Leduc, played a few words from a recorded speech by Bernard Q. Jorgensen, President of the Church of Jesus Christ of Latter Day Saints, dated April 13, 2093:

Brothers and sisters, more than ever before in the history of our marvelous world, we are experiencing the sorrow and despair that have, at times, consumed mankind. Likewise, more than ever before, we have need of the loving and tender mercies of our Heavenly Father, who wants nothing more than for us to return to His presence following our sojourn on this Earth.

Through this time of terrible tribulation, when many around us, even ourselves, are sick and dying, let us cleave unto the Word of God and our knowledge of the eternal blessings that await the righteous in the next world. Let us repent of our wrongdoings. Let us come unto Christ through service, love, peace, kindness, and in all other respects, a Christ-like attitude.

We may yet have opportunities before us to love and serve our families and neighbors. The pandemic which now infests and floods all the corners of this Earth, like the waters at the time of Noah, may be too strong for our modern medicine and science to hinder; but it is not so great as to destroy our faith, our spirits, or our ability to give of ourselves for the common good. Remember that while our physical bodies will surely die, through the suffering and death of our Lord, Jesus Christ, we may all receive eternal life!

I plead with you, my brothers and sisters, to turn to God, and to lead your families toward His throne. In your last hours of mortality, pray, read the scriptures, follow the words of Christ as revealed by his prophets, both modern and ancient, and spend your remaining time here on Earth teaching your children the principles of salvation.

Be of good cheer. Your Heavenly Father loves you! He knows the desires of your heart. Have faith, repent if you need to, and endure to the end. Let us be as the Savior who, when faced with impending death, had a sure knowledge that He had performed the work for which He had been sent to Earth. Let us continue with faith to finish our earthly work, so that when we are called home, we will be welcomed by our Heavenly Father, His son Jesus Christ, and our loved ones who have already passed beyond the veil. May the Lord bless us all.

Finally, Dr. Nelise Fabrisio, an astronomical physicist from California, quoted from a speech by Charles Parham Lightfoot, a popular American Evangelist, dated April 18, 2093. He was interesting to listen to as he mimicked a southern accent while reading:

The words of God through the prophet Joel are now being fulfilled, when he foretold of the last days saying: 'I will show wonders in the heaven above and signs on the earth below, blood and fire and billows of smoke. The sun will be turned to darkness and the moon to blood before the coming of the great and glorious day of the Lord. And everyone who calls on the name of the Lord will be saved.'

Without doubt, the Lord has begun to show his strength and to show the world that He is, and that He rules from on high. The moon has, although figuratively, turned to blood with the descent of the plague therefrom. To the Christian, you need not fear, for Jesus will welcome you home! You have believed in Him, even through your trials. You are saved through your belief in Him! To the unbeliever, we pray for your soul. It is now too late to call upon your God and beg for His mercy. The hour has passed.

The Rapture is nigh! Many of those who believe have already been taken up to Jesus and spared this time of great trial which remains for those left on Earth. Many others will continue to be spared; But woe unto you who do not believe, for death and hell await you for an everlasting torment.

Okay, the last part of that one was less inspiring—a little creepy really; but the messages were all similar. This life is not the end. We continue to live, although without our disease-ridden bodies, after this life. "Church" was good today. I'm feeling better, although I'm sure it will be short lived. Maybe I'll go again, and get Anta to go with me.

55

"We're exhausted Shift," John said, stifling a yawn. "We've all been working around the clock for days. I've hardly slept since we got the animals."

It was true. Nobody had slept much since the animals arrived because the animals can't shut it. But Yurgi and his crew really had been working, with very little sleep, since Street and Lucky brought in the animals for testing.

"Are you getting close? I asked. "I mean, are there any positive results?"

"Yeah, Yurgi said he's going to announce his test results tomorrow at the meeting," John said.

"That's great, I hope. Why aren't you excited? Is it bad?" I asked, nervously.

"Actually, I don't know the results," he replied. "I haven't been part of that phase of testing. So I don't know either. So what's up with Anta's family?" John asked, changing subject abruptly.

"Actually, her parents both died a couple of days ago, but Anta didn't even tell me until today."

"That's kinda weird, isn't it? John asked.

"Well, maybe. She's pretty private about her family. I've been so worried about her, but I wasn't going to ask. Maybe I should have, but it tore her up when she first learned they were sick. I hoped that it wouldn't be so bad for her when they actually died."

"Haven't you talked to her? I thought you liked this girl."

"Uh, yeah, I do, but . . . anyway, I haven't seen her much lately. She hasn't come to talk to me, but I haven't seen her moping around either. She told me today that she's sad, and that was about the end of the discussion."

"Man, if I had a woman like Anta around, I'd make sure I was the only one giving her any comfort. I'd go talk to her if I was you."

"Yeah, you're probably right. I think I better do that."

I didn't know what I would say to Anta. It was foolish of me to have waited so long. Now, it would be awkward. John was right, I'd been an idiot. It should have been me comforting her. I knew that none of the men here still had wives or girlfriends alive on the outside. And it was impossible to know how many women would be alive out there when this was over. I needed to let Anta know of my feelings for her before some other guy beat me to it.

But how could I be thinking about scoring with Anta when the entire world was on the brink of collapse? Nearly every person in the bunker had lost his or her entire family. Those with family remaining alive on the outside don't expect any miracles to occur. Even if Shevchuk had awesome news to announce tomorrow, it would be too late for just about everyone. There won't be any way to get a vaccine out there to the people with any real speed. Who would do it, and how?

By now, it's almost certain that no safe haven exists on our planet, save the bunkers like this one. Nine days ago, it was estimated that more than two billion people were already infected or dead. With the inclusion of the world-wide violence, death and infection rates must be nearing, or even surpassing, three and a half billion. The world's living human population could be down to hundreds of thousands within a month. And those still alive by then will be spread out over the entire globe. How many people are immune? Will they figure out that they are immune? There has to be more than just Neirioui Safar and her daughter Suvan. Other people will be safe, at least for a while because they're hiding out in bunkers like us. Others will be safe if they've found a place to hide, and no wind or birds have brought the plague near them; but for how long?

I pondered this as I walked down the hallway toward Anta's room. When I arrived, I stood there a moment, listening. Hearing nothing from inside, I knocked quietly on her door.

"Down here," a voice replied from a darkened corner at the end of the hall.

I walked toward the voice and found Anta there, with Dr. Andrew Jones' arms wrapped around her. Anta didn't look up. She was crying into Andrew's chest. Apparently, Anta and Jones had made up after Jones' insults a couple months ago.

Jones winked at me, knowingly, as if to say, "You blew it and now she's mine." My heart crumpled as I took in the scene. I felt dejected. An inner conflict was beginning to brew. I didn't know what to do next. But I did know that I needed to respect Anta's wishes, whatever they were. So I didn't say anything more. I turned on my toes and quietly walked back down the hall in the direction from which I had come.

APRIL 25, 2093
STAFF MEETING
HIDDEN BUNKER NEAR BOSTON

"Ladies and Gentlemen, we have had a significant breakthrough!" The room was quiet, almost silent, until Dr. Yurgi Shevchuk said those words. Then the quiet broke and 17 voices began to speak at once. From four separate holos along the wall at the front of the room, the voices of Street, Lucky, Mrs. Neirioui Safar and her daughter Suvan Safar joined the cacophony of noise.

The tension that had at first existed in the cramped conference room broke like a dam, letting the nervous waves of energy free. But nobody was listening to what anybody else was saying.

After several long moments, the group began to quiet, realizing that Yurgi was standing there, smiling, and waiting to continue.

"Although it was over a week ago that we finally succeeded in the creation of a difficult process that appeared to offer us the ability to proffer a life-saving vaccination to living cells, not until yesterday did we have near-conclusive data confirming that such a process may prove useful in aiding the living cells of human beings in the creation of an antibody to ward off the effects of Anthrax E!

"English please," Street begged.

"Of course, Street. My apologies to you and our other non-technical team members." Yurgi looked around the room, then turned back to direct his next comments to Street on the holo. "As a result of yours and Lucky's efforts 10 days ago, Street, to collect and bring us live animals, we have been able to test immunity to Anthrax E by injecting some of the animals, under controlled conditions, with a concoction made, in part, from the living cells from our immune donors. Then we exposed the animals to the live bacteria. The testing appears to be successful. The animals appear to be immune. But there is still work to be done. Just because the procedure works on animals doesn't automatically mean it will work on humans; nor does it mean that all humans will respond in the same manner."

"Touchdown!" Street cheered, throwing his arms into the air, while everyone else cheered. Even Yurgi was excited. His usually calm persona was gone, and in its place, a happy child stood, bouncing on his toes.

"But there's also some disturbing news," John said after allowing the crowd a few more minutes of excitement. The group quieted again.

John continued: "We haven't received any communication from any United States governmental agency in more than three weeks. The IWO hasn't contacted us in nearly a week. Even the U.S. leaders we believed were tucked away safely inside bunkers like ours have stopped talking."

"Where have they all gone?" Mrs. Chrissy Houghton asked.

"Well, as you can probably guess, it seems possible, even probable, that the lack of communication is the result of illness and death. But what is curious is that we were told that the top ranking U.S. leaders, just like leaders around the world, were all in bunkers like ours."

"So do you think Anthrax E got into some of those safe-houses?" Anta asked. "Or are they just so despondent or afraid that they aren't talking."

"Would you like to know what I think?" Mike asked. When nobody responded, he continued. "I think they may be dead." He said no more as all faces turned to him, most staring blankly.

"And why is that?" Shift prodded after several seconds of silently waiting for Mike to continue.

"I didn't want to say it in this group meeting without doing some more checking, but I saw something strange this morning."

After a short pause, and a sigh, Mike continued, clearly uncomfortable with the news he was about to share. "Let me start a little differently. As you know, we don't know exactly where any other bunkers are located. It's all pretty secretive. While I haven't been able to learn exact coordinates of other bunkers, I have been able to decipher enough information to find cities where some other bunkers are located.

"One of the bunkers is in New Jersey. I've developed a friendship with my counterpart in that bunker over the past few weeks. They have 13 people in there, but I don't know if any are government. Anyway, recently my colleague gave me his exact coordinates, and I gave him ours."

There was some murmuring, but nobody said anything out loud. Yurgi's mouth tightened just a little. The trust and respect for Mike and his abilities had grown tremendously over the weeks, but this was a breach of security protocols. Everybody waited for Mike to continue.

"I know that was something I wasn't supposed to do, and it could be dangerous, but I had a theory and I wanted to test it. My colleague and I decided to watch each other's bunkers to see whether anything came of it. There was a very specific reason for this.

"I'm sure you all remember the bathroom incident a couple weeks ago where the ventilation system screwed up. Well, the same thing happened to the New Jersey bunker a few days before ours. After our incident, because my colleague had told me about their malfunction, I did some checking in online records from the various bunkers. Because I knew the cities where many of the bunkers were located, I could see a pattern. Starting with a bunker in Alabama, ventilation systems started malfunctioning. After Alabama, bunkers in Tennessee, North Carolina, two in Virginia, Maryland, Arkansas, the one in New Jersey, our bunker, and then finally, a bunker in Ohio all had ventilation malfunctions, in that order. Since the Ohio malfunction, there haven't been any others that I'm aware of, but I haven't checked for a few days.

"There are some bunkers with no problems. Those bunkers appear to be newer. The older ones like ours are the ones having ventilation problems. I haven't been able to learn what was happening to the other ventilation systems, but their computers showed a malfunction of some kind. I presumed that the malfunctions were probably all the same.

"The interesting part is that the sequence and timing of the malfunctions seems to coincide with the timing and sequence of the spread of Anthrax E throughout the eastern states. So, the theory I developed after my research in the day or two following our ventilation malfunction was that, perhaps, the malfunctions had something to do with the spread of Anthrax E. It was a strange idea, but this whole thing is strange, so I followed up on my idea.

"My concern was whether the ventilation malfunction could be bad for those inside the affected bunkers. Obviously, if the malfunction had something to do with Anthrax E, it could be problematic for those inside. But I couldn't figure out how Anthrax E could be related.

"So, I talked with Carón about it. He didn't think there was any relation. But he didn't rule out one possibility, albeit very slim. He thinks there's a remote possibility that the various ventilation systems, while attempting to perform the function of cleaning out the air from the inside, could have actually been struggling with that process due to some kind of altered atmospheric pressure on the outside. That theoretic struggle may have then led to a malfunction.

"Carón confirmed that, when he worked on our ventilation system, it was not actually plugged up like he originally thought. It wasn't working and the computer said it was clogged, but that wasn't the case. He was able to get it going by simply reentering access codes. I then confirmed with my friend in New Jersey that the same fix was enacted in their bunker. So, something appears to have caused the systems to stop working, and it likely happened the same way in the other bunkers.

"Talking with Dr. Justin Case, our resident computer science professor and fusion physicist, he said that, although unlikely, it is remotely possible that Anthrax E spores may be dense enough to cause a shift in the air pressure outside. If so, then the theoretical variance from the usual air pressure outside each bunker, in sequence, could have resulted in ventilation system malfunctions."

"Wow!" Shift said. "That's quite a theory. So, what is it that caused you concern this morning?"

"Well, this morning, I started to wonder whether that kind of problem, or something else like it could allow for a reverse flow of some kind—like a back draft from a burning building. I talked with Carón about this too, and he didn't think this was likely either, but again, he didn't dismiss it outright. So, here's the thought I had, but simplified. And, Dr. Case confirmed the *possibility* just before this meeting.

"A back draft occurs when a compartment fire has little or no ventilation, leading to the slowing of gas-phase combustion due to the lack of oxygen. If oxygen is then rapidly re-introduced to the compartment, by opening a door or window to a closed room for example, combustion will restart, often very quickly. The gases will be re-heated by the combustion and will expand quickly because of the rapidly increasing temperature.

"Here's the part that I was worried about: in a fire, firefighters are looking for instances where a room may be pulling air into itself, like through a crack. If they see that phenomenon occurring, they evacuate immediately because that's a strong indication that a back draft is imminent. Due to pressure differences between the closed room and the outside of that room, puffs of smoke are sometimes drawn back into the enclosed space from which they came. That's how the term back draft originated.

"So, my thought was, while the ventilation system was malfunctioning, it wasn't expressing air. It was holding the air inside. If the pressure difference between the now-closed-up bunker and the outside became too disproportionate, could air, like the puffs of smoke from a fire, be drawn back into the bunker?"

Suddenly, there were several voices talking at once.

One voice rose above the crowd. "Why the hell didn't you tell us about this before, Mike?" Dr. Latisha Bodily, a virologist from Connecticut, shouted to be heard above the crowd. "Do you think we're too stupid or something?"

Several others murmured in assent to Dr. Bodily's question.

Dr. Shevchuk had been quiet since his announcement, but spoke up, forcefully, "I need for all of you to be quiet . . . now." The silence was instantaneous, except for Dr. Bodily.

"Why should we be quiet? This man may have put our lives in jeopardy, and for what? And what gives you the right to tell us what to do?" Dr. Bodily's questions were asked with such hostility that even Dr. Shevchuk appeared surprised, momentarily. But this wasn't the first time Dr. Bodily had questioned Dr. Shevchuk verbally in front of the others. This would be the last.

"Dr. Bodily," Dr. Shevchuk said slowly and quietly, but with such energy as to cause every person in the room to feel the force behind his words, "I need for you to understand something, now. This is *my* lab, *my* facility, and *my* operation. You will listen when I talk. You will jump when I say 'jump', and you will shut your mouth when I tell you to shut your mouth. Am I understood?"

Dr. Bodily's body was shaking, but she slowly and painfully nodded her head. Then she looked at the ground and didn't raise her eyes again until the meeting had adjourned.

"Thank you. Now, Mike, Dr. Bodily asks a good question. Why haven't we heard about this until now?"

"Well, I just put it all together this morning Yurgi. I only thought about the back draft theory very late last night, and Dr. Case just confirmed the possibility this morning. I'm sorry I didn't speak up before, but my theory was only that—a theory. And it didn't even seem like a very good theory until now. I'm sorry. Really."

"I understand," Yurgi replied. "And the rest of us will try to understand if we don't already. But more importantly, even if we knew before, what would we have done? Would we go outside so as not to risk being infected inside? No. Nothing has changed but our knowledge. Ignorance, at least for a while, was bliss. But now, the next question is, Mike, what did you see today that made you worry?"

"Well, because of what I saw, I approached Dr. Case this morning. Before witnessing this strange occurrence, I hadn't been able to piece it all together enough to even form a coherent question."

"Mike, what did you see?" Yurgi was becoming impatient, clearly worried like everyone else. But Mike didn't feel any anger coming from Dr. Shevchuk—just urgency.

"I was checking current and past video feeds from some of the cities where I know bunkers are located. Mostly, I was just looking for anomalies of any kind. I didn't know what to expect or even what I was looking for.

"When I got to Cheyenne, Wyoming, I started with a city-wide overview, as usual. I was just about to zoom in on the downtown area when I noticed heavy smoke on the east side of town. The smoke wasn't strange by itself—buildings are burning all over the world. What was strange was that some of the smoke looked like it was falling rather than rising. I zoomed in. The smoke was coming from a small burning building and actually looked like it was being sucked into the house next door. I immediately checked online records and saw that the Cheyenne facility, another old bunker, was experiencing a ventilation malfunction at that exact moment."

"Damn!" John said. Others exclaimed similarly. The volume again rose as the group began speculating again.

"Quiet!" Yurgi shouted, but not in anger. Again, nearly-instantaneous silence.

"Indeed, John," Mike replied. "That's just what I thought. I immediately called Dr. Case. He looked at the images and that was when he confirmed the possibility that I had, until then, only speculated about. It appeared that a back draft-type event was occurring in Cheyenne. This was less than an hour ago."

"Mike, are you saying that any bunker with a malfunctioning ventilation system could have possibly been infiltrated, or could still be infiltrated by Anthrax E spores?" Shift asked. He, like the others, was hardly able to grasp what he was hearing.

"Yes, that's what I'm saying," Mike replied, solemnly. "But the good news, at least for us, is that Anthrax E never got in here, right?"

"The ventilation problem occurred on April 14th," Carón said. "And I had it back up and running late that evening. That was 11 days ago."

"We should be fine then," Yurgi said, speaking calmly again. "Let's pray the others are too. Mike, I want you, Carón, and Justin to call Cheyenne. Tell them what you've seen and what you suspect could occur there. Just so they're ready. Mike, find records for every other bunker you can, worldwide. I know that will take some time. Get help from others. Start with the places where the infection first arose, then move on to the more recent sites. It seems obvious that the older sites are more vulnerable. Once you start compiling your lists, I want the three of you to begin making contact with as many sites as you can. Everybody else, let's get back to work."

56

Wow! What a meeting. I'm beginning to think Mike is a genius. And Dr. Shevchuk, even though he's been our de facto leader for months, has just shown us how great he can be. He's no tyrant though. He's a good man, and I'm certain he won't ask us to do something that doesn't need doing. At the age of 74, he's also the oldest among us. Thankfully, his health is full and his habits, assuming he maintains them, should help him continue in health for thirty or forty more years, unless Anthrax E has its way.

Unfortunately, there's one person here who doesn't play well with others. Dr. Latisha Bodily, a virologist from Connecticut I think, really got under Yurgi's skin today. She's such a smartass. Yesterday, she and Shift almost had an actual fist fight. It would've been cool! I would love to see Shift beat that lady down, even though he's probably too gentlemanly to hit a woman.

Anyway, their argument centered on the potential methodologies for the distribution of any vaccine that might be created. That's something we've been talking about these days—a lot.

Shift had suggested again, as we've all discussed several times, that the best approach would be to travel around in a small group, or several groups, loaded with vaccine, and administer the vaccine to every living person we see. His thinking is that, if someone can be saved, he or she should be.

Dr. Bodily vehemently argued that such a method would be "madness". She insisted that only those deemed fit and able should be vaccinated in order to ensure the "survival of the fittest". She seemed so angry about it.

Upon Shift's suggestion that all life has value and that each person, regardless of their current situation, should have the opportunity to live, Dr. Bodily became enraged. I don't know why. Taking several steps toward Shift, who bests her in height by more than six inches and in weight by at least 50 pounds, Dr. Bodily began to rain down flawed arguments, in virtual torrents, in favor of the survival of only those who have the health, stamina, appearance, intelligence, energy, and motivation to ensure that our race can continue after this crisis. She said this is the perfect opportunity to purify the human race. Yeah, she actually said that—out loud.

Shift reminded her that Adolf Hitler had the same agenda, which caused her face to go bright red and her body to quake with rage. I guess she knows enough about history to know who Adolf Hitler was.

Thankfully, some of the gentlemen around, who had until this time listened attentively to the arguments of both sides, stepped in and restrained Dr. Bodily. It's a good thing too; if it had come to blows, she would have faired much worse than Shift. I wouldn't have cared though. She's psycho.

After Dr. Bodily was physically escorted to her room to ponder her approach to verbal disagreements, a small group of us who had listened to the arguments on both sides of the debate sided with Shift, again.

Today is the second time, in two days, that Dr. Bodily has appeared unstable. Yesterday it was Shift, but today, she chose an even more formidable opponent—one she didn't see coming. I hope Yurgi's reproach humbled her a bit. Otherwise, she might pick a fight that doesn't end only in a verbal reprimand.

In any event, even though Shift's approach is how we'll likely proceed, as it stands, only the "fittest" will survive anyway, since not many people beyond those already housed in bunkers are likely to live;

and, we know that most of the government-built and operated bunkers were housed with people whom the government deemed to be among the "fittest" in our society. And now we have reason to believe that even some of the "fittest" may have died. Of course, even amongst our small group, I'm sure there would be disagreement in opinion as to what constitutes "fittest".

APRIL 30, 2093—SHIFT

Three days ago, Mike was finally able to access the last IWO USCAN system—somewhere out in China. Even though we've been looking at USCAN daily for weeks, taking turns, for hours on end, we've spent the last three days carefully looking at live footage from around the world. We've been systematically documenting what we see in each country and in the various major cities across the globe.

It's been a miserable and depressing task. Dr. Nelise Fabrisio and Dr. Annabelle Wentworth, a couple of geniuses, have done some crazy, complicated calculations. Based upon our records and viewings, they estimate that as many as 5.5 *billion* people have now died from Anthrax E and/or the widespread violence that exists outside our protected bunker!

Using those same mathematical calculations, the good doctors estimate that, by May 15, just over two weeks from now, over 9 *billion* people will be dead. By the end of May, all that will be left alive are those who are immune, those left in bunkers, those who may have found some kind of temporary shelter, and those who may be vaccinated, if any. The prospects are awful. Even though the mood around here has become better as a result of Dr. Shevchuk's recent successes, this news is awful and frightening. I don't know how to express it in any other way.

The Net these days has very little new information about anything of substance. There aren't many people left to input the stuff. What *is* going up on the Net, besides disgusting images of death by still-living psychopaths, are speeches from religionists around the world who are preaching fire and damnation. Others are preaching salvation and eternal life. Political leaders have mostly vanished. Either they're dead or they've gone into hiding, using their status to secure placement in one of the several bunkers that have been built over the past 60 days worldwide.

Where do we go from here? Anta and I have talked about that question a dozen times over the last month. What is there to do? I feel such a pull of intense emotion threatening to drown me in sorrow. But I also have feelings of hope.

Dr. Shevchuk's team is getting closer and closer to a human vaccine. The animals they began testing about two weeks ago are still alive! We expect that, any day now, Dr. Shevchuk will announce a plan to test his vaccine on a human subject. Who that will be is unknown. Perhaps it should be me.

While I could easily suffer a horrifying and painful death under the tests, my chance of survival is slim anyway, just like everybody else. Certainly, any person's survival will be limited and miserable into the foreseeable future. I imagine there are others who are thinking similar thoughts. It may be that many of us will volunteer to be tested. I'll be thinking and praying on the matter.

57

MAY 1, 2093—DR. STEVEN PORTER

Jon is alive!! At least he was 3 weeks ago. I can't believe it! I've got to get to him!

How can this be? Maybe he's immune. The young mother and her daughter who are here from Egypt are each immune, so we know it can happen. The medical doctors here tell us that the Safars' immunity is genetic and was passed from mother to daughter. That means that maybe I'm immune too, because, clearly, my sweet wife was not.

Mike came across a post from Jon this morning while scouring the Net for survivor posts. Apparently, Jon's been using different message boards to try to contact me, or anyone.

APRIL 9, 2093
NET POST: JON PORTER
(14-YEAR-OLD SON OF DR. STEVEN PORTER)

Mom is dead. Katie and Shanna died soon after. Baby Justin died last while I held him in my arms. I cried all the tears I had when he died last week, just after my sisters. Then came the fear. Dad is somewhere on the east coast, but I don't know where. I was trying to contact him using the access ports Mom was using, but that didn't work. Mom never told me how to contact Dad. I think she wasn't supposed to.

The heating at the house went out for some reason yesterday. I don't know how to operate the heat, but we have an old, portable natural gas heater in the basement that grandpa gave us a few years back. I brought it upstairs. While I was trying to start the little fire with some matches, I made a mistake or something. The awesome house Dad built for us is now a heap of garbage. I blew up my house. The fire from that little match should not have been so big, but somehow it was.

I burned myself a little, but it's cool. I'm now across the street at the Sorenson's house. They aren't here, neither are their bodies. So I don't know what happened to them. Nobody burned the Sorenson's house down though, so I guess I'll stay here for now. I'm using Mr. Sorenson's computer to upload this journal entry to a ton of public Net servers, hoping that Dad will find it, read it and know what happened to us.

I've been alone for eight days. I don't know if anybody on my street is alive. I look out the windows and I can't see a single person, alive or dead. I feel really good though, except for the fear. I hear sounds in this big, strange house, and every sound I hear seems like it's coming from behind a closed window or door. There's probably some maniac trying to get in, grab all of the Sorenson's fancy stuff, and then kill me. I'm not too valuable, but I feel like I have to protect this house I'm borrowing. I guess there's probably nobody out there anyway.

It's kinda weird that I'm alive. The news channels, before they crapped out, told us that the infection spreads so fast that if we get anywhere near someone who's sick, we'll get sick too. I don't know if that's all true though, since everyone in my family is dead (except Dad I hope) and I'm not even sick. Maybe I'm immune to it or something. I don't know if that would be good or bad. How would I know? Do I have to stay in my neighbor's house by myself for the rest of my life?

Dad, if you read this, I don't know how you can contact me, or whether you can. If you're safe and can reach me, I'm at the Sorenson's house. I can't find any kind of communicator to give you their numbers. I'll probably stay here for a long time, until everyone else in town is dead. Then, I don't know what I'll do.

Jon's post gives me hope! I grieve for my Mary and the kids, but I've spent all of my tears on them already. I've assumed they were dead for a long time, since I haven't received any communication from Mary since March 30, when all was well in my home. Thereafter, they must have gotten sick right away since I didn't hear from them again. I know that this will hit me tonight, as I lay in bed preparing for sleep, but for now, even though Jon was with them when it happened, he didn't get sick.

I have to go to him, but that can't happen until there's a vaccine. Maybe Yurgi will let me out of this bunker if I'm immune. But the only way to find that out is if I'm purposefully infected. Can I volunteer to test the vaccine? I don't know if they'll let me. Of course, I'll be posting messages daily, on every public message board I can find on the Net, hoping that Jon will see that I am waiting for him, and reply.

MAY 2, 2093
NET POST: JON PORTER
(14-YEAR-OLD SON OF DR. STEVEN PORTER)

DAD! I saw your message! I'm still alive! The Sorenson's house is great, but I'm scared and want you to come home. There's nobody on our street. I haven't gone outside in a long time and I want to play ball or golf, or do anything really. Come home, please!

MAY 2, 2093
NET POST: DR. STEVEN PORTER

Jon! It's so good to hear from you! I have thanked God a hundred times in the last few minutes for the fact that you are alive! I want you to know how proud I am of you! Your age hasn't allowed you to experience all the things that would be required to survive in this world, and yet, you've done it! My wonderful son!

I will come to you as soon as I can. I can't possibly know how hard things are for you, but please understand that I can't leave this compound until there is a vaccine. I have learned that immunity to Anthrax E is inherited, meaning that IF you are immune (which we don't know), then there is a good chance that I am too. But there's no test for that except to purposefully infect myself with the bacteria. I'm not prepared to do that, because if I'm not immune, I'll die; and I can't possibly do that to you and leave you alone.

There's good news though! The doctors and scientists with me have been able to finally figure out what they believe will be a vaccination. They're going to begin testing today! If all goes well, then perhaps I'll be able to leave here within 10-12 days.

Stay strong son. I love you! I am so proud of you and I miss you so much. I'll write on this board every day until I'm able to see you in person. In the meantime, I'm attaching to this post some directions for using the communication system so that we can talk through the Holos like we did when Mom and your siblings were still alive. The only problem will be if the Sorenson's house isn't set up to operate that kind of technology. You'll have to figure that out with my instructions. Until then, I love you!

58

The time has arrived for the testing of Shevchuk's vaccine! Scientists around the world have been largely able to duplicate his results on animals of various types, depending upon what types of animals were available at each location. Shevchuk tells us that mammals of all sizes and shapes have proven immune after injection with the vaccine. He also says that some birds, reptiles and salt- and fresh-water aquatic animals have shown immunities.

Apparently, no testing location wants to be the first to test on humans, so Shevchuk has asked for volunteers. We just met and had a frank and exciting discussion of the potential ramifications of the testing. Shevchuk and his team answered every question as honestly as they could, or so it appeared. We'll be meeting in three hours to determine who will be among the first test subjects.

"Why?!" I asked, unable to mask either my surprise or my disappointment.

"I needed to," Shift repeated, more quietly this time.

"You crazy son-of-a—! Sorry," I said, trying to calm my emotions. "Why did you need to?"

"Well, somebody has to do it. My life is no more valuable than any other, is it?" He asked.

"Yes, Shift," I replied. "Your life *is* more valuable than others, at least to me."

"Oh." He looked down at his feet, clearly uncomfortable.

"'Oh!' That's all you have to say?" I asked, feeling frustrated.

"Well, no, that's not all I have to say," Shift replied. "But if I tell you what I really think, things may become awkward."

"I think things are already awkward," I said. "I don't want you to risk your life. I want you to be with me, safe."

"Anta, I want to be here with you too, safe; but what kind of life will we have if we have to stay in the bunker forever? We'll die in here as surely as we could die out there. Someone has to stand up and make this happen. I can't escape the feeling inside that it should be me. I'm sorry."

"Well," I said, "at least that's better than 'oh.'" I smiled, a bit sheepishly. I couldn't help but feel proud of him for his bravery, even though the thought of him risking his life was killing me on the inside.

We spent the next few minutes discussing the situation. I tried, half-heartedly, to talk him out of it. Thankfully, six other people have also volunteered to become the first test subjects of Dr. Shevchuk's possible vaccine. The ancient process of "drawing straws" will be invoked later today. At that time, any of the seven volunteers can withdraw their names from consideration. I don't think Shift will withdraw. Of those remaining, the two with the shortest "straws" will be injected with Shevchuk's vaccine, dubbed "E-rase". I may literally pass out if Shift draws a short straw.

In addition to Shift, "Lucky" Rabene, Dr. Bodily, Dr. Case, Dr. Treggor, Dr. Porter, and "Street" Kimball have each volunteered. I knew that Street would. He's become so incredibly helpful and wants to do anything he can for any of us. Dr. Porter is an interesting candidate. He may be immune—if his son is—which Dr. Shevchuk believes may be true. So, testing on him is probably not worthwhile because it could skew the results.

The thought of losing any of them saddens me, but the thought of losing Shift fills me with so much more sorrow—in an unimaginable way. The moment he raised his hand to volunteer, I felt a great weight press down on me, like that pressure when you turn really sharp, really fast in a hover, but more powerful. I had to hide my tears, as I'd done on more occasions than I liked to admit. After our conversation, I felt a little better, knowing that he was not doing it for any reason other than because it must be done.

What's up with my feelings for him? He's my colleague, not my lover. I'm desperately trying to push these stupid feelings down into the cracks between my toes unless and until Shift is ready for a relationship, if ever. But it kind of seems like it may happen, if he's not dead in 10 days.

MAY 2, 2093—SHIFT

Although I volunteered, I wasn't selected to be one of Shevchuk's first two test subjects. I'm a little relieved. Lucky and Dr. Case drew the shortest "straws". They were then placed into isolation bays and remotely injected with "E-rase". Five or six days from now, if they haven't developed any signs or symptoms of Anthrax E, we may be in luck.

In the meantime, we'll continue to monitor the situation outside trying to locate any location to which we might be able to travel to give inoculations in the event E-rase is successful. I hope Lucky is as his nickname says.

Upon the wise suggestion of Mrs. Houghton, Mike and his team have also been looking for farms nearby with living animals. As Mrs. Houghton pointed out, if any of us live, we need to be able to survive for more than a couple of weeks. While the food processors may last a long time, we will still probably face a day when meat becomes necessary. Plus, who wants to live in a world without animals? I could probably do without some of the bugs, and maybe rats, but life would be less exciting without most of the others.

59

"Damn it!" Yurgi yelled angrily as he marched into the conference room for an emergency staff meeting he had just called. His face was red to match the velvet of the upholstery in the conference room. "Who did this? *Who did this?*"

"Who did what?" Mike asked quietly. None of them had ever seen Yurgi mad. Upset, yes. Firm and demanding, certainly. But angry? Never.

"Anthrax E has been released into the air *inside* this bunker!"

Shouts of surprise echoed around the room. Instantly, several members of the group covered their mouths and noses with hands, shirts, jackets and pillows. Ms. Star Lawrence, a housekeeper from Massachusetts fainted. She fell and hit her head on the edge of the folding chair in front of her. General chaos continued for several moments until Dr. Shevchuk spoke again, this time more slowly and quietly, but with equal intensity. "Who. Did. This?"

The commotion and confusion stilled, almost instantaneously. Dr. Shevchuk's mere presence in the room usually engendered respect and quiet. But now, with eyes burning, and a gaze so intense and fierce as to provoke total fear among the occupants of the small conference room, the silence was absolute. Not even the new, deep, ragged breathing of several members of the group could be heard for several seconds.

Finally, after looking into the eyes of each person in the room, Dr. Shevchuk said, "Anthrax E has been released here, inside our home. Monitors throughout the bunker have picked it up. John and Angel have confirmed its presence. The isolation chambers holding Mrs. Safar, Suvan, Dr. Case and Mr. Rabene are each wholly intact. Who did this to us?"

Suddenly, or so it seemed, many of the members of the group began casting angry glances at their companions. Nobody spoke, but the eyes of the people certainly made it appear that everyone was a suspect.

"Nobody leaves this room until I say so," Dr. Shevchuk said with authority. "Shift, Anta, John, Angel—come with me. The rest of you will remain. Anyone who leaves this room, for any reason, will suffer consequences too great for me to say aloud. Mr. Kimball, keep them in here. Am I clear?"

Every head nodded. Every mouth remained closed.

Dr. Shevchuk turned abruptly and stormed out of the room. Shift, Anta, Angel and John followed, slowly, each more worried about what Dr. Shevchuk had in mind for them than about what may become of their lives as a result of the Anthrax E release. Street Kimball stood, walked to the door, then turned and faced the group. He folded his muscular arms across his bulky chest as the door closed behind him.

The small group walked into the laboratory adjacent to the room with the isolation chambers where the Safars, Justin and Lucky had all watched and listened to Dr. Shevchuk through the holos.

"Have a seat everyone," Dr. Shevchuk said sternly as he closed the sound-proof doors.

When all four people had sat, Dr. Shevchuk said, "I assume that none of you had anything to do with the release of Anthrax E, be it accidental or purposeful. Is there any reason I should assume otherwise?"

Dr. Shevchuk looked deep into each of their eyes before continuing. "I have my reasons for not suspecting any of you. But you are not in the clear, yet. But for our purposes, I need your help to figure out what to do next. Any suggestions?"

Nobody spoke. Even though Dr. Shevchuk appeared to be keeping his anger in check, nobody felt comfortable.

Finally, Shift asked, using the doctor's formal title, rather than the friendlier version of the man's name, "Dr. Shevchuk, do you know when it was released?" Shift's voice wavered as he asked the poignant question.

"John?" Dr. Shevchuk said.

John wiped beads of sweat from his brow as he looked up from the floor where his eyes had rested since the moment he sat down. "Well, the monitors just picked it up a few minutes ago," John stammered. "So, we assume it just happened."

"But how did it happen?" Anta asked. "Who else, besides the three of you and Andrew have access?" Anta was referring to Dr. Shevchuk, Dr. Angel Robertson, Dr. John Silitzer and Dr. Andrew Jones. The four doctors had full control of the operations of the testing center and laboratory. But access wasn't necessarily restricted. Security measures were in place, but they were not absolute.

"Nobody has access to the labs but the four of us," Angel replied. Her face masked the fear she had felt since the alarms first sounded in the lab.

"Then how did this happen?" Shift asked.

"That's what we intend to find out," Dr. Shevchuk said. "Starting now."

"I don't understand why Shift and I aren't potential saboteurs," Anta said.

Shift looked sideways at Anta, hoping she didn't say something that would get either of them in hot water. He had done nothing wrong, and didn't want to be lumped together with those that may have.

"Anta, I know you didn't do anything wrong because I have come to know you on a deep, personal level," Dr. Shevchuk said. "If you were evil, or had any evil intent, you could have wiped out the entire world by releasing the disease in Egypt outside the quarantine zone. You could have released it on the plane, or in Boston, or in the bunker at any time. You could have maintained possession of some quantity of the disease without any of us knowing it. Any action you may have taken, to destroy lives, most certainly would have been taken long before now, on the eve of the creation of a vaccine. Because you didn't know when a vaccine might come to fruition, you could have prevented any research at all with the simple act of killing us here, long ago. That is why I don't suspect you. Am I wrong?"

"No, you're not wrong," Anta replied. "I didn't do this."

"Neither did I," Shift said hastily.

"Good, let's move on then, shall we?"

"What about them?" Angel asked, pointing a thumb over her shoulder to the room where Lucky, Justin and the Safars were cooped up in isolation chambers.

Dr. Shevchuk began slowly, thoughtfully, "It seems it would have been impossible for either Dr. Case or Mr. Rabene to have done this personally. They were placed into the chambers yesterday. Obviously, the Safars did not do this. They haven't been released from their chambers once since they got here."

"But they could have had someone else do it for them, right?" Angel asked. "All four of them know, or at least *think* they're safe."

"But that would be quite a risk for Lucky and Justin," John countered. "We don't know if the vaccine works yet. Any release by either of them would be rather premature, and either of them, if they held such evil intentions, is too smart to attempt a release at this time. I think."

"I agree," Dr. Shevchuk said.

"Excluding them and us, that leaves 18 potential saboteurs," Angel said. "But isn't it possible that this was accidental—a mistake somehow?"

"Of course that's possible, Angel," Dr. Shevchuk replied. "But how such a mistake could have been made is beyond my ability to speculate."

"When was the last time any of you were in the lab?" Anta asked. "Could someone have snuck in and breached the security systems around the containment facilities?"

"Not today. I was in there not two minutes before I called the emergency meeting," Dr. Shevchuk replied. "John and Angel were with me at that time trying to figure out why the silent alarms were going off in the lab, and why alarms around the bunker were being registered on the computers. All three of us had been in there for several hours straight before the alarms sounded."

"Anta and I haven't been in there in days," Shift added. "Well, I guess I shouldn't speak for Anta."

"You're right," Anta added. "It's been several days. What about Andrew?"

"He's been in and out," John replied. "His tasks have become more routine and he isn't required in there as often as the rest of us."

"Could he have some kind of vendetta because of that?" Anta asked. "I mean, if he feels like he's become expendable, or less important, could he have gone nuts?"

"That seems unlikely," Dr. Shevchuk replied. "I've known Andrew for many years. He is a close friend and colleague. That's why I selected him to join me here in the first place many months ago. I don't believe he would do something like this."

"What about Mike's back draft theory?" Shift asked, suddenly remembering.

"No," John replied. "I had Carón show me how to look at the systems operation center after his big theory proved likely. I checked while Yurgi was calling the meeting a few minutes ago. The ventilation system is working fine."

"Then that leaves the other 18 people," Angel said. "How do we go about eliminating them as suspects?"

"More importantly," Shift said, "how do we go about protecting ourselves now? We can assume that we've all been contaminated by now, right?"

"Yes," Dr. Shevchuk said. "The only thing I can think of is to vaccinate everyone and hope that it works. And I think it will. If it doesn't work, it now makes no difference," Dr. Shevchuk said solemnly.

"I'm game," Angel said.

"Me too," John and Shift added in unison.

"When do we start?" Anta asked.

"We better start right now," Dr. Shevchuk said. "While we know how long Anthrax E takes to germinate before symptoms show, we don't know how long we have between the time of infection and the point of no return. There isn't any information about that presently, from any bunker."

"I'll start prepping vaccines," John offered.

"But we also need to know who did this," Anta said. "If someone did this on purpose, that person is very dangerous."

"If everyone is going to be vaccinated now anyway, because we've all been exposed, then can't we let those guys out of isolation?" Shift asked, pointing to the next room.

"Yes, I think we should," Dr. Shevchuk replied. "Do any of you have any reason to suspect Mr. Rabene? I would like him to spearhead our investigation, unless there's any chance he's involved."

"I don't think anybody knew him before we came here," John said. "But he did go outside with Street to capture animals. And there's no way Street is involved, in my opinion. So, let's get him in here and talk to him about Lucky. Maybe he can offer some insight."

"Get him in here," Dr. Shevchuk said.

Three minutes later, John and Street entered the lab. Street's face was ghostly white, his limbs moving slowly as if petrified by fear.

"Nobody left the conference room Dr. Shevchuk," Street said as he stepped into the room.

"Thank you. That's good. Sit down Mr. Kimball," Dr. Shevchuk said kindly. "We need to talk."

60

After yesterday's fiasco, every person in the bunker elected to be inoculated against Anthrax E. Justin, Lucky, Neirioui and Suvan were all let out of their isolation booths, voluntarily. Either we all die or we all live. I guess Neirioui and Suvan will live either way—they're immune. But now, either the vaccination works, or it doesn't. We'll find out soon enough.

Street gave us no reason to distrust Lucky. So Dr. Shevchuk put Lucky in charge of the investigation. His job is to find out how the release occurred and if any person here is responsible, either inadvertently or purposefully.

"We're screwed, Anta," I said, "even if E-rase works, and it appears it might."

"What do you mean?" Anta asked.

"I know you haven't spent a lot of time with Mike lately, but I have. USCAN reveals a lot, and it shows loads of dead bodies out there. We haven't seen hardly any movement in the streets anywhere over the past couple of days."

"Is *anyone* alive anywhere near us?" Anta asked.

"Yeah. There are a couple of small towns in northwest Canada. There's obviously human life there even though we can't see the people. Lights are going off and on at appropriate times to coincide with day and night, and not in any pattern which would suggest that the lights are on automatic timers. There's also movement in windows on occasion. We can't tell how many people are alive, but Mike's estimate, based on the locations in which he's tracking movement and lighting changes, is approximately 31 households. That's the best place we've found right now."

"Well that's good at least. Any place else?" she asked.

"Sure, but the prospects look more bleak in other places. Mike's keeping detailed records which show that, in many places with people still living, the numbers seem to be going down. Kinda sucks really."

"That's quite the understatement," Anta replied, without any hint of humor.

"Yeah, I guess so. But if E-rase works, we'll get to each of those places and vaccinate whoever is still alive. All the other bunkers like ours will soon have access to Shevchuk's information and will hopefully be able to develop the vaccine. Then they can get out there and save some lives too.

"Of course, we may all die in here. If so, then the vaccine didn't work and all the other bunkers will be left to continue the work."

"Well, I suggest we don't die then," Anta said, smiling.

61

I feel strangely alive, four days post-injection. Not only do I feel no negative effects—yet—from the E-rase injection or from Anthrax E, but I actually feel invigorated! It's really weird actually. I know that's not a scientific way to explain my feelings, but it's accurate. Perhaps it's only in my mind. The other alternative is that E-rase may actually be changing something physically within my body. In either event, I can't complain. I feel like I could run a marathon, or maybe one of those Iron Man races!

MAY 8, 2093
ENTRY IN THE ANTHRAX E DATABASE
DR. YURGI SHEVCHUK

Our test subjects (Dr. Case and Mr. Rabene) are well—very well actually. Presently, we see no sign of infection, nor does either complain of such. Strangely, Dr. Case reports feeling better, stronger and healthier than he did pre-injection. His vital signs and objective test data conclude that he is slightly more fit than pre-injection. This phenomenon will be closely monitored.

Following the 'accidental' release of the bacteria in our bunker and subsequent inoculation of the remainder of the residents, all residents are now being tested and monitored. Only two illnesses have appeared. One, we concluded was a stress-induced headache. The other, Dr. Bodily, showed some of the early signs of Anthrax-E. However, we have concluded that her symptoms are psychosomatic rather than physical.

Following the submission of our test data to the Anthrax E database earlier this morning, testing centers in Japan (2 of them), England, France, China and India have now each announced their intent to test human subjects tomorrow. Each center intends to inject two healthy subjects, as we have done. There will be a total of 14 intentional injections including ours, plus our 23 subsequent inoculations. Additional injections are planned in the next few days at other testing centers.

Preparations are underway for the mass production of E-rase in our facility, subject of course, to confirmation that the vaccine actually operates to inoculate the human body.

Because each of us was exposed to Anthrax E, in all its strength, five days ago, within one to three days, we may have conclusive data proving that our vaccine is proper for human inoculation. Nobody is sick, so at the least, the vaccine acts to extend the period of infection. If we die, may God help you all.

MAY 8, 2093—SHIFT

"Well dudes, it's been six days since Lucky and Justin were injected with E-rase," I said, trying to make conversation. John, sitting next to me, and Anta and Street, across the table, were all eating. All of us except Street ate lazily; Street ate with gusto. I don't know where he gets his appetite.

Our time hasn't been required so urgently these last couple of days. Most of us are just waiting around now, except for Mike and his team who continue 24-hour surveillance of the world outside. The waiting seems to be causing depression. Or maybe everybody's just so tired from all the work that their bodies are shutting down after the months-long adrenaline rush. I don't know. I'm not that kind of doctor. Me? I'm mostly just apprehensive. I don't want to die.

Receiving no response, I continued, "Dr. Shevchuk says that neither of them has shown any symptom of disease from the vaccine. They both appear healthy and normal. He says he's tested, retested, and tested again for both the presence of the disease in their systems and any signs of infection from the disease. And aside from Dr. Bodily, maybe, no one else has shown any negative effects from the accidental exposure and vaccination either."

John and Anta looked really bored. Street was so busy stuffing his mouth, I don't think he even knew I was talking. That, or he doesn't care what I think.

"How does it work anyway?" Anta finally asked. "Is the vaccine just like others?"

"Yeah," John replied. "It's just like others. Nothing special really. It just took a long time to make it work."

"How *does* it work John?" I asked.

"It might be too complicated for your small brain Shift, but I'll try to dumb it down."

"Thank you, oh great one." He's such an arse.

"It works pretty much like the influenza vaccine. E-rase is composed of dead Anthrax E cells which are injected into the human bloodstream; except we had to modify the cells because they aren't naturally-occurring. Because Anthrax E is manmade, we had to adjust our method of creating the vaccine. We couldn't just use plain old dead cells. That would have been too easy.

"Anyway, we hope our bodies will create antibodies to fight the modified dead cells and, in the process, become able to defeat the disease itself. With the influenza vaccine, the human body typically took about two weeks to develop any kind of immunity to the flu. Unlike the influenza vaccine, though, current science allows for most immunizations to begin to work within 12-24 hours."

"That's awesome!" I said, trying to show enthusiasm and maybe get some reaction from Anta.

"Yeah, pretty awesome," John replied; although the way John said "awesome" and the way I said "awesome" were completely different. He looked like he was falling asleep with food in his mouth. He could have choked. That would have been adequate punishment for his earlier rub I think. "So, what does that speed mean for us now?"

"Based upon that timeframe, Shevchuk appropriately estimated that Dr. Case and Lucky would either show symptoms or not show symptoms within 5-6 days of the injections, or, approximately one day longer than the billions of people who have succumbed to the disease. That's today."

"So far so good!" I said.

We've all been exposed to *live* Anthrax E now. John explained that we'll have to wait another six days before Shevchuk will pronounce Justin and Lucky, and the rest of us, clean. During that time, numerous tests will be run, most of which I wouldn't likely understand.

"Has Lucky's investigation gone anywhere?" Street asked, finally looking up from his plate.

"Not that I'm aware of," I replied. "He's interviewed everyone and he and Mike have checked all the entry logs and databases trying to find unauthorized access to the lab. Nothing yet."

"Well, someone did something bad," Street said. "I hope Lucky nails the bastard, even if the vaccine works and we all live happily ever after."

"I couldn't agree more, Street," I said.

62

"Unfortunately," Dr. Wentworth began, "our estimates from several days ago, of the death resulting from Anthrax E worldwide, appear to be right on track. Ten days ago, Doctor Fabrisio and I ran numbers that seemed to indicate that, five days from now, approximately 9 billion people will be dead. Based upon the data we are amassing and which is being collected worldwide from bunkers like ours, approximately 8.2 billion people are likely already deceased. If that's accurate, then only 2.2 billion people remain alive on Earth." Nobody spoke.

"I know that seems like a lot of people still alive," Dr. Wentworth continued, "but the problem is that there is no way to save most of them. Nearly all of the remaining 2.2 billion people will likely be sick or dead within days or weeks."

"Mike," Dr. Shevchuk said, "tell us about your progress please. Can you confirm those estimates?"

"As you know, we have incredible surveillance access to the largest cities of the world," Mike said. "In smaller communities, though, where our surveillance is less perfect, there could be abundant life or complete destruction, either of which could change the estimates. So, no, I can't confirm the estimates. But I can't say they're inaccurate either."

"It seems logical," Mike continued, "to assume that smaller communities, especially in rural areas many miles outside population centers, might be more protected. But if one person in a community is sick, the rest are going to be eventually, right?"

"Plus," Dr. Porter interrupted, "the darn wind is really hard to stop."

"It seems, realistically, that the only communities that may be safe are those that are completely isolated from others, perhaps in high, secluded mountain valleys, or some of the native populations in the Amazon River Basin or the Australian Outback or the African Savannah," John added. "But even those communities may be contaminated by the wind or the birds. We'll probably never know the extent of death in those areas unless Mike can figure out how to hack into the IWO's global surveillance satellite system."

"Which I've been working on for a while now," Mike said. "Apparently, the IWO is much more secretive than I had originally thought."

"Not that it really matters now," Shift said. "Whoever survives this will be governing themselves, I think."

63

The group eagerly anticipated the arrival of Dr. Yurgi Shevchuk. He had kept everyone out of the testing center since the release of Anthrax E, 10 days earlier. A select few had an inkling of what might be revealed, but nobody knew for sure save Dr. Shevchuk, Dr. John Silitzer and Dr. Angel Robertson, who were each conspicuously absent at the moment.

Every other person in the bunker was in attendance at the meeting. While most of them were still nervous about who released Anthrax E, and why, it didn't matter to the health of the group anymore. They would live or die, and nothing could change that now. But nobody had gotten sick yet, which meant that, at the least, the vaccine held the disease at bay for a time. At best, the vaccine would protect them forever. They now waited anxiously for Dr. Shevchuk to tell them their fate, if he knew.

No person from outside the bunker was connected remotely to the meeting. Dr. Shevchuk had given the order that the information shared in this meeting should first be shared with those who contributed so much to the process.

The excitement and nervous energy was palpable. Knees were bouncing, foreheads were shiny with sweat. Shift sat by Street and glared as he watched Andrew reach over and take Anta's trembling hand. Dr. Porter was praying a silent prayer, head bowed. Others were also praying or mumbling to themselves. Dr. Shevchuk was taking too long.

When Yurgi, John and Angel finally walked through the door into the crowded conference room, stifling with a mixture of sweat and humidity, the group immediately fell silent. Not a sound was heard except for the deep, ragged breathing of someone in the back.

Dr. Shevchuk, face serious and unreadable, started slowly. "My friends, there is news, as you know." He paused, causing several members of the group to suddenly lose hope. "Testing has been thorough and complete. As you all know—very well—the results I am about to present to you have serious ramifications for the survival of the human race." Again he paused. "If we fail, our race may not survive. If we succeed, there will be much work to do, and even then, our race will be so decimated that survival will be harder than it has been for centuries."

Shift couldn't contain himself any longer. "Yurgi! Great speech, but come on man! Out with it!"

Dr. Shevchuk smiled. "Ladies and Gentlemen, we have succeeded!" Then he laughed, triumphantly, not even attempting to hide his euphoria.

The room erupted with cheers and applause.

Carón and Mike wrapped each other in a huge bear hug, clapping each other on the back, then moved on to do the same with others.

Street ran around in a tight circle, as the room would allow for nothing more, high-fiving everyone who looked at him, and some who didn't. Then he circled back and began again. He even gave Yurgi a quick pat on the butt as if he was celebrating an amazing play on the football field. Yurgi laughed.

Dr. Steve Porter wept, as did many others.

Andrew Jones squeezed Anta's hand, then jumped up and joined Street in his celebratory run.

Lucky Rabene, usually more calm and composed than others, pounded on the back of the chair in front of him then jumped up and down with excitement.

Dr. Angel Robertson smiled, mischievously.

Shift approached Anta tentatively. "Well, that's great news."

"Yes, it is," Anta replied, looking curiously at Shift with her head tilted slightly to one side.

"Things have turned out differently than I hoped . . ." Anta noticed Shift's gaze move toward the celebrating Andrew, then back again, "but there's some real hope now that we can help some people, including Hasani."

Anta didn't answer. Instead, she smiled sweetly as she leaned in and kissed Shift on the lips. Shift kissed her back. Nobody else even noticed.

Dr. Latisha Bodily sat in the back row, face stoic, as sweat trickled down the back of her neck.

MAY 14, 2093—ANTA

Yesterday, Dr. Shevchuk's team began the mass production of E-rase before our staff meeting had even finished! He has called for four volunteers to leave the compound to begin vaccinations. I intend to volunteer, and I intend to take Shift with me.

There's no news from the moon. My last communication with Hasani was March 21. Some time shortly after that communication the message board link between the IWO and the moon was severed. Mike and his team have been trying to repair the connection, but have been frustrated at every turn. Mike thinks the physical components that work to operate the wireless connections may have been intentionally sabotaged. He believes that, if it were just a bad connection, he would have been able to get it back online by now. That presents an interesting problem. Mike has traced the connection away from our bunker but can't tell where, or why, the connection is lost. He is completely baffled, which is strange.

In any event, the five people on the moon, whether they are alive or dead, have only partial knowledge of the conditions here on Earth. While they're probably alive given all the information we had about their circumstances, what hope do any of them have of any semblance of *real* life on the moon, without family and friends, and with little hope for return to Earth.

64

Four days ago, Anta and I, along with Dr. Angel Robertson and Mr. Threet "Street" Kimball were selected to go to the surface. Owing to the intelligent designs of Dr. Shevchuk, only four of us will be leaving the compound tomorrow morning, with others possibly leaving later after we work out the kinks and make sure the search and rescue process actually works. We'll proceed above ground and then head northwest toward Canada, away from the bigger cities of the East coast and the Midwest.

Dr. Wentworth's estimate of life is now under 50 million people worldwide, and more than half of those people are in northern Africa, of all places. It's extraordinary that, in the countries and communities surrounding El-Alamein, more human life can be found than the rest of the world combined. The containment measures taken in El-Alamein were completely successful. I am sooooo glad we weren't there. Clearly *nothing* escaped the foam. Even though southern Africa fell early, the desert that kept the disease at bay for so long must have continued to protect northern Africa.

Most of the remaining survivors may still die though since there aren't any active research facilities anywhere near northern Africa. Not one person among us is a pilot or has had any pilot training; nor do we have access to the clearance encryptions required to start up any modern aircraft. Mike could probably get his hands on some, but then what? Even if we do access a modern craft, or if we find an old craft that still works, we still can't fly. We thought Lucky might have received some flight training as part of his government employ, but no luck. There are other bunkers closer to northern Africa than us, and maybe some have pilots. If so, it will be up to them to reach northern Africa—hopefully before it's too late.

Dr. Wentworth theorizes that, even though our small group and small groups from other bunkers will be saving some people, and even though several thousand people are located in bunkers like ours, within 4-5 days there will be less than 40,000 survivors worldwide. Within 8-9 days, there could be as few as 10,000, and nearly all of them will be located in bunkers and other, presently-unknown safe havens waiting for teams like ours to reach them.

Hasani and the others on the moon don't know that a vaccine has been created. They don't know anything about what's occurred here over the past few weeks. With communications out we don't know how to even begin to solve the problem of those trapped on the moon; maybe the IWO or someone else is already working on that.

Dr. Porter hasn't been able to reach his son in four days. He's bursting at the seams to get out of here. I suspect Yurgi won't be able to contain him once we've left.

"So, John," I said. "What do you plan . . . ?" John wasn't looking at me. He was looking at Andrew as he walked into the mess hall where John and I were just beginning to eat.

A quick look and I could see why John was staring. Andrew had a black eye. His self-conscious, head-down posture was so unusual that he immediately drew attention to himself. A couple of people asked if everything was okay with him, but he just grunted and looked away. After quickly grabbing some food, he slouched at a table in a far corner by himself.

"I wonder what happened," John said.

"Beats me," I said.

"Looks like someone has been *beating* Andy," John replied, snickering.

When Anta came in a couple minutes later, she was also acting unusual, but in a totally different way. She held her head high and had a pasted-on smile. She responded to greetings with a curt nod and a 'fine, thanks'. After carefully selecting her food, she looked around briefly then marched off to an empty table about as far away from Andrew as she could get and still be in the same room. She set down her food tray and handbag, removed a paperback book from her bag and started eating and reading, as if defying anyone to disturb her.

I was confused. John, sitting next to me, elbowed me in the ribs and told me to close my mouth or I might catch a fly. That broke me from my trance. I slowly turned to face John with a "what gives' expression, which made him laugh.

"I'll go ask." John continued laughing at my obvious confusion and got up from the table. I looked from Anta to Andrew and back again several times, trying to understand what I was seeing. John reached Anta's table and said a few words, pointing to the seat opposite Anta. Anta looked up briefly and nodded without answering. John sat down. They spoke briefly, Anta's eyes never leaving John's, her expression not changing. Then John got up and returned to our table, smiling. Anta returned to her book.

Looking around the room I noticed there were a few curious looks, at Anta, at Andrew, even at me and John.

"What?" I asked quietly once John was seated and eating again.

"Not here," was his reply. "Too many eyes and ears."

I stood up and grabbed my food tray, my lunch half eaten. With my free hand on John's elbow, I pulled on him to get him to stand. "Let's go, then."

John, who had his mouth open and a forkful of pasta halfway to his mouth, lost the noodles to the floor and groaned as he hurriedly grabbed his tray and followed. We deposited our trays with the other dirty dishes and left the room.

Out in the hallway I stopped and turned on him. "Ok, what happened?"

"She was not real forthcoming. All I will say is that you better make time to talk to her . . ."

I was already turning to go back into the cafeteria when John grabbed my arm and stopped me. ". . . after she finishes lunch man. Find her alone and be polite, not demanding like you're being with me." These last words were said in mock protest, as if I had damaged his pride.

"What did you say? What did she say? Word for word."

"Oh, come on Shift! Everyone knows she loves you, except you. She's been through some tough days here, just like you and the rest of us."

"I know she has. I've been trying to push the pain aside and get things done. Just like you and the others."

"Well, maybe you've been too busy to notice that she needs you right now. Andrew saw it and tried to be sympathetic. He just had the wrong motive."

I stared at John, trying to grasp what he was saying. "Shift, Anta told me that Andrew came to her room this morning. She slugged him for misinterpreting their relationship and trying to take advantage of her—Anta's words."

"What have I done, John? Will I lose her before I even had her?"

"Don't add insult to injury, Shift. Just go talk to her. No, actually, go listen to her. Let her talk."

John walked away, down the hall. The thought crossed my mind that neither of us finished our lunch. Then I shook my head in wonder that I could think of something so trivial when what was left of my world was falling apart.

Anta slugged Andrew. Andrew is sulking. Anta loves me? And how have I acted toward Anta? "Idiot!" I said out loud to myself. *I'll go talk to her right now*, I thought. *No, I'll wait here and talk to her as soon as she's done eating. No . . . I don't know what I'll do.* I was getting a headache thinking about it.

I went to my room, paced back and forth in the four feet between the door and my bed. Then, noticing that was the shorter distance in my room, turned 90 degrees and paced the ten feet between my desk and the dresser at the other end of the room. After pacing for a while I busied myself doing . . . actually, I don't remember what I did, but it took about twenty minutes to do it.

Finally, I couldn't stand it anymore and went to Anta's room. I stopped outside her door, raised my hand to knock, and then started second guessing. Had I waited long enough? What was I going to say when she answered the door? Was I capable of just listening? While I was standing there with my hand in the air a female voice spoke immediately behind me.

"Are you deep in thought or frozen in place?" Anta! There was laughter in her voice. I spun around, almost hitting her in the head with my raised arm that had been poised to knock. It made her flinch, but the smile didn't leave her face.

"I . . . I . . ." What was I going to say?

"Not frozen, but the cat has your tongue, I see."

Then it all came out at once. "Anta, I wanted to talk to you in the cafeteria, but John said I shouldn't, that I should wait until later . . ." Anta raised her right hand and placed her index finger to my lips. "Shhh . . . It wouldn't have been a good result. I needed time to think things out." I just stared, speechless.

"You're here now. Come in and we'll talk."

She was so calm about it. Didn't she realize that I had almost ruined everything? Or maybe I *had* ruined everything. We went in and she pulled me down next to her on the bed instead of sitting in the two chairs.

"Anta, I need to apologize . . ."

"No, you don't. I need to explain, so just listen. I knew you were struggling with the deaths in your family, so I tried not to bother you with my problems."

"But . . ."

"Quiet! Me first. I know you care about me and I care about you. This whole Anthrax-E mess could ruin a beautiful relationship if we're not careful. We're going out on the surface tomorrow and there's a lot to focus on. I want our relationship to progress, but some things may have to wait." I was not only speechless, but feeling so stupid. I had no idea she had thought this through as she had.

She continued. "We still may not survive this. We don't want to go too fast. But I believe there will come a time in the near future when we can think seriously about ourselves." Then she stopped talking and smiled, that beautiful smile that lights up her face.

"What about Andrew?" I asked hesitantly.

"I allowed Andrew to get close to me because I needed someone and didn't want to bother you with my problems when you were still so upset over your own problems. It was a mistake. He misread my needs and pressed the relationship to be something I didn't need or want. I'm fine now."

I felt so stupid. We sat side by side, our thighs touching, her two hands wrapped in my hands, and a careful smile slowly lit my face to match hers; but it quickly began to fade.

"I am scared to death Anta! What's going to happen?" I asked self-consciously.

"We're going to the surface . . . together . . ."

"With Street and Angel," I added.

Anta laughed, a deep, happy laugh. It sounded wonderful. "Even with those two around, I think we can find a little alone time, don't you?" After a pause, she added, more seriously. "We'll help each other get through this." Then she leaned in and kissed me softly on the lips.

We're going to the surface, together. Anta will be with me, but that's almost as scary as rising to the surface.

There's still a little shyness between us. But we can work out our relationship, slowly—because there are too many other things to do right now. We've got to get ready for our expedition to the surface with the 'first string', as Street calls it. And with so much going on, our budding relationship will continue to take a back seat for a while.

My feelings for her, and my inability to do much about those feelings right now, are irritating, like a pebble in a shoe. Even if the pebble doesn't hurt at first, it keeps rubbing and rubbing until it hurts so bad you have to finally sit down, remove your shoe, dump the pebble out, and then throw it far away out of spite. Yeah, that's what this feels like. But I don't want to get to the point of pain. I think I love her.

In the meantime, it appears that our world will survive! Barely. It's amazing that less than five months ago, my life and the lives of ten and a half billion people were silently, unknowingly creeping toward a disaster that none of us knew existed, or could have ever fathomed. The greatest disaster since . . . when? Noah and the Flood? What fragile lives we lead.

Now, however, we see a light at the end of this short and disastrous tunnel. Life will go on. We'll find anybody still living, although it may take months or years, or maybe even lifetimes to do so. What remains of our lives, however, is yet to be seen. Will the remaining population of our world, whatever numbers of us still breathe, be able to come together and form a new world? Will we be able to recreate the peace and harmony that had existed until only months ago?

What of the handful of people stranded on the Moon? What's to become of them? And I still have a nagging concern about how the plague got free in the bunker just on the verge of a vaccine. I don't know. I have doubts and suspicions. I know enough about human history and human nature to understand that we, as humans, will fight to survive. Unfortunately, our fighting is often amongst ourselves.

Maybe we've learned from lessons of the past. Maybe this human tragedy will bring us together, unlike tragedies of long ago. Maybe, ultimately, we'll be able to live meaningful lives, once the sorrow and despair run their course. I really, really hope so.

Tomorrow we rise!

AUTHOR'S NOTE

The premise of this story is that Germany planned to test a lethal strain of *Bacillus anthracis*, the etiologic agent of anthrax developed by Japanese scientists, against unsuspecting villagers in Northern Africa, then use it against Allied forces during World War II. I don't know whether anything like that ever happened. In other words, I made it up. While many of the pieces of information included in this story are factual or based upon factual events, and I have attempted to be as accurate as possible in regard to those events that actually occurred in the past, much of this is the fiction of my mind. This story is not meant to be an historical treatise or anything like it. It is just a story. And it is fiction.

Of course, I spent a great deal of time researching past events. But I cannot vouch for any of my sources. I don't know whether they are accurate or not. With that in mind, my reading leads me to believe that Nazi Germany's biological weapon research program was severely limited throughout World War II due to Adolf Hitler's strong feelings about such weapons. Many of the books and websites I've read indicate that Adolf Hitler, German Führer and Reichskanzler, and supreme commander of the German Armed Forces during World War II, initially prohibited the development of biological weapons as a result of his own devastating experiences with chemical weapons during World War I. Again, I don't know whether that's accurate, nor does it really matter for purposes of this fictional story.

If my unverified sources are accurate, however, it would appear that Hitler's stance on the issue of biological warfare appears to have been unpersuasive. As was the case with other issues during that time, it seems that Hitler wasn't influential enough to compel strict obedience and, with the support of high-ranking Nazi officials, it seems probable that German scientists eventually began biological weapons research. Most historians and political archives (at least those that I looked at) agree, however, that German success with biological weapons was minimal at best.

Joseph Goebbels, German politician and Reich Minister of Propaganda in Nazi Germany from 1933 to 1945, and one of Adolf Hitler's closest associates and most devout followers, accused the British of attempting to introduce yellow fever into India by importing infected mosquitoes from West Africa. I don't know whether that occurred—I wasn't around in those days. But several sources state that the British were, indeed, *experimenting* with at least one organism of biological warfare: *Bacillus anthracis*.

It appears, again based upon my readings, that only the Japanese successfully *used* biological weapons during World War II—against Allied forces in China between 1937 and 1945. Although I haven't come across any other use of biological weapons during World War II, it appears that many countries had active research and development programs, including the United States and the former Soviet Union. It wasn't until late in the 20th century that the super-powers signed a chemical demilitarization agreement to destroy stockpiles of Mustard gas and other biological weapons that were aging and corroding in storage facilities around the globe, threatening to escape into unsuspecting neighboring communities.

SECOND AUTHOR'S NOTE

Because It's My Book And I Can Write As Many "Author's Notes" As I Want

Long before this book was written or even conceived (back when I was 13 years old), I began writing a book about a group of teenagers who had to survive during a Second Great Depression. My friends (Justin Bath and Brian Martin) helped me write it. In the story, six boys left home to live in the mountains outside Salt Lake City, Utah. They were going to build cabins and hunt for their food. It was going to be an incredible story. We got about 14 pages written, by hand, before we got bored. We had girls to flirt with and BB gun fights to engage in. Seriously, there isn't time for everything.

Nevertheless, in my young teenage mind, I thought that, even though the reality would be awful, it would have been an amazing adventure. That short-lived dream died, but the idea never left me. Eventually, the dream of writing a book returned. It took me four years to write this book. It took another two years to write the sequel. It may not be the best story ever written (perhaps top 5 ;-)), and the writing style may not be everyone's favorite, but I'm proud of the result.

While this story is vastly different than the original concept 27 years ago, and hopefully a bit more polished, the concept of surviving against the odds is the same.

I had a lot of help getting the story ready to publish, and each of the following people deserve my thanks. Perhaps this little tribute is enough for all of these people to feel loved and appreciated, but I'll probably send them a free copy of this book too—I'm pretty generous like that.

Anyway, thank you Steve Wilde (or, as I call you, "Dad"). Dad spent hours and hours helping me edit and polish the story. Some of the great ideas, like the hurricane dispersing the disease, were his. That part is pretty cool. So, hat's off to Dad for that!

Thank you Ron Beach for financial and emotional support. Ron's praise and support encouraged me greatly, and his cash was quite useful as well.

I also had a few people test-read the book and offer valuable insight into the various facets of the plot and characters. These people also contributed to the editing process in various ways. Thank you Jamie Richens Kirkham, Susan Niedert, Jac Cooper, and Brandan Morgan. My daughter (Sage) and my son (Roston) also tried to read it and give me feedback, but in the end, they decided that their own agendas were more important than mine—typical teenagers.

Thank you to my son, Roston, who spent a cold weekend in the desert with me taking pictures, one of which ended up as the cover for this book. Those are even his footprints in the sand!

I also want to thank the guys at IndiBookLauncher for their help getting a cover designed and this published and out there for you to read.

Finally, I want to thank my wife, Chandi. While she didn't offer much help with the story itself, she happily (I think) listened to me talk about it over and over and over again. She encouraged me and let me stay late at the office to write since doing so at home would have been fruitless (remember, I have a lot of kids).

Now, go read the second book. It's even better. I know that self-endorsement is no endorsement at all, but seriously, the second book is better. Take a look below at these awesome passages from book 2, "Tomorrow We Rise"! (You see what I did there? Last line of book 1 is the title of book 2. Clever, huh?!)

TOMORROW WE RISE

"Look," she replied, shining the flashlight onto the floor at her feet.

I peeked around her shoulder into the hallway, placing my hand on the door frame. My little finger slipped into a small hole, about the size of a pea. Dried blood stained the floor immediately at our feet, and the walls on both sides of the hall. Anta and I each took a small step backward away from it. Several seconds later, having gathered my nerves, I quietly stepped around Anta and entered the hallway.

A short way down the hall to the right I came upon the shadowy remains of conflict. Two long streaks of dark, dry blood ran parallel to each other along the hallway floor for several meters. At the end of the left-most streak sat a lone Adidas tennis shoe. Just beyond the shoe, a silver Smith & Wesson handgun lay on the floor in what was once, surely, a large puddle of blood. It looked as though a body had been dragged down the hallway.

"What do you think happened here?" Anta asked, quietly.

"Everything's still clear from our vantage point," Hasani said quietly though Shift's MEHD. "Nothing outside yet. Wait, the door's opening. Looks like your guy."

"Keep an eye on him," Shift said. "If you see anything approaching, even a long way off, let me know ASAP so I can get him out of there."

"Got it. He's at the rear tires now. He knows what he's looking for, right?"

"Yeah, we went through it carefully," Shift answered.

"Okay, he's moving forward now."

"Everything still look good out there?"

"Yeah, still good . . . No, not good. I can see them. They're moving very fast."

"Andrew!" Shift called out through the MEHD. "Get in here now!"

Andrew didn't hear Shift issue the warning. Communications had just gone down, but nobody knew it yet. Andrew was alone, unknowing, and the Skins were almost on top of him.

Andrew saw them before they saw him. He wondered why he hadn't been warned as he saw the horde of demons climbing over rooftops and coming around the buildings on both sides of him. Then they saw him. Andrew was already running toward the bay doors. If he could get there, if he could get inside, he would be okay. His heart raced and his blood pumped as he approached the doors. But the horde was moving too fast—they could smell his blood. They were right behind him. He turned and fired several shots into the throng as he ran backward toward the doors. Moments later, he ran into the door, cracking his elbow on the hard metal casing. Still firing, he reached behind him, sending pain up through his elbow and into his shoulder. He was searching for the sensor. He almost touched it.

"Oh shite!" Hasani cried out as he watched the naked human-like beasts swarm over the man below on the tarmac. The man had been so close—he was almost there. But the Skins were so fast. Hasani had never seen anything like it. He'd heard what the others had told them about the Skins, but seeing it was something entirely different. Then the man rose from the ground, reached out his hand, and touched the door sensor. It opened.

"They're inside!" Jonas yelled down the corridor to the people coming toward him. "Run!"

Tomorrow We Rise is available now in Kindle format from Amazon.com and in paperback format from major booksellers.

RONIX
WA

ABOUT ME

I'm Dan. I'm writing this myself because I couldn't persuade anybody to make me seem as awesome as I hope to make myself appear.

I grew up in Taylorsville, a suburb of Salt Lake City, Utah. My teenage years were spent skiing, golfing, mountain biking, hiking and camping (and attending high school now and then). After high school, I spent two years in Scotland on a religious service mission. During college, I met and married Chandi; and we started our family shortly after that. I graduated from the University of Utah with a bachelor's degree in mass communications. Since the best job I could possibly hope to land with that degree would be writing obituaries, I went to law school in San Diego, California. Boogie boarding became my favorite pastime. I graduated from law school in 2007 and was offered a sweet job at a small firm in St. George, Utah, in the southwest corner of the state. I practice law in both California and Utah.

I've been in St. George with my family for 10 years now. It's hot here. I'm perspiring just thinking about it. But my life couldn't be better. I'm a husband and a father of six. My wife and kids are amazing and keep me busy and young-ish. My wife is hot. I'm a lawyer, a pianist, a percussionist, a Sunday School teacher, a soccer dad, an armchair quarterback, an outdoor enthusiast, and now, an "author". In the very little free time I have, I camp, cliff-jump, kayak, golf, do yardwork, and hike with my family. On the rare occasion I have free time after all of that, I write. That's why it took me so long to get this story out.

Keep up with me at *www.danielpwilde.com*, *www.facebook.com/danielpwildeTKS*, or e-mail me at *danielpwilde@gmail.com*.